Broken Match

RENÉE ARONIS

To Scott: my love,
my motivation,
and the man who brightens my darkness.
The star by which I sail my life to—
Oh, and also my favorite.

Other Books in this Series:

Meet Your Match

Striking of the Match

CONTENTS

Chapter One

FAREWELL FOR NOW

Erin March didn't look back at her new friend, Roger Blackwood, as she entered the terminal at Edinburgh Airport. She knew she might not stop crying if she did, and she needed to stop. It seemed to her that all she'd done was cry since meeting David Elliott, the forty-five-year-old tall, dark, and handsome Scottish actor who just happened to be the treatment match for her disease, the Fertilis Defect.

It was difficult for her not to dwell on the events of the last week, especially the reason she was leaving his mother's beautiful home, named Owlgate. Memories of her horrible encounter with David's nearly identical cousin, Bran, tried to overwhelm her as she stood in line at security. His putrid breath on her face and the eyes of the snake tattoo on his chest, just barely visible in the dark spare bedroom in Roger's flat, assaulted her at random and without warning.

That experience was bad, very bad, but David's reaction to the news was even worse. He'd been at his wife's funeral with their children when it happened and wasn't there to protect her from the man who had terrorized his life since childhood and whom he hated with a passion. Not only had he not been able to protect her, but Bran had already been taken away to an in-patient rehabilitation hospital, so he wasn't able to exact his revenge.

In his frustration and rage, he chose to lash out at everyone, including her. Roger had tried to defend her, but David insulted her and broke her heart. Once he finally calmed down and realized what he'd done, it was too late to take it back.

She'd decided to go home and get some things settled, promising David's mother, Annis, and her partner, Millie, that she would return. She had also spoken to David and assured him that she still loved him, and all she needed was a little time to sort out her feelings, vowing to come back as soon as she could.

In all honesty, what she really needed to do was prove to herself that she was strong enough to leave. Her nature was to run back into her lover's arms, no matter how he'd hurt her, but she had to take a stand for her own self-esteem and find out if she could trust him and her heart. Her heart palpitated as she thought of her true love. He'd begged her not to leave, but she had always been too quick to forgive and forget in past relationships, only for the pattern to continue.

There was no question of her returning, though she knew David and his family weren't convinced. The way Roger had asked about it in the car had proven that to her. When he said that they'd miss her, her heart hurt, knowing just how much she'd miss them too.

The flight was on time, and Erin boarded her first-class flight from Edinburgh to Green Bay, Wisconsin, with a heavy heart. She hoped she was doing the right thing by leaving David after his horrible fit of temper. She just needed a day or two to heal and get the divorce from her husband, Todd, started.

Thankful for the first-class seat, she settled in for the long flight home. Outwardly, she was pleasant and friendly; however, that was just her own autopilot kicking in. Inside, she didn't care. She tried to sleep, but her mind was too worked up. As soon as she'd doze off, a memory would wake her with a gasp.

The layover went smoothly, and her flight landed in Green Bay at six-fifty pm, which was only a few minutes late. It was nearly one am in Edinburgh, and she was exhausted. She was fed up with all the flying and waiting, with too much time to think and do nothing. At seven-fifteen, she finally got off the plane and made her way to the baggage carousels in the small, open airport to wait some more.

After twenty minutes, the bags and luggage began to appear, riding around the track. Too tired to fight the crowd, she waited, leaning against the wall. She watched the people in line for rental cars at the far end of the room, glad she'd be able to use her own. When the crowd at the carousel thinned, she saw her bag coming her way, so she walked over and picked it up.

She made her way toward the exit, wanting to find a taxi and get to the hotel as quickly as possible. "Erin?" she heard behind her and turned. She saw a woman she and Todd had gone to church with many years earlier, although she couldn't for the life of her remember her name. "How are you, and how's Todd?" she asked, smiling and expecting a nice, happy answer.

Erin knew her next question would be 'And what church are you two attending now?' and when Erin said 'none,' she'd *tsk* and shake her head. Then, she'd encourage her to find one, telling her how they'd just started going to such and such church. She'd tell her to check it out because the pastor was really great or the music was amazing or whatever.

She didn't want to stand there that long, so she answered with full disclosure, "Honestly, I'm really quite exhausted right now, and I don't know how Todd is because we are no longer together. Actually, I need to go, but it was nice talking to you." It was apparent the woman wasn't expecting that response. The woman stood gaping as Erin hurried out the sliding doors.

She made a beeline for the row of waiting taxis and stopped at the first one she saw. While she got into the car, the driver put her suitcase into the trunk; however, when the driver returned and asked where she was going, Erin realized she didn't know. The hotel information was in her UK phone, and it wouldn't open the forwarded message David had sent her. Her US phone was dead.

"Shit!" she said, and the driver looked at her in the rearview mirror. "Sorry, uh, please take me to 1324 Whistlers Way." If she went to her former home, she could at least get her car and wouldn't have to mess with that in the morning.

She nearly fell asleep in the taxi and realized it was almost two-twenty in the morning back at Owlgate. The house would be quiet; David would be asleep in his fantastic bed, naked, and— Her thoughts were cut short as they pulled into the driveway. The driver got out, took her suitcase out of the trunk, and Erin gave her a tip before she left.

It was eight-thirty, and she figured Todd would be getting ready for bed since he had to wake up early for work the next day. She didn't see any lights on in the house, so she hoped he was already asleep. Using her house key, she quietly let herself in.

As soon as she opened the kitchen door, the lights came on. Todd was standing in the opening to the hallway that led to the bedrooms in only his pajama bottoms, smiling at her the way he'd done for fifteen years. "Hello, Erin," he said. "You look good."

"Hi, Todd. Sorry if I woke you, I just thought I'd get my car—" she began.

"You didn't wake me. I took off work tomorrow so I could get the paperwork ready. I also filled your car with gas and took it through the carwash," he interrupted.

"You didn't have to do that," she said, wishing he wasn't being so nice to her.

"Wasn't a big deal. I thought you'd go right to your hotel."

Erin lay her purse on the kitchen table, took out her old American phone so she could read David's message, and then searched for the charger, but it wasn't in there. "Fuck! It's dead, and of course I forgot my charger!" she said, sitting hard on one of the dining chairs. "I'm too tired for this crap!" She lay her arm on the table, placing her head on top of it. She was starting to feel jet lag creeping ever so slowly upon her and needed something to go right.

"You can use mine; I'll get it," Todd said and left the room. A moment later, he was plugging the charger into an outlet above the kitchen counter and then took her phone from her to plug it in.

"Thank you. I'm just so tired. It's past two in the morning in Edinburgh."

"Why don't you stay here? You can use the spare room. You know—you... don't want to be alone when the jet lag hits," he said carefully.

She knew he was right; she hadn't thought of that when she'd decided to run away on this foolish trip. "Let me see where I'm supposed to be staying." She could feel herself falling asleep where she sat and fought it vigilantly until she heard her phone making noises on the counter. She stood wearily and found the message, though there wasn't a hotel in the itinerary at all.

"What the— Are you kidding me?" she said. It was then she remembered she'd asked David to have Tina add it, last minute, at breakfast. "He forgot! Good night nurse! I don't have energy for this—I just don't." She looked at Todd and realized she was going to have to surrender. "Fine, I'll stay here." *And David is going to be livid about it!* she thought.

"Good, now let's get you into bed before you fall asleep where you stand."

———

Todd took her phone out of her hand and set it on the counter. Then he led her like a child to the spare room. He turned down the covers and stood, not sure what he'd be allowed to do next. He wanted to help her off with her clothes and then have her say she missed him and wanted him back so he could make love to her.

"My suitcase," she said.

He left the room and returned, bringing it with him. He put it on the bed and unzipped it, ready to help find whatever she needed. "Todd," she said softly, "You should go now; thank you for your help."

He acted as though he was okay with that and turned to go. "Goodnight, Erin, sweet dreams."

"Night."

He walked out of the room, his heart aching as it had when she'd left two weeks earlier. He took off his pajamas and got into the bed they'd shared for so long. He lay staring at the ceiling, trying not to think about the love of his life in the next room or what he wanted to do with her.

Todd didn't know how long he'd been asleep, but it didn't seem that long when he heard a noise coming from the other room. Without thinking, he rushed into the spare room. Erin was sitting on the edge of the bed, crying, and holding something on a chain around her neck. He knelt in front of her, took her hand in his, and brushed a hair off her face.

"Erin! Are you alright? I heard a noise," he asked tenderly. She looked at him and stood, trembling like a frightened child. He stood and held her by the shoulders. "Erin, calm down." He knew it was jet lag, but she looked truly scared of him. "What's the matter? It's just me," he said as she launched herself over the bed to the other side of the room, knocking the bedside table over in her rush, and cowered in the corner.

"Go away! I don't want to have sex with you! Please, go away, please!" she pleaded with him. She was shaking and crying, her words sounding like someone begging for their life.

"Who said anything about having sex, honey? I was—" He then realized he was naked. "Shit! I'm sorry! I didn't mean to—" He left the room to put his pajama bottoms on. When he returned, he stood at the spare room door and watched her try to make herself as small as she could, seemingly to hide from the maniac who wanted to molest her. "I'm so sorry. I—I didn't think—It was stupid of me. Can I come in now? I put my PJs on," he said apologetically.

She was shaking her head and trembling. "Erin, are you okay? I'm coming in, but I won't hurt you." He'd seen the same behavior in cornered animals. They would either lash out and attack whatever they found threatening or cower and try to hide. Even with the jet lag, he couldn't understand why she'd be that afraid of him.

Then he remembered what he'd done after the game night. He'd tried to take her against her will, and he felt truly ashamed of himself. "Oh, Erin, I promise I won't hurt you or try to make you do anything—I was so wrong when I tried to force you. It's not like that now, I swear!" He walked to the table on the side of the bed nearest him and turned on the lamp. He went to where she was curled up and sat on the floor next to her. "Please trust me. I know you're suffering from exhaustion and jet lag, but please, let me help you."

"There's nothing you can do!" she cried, "I shouldn't have left, and I shouldn't be staying here! I'm an idiot! God! What time is it? Can I—Is there a flight back home tonight? I need to go back! Where's my phone? Surely David's awake by now—I need to talk to him! I need to be with him! What is wrong with me? Why was I so stupid to leave like I did? God, Erin! Oh my God, what if he— What if he changes his mind—What if I'm really not good enough?" she said, sounding panicked. She was talking very fast, not giving any space for a reply between her thoughts as she spoke. She eyed him, then suddenly bounded over the bed and ran out of the room in nothing but her underwear and a light t-shirt.

He watched her grab her phone and start typing while she sobbed, muttering to herself. He went to her and took the phone out of her hands, seeing a message to David. He knew anything she sent in that state wouldn't be wise, and she'd regret it when she was back in her right mind. "Come sit with me. Tell me what's wrong, and I'll listen to you, alright? You can send your message in the morning," he said as he led her to the living room and sat next to her on the couch.

She stared at the floor, crying. "I was angry, and I thought a few days away would be a good thing, but I was so wrong. He's going to hate me and find someone else. I'm so stupid! What am I going to do?" she said and then put her face in her hands and sobbed.

Todd touched her shoulder and watched her heart aching for whatever had happened over there with *him*. He leaned closer to her and pulled her toward him. She put her head on his chest and cried, wrapping her arms around him. He could feel her tears running down his stomach and wanted it to last forever.

Her breath cooled the hot tears as she gasped. He kissed the top of her head and put his arm around her shoulders, feeling them shudder as the sobs wracked her tired body. He held her until she became quiet, remembering the many times he'd held her while she struggled for air during one of her episodes. He'd also held her, years earlier, when they'd gone to England together, helping her through the horrible effects jet lag had on her.

She would be alright in the morning, but she needed him then, and he was so glad to be there for her. *This is probably the last time you'll be able to hold her; make it count!* he thought sadly. He felt her breathing become more regular, with only a few shuddering breaths as evidence of her earlier distress.

He knew it was wrong to be thinking about it, but he could feel her breast against his arm through her t-shirt, and it felt so good. *Knock it off, you idiot! She won't appreciate you getting a stiffy like this!*

But it was too late, his loose pajama bottoms were tented in the front, and he was very aware of it. He didn't want her to get upset again, so he tried not to move and to think of anything other than her soft skin and bare leg against him.

Unfortunately, she slid down his chest to put her head on his lap, as she used to do while watching movies together. She scooched her hips away from him, wanting to stretch out on the couch. When her head found his lap, she froze. He could feel her start to breathe heavily and presumed it was in fear, not excitement. "I'm sorry. I can't help it... you're just so lovely, and—"

She sat up, looked at him, and then at the tented pants. "I have to go. I can't stay—" she began, but he couldn't help himself. He could see her nipples through her light top; they were so close, and he longed to touch them. He knew he'd regret it, but he leaned over and kissed her, placing his hand over her soft, full breast.

To his utter astonishment, she didn't bolt or fight him. No, it was worse; she became rigid and held her breath, not kissing him back. He could feel her trembling and regretted his decision, but his cock was thinking by then, and he was having a hard time controlling himself.

He was getting angry that she wasn't responding to him, even though he also knew she wouldn't. *If I could just make her remember me, she'd relax and let me take her—I just know it!* He slowly moved his hand down over her underwear, foolishly taking her lack of movement as acceptance. She started to shake violently. *Just one more second!* he thought, desperately. "Just remember me and how I used to love you, please," he said, not meaning to say it out loud.

Somewhere in his fogged-up mind, he heard her say, "I remember, and I want you to stop." She was trembling, and yet still, as if she were standing on an IED she'd just tripped, knowing it would explode if she moved and she'd be dead, blown to bits. "Please take your hand off me." She carefully took his hand and lifted it off her crotch.

Again, he was thoroughly ashamed of himself and his lack of self-control. "I'm sorry. I'm so sorry," he said. "Yeah, you should go now—I just thought—Never mind."

———

Erin stood, hardly able to walk for the tremors running through her body. She made it to the spare room, then ran to the master bathroom, heaving into the toilet. Whether it was morning sickness or sheer terror, she didn't know. *How will I ever be able to tell David? He'll never get over it!* she thought.

After flushing the toilet, she walked back to the spare bedroom feeling drunk and woozy from the adrenaline coursing through her body. She hadn't known if he'd force her or not, and yet, somehow, she'd kept her head and managed to get him to stop. Driving in the state she was in was a bad idea, so she locked the door and put the chair under the doorknob, hoping she would be safe enough to get a few hours of sleep.

———

Todd saw her phone sitting on the counter. He decided to read what she'd written to her lover, the one who stole her away from him.

E: *David, my live! I'm sorry I left*
yipee! I cant believe I was do stupid.
Please din't be mad! I want too
come home right new. I'm at my

*horse. There wasn't a hotel on the
message from Tina, so I an here. I
ned you, and I won't lane yippee
again. Please don't be angry. Oh,
good! I'm do stupid!*

Sounds like they had a fight; maybe he'll leave her, and then she won't have anyone to hold her while she cries! he thought bitterly. He unplugged her phone, took his charger back to his room, and plugged it into the wall. Then he sat on the edge of the bed. *You're an idiot! A damned, fucking, idiot. What in the hell were you thinking! She deserves someone better than you'll ever be!*

He was actually afraid of his behavior. He'd never, in all his life, been that way before she'd started treatments, and he didn't know where it was coming from. He never wanted to be out of control like that again; it truly scared him. The clock read four-twenty am, and he wasn't tired, so he got dressed. *I'll just have to find something to do until the divorce attorney's office opens and then they draw up the paperwork. Hopefully, she won't leave town before she signs the damned thing.* Just before he left the house, he thought he'd better leave her a note, so she didn't just up and leave.

Chapter Two

LOOSE ENDS

E rin woke at ten-thirty, feeling groggy and exhausted. Once dressed, she moved the chair away from the door. Though she didn't think Todd was still there, she was nevertheless cautious about leaving the room, just in case. She opened the door and took a few timid steps out into the hallway, saw the note on the kitchen table, and read it.

Erin,
I will be getting the paperwork ready while I'm gone, so please don't leave town. I'll let you know when it's ready.
-Todd

Sounds like HE'S angry at me! She made herself a cup of tea and looked at her phone, seeing her unsent message to David. *Good night nurse! I'm glad I didn't send that!* She began a new one.

E: *I arrived safely and am at my house.*
It was late when I got here, and
there wasn't a hotel in the itinerary.

I had a rough night and want nothing more than to be back home with you. I'll be back as soon as possible. I love you.

Just thinking about him made her want to cry, but she had a lot to do before Todd got back. *As soon as the stupid papers are signed, I'm going straight to the airport.* She'd just noticed the stack of boxes and rolls of tape Todd had obviously set out the night before when she received a reply.

D: *I'm glad you arrived safely. I'm sorry I forgot about the hotel. I'll ask Tina to arrange one for you tonight, unless…Well, let me know what you want to do, and I'll have it arranged for you. I hope all goes smoothly whilst you're there. I miss you terribly, and I love you, darling. X*

E: *If Todd can get the paperwork in order today, I won't need a room. If I do, I'll get one myself using the card you gave me. xoxo*

She taped several boxes and took them to the living room to pack her Pop Vinyl figures and some of her other tchotchkes, but they were gone. She searched the cabinet under the shelves, and there they were, looking out at her. When the box was full, she took a picture of the contents for insurance reasons. This wasn't a trip across the state, it was across the world, and she wanted to make sure everything arrived intact. She taped the top then wrote David's London address on it.

She went through the whole house, including the attic, which was empty except for a few tattered porn magazines, and finished in the basement. The safe held her birth certificate, social security card, and two old savings bonds she could cash out while she was in town. A few other bits and pieces of her life, mostly jewelry, were put into her purse for safekeeping.

She wasn't filled with sadness and regrets that time as she came back upstairs into the kitchen, only urgency to return to Scotland and her true love. There were a few fragile things in some of the boxes, so she left them open; she'd have to buy extra padding at the FedEx when she got there. Everything else was taped and labeled, so she started taking them to her car. As she set the last one down, she heard a notification on her phone. It was Todd.

T: *Papers are ready. Come sign them.*
   Here is the address.

The place wasn't far, so she went inside, grabbed her purse and suitcase, did a quick sweep of the house to make sure she hadn't missed anything, and then responded to Todd.

E: *Be there in ten minutes.*

She took one last look at her home of fifteen years. There were so many memories, though she knew she'd make new ones, and everything would be okay.

——

Todd sat in what seemed like the largest conference room they had at the attorney's office. His stomach was in knots as he watched the condensation bead up and then roll down the side of the bottle of water he'd accepted when he arrived twenty minutes earlier. After he left the house, he'd driven around aimlessly, taking turns trying to figure out why he'd behaved so stupidly and beating himself up over it. Finally, he decided to go there to wait.

His phone chimed, and he saw Erin's message, which made him feel a bit nauseous, knowing he'd have to face her after assaulting her. He stood and began pacing while the legal aid set out the paperwork on the table. *It's all so final,* he thought as he stepped up to the open manila folders lying on the desk.

A memory came back to him of seeing two similar folders on Doctor Nanavala's desk, only a few months earlier. *I should've known this would happen. We really were stupid to think we could go back to our normal lives after something like that.*

Yeah, and who could blame her? You weren't the best husband, were you? You took her for granted and resented having to be her caregiver. You knew how much she hated those fucking magazines, and you just couldn't resist—

I should've used my phone! She'd never have known if I'd used incognito mode!

You idiot! She always knew! You're such a fool!

"Can I get you anything else, Mr. March?" the aid said, interrupting his thoughts.

"No, thanks. My wife... I mean... Erin will be here in about ten minutes."

——

Erin's emotions were scattered as she entered the attorney's office. Feeling tired, she told the receptionist she was there for the March divorce and was led into a room where Todd and the lawyer were sitting. She took a seat and listened as the woman explained, in boring detail, what each of the many pages said. When that was over, she asked if Erin was satisfied with everything.

"Yes," she said and then signed her name under Todd's. She was then asked for an address where the official documents should be sent once they were officiated by a judge. She gave them David's London address since it was still in her mind, adding, 'Care of Mr. D. Elliott.' "Are we done here?" she asked impatiently.

"Yes—" the attorney began.

"Good. Todd, please do not follow me; thank you." She just wanted to go. There was a lot to do before she could leave town and she didn't want a fight. She was out the door and halfway to the exit when she heard him behind her.

"Erin! Wait!"

She turned to face him, seething with anger. "You—can stay away from me! Don't come another step closer, or so help me God, I'll take you to court for sexual assault," she said, making sure the receptionist could hear her.

He stopped and stood with his hands out. "Okay, I won't come any closer. I wanted to say that—I'm sorry, and—Well, I hope you have a good life with him. Goodbye, Erin," he said, then he turned and went back into the office.

Erin hurried to her car and drove to the FedEx building, where she mailed the boxes with insurance, which cost a bloody fortune! She put it on David's credit card and left feeling like things were finally going in the right direction. After that, she stopped at her bank and cashed her EE savings bonds, which didn't take long, then she took out the money she'd been saving for another trip to the UK and closed her personal account. Next, she stopped at the post office and changed her address, forwarding her mail to London.

She couldn't think of anything else she needed to do, so she drove home and called for a taxi to pick her up. A thirty-something man picked her up and helped her get her much heavier luggage into the trunk. Twenty minutes later, they arrived at the airport, and the driver took her suitcase out of the trunk for her. She gave him a tip, thanked him, and rushed into the small terminal. At the ticket counter, she explained to the attendant that she already had a ticket leaving the next day but wanted an earlier flight.

The woman informed her of a flight leaving at three-twenty with only a two-hour layover in Chicago. That meant she'd be in Edinburgh at seven-fifty the next morning. Erin was ecstatic. "Perfect! Thank you so much!" she said and waited for her new boarding passes.

As she walked away from the check-in desk, she realized she hadn't eaten anything, so she went through security, then grabbed a cold sandwich and a bag of chips from the vending machine near the waiting area. There was no way she was going to miss the flight!

At three-eighteen, they started boarding the plane and everything went smoothly. The layover at O'Hare went well; she bought a magazine and kept her purse close to her. The next flight boarded on time, and seven hours and thirty-three minutes later, she was in Edinburgh!

She knew she'd probably go through jet lag again, but she also knew David would hold her, and he wouldn't try to hurt her. She nearly kissed the ground when she entered the airport! Wanting her return to be a surprise, she didn't call Roger to come for her; instead, she found a taxi and had it take her directly to Owlgate. She could have cried, being back where she should be.

Chapter Three

SURPRISE! I'M HOME!

Erin gave the taxi driver a generous tip, then stood in front of the old door in the brick wall with the wrought iron owls decorating it. It was early enough that the street was free from the reporters who were trying to cover both Susannah Elliott's untimely death and the photograph of the woman kissing David at her funeral. That was a relief, though, for all Erin knew, they might have given up by then.

She pushed the heavy door open, closed it behind her, and then rushed up the horseshoe-shaped drive, moving as fast as she could, hindered by her heavy suitcase, to the grand entrance stairs. The large house with its pillars and climbing ivy looked more beautiful to her than it had ever done. She left her luggage at the bottom of the staircase for Roger to bring in later and ran up the nine stone steps.

She rang the brass doorbell and laughed when she heard the dogs going crazy. She admired the brass knocker, toe plate, and doorknob as she stood, wiping her shoes on the rough doormat, though she knew they weren't dirty. The door opened to a shocked

Millie, who put her hands over her mouth and then pulled her inside.

"Ach! Praise be tae God for bringin' yeh back tae us in one piece!" she exclaimed. "Ye're a sight for sore eyes! David's been beside himself—Well, he'll tell yeh, I reckon. He's no' come down yet, so why don't yeh go up and tell him ye're home! You can greet everaone else afterward. I'll give yer excuses at breakfast," she said and then gently pushed Erin toward the staircase.

"Thanks, Millie," she whispered and then ran up the stairs, so excited to be back! She hurried down the hall, put her hand on the door to his room, silently turned the knob, and pushed it open. He had the curtains drawn, so she could barely see the shadow of his body under the blankets. She closed the door and stood at the side of the bed, listening to his breathing. It was staggered and choppy like a young child's when they've been crying for a long time, and her heart was torn apart.

"David," she whispered, and he froze as though he'd heard a ghost and needed to be still to find out if he'd hear it again. "I'm home—"

He sprang off the bed, holding her in his arms, weeping, just as he'd done the night before she'd left. "Oh, thank God! Ye're here! I thought I'd have tae wait another day!" he said, trembling and crying with joy.

"I—learned something, David. I can't live without you; I love you, and I need you," she said. They stood, forehead to forehead until finally, Erin put out her hand and touched his chest. His heart was beating hard and fast, and she looked up at him. "I'm glad I'm home."

"Please dinnae leave again! Stay with me forever," he said tenderly. "I need you as well; ma heart feels dead without you near me. I was just repentin' tae God for not keepin' ma end of the bargain I'd made with Him. He brought yeh back tae me after the fire, and I've treated you so wickedly. Please, ma love, please forgive me and stay."

Erin took her clothes off and lay on the bed. "I forgive you," she said as he got in behind her and held her tightly, his body wrapped around hers, flesh to flesh. "*Just wait till she's asleep, and she'll open her legs right up for yeh!*" The words attacked her. She hadn't thought about them since she'd left, but they were back, trying to rip out her heart again. She began to cry softly at the memory. "I can't stop hearing what you said. It won't go away. I thought I'd left them behind, but they keep chasing me," she said quietly.

'Aye, I can't stop hearin' maself say et, and seein' the look in yer eyes; I'll never forgive maself."

"Say other things, things to replace it. Cover it with something good and beautiful and lovely," she said.

"Ach, Erin, I wish there were more words, words to express just how much I love yeh.

"*...Love is not love that alters, when it alteration finds, or bends with the remover to remove...,*" she said.

"*...Ah no, it is an ever fix'ed mark, that looks on tempests and is never shaken...,*" he replied.

"Is our love an ever fix'ed mark, like the stars in the sky, David?"

"Aye, Erin. I believe et is. I love yeh more than anathin' I have or own or have accomplished. The only things I love *more* than you are ma five bairns, and I intend tae show et from now on. I'll not hide yeh from the media anamore either! If they dinnae have anathin' tae find out, they won't have a reason to stalk us. I'm gonna go tae those reporters and tell them just how I feel about yeh, and if they've all gone, I may just make an official announcement today!" he said boldly.

"Whoa! You shouldn't do that! It's too soon after Susannah's death! I appreciate the feelings behind it, but you need to wait at least a month or two. *Then*, you can tell the world, alright?"

"Humph! A'right, but I won't wait any longer than that! Now be still and let me hold yeh," he said.

"Wait—One more thing I've been meaning to ask you since the night before I left."

"What's that, ma love?"

"How much does a stone weigh?" she asked, and David chuckled softly.

"Did yeh use Millie's bathroom scale? A stone is fourteen pounds, so ten stone is one hundred forty pounds, yeh ken?" he explained.

She quickly did the math in her head *thirteen times fourteen was—one hundred eighty-two*. "I've lost twenty pounds since I met you," she announced, then she closed her eyes and relaxed into his arms.

The next thing she knew, she woke, needing to run to the bathroom to be sick. Once she'd recovered and brushed her teeth, she left the light on and stood in the doorway, watching David breathing evenly, his tall, lean form silhouetted under the covers.

He stirred and rolled toward the light. "Are yeh a'right, hen?" he asked, and the sound of his voice filled her with joy.

"Yes, I'm fine," she said as she walked across the bedroom and got back into bed with him. "I was thinking about it, and I can't believe my whole dream came true."

"I… hadn't thought of the dream," he said quietly. "Aye, Bran wasn't at the funeral; he was here, posing as me."

"I… don't think he meant to do that. I think he didn't know I was… in the bed. He just took the opportunity when—"

"Aye, typical Bran," he interrupted. "If it's all the same tae you, I'd rather not talk about et; the whole thing makes me sick to ma stomach."

"Me too."

David became very still. "I… need tae ask you somethin', and I need yeh to be patient and honest with me, a'right?" he said, and she didn't think she'd like what would come next.

"O-kay… patient and honest? That sounds—"

"Did yeh—" he interrupted but then hesitated.

"Did I… what?" she asked.

He was silent for a moment and then let it all out at once. "I just need tae know… if yeh tell me yeh didn't, I'll believe you. Did you… sleep with Todd?" he asked.

Erin was gobsmacked; she rolled over and looked at him, not sure what to say. "Or… I mean… did he try anathin' on yeh? Did he force yeh?"

"No, David, I didn't—I didn't want to. I don't want him at all anymore, don't you understand? Did I ever ask you if you fucked Susannah all those times you stayed in London?"

"Erin, I'm sorry for askin', but I had a nightmare last night, and... I need the truth, please. Ma mind won't let it go, and et's drivin' me mad. I... went tae London after Susannah died without any thought of you... havin' tae deal with Bran, and when I came home, everathin' seemed a'right, but it wasn't, was et? I just need yeh tae set ma mind at ease," he said, sounding miserable. "Also, yeh ken I didn't do anathin' with her, now, please don't be angry, but yeh didn't answer ma whole question. Did he—do anathin' to yeh?"

She didn't want to tell him. It was over, and there wasn't anything to be done about it anyway; what was the point? However, she knew she needed to be honest, so she rolled onto her back and took a deep breath. "He... did," she admitted slowly. "I had terrible jet lag, and at first he tried to help me, but then, when he got me to sit with him on the couch, he... well he tried to take advantage of me." David rolled onto his back, away from her; she heard his breathing deepen and thought she could feel the bed shaking.

"And just what did he *do* whilst tryin' tae take advantage of yeh?"

"Do you really want to know? Why, so you can torture yourself, or—me?" she said and sat on the edge of the bed. "I didn't let him do what he wanted to; isn't that enough?" She waited for a reply, but he was silent for a long time, so she stood, ready to put her clothes back on.

"Wait, don't go!" he said. "I'm tryin' tae keep maself from goin' mad. I wasn't there; I couldn't help yeh... again. I wanna know how far he got with you, so I know how angry to be. I know that sounds mental, but I need tae know."

She turned to face the bed. "Fine," she said hotly, "but if you use it against me—ever, I'll be gone forever, do you understand me?"

"Aye."

"I woke up in a strange bedroom and started freaking out, so I reached over to turn on a lamp, and the alarm clock fell to the floor. He must have heard it and ran into the room, trying to find out what was wrong, but... he had no clothes on. Well, I panicked, and the next thing I remember, he had his pajamas on and was trying to coax me out of the corner I'd ended up cowering in. I managed to escape what I thought was a trap but wasn't, and he somehow managed to calm me down and get me to sit with him on the couch.

"He was holding me while I cried, wishing I hadn't left you, and imagining all kinds of horrible things about how you would find someone better than me while I was gone, and... he—I don't know what he was thinking about, but when I went to put my head on his lap to sleep—I was just so tired; It was three-thirty in the morning here, and I was utterly exhausted! I just wanted to sleep, honestly, but he was... physically... excited," she said, feeling sick at the memory.

"I moved away from him as fast as I could, but he somehow ended up with his hand on my breast and was trying to kiss me. I couldn't move! I froze, and he put his hand on my... well, over my underwear, of course, but I managed to stop him, and he didn't do anything else. I ran to the spare room and locked myself in. I swear, nothing else happened. After I signed the divorce papers, I told him not to come near me, or I'd take him to court for sexual assault. And you know what? I don't care if you don't believe me. I know what happened, and I have a clear conscience, so… so—" She was angry and could feel hot tears welling up.

"I do believe you, and I'm so sorry yeh had tae go through that—again. From now on, you'll not need tae worry about anathin like that happenin'! I'll do everathin' in ma power tae keep yeh safe. Now come here and make love tae me; it's been too long, and I need you!"

Erin was still a bit upset at having to recount everything that had happened, but she was also nervous. She wanted him to make love to her, but there were so many things to factor in. She still had flashbacks of Bran, and now with what happened with Todd, she didn't know if she could, but she didn't want to say no either. She could feel a cold sweat break out all over her body. Then she started to shiver like she was coming down with the flu.

"I—can we wait till tonight? I'm just so tired and stressed out," she said. "I need a little time." Just then, her stomach started to growl loudly. "Not only that, but I'm starving!" she said, thankful she had an excuse to put him off for a while.

"Aye, we can wait, darling."

Chapter Four

INSECURITIES

David and Erin got dressed and went downstairs, hoping they hadn't missed lunch. They headed to the dining room, and as she got to the door, Erin said to him, "They're already eating."

When she walked into the room, Roger stood and pulled out a chair for her while Millie ran to lay two more place settings on the table. "Ach, ye're just in time; we've only just started. Did you sleep well?" Annis said with a smile and a twinkle in her eye."

Erin smiled and sat in the chair Roger was holding for her. David sat next to her and placed his hand on her leg under the table. "Aye, we did," she said softly.

As Roger pushed her chair in for her, his smile betrayed how happy he was to have her back. He offered to pour her tea and was being more than slightly over-attentive. At one point during the meal, he put his hand over hers and smiled warmly at her. "I cannae tell yeh how glad I am tha' ye've come back tae us! The place isn't the same without yeh," he said tenderly.

"Thanks, Roger, I might go up to Arthur's seat again, or maybe to St. Anthony's Chapel sometime today... if you'd care to join me?" she said, her cheeks suddenly rosy.

David was becoming uneasy and wondered how their earlier climb to the top of Edinburgh's mountain, Arthur's seat, and then the drive to the airport had actually gone? *Was there more involved than I realized?* He cleared his throat just enough to let Roger know he'd prefer that he didn't. "I will be out tae speak tae the reporters after lunch today," he said. "I won't be a prisoner in ma own home... er, ma mother's home."

"Well, good," Erin said, "I wasn't trying to exclude you, David. You can join us if you want to; you don't need to change the subject."

Annis raised her eyebrows and gave Millie a look while Roger smiled at her and said, "Aye, if yer sure I won't be a third wheel, then I'd like tha', thank you. Find me when ye're set tae leave."

"There weren't any cars out there earlier; what are you going to say to them?" Erin asked, and David looked confused for a second. "To the reporters," she said in explanation.

"Ah, well, I have a plan," he said. "How many cars are out there now, Roger?"

"I reckon there were three or four, last I looked," he said.

"How many garden sprinklers do you think you could find?"

"I believe I know of four off the top of ma head; why?" Roger said, and David smiled.

"That should do nicely, I reckon. I intend tae simply ask them tae go. I'll tell them the photo was a setup, and that's the only thing I'll say on the subject. If they leave, brilliant, if they don't, I shall make et difficult tae obtain a suitable, saleable photo. If we place the sprinklers on the wall, end tae end, pointed at their car doors, they will be hindered or at the least require their brollies! I reckon a wall of water would keep a photograph from turnin' out," David said.

Roger looked at Annis. "Et may just work; it'll make their lives miserable, that's for certain," he said.

After lunch, David and Roger went to the garage to arrange the sprinklers, while Erin helped Millie with the dishes. After about an hour, she saw David walking down the driveway from the sitting room window, so she moved closer to watch him. As he reached the gate, the reporters left their cars and started a barrage of questions.

David held out his hands to quiet them. "The woman in the photograph was part of a setup. I don't know who she was, nor where she's gone, and I don't care to know. I will not be held hostage in this house any longer, so if you don't leave, I will take measures to deter you." The crowd ignored him and started hurling questions once more. "This is the last thing I will say to you; I won't be answering ANY of your questions, so you're wasting your time here," he said, then he turned and headed toward the front door.

"Who's the big girl seen here over the last few days? Is she the woman you were with in America?" One of the reporters yelled out. David stopped. The cameras started clicking and flashing, but he kept his composure as he ascended the stairs to the front door and went in.

Erin watched Roger drag a garden hose to the front gates. He returned to the garage, and using a wheelbarrow, brought out a snake of garden sprinklers attached end-to-end with sections of cut garden hose, wire, and waterproof tape. He laid the sprinklers on the lawn and aimed them over the wall so they'd make as heavy a water curtain as possible. Then, he hooked the contraption to the main hose and walked back to the house. Starting out slowly, he turned on the water tap, making sure the short bits of hose held. It seemed to be working, so Roger smiled and waved at the reporters who stood looking through the gates as he turned the water all the way up and then went out to adjust the aim of each sprinkler. Two of them rushed to their cars, but a few, who weren't afraid of a little water, got a soaking that morning.

Annis had already called her neighbors and the police to tell them the situation. When the reporters called to notify them of the water on the street, hoping they'd be forced to shut it off, nothing happened. Eventually, they got sick of sitting in the deluge and left. Finally, Roger shut off the water but didn't bother bringing the contraption in, as they knew some of them would return.

At about four o'clock, Erin told David she wanted to climb Arthur's seat again and was about to run to the garage and let Roger know. "Wouldn't it be nicer if et were just us two?" he asked.

"I've already invited him, and I'm not going back on it, plus, he was so kind to me on Tuesday when I was at a very low point—"

"Aye, I'm sure he was," he said under his breath, and Erin frowned.

"Really? Is that how you're going to be? What's come over you? You were never jealous before, saying things like that about a trusted member of, well, in essence, your family. Not to mention it... well it makes me feel like you no longer trust me, like... like you really do think I'll just spread my legs for anyone," she said, her face growing red.

David's eyes grew large. "I didn't mean et like that," he said. "I'm sorry, Erin, and you're right, it's not fair of me tae take out my insecurities on Roger. He's just been so... attentive tae yeh, yeh ken? Holdin' yer hand and such; I know I'm bein' foolish, but everathin' has me worked up lately."

"Insecurities?" she said, frowning, "But, David, don't you understand? To me, you are the most beautiful man God ever made, and when you're not being a jealous nincompoop, I like you as a person, too. I'm not looking for, or at, anyone else. I swear that I wasn't trying to sleep with Bran; I ONLY want to sleep with you, ever, from now on, until I die!" she exclaimed, sounding exasperated. Her eyes were closed, and her fists were clenched into tight balls at her sides.

He stood in front of her, took one of her fists, and held it gently, lest it should lash out and strike him unannounced. He scanned her face; the bruises were much lighter, with only small bits of dark purple and the slightest yellow-green marks under her eye and over her cheekbone. She opened her eyes, and he touched her hair, putting a stray strand behind her ear. "A'right, ma love. Yeh dinnae need tae convince me of that again; I'm just an old fool. Go, find Roger, and I'll ask Millie tae send somethin' along with us," he said lovingly.

He kissed her and let go of her hand, which she had unclenched and allowed him to hold with their fingers entwined. She took a deep breath and turned to walk away. "The most beautiful man God ever made, eh? I think I'll have that put on my business cards!" he said and laughed.

She turned around and rolled her eyes, "Just watch it, or it may end up as your epitaph!" she teased.

Roger was in the garage, as usual, and smiled when he saw her. He truly liked Erin and wanted David to get things right with her. "Hello," he said.

"I was thinking of leaving soon; are you still interested in joining me?" she asked as she approached him, and he narrowed his eyes a bit. "If you're concerned about David's say in the matter, he doesn't have one. We've had a wee talk and settled some very important things between us. Now, I'd like it if you came along."

"Well, if that's so, how can I say no tae yeh then? Let's fetch the walking sticks; will David be joinin' us?" he asked.

"Yes, he will."

He pointed to the stairs in front of them. "After you." He followed Erin up the stairs to the flat. It seemed awkward to him as they stood there, remembering the last time they were in the flat together. Then, she had been naked, and he'd pulled Bran off her. He could still see her face, and—well, he tried not to think of the other parts of her he'd seen. "I'm glad ye've made up; ye're so good together. Broke ma heart tae see yeh hurtin' as yeh were," he said sincerely, and Erin's cheeks bloomed pink.

"Yeah, well, I'm embarrassed about that. Anyway, I think it may be a while before things are a hundred percent again between

David and me, but I'm glad the worst of it is over," she said, standing at the window that looked out onto the large front garden.

He went to his room, took off the dirty work shirt he was wearing, and put on a clean one with a flannel over the top, just in case it was chilly again. Then, he took the two walking sticks from the corner of the tiny sitting room and handed the one with the little seat to her. "We'll have tae get the third one from the main house; I've only two of ma own," he said.

Erin saw David standing at the bottom of the stairs as they descended. He was holding the same satchel she and Roger had used a few nights before and was also carrying his own walking stick. She noticed the tiniest little… something in his face which said, without meaning to, that he didn't like the fact she'd been in the flat alone with Roger. She was starting to realize that it really would take a long time for things to get back to normal.

"Oh, good!" she said. "Then we're all ready to go."

David took her hand but let it go as he approached the door. "For fuck's sake!" he said. "Now what?"

Erin peeked out the door. A reporter was parked in front of the gate, his camera aimed at the house. "Well, I think we have maybe three options," she said. "Number one, Roger turns the water back on, but they will just follow us. Number two, I can walk with Roger, so they think I'm with him and not you, and number three, you can go back in the house and remain a prisoner."

David looked at them both, seeming to consider the options given. "There's another option yeh didn't mention," he said. "I could confess ma love for yeh with a show that'll earn them their million quid."

Erin laughed and shook her head while Roger looked at him like he'd gone mad. "Aye, and then ye'll have every reporter from here tae Timbuktu on the doorstep! I think the best option is tae act as though Erin is with me," Roger said. "They've already seen us together several times now."

Erin noticed David grow ever so slightly tense and take a deep breath. "Come here," she said and pulled him to a corner, well away from sight. She kissed him, a passionate kiss that had them both out of breath and wanting more. "Don't be a nincompoop! I love yeh!"

"A'right, I'll walk behind yeh," he said.

Erin and Roger walked out of the garage together, and then David followed, looking sad; he was supposed to be in mourning after all. The three of them walked to the gate, David with his head down, while the reporter took pictures. Then, seeing they were going for a walk, he hopped into his car and started the engine.

David stopped and tapped on his window. "Please," he said, "we'd like to go for a walk; can't you leave us be? I'm not going to do anathin' worth you following us around, and I'd like to grieve in peace." The man opened his mouth to argue, but David interrupted him. "I'll make a deal with you; if you go away, and I mean don't come back, I will give you a heads up on the next story-worthy thing I do. Give me your contact information, and I give you my word, I'll do it."

The reporter thought about it and then handed David his business card. "Are you plannin' to do anything soon"? He asked, and David smiled.

"Aye, I might just!" he said, so the man raised his window and drove away.

Erin and Roger had stopped together and waited as David bargained with the man in the car. As the car drove away, he approached them. "Wow," Erin said, impressed.

"Ach, I promised him my next big story if he'd bugger off," he said.

Erin laughed and hugged him. "Yes, I heard you. And what will your next story be, hmm?" she asked, linking her arm with his.

He gave her a wily grin. "Dunno, maybe announcing that I'm in love with you, or that ye're having ma bairn, or the first photo of said bairn, or perhaps our first official weddin' photo," he listed. "That's just off the top of ma head."

Roger raised his eyebrows, "Looks as though ye've got a few bargaining chips goin' for yeh," he said.

Chapter Five

UP THE MOUNTAIN

Roger, Erin, and David walked to the footpath that would lead them to the top of Arthur's Seat. David was wearing a disguise of a baseball cap and sunglasses. It worked well enough that he could hold Erin's hand and even snuck in a kiss or two when he was sure no one would see them.

It was foggy that afternoon, but the day was warm enough until they got to the apex, where it was windier. Erin had brought a sweater, but it wasn't heavy enough. David had a long-sleeved sweatshirt with him, but it was far too small for her. Roger had a bit more bulk in his shoulders and arms, so his shirt fit her pretty well, as long as she didn't need to button it. He let her wear it as they stood on the mountain's peak and looked out as far as they could.

Without warning, they watched as a bank of thick fog rolled over them and stayed there. They couldn't see their hands in front of their faces, so the only thing to do, unless they wanted to fall off the mountain, was to stand still or sit where they were until it blew away or lifted. Erin and David took full advantage of the fog to do a little snogging. They wrapped their arms around each other and kissed, continuing what Erin had started before they'd left the garage. She felt a bit bad for Roger since she was sure he would hear them making out. David took hold of her ass and pulled her tight against him. She gasped when she felt his erection against her.

"When we get home, supper or not, I wanna bed yeh and please yeh. May I do that?" he whispered in her ear.

She wanted him to so badly, but she also didn't want to risk the wrath of Millie. "Aye, unless supper is ready, or very nearly ready, then I'd like to wait so we can take a little bit more time and enjoy ourselves. I'd rather not have a 'wham bam, thank you ma'am' scenario," she said, making David laugh heartily.

"Wham bam, thank yeh ma'am, eh? I'd give yeh one of those right here and now if I could. If I were wearin' ma kilt ye'd be able tae feel et, yeh ken? I'd let yeh reach under ma sporran. Mebbe I'll wear it for supper tonight," he joked.

They hadn't made love when she'd surprised him that morning. It had been four days before that since they had, and David was behaving like a seventeen-year-old kid, all horny and desperate. "You don't need a kilt for me to feel you up; your trousers are pretty loose," she whispered and unzipped his fly, which she knew caught him off guard. After making sure the cloud cover was still thick, she managed to slip her hand in and at least fondle him over his underpants. That was as brave as she was willing to be out in public, even if they were under cover of fog.

"Ach, woman!" he whispered urgently in her ear, "Stop now, or I won't be able to, and et'll be a right mess!" He took hold of her hand, carefully extracted it from his fly, and zipped it back up. He was breathing heavily and stood with his forehead against hers. "Just don't move, a'right?" They stood like that for several moments before he sighed in relief. "That was far too close for comfort!"

The fog began to lift, and soon they could make out Roger standing about five feet away from them. A few minutes later, it was clear enough to see their way, so they headed back toward Owlgate. That time, Roger walked ahead until they were a few blocks from the house, then Erin caught up with him, resuming the pretense that they were the ones who were together, just in case there was someone with a camera hiding somewhere.

When they stepped into the house, they could smell something delicious cooking. Erin's mouth started watering right away, and within moments of their return, Millie told them there were only twenty minutes until the meal was ready. Erin handed Roger his walking stick and thanked him for coming with them, then she and David went upstairs to change before supper.

They got to the room, and David shut the door, pinning her against the wall in a flash, but she wasn't about to rush it that time. "David!" she said and tried to push him away. "David, please stop." He was groping her, and it wasn't pleasant.

He reluctantly paused what he was doing and looked pleadingly at her. "Ach, Erin, dinnae torture me!" he moaned, but she smiled and unzipped his fly again. That time she unbuttoned it as well.

She let his trousers fall to the floor and then knelt to pull off his underpants. "Just relax, while I—" She didn't finish her sentence before putting her lips around him and taking him all the way into her mouth. He gasped and grabbed hold of her hair as his knees buckled. She knew it wouldn't take long, and within a few moments, he was finally able to release into her mouth. She stood and spit it out into the bathroom sink, then rinsed her mouth out quickly. That wasn't her favorite thing to do, but sometimes it had to be done. She returned to the room to find David laid out on the bed, obviously feeling much more relaxed and content than he had been before.

"Ach, thank yeh. I was about tae burst!" he said.

"Really? I'd never have guessed!" she said and laughed.

"Ha. Ha. Ha. Just yeh wait until after supper; I'll make you burst!" He sat up and pulled her to him, so her chest was at his eye level, though he didn't grope her again. Instead, he lifted her top and kissed her belly. "I only have a minute tae speak tae yeh just now, but yeh need tae know somethin'. I love yer mummy verra much, and I love you as well," he said to her stomach. He gave her a light raspberry, which tickled, and she pulled away, laughing.

"Okay, go and change!" she said, trying to rub away the tickle. She went back to the bathroom and brushed her teeth before changing out of her sweaty clothes.

"I've taken two small jobs in London on Tuesday and Thursday next week; would yeh like tae come with me or stay here?" David asked on the way to supper. "We'll return at the weekend tae retrieve the children from school, and then we can decide where we'd like tae spend their holiday."

"I'd like to go to London with you," she said and took his hand.

Supper that night was cottage pie filled with meat, veggies, and a delicious homemade gravy, all piled high with creamy mashed potatoes. "Millie, you're spoiling me! This is too good! What will I do when we leave here?" Erin asked. "Probably too much take-away, I guess; fish and chips and curry."

"I do have a cook, remember?" David said as he spooned another helping onto his plate. "She's not as good as our Millie, but she's not half bad."

Erin looked at Millie and smiled. "Not half bad means not half good as well. Millie, would you mind teaching me a few of your tricks someday? Things like this gravy and maybe your meat pie?" she asked. "I'm devastated over the loss of the one that burned in the cottage fire."

Millie smiled at her friend. "For you, Erin, I will. Ye'll have tae wait for the meat pie, as we've jest had et, but I can teach yeh the gravy at the weekend."

"Okay, I look forward to it. Ooh, David, will Kitty be there? I'd like to talk to her some more," she asked, and he smiled at her.

"Aye, I'll arrange for both her and Francie to be there when we return. At some point, we should discuss what tae do with the house, whether tae keep or sell et, though that's not a subject for the supper table," he said.

Once the meal was finished and the pudding half-eaten, David stood, getting everyone's attention. "I... would like tae... uh, apologize for my... behavior on Tuesday," he began haltingly; it was clear he was trying to choose his words. "I was immature and rash, and I'm embarrassed at the things I said and did. I... must also thank yeh for supportin' Erin as yeh have. He took her hand in his and gazed into her eyes. "She's been gracious enough tae forgive me...

and… well, I couldn't live without her, so I'd like tae raise a toast, if I may. To family."

"To family!" The whole table said together, and then Erin said, "*Slàinte mhath* (slange-eh vah)," as she was accustomed to doing in her household. Everyone looked at her, smiled, and echoed, '*Slàinte mhath*,' then raised their glasses and drank.

———

Annis smiled at her son, and the woman she hoped would soon be her daughter-in-law and mother of her newest grandchild. *Aye, they are lovely together,* she thought happily. "Thank you, David," she said. "That was well braw of yeh. Since this seems tae be a night for toasting, I'll ask everaone tae raise their glass once more tae David and Erin; may they have many, many happy years together, and to the bairn, may it grow tae be as bonnie and braw as its parents!"

"Hear, hear!" Roger said, and they all drank to David and Erin.

Erin raised her hand awkwardly and then stood. "I might as well join in, right?" she said. Everyone around the table smiled warmly at her. "I'd like to raise a toast to my new family. All of you at this table, and the children; those far away from us and the one very near." She put her hand on her belly and raised her glass of ginger ale. "To kith and kin, *Slàinte mhath*!" Everyone stood and gave a hearty "*Slàinte mhath*!"

Chapter Six

WHAT MUST BE DONE

Erin was determined to be done with drama. D-O-N-E-done! She didn't care if there was a hurricane, a tsunami, or if she lost her right arm, she would not cry again for as long as she possibly could, and she couldn't even imagine it after a night like that one!

After supper, she helped Millie clear the table, knowing full well David wanted to go right back upstairs, but she liked making him wait—building the anticipation of things to come. He waited for what she presumed he thought was an appropriate length of time, then came into the kitchen and asked to speak with her. She and Millie exchanged knowing glances and smiled as she left the room with him.

"Am I really that irresistible, David?" she asked him, half kidding and half really wanting to hear him say it.

"Erin, you are the air tae this drownin' man!" he said.

She laughed as he led her back upstairs for round two, though when they reached the first landing, Erin's heart began to palpitate. As they reached the second landing and started down the hall, she was sweating, and her breathing became short and rapid. They entered the bedroom, and after David closed the door, she told him she needed to freshen up first and made a beeline for the bathroom. She found herself hesitating to take her clothes off, and when she finally managed it, she took her time washing herself.

"Please come tae bed, love," he said tenderly from the bedroom.

She couldn't understand her reluctance to be intimate with him. At first, all she wanted was for him to make love to her, erasing the feeling of Bran, but now, just the thought of it made her remember everything and feel suffocated. How could she possibly explain it to him though? "I'll be out in a minute," she lied, trying to find something else to do, hoping maybe he'd fall asleep or something. She brushed her teeth to stall, but apparently, he wasn't giving up that easily.

———

David came to the bathroom door and saw her standing over the sink with her hands firmly gripping the edge of the countertop. Her head was down over the sink bowl, and she looked pale. "Erin?" he said, making her jump "What's the matter? Why aren't yeh… coming tae bed?"

She looked at him and then held out her hand, which had an obvious tremor. She shook her head and tried to take a deep breath. "I… don't know… what's wrong with me. I long to make love to you, more than anything, but… I can't stop the flashbacks. He's the very last person I want to think about, ever, but there he is, with his pockmarked face and… and greasy hair, speaking to me with half-rotten teeth and breath that could kill. I don't know how to make it go away!" She closed her eyes and hung her head once more.

"Do you think it might help tae keep the lights on or open the shades?" he asked, knowing how selfish he was being. He wanted to help and support her, but he also desperately wanted to make love to her.

"I don't know," she said with a shrug. "My irrational brain has been trying to convince me to… sleep in the tub." One tear rolled down her cheek; she wiped it away in frustration, and no more followed after it. "I'm so sorry."

He walked in, touched her arm, and she turned toward him, allowing him to hold her. "I dinnae ken what tae do tae help yeh, but I'll wait if we need tae," he said, hoping he'd be able to even as he said it. The feel of her in his arms made his heart beat faster. "Is et the bed? We could sleep on the floor if yeh think it might help?"

She looked at him sadly. "It's more than that—I'm afraid… to fall asleep, or maybe I am asleep now, and… when I wake up… will it be you or… someone else on top of me?" she said, her breath coming out shaky and uneven.

He knew it was his fault she was so afraid; if he hadn't said what he had, she might not be so frightened of it repeating. "Erin, we don't have to have sex if you don't feel ready. Just let me hold yeh, a'right?"

"Okay," she said and allowed him to lead her to his bed.

As he spooned behind her, he could feel the tension in her body and kissed her shoulder. "Relax, darling, ye're safe with me and I'll not do anathin' tae harm yeh." He felt her body gradually settle and her breathing slowed until she was asleep.

In the middle of the night, David woke as Erin began thrashing beside him. She was on her back, acting as though she were being held down. "No! Please! I don't—Please—please stop—stop!" she said, then suddenly lay still. Just as he was deciding whether or not to go back to sleep, she yelled, "Help me, Roger!" and then got out of bed, panting and clutching at her chest. She fell to her knees as sobs racked her body. Not knowing what to do, he got out of bed and knelt beside her. He put his hand on her arm, and she jumped. "Who—" she began and then ignored him.

David was shocked; he hadn't seen her like that since her episode in New Orleans. *She called out for Roger, not me*, he thought sadly. He understood Roger was the one who had saved her, so it made sense she'd call for him, but it still stung. "My darling, are you a'right?" he asked gently. She shook and cried until eventually she lay on the floor and wouldn't let him help her up.

He covered her with a light blanket then carefully put her pillow under her head. "I love yeh, Erin," he said and lay on the floor next to her, watching her. After some time, he saw her breathing slow and could hear it become steadier as she fell asleep again. He lay there wondering what he could do to help but could think of nothing.

In the morning, Erin woke on the floor, stiff and chilly. She opened her eyes and remembered the events of the night before, but not the nightmare or how she had ended up where she was. When she heard David come back from the bathroom, she crawled back into bed, and he snuggled up to her. "What happened? Why was I on the floor?" she asked.

"Shh, never mind that now, just let me hold yeh, and I'll tell yeh later." He buried his face in her hair and took a deep breath. "I want to be close to you—to feel yer skin." He lifted his head and nuzzled her ear with his nose, moving down to her neck. His hand made its way down her thigh to her knee then he bent her top leg so that it lay in front of her. He ran his hand along the inner thigh of her other leg, making her shiver.

His touch made her breath quicken, and she couldn't help but make approving noises. She wanted him as he pulled her shoulder toward him; however, when her back touched the mattress, panic rose inside her. She tried to hide her fear and allowed him to get on top of her. He had just gotten into position to enter her when she began weeping softly. "Stop," she said almost inaudibly at first. "Please stop," she said more forcefully and pushed him away. She sat up, panting and gasping for breath.

"What did I do? Why did yeh... stop me?" he said with a mixture of concern and a hint of frustration. She stood and walked into the bathroom, closing the door behind her. "Erin. I'm sorry, I didn't mean for et tae come out sounding like that."

She sat on the tiled floor against the door and tried not to cry. She held her breath, wanting to slow her breathing.

What in the fuck is wrong with you? He's done that twenty times or more; why can't you just get over the thing with Bran? Why do you have to torture yourself and him? He's going to stop trying soon, so get over it already.

She wasn't going to allow Bran to control the rest of her life. She was going to allow David to make love to her if it killed her, so she stood and opened the door. David was sitting on the edge of the bed; he looked up, and she went to him. She ran her fingers through his dark chestnut hair, and he laid his forehead on her chest.

"I'm sor—"

"Get all the way onto the bed and lay on your back," she said. He looked at her with his eyebrows knit together, and she kissed him. "Please." He did what she said, and as she straddled him, she started trembling, but she didn't let it stop her. She took his hands, placed them on her breasts, and when he was fully erect again, she put him inside of her. She was still shaking, and a few tears escaped her eyes, but she continued. She looked at his face, watching his reactions to her movements, which helped her to allow herself to relax and enjoy how she felt as well.

She concentrated on the feelings building within her and could sense they were also doing so in David. She moved a little bit faster, and finally, she felt their electricity again, pulsing through her, moving from him, and filling her once more. Her body reached the point of release, and then she felt his orgasm reverberate in response.

"Oh, Erin! Ma Losh!" he said as their bodies became one again.

Erin was weeping, not from being sad or upset, but because of the intense joy and fulfillment she felt with him. Once again, she couldn't imagine going a day without making love to him instead of the dread she had so recently felt at the thought. She laid her head on his chest, feeling his carpet of dark brown chest hair against her smooth, bare skin. "David, I'm sorry; I love you so much!" she said. He wrapped his arms around her and held her. "Thank you for loving me."

"I think I ought tae be thankin' you."

"Well, what's stopping you?" she said and rolled onto the bed, snuggling up to him.

"Alright," he said and took her hand in his. He put it to his lips, kissing the back of it. "Thank yeh, Erin, for puttin' up with this old man! For bein' patient and forgivin' me, as well. And for makin' love tae me just now." He closed his eyes and sighed.

"You're welcome. I... just had to force my way through it until it felt like it always did... before. I—I can't promise I won't have another difficult time, but if you're patient with me, I'll get past it," she said. They lay together, drifting in and out of sleep until Millie knocked at the door.

"Brekkie will be ready in twenty minutes," she said cheerfully.

David chuckled and answered they would be down soon. "Well, she's in fine spirits this mornin'. She hasn't called et 'brekkie' since I was a lad."

"Not to change the subject, but you said something about selling the house in London?"

"Aye, I wanted tae talk tae yeh about et. Do you wanna keep et or find somethin' else?"

"I don't think you should sell it. I mean, after all, you have that amazing office, and the kids have their rooms, and it's a lovely old house. I really do like it, except—"

David looked at her. "Except?"

She didn't like to criticize, but she couldn't help it. "Except... well, the kitchen. I don't like it at all. I'm sorry; I hate to—"

"Dinnae worry, love, I hate it too. It's funny, I just remembered ma Gran's kitchen, in Dorset. It was lovely, as far as kitchens go. I wonder if I could find some old pictures. I think ye'd like et."

Erin propped herself up on her elbow. "Old photos! I LOVE old photos, especially of people I love! Especially when they were little kids! Hint, hint."

David laughed as he got up. If they were late to the table, Millie would be irate. "I'll see what I can do. Now, up you go; time, tide, and Millie wait for no one!"

Chapter Seven

MEMORIES OF DAYS GONE BY

After breakfast, David asked Millie if she knew where the old family photo albums were stored. She looked at Erin and smiled. "Aye, I know jest where they are. Ach, dearie, ye're gonnae love our Davey as a boy! He looks like Peter, only more like his father. He was a verra handsome man, our Charles," she said and led them to an accent cabinet that had been hand-painted with green and blue parakeets in tropical vegetation.

"Good night nurse! That's breathtaking and so lovely," Erin said, noticing it for the first time.

David smiled and ran his hand over the smooth, polished mahogany top. "Aye, it was an anniversary gift from my da. I've always fancied et as well."

"Well, you have good taste; you like me, after all!" she said.

"True! There's no denyin' that," David agreed. He put his arm around her shoulders and kissed her cheek. Millie began pulling the old photo albums out of the cupboard, but he stopped her. "Ach, Millie, I'll do that."

Erin noticed that she looked a bit disappointed and presumed she'd wanted to have a look as well. "Do you mind if we use the kitchen table to look through these, Millie? That way, you can peek over our shoulders if you want to," she asked and saw a smile on the older woman's face, though it was fleeting.

"Aye, et's a'right with me. I'll make sure et's clean," she said with feigned indifference and left them.

There were quite a few albums; some of them appeared to be very old. David set them on the table and opened the oldest looking one, first. On the first page, dignified, well-groomed, late nineteenth-century men posed sitting or standing next to finely dressed women, children, and babies. In that photograph and the ones that followed, the women wore corsets under their long dresses, giving them an ideal shape. The men were clothed in perfectly tailored suits and ascots or some form of a tie, along with tall, black top hats and fashionable walking sticks. Several men had watch chains hanging from their waistcoats, some wore little round glasses, and one dapper older gentleman had a monocle.

Near the back of the album, there was a portrait of a fine-looking man with a glorious example of an Edwardian mustache in an ornate military uniform; he was very handsome, and his smile reminded Erin of David's. "Oh, I like him," she said. "I mean, I know I'd have liked him if I'd met him. He has your eyes, David, but with Charlie's nose and the little gap between Rosie's front teeth."

David smiled broadly. "That was ma great grandad, and namesake, David Peter Elliott. He died when I was small, so I dinnae remember him," he said while Millie looked over Erin's shoulder at the picture.

"He wouldae loved yeh, Erin!" she said. "He lived here for a few months before he died... when our Davey was wee; he stayed in the room ye're usin' now. He was a lovely man! Charming, funny, and smart; everaone who met him liked him. He'd have everaone laughin' so that they couldnae stand upright! I loved him, maself."

"He was nearly one hundred when he died, right, Millie?" David asked.

"Eighty-two, and jest as witty and loveable as he'd ever been. Ach, seeing that old photo brings back the memories; does ma heart good, seein' 'em," she said.

"This is gonna sound childish, but wouldn't it be wonderful if we could talk to portraits, and they could talk back like they do in Harry Potter? I'd love, with all my heart, to sit and have a conversation with this man. To hear his voice and have him respond to what I was saying," Erin said and felt her cheeks turn pink.

"Aye!" David and Millie said in unison, which made them all laugh.

"Ach, what I wouldnae give tae speak with ma sister, Eleanor again!" Millie said. "We called her Ellie, and she was the person whom I loved most in the world. She died when I was seventeen; I still miss her, and I'm nearly forty now," Millie teased, and her eyes sparkled with concealed laughter.

"Well then, Ann is a cradle robber!" Erin said and then put her hands over her mouth. "Good night nurse! I didn't mean to say that!" She bit her lip and looked at Millie, her eyes huge, hoping her friend wouldn't be angry. Thankfully she was laughing, while David seemed confused.

"What on earth does—" he began, and then the realization hit him. "Oh! Ma Losh! Is—Is et true?" He looked at Millie and then at Erin.

Conveniently, Annis walked in and saw the astonished and befuddled look on David's face. "What did I walk in on?" she said light-heartedly.

Erin looked at Millie and then at the tabletop. "I'm sorry, Ann, I spoke without using my brain," she said, feeling like she'd betrayed their trust.

David's gaze was darting, back and forth, between Millie and his mother. "But I didn't know—When did this happen?" he asked, and Erin thought he looked a little bit like a confused child.

Annis seemed to realize what he'd just learned and put her hand on his. "Ach, son, a verra long time ago," she said gently. "No' long after yer father died. Millie helped me get through it, and I soon realized I loved her, no matter that she wasn't a man. She's been stayin' in ma room evera night for over nine years; did yeh never notice?"

"It honestly never occurred tae me," he said with a frown, but then his expression changed. "Frankly, I'm a wee bit relieved—"

"Relieved?" Annis said with her eyebrows raised.

"Aye. All this time I've felt as if I should... I dinnae ken, visit more often, worried you were lonely. Now I learn I needn't have worried," he said with a smile.

"Ach, ye've done a fine job making sure I was alright. You may relax, now," Annis said and patted his hand. "What're yeh doin', anaway?"

David smiled at his mother and Millie. "I'm verra happy for yeh both. Shocked and a wee bit gobsmacked, but chuffed all the same," he said and kissed his mother's, then Millie's cheek. "Now, as for what we're after, I was hopin' tae find a photo of Gran's kitchen in Dorset tae show Erin. She doesn't particularly care for the one in London."

"Aye, I dinnae blame yeh!" Millie said.

"Ach, it's an eyesore!" Annis said at the same time.

David laughed. "I couldn't agree more. We came across this picture of Great Grandad Elliott in our search," he said, pointing to the sepia-colored picture which was held in place by small black triangles glued onto the page of the album.

Annis looked over his shoulder and sighed. "Et's funny; I'm sure yeh didn't know, but the reason I married your da was because of him. I reasoned that if Charles turned out tae be even half the man his grandfather was, I'd be a lucky woman," she said with a twinkle in her eye. "He was brave and fearless, as well as charming and kind; the most generous and agreeable man I've ever known." She lifted several of the albums off the top of a stack and picked up a navy-blue one with a gold pinstripe around the edge of the front cover. She set it in front of Erin, opened it, and smiled.

In a faded color photograph, Erin saw Annis and a very handsome man as a young couple standing on the beach, with high red cliffs behind them. A small boy was holding her hand, and she instantly knew it was David. "Awww! Look at you!" she said, her voice pitched higher than usual. "You're so sweet! And look at you, Ann!" She gave a soft 'cat call' whistle. "Good night nurse! Don't you and your husband make a handsome pair!"

Annis tried to look unphased, but her cheeks were a bit rosier than they had been a few moments earlier. "Pshaw!" she said, then smiled brightly. "That was one of the best summers I've ever had." Her voice betrayed a bit of melancholy. "Our Davey was past his naughty years and could play without us havin' tae be right next tae him. Charles and I would sit on a blanket and watch him run up tae the water and then try tae run away before the frigid waves touched his wee feet, but the water was always more clever."

Erin looked at David, who was watching his mother's face and smiling. Annis flipped through the pages slowly. Erin could tell little movies of the events in the photos were playing in her mind. She'd smile and sometimes laugh when she saw something that made her remember the past events which had been pushed to the farthest corners of her mind.

"I loved goin' tae Gran's," David said, "I reckon they were the best times of ma life as well." Annis glanced at her son, and they exchanged knowing looks. "So many things changed after she passed. No more carefree summers by the coast."

"Aye, and soon afterward, you had Bran to contend with," she said with a sigh.

The next page showed his grandmother, dressed in an old-fashioned house dress with an enormous floral apron over her entire front. She looked sweet and kind, and Erin liked her right away as well. "That's her; Dora May Elliott," David said. "She was Great Grandad's daughter-in-law," he said. "Her maiden name was Douglas, correct?" he asked his mother.

Annis was staring at a faded picture of her and Charles. He was sitting in a high-backed chair, and she was sitting on his lap. Her head was on his shoulder, and her hand was on his chest; they were both laughing. "Aye, Douglas," she said absently as she gently touched David's father's smiling face and sighed.

"Are you okay, Ann?" Erin said, noticing how far off she seemed.

Annis looked up and walked over to Millie. "Aye, et's just memories of happy days and youth gone by. Now, let's find a picture of the kitchen for yeh," she said and turned around with the pretense of moving something out of the way, but Erin saw her hand come up to her face to wipe a tear away.

She turned around and flipped the page. People were standing in a kitchen in one photo, but it was too close-up to see any details. A picture on the next page was much better, though. She saw the lovely old farmer's sink and some pretty floral fabric gathered on a string below it, covering the pipes and such. There were adorable little shelves that held things like an egg timer and a small vase filled with violets.

"YES!" Erin said excitedly; this is perfect! I love it."

David smiled at her. "I knew yeh would," he said and placed his hand on hers. They looked at more photos in that album, and every time little David's face appeared, Erin would squee and comment about how adorable he was.

"Millie! Is that you?" Erin said as she turned the page and saw a young woman wearing plain clothes and a starched apron. Her hair was in a tight bun that rested on the back of her neck, and she was holding David's little, chubby hand. "Oh my gosh! I hate to say it, but... you're so young!"

"Aye, I reckon I was," she said and laid her finger over the image of her and David's hand.

They continued looking through the albums; David went from a tiny baby to a teenager, with freckles and a few pimples, but he was always remarkably handsome. "It's amazing how much Peter looks like you at his age. It's striking!" Erin said, looking at a photo of David in swimming trunks, getting ready to run out into the sea in one album.

"Thank God for good genes, aye?" he said.

In the next album, there were several photos with Bran in them. Erin felt a chill run down her spine to see the two boys, looking so much alike, standing together. She didn't want to see any more of him, so she turned to Annis. "Do you have any pictures of your sister and Charles' brother?" she asked, curious to see just how identical they were.

Annis smiled at her, "There is an album of us together," she said. "David, please fetch ma wedding album from my bedroom. It's in the closet on the top shelf nearest the door."

"Aye." David stood and left the room.

Erin turned the page and saw a picture of David and his father, with Roger in the background. It looked to be from the time he'd first started working for them; he was thin and scraggy, with an unkempt beard. She thought about his wife having just died and how sad he must have been in those years.

David quickly returned, carrying a satin-covered wedding album that had once been white. However, due to age, it had turned a delicate cream color. He set it on top of the album they had been looking through, and Erin lightly ran her fingers over the cover. Around the words, 'Our Wedding Day,' embroidered in dark blue floss, was a frame of hand-stitched silk ribbon flowers and greenery. "Oh! This is lovely!" Erin said, afraid to touch it.

"Ma sister had an identical album and did the handiwork on both. She was verra talented with a needle and thread. Go on, love, ye'll no' break et," she said to Erin, apparently noticing her hesitancy.

"I'm just afraid it'll get dirty, or the delicate silk will rip."

"Dinnae worry, love."

Erin opened the cover and sighed; the first picture was of a couple she assumed were Annis and Charles, posed in front of the altar. Annis was smiling, holding her bouquet in front of her beautiful, white lace wedding dress. Charles was smiling David's smile at them in his kilt and formal jacket. She laughed at her inner dialogue and then blushed, wishing she'd kept her mirth hidden a little better than she had.

"What's so funny?" David asked, his eyebrows furrowed.

"I'm sorry, I wasn't laughing at the photo. I was thinking how your father, or at least this man... looks so dashing, like a movie star," she said, and then everyone laughed with her. "Ann, if this is you, you're stunning!" Erin said, touched by the youth and beauty in the picture.

Annis smiled and turned the page for her. The next photo was of the two couples, as they had both gotten married on the same day. Erin studied the picture; they were wearing identical dresses, and the men wore the same kilt and jacket. She tried to figure out which couple was which, but she couldn't. She put her head close to the album, trying to see their faces, and Annis laughed. "Ach, turn the page, dear; there are close-ups soon enough," she said.

The next page had close-ups shots of each couple, side by side. Erin looked at the older woman before her and smiled. "Now, which do you reckon is me?" Annis asked, seemingly amused.

Erin shook her head, not able to tell at all. Annis smiled and pointed to the woman on the right. "It would've been a coin toss," Erin said, gazing intently at each photo, trying to see the differences. "I bet you could tell, couldn't you, David?"

"I could, but I'm not gonna tell yeh *why*; not quite yet," he said and turned the page.

The bridesmaids, in light blue, were standing in a row, smiling. "Oh, I like that one!" Erin said, pointing at the lineup of kilted groomsmen. "I love Scotland! Where else in the world would men look so manly in what's essentially a pleated skirt?" She turned the page and laughed until she snorted, which made everyone else laugh. Before them was a photo of the two brides lifting their skirts to show their garters; next to them, the two grooms stood, lifting their kilts in like fashion.

"I'd forgotten about that one!" Annis said. Her cheeks were slightly flushed, and she was laughing softly. "Tha' was Henry's idea; he saw us in the pose and ran up with Charles tae get in on et. He was funny, our Henry, before—Well, never mind."

They went through the album, Erin exclaiming over the size of the cake and wincing at one of the couples, who'd both mashed cake onto each other's face, while the other two were still neat and tidy. "Let me guess, Charles wasn't the kind of man to do that, was he?" she said, and Annis smiled.

"Good call. I told him he'd best not if he wanted tae share the wedding bed with me," she said and laughed at the memory.

"He was a wise man!" David said.

"How did you meet? It must be a fascinating story," Erin asked as they turned to the last page in the album, seeing the back end of an old car driving away with cans and old shoes tied to the bumper.

"Not so interesting, really," she said. My sister and I had dance instruction with Mrs. Williams for six years. For some unknown reason, she kept all the same age group together, except when we graduated; then she threw a party, inviting the older students.

Charles and Henry had graduated two years earlier, and as soon as I saw Charles, I knew—I just knew. I was never attracted tae Henry, even though they were as identical as ma sister and I were. Charles told me he'd felt the same way for me as well. We had something special; et's hard tae put tae words."

Erin and David looked at each other. "Aye, we understand," David said.

"Of course yeh do! Et's undeniable ye're meant to be together," Annis said.

"What were Olive and Henry like?" Erin asked.

"Both my sister and Henry were the wild ones in our group. Charles and I were content tae play skittles or tae see a film, but they needed tae be causing a ruckus. They became activists for any and all causes. They smoked marijuana and more than likely other things I wasn't privy to. I suspect they allowed poor wee Bran tae do things a young boy should not be doin'. They were headed back home tae Glasgow after a rally or protest when... the train they were on derailed... and were both killed," she said sadly.

"That's so sad," Erin said.

"Aye, et was."

"How old were you when you had David?" she asked, abruptly changing the subject. There was something she had to get off her chest.

"I was twenty," she said.

Erin nodded and tried to smile, but her heart was heavy. She now knew Annis was sixty-five since David was forty-five, and it occurred to her that she'd be eighty-five when their child was his age.

"What's troubling you, dear?" Annis asked gently.

"Oh, it's nothing," she said, but both Annis and David gave her a look that plainly said they didn't believe her. "Okay, I just feel like I'm too old to be pregnant. I'll be forty in September, so when our child is forty-five, I'll be eighty-five, and David will be… ninety! Good night nurse!" she said, wanting to cry.

"Ach, dinnae worry. My mother was near your age when she had twins. I reckon ye'll be just fine, dear," Annis said, trying to console her.

Erin was still worried; she didn't want to get old. She felt time flying past her and wanted it to slow down. They moved on to the next album, which had quite a few of David and Susannah; she tried not to focus on them. "So, you were twenty-seven in these?" Erin asked and saw the confused look on his face. "Roger told me you didn't meet Susannah until you were in your mid-twenties."

"He did, did he?" David said, sounding slightly suspicious.

She could see the question marks all over his face and wished she hadn't said it. "Now, don't get upset," she said. "He had just helped me move my things back to your room… when the reporters were outside the house. I invited him to stay and rest while I unpacked, then I asked him how it was he'd started working here. He told me that after his wife died, he'd been homeless, and your dad took him in and gave him a job. I asked how old you'd been back then, and he told me. It was nothing."

"I didn't know about Roger bein' homeless or that he'd a wife who died. He told yeh all that while he sat watchin' yeh unpack?"

"Well, no, not all of it. He told me about his wife when you were at the hospital after Susannah died. I… felt a bit lost and started walking. I ended up at Dr. Neil's. Roger followed me and told me the story to encourage me to give you time to grieve. He's a very wise man, you know?"

"I hadn't thought about what ye'd done after I left that day. I'm glad he was there for yeh," he said sadly. "I'm ashamed for so many things that happened in the days following her death, especially how I'd started questioning Roger's motives."

"Dinnae fash, *Mo ghràidh (mo gry)*; it's all water under the bridge now," she said and kissed his cheek. "I'm a bit tired; I didn't sleep well last night. I think I'll take a nap if no one minds?"

"I'll follow you; I'd like to discuss when we should leave for London," he said, clearly glad for the subject change. He picked up the albums, ready to put them away, and

Erin stood, keen to get upstairs.

"Alright." She yawned and turned to Annis and Millie, "Thank you for sharing the lovely memories with me; I really enjoyed it."

"Aye, it was nice," Annis said.

Erin started up the stairs, and by the second landing, she was very tired. When she reached David's room, she was dragging and was leaning on the doorframe when he caught up with her. "Are yeh a'right, love?" he asked.

"Mmmm, I'm just so tired all of a sudden." It was a familiar tiredness; it was the way she'd felt for so long before starting treatments. *It's only been a few days; how could my symptoms be back so soon?* "I'm sure it's all the traveling in such a short amount of time," she fibbed, hoping that was the reason.

Chapter Eight

GETTING THINGS SORTED

David helped Erin into the bedroom and onto the bed; he would've helped her take her clothes off, but she was half asleep when her head hit the pillow. "I'm fine, g'night," she said.

He stood for a few minutes, watching her sleep, then he bent over her, kissed her cheek, and left the room. He stepped into Millie's room and looked at Erin's things scattered around it. His heart still ached with the memory of sitting outside the bathroom trying to apologize to her. Then, as he stood, watching her get out of the tub. *Yeh ken yeh nearly lost her this time? She may not return if she leaves again; ye'd better be mindful of what yeh say tae her from here on out.*

Taking her to his home in London was his next thought. *It'll be splendid havin' her there!* Smiling, he thought about something in his office safe that he wanted to give her. A few ideas of how he wanted to go about it swam through his mind, though some organization would be helpful for everything to be perfect. He sent a text message to Kitty, asking her to prepare the house for him, then, he thought to send a message to Francie, asking her to set the table for two starting the next day. Once that was sorted, he went downstairs to the back patio to wait for Erin to wake up.

—

An hour and a half later, Erin poked her head out the patio door. "David? Oh, there you are," she said. She stepped out into the red brick paved seating area bordered by flagstones, bricks, and light-colored, soccer ball-sized rocks. She sat next to him on the swinging bench and put her head on his shoulder.

"Are yeh feelin' better now, hen?" he asked.

"I think so; I'm still tired, but I'll be good and ready for bed later. What did you want to talk about?" she asked.

"Ach, yes; when to leave for London. Tomorrow, after breakfast, might be a good time."

Erin had mixed feelings about going to London. She wanted to, but she also wanted to stay there with Annis, Millie, and Roger. "Okay, though I'll be sad to leave; it feels like home here."

David put his arm around her shoulder. "Aye, it *is* verra nice, though we'll be back in a week to retrieve the children from school."

"That's true. Okay, tomorrow after breakfast then." She sat up and turned to face him. "So, I'm still pretty tired, but do you want to climb Arthur's seat again after lunch today, just you and me this time? Actually, that might be part of the reason I'm so tired; I'm not used to mountain climbing and *then* David riding." She gave him a wicked grin, and he bent down to give her a very passionate kiss. "Mmm, I like that! More please!" she said. He continued kissing her for a long time until eventually, Millie came to the back door and cleared her throat.

"Ahem! Lunch will be served in thirty minutes," she said with a smile.

They broke away from their snogging to acknowledge her and then continued. *Holy Moses, it's nice to make out like this!* Erin thought, thoroughly enjoying herself.

"We've a whole half hour before lunch, would yeh care tae come upstairs with me?" he asked as he took hold of her hand and pressed it against the front of his trousers.

Feeling his full erection, she smiled at him. "Half an hour? Okay."

David stood, pulled her up to him, and continued kissing her for a bit longer. Trying to be quiet, they snuck inside and were halfway up the stairs when Millie yelled, "Jest be sure tae come down on time!"

In the bedroom, they resumed kissing and feeling each other up while undressing and somehow made it to the bed. Erin lay on her back and David paused before getting on top of her. "Are yeh sure yeh want tae do et this way, love?" he asked.

"Yes, I'm sure, now come here!" she said urgently, wanting to get past all the bad stuff. He lay on top of her, missionary style, and entered her. At first, she was rigid and started breathing hard in fear, though as soon as he began to move, she felt their connection and relaxed.

———

David looked into her eyes as he thrust, over and over again, causing her to moan and making him feel like the luckiest man on the planet. "I was afraid yeh wouldn't come back tae me," he said quietly. "I thought I may never be allowed tae do this with yeh again, and et filled me with terror." A tear fell and hit her on the nose. "I dinnae want to feel that fear again. I wanna know we're in this forever, yeh ken?" He thrust his cock harder and deeper, filling her so that he could feel the back of her—solid and yet supple against the head of his cock.

"As soon as I got there, all I wanted was this... was you. I knew I'd been wrong to leave you, and I was so afraid you might not take me back after I walked out like I did. I was sure one of those fangirls would come and take my place," she said and laughed, which he could feel from her insides out as he made love to her. "I know it's silly to think of now, but I was terrified too," she said.

He moved ever so slightly and started hitting a spot that made her gasp; then, she made the primal noise she had in New Orleans. He felt her body begin to spasm, and her hips started moving so that he thrust more deeply into her each time. Though he didn't want it to end, he allowed himself to climax with a deep, almost primal groan of his own.

David held her, not wanting to move, though he knew at least fifteen minutes of their thirty were gone. No matter how happy Millie was at Erin's return, she would not be lenient if they were late, so he sighed, ready to get up.

"I promise I'll never leave you like that again," she said.

"And I promise tae never tae speak to you as I've done again," he replied. Her arm was over his chest, and she squeezed him in a sort of half-hug, then began absent-mindedly playing with his chest hair. He was just drifting off to sleep when he started and sat up. "We can't be late!"

Miraculously, they managed to make it to the dining room with only moments to spare, out of breath and laughing. They sat next to each other, completely absorbed in one another.

———

Roger walked into the dining room and nearly turned around, feeling like he'd interrupted something he shouldn't have. Erin looked at him, and he could've sworn she was glowing; her cheeks were pink, and her smile was carefree.

"Good afternoon, Roger!" she said with enthusiasm, making him laugh.

"Good afternoon tae you as well. Yeh look as though ye've shed ten years! I need some of tha' energy!" he said.

He watched David's happy face light up when he laughed. "Sign up for the Fertilis Defect Registry; yeh may just find the love of yer life!" he said and smiled at him, then at Erin. When Annis came into the room, David smiled at her then he gave one to Millie when she sat at her place. "Isn't et a bonnie day today?"

They all agreed it was indeed a verra bonnie day. Roger knew the household was collectively glad they had made up, and things seemed to be going quite well for them. He and everyone else at the table felt younger and livelier than they had in a long time.

"We will be leaving for London tomorrow, after breakfast. Roger, would yeh mind—" David began.

"Aye, not a problem, as yeh already ken," he interrupted. He was a bit sad; he would miss the two of them, but especially Erin. She brought something new to the house; a fresh energy that the old place needed. "Just let me know when."

"Aye, I will when I know. I'm waitin' on a reply from Tina."

They ate their cock-a-leekie soup and homemade bread with butter, which was delicious. As they neared the end of the meal, Erin cleared her throat. "David, please remind me to give Millie a hug and kiss for this meal when we're done," she said, loud enough for the whole table to hear her and with a twinkle in her eye.

"Ach, be forewarned, Millie! But I shouldn't worry, as her hugs are quite pleasant," he said with a laugh.

"Humph!" Millie said in a clear attempt at being off-handed and acting as though she didn't care for all the sentimental stuff, but she smiled and then laughed as well. "Ach, yer somethin' else, Erin, yeh are."

"Aye!" Both David and Roger said in unison, which made Erin laugh.

"You're all so sweet! How will I be able to leave you?" she asked. "I genuinely want someone to tell me how."

When no one gave her an answer, David turned to Roger and said, "Ach, we'll be headin' up the hill after lunch today. If Erin's alright with et, you can join us."

"Aye, and be the third wheel?" he said, remembering how he could hear them snogging and whispering through the fog the last time he joined them. "I don't think—"

"Wait! What happened to the reporters? Are there any out there today?" Erin asked.

"Nae, another story has pulled them all away for now. Ye're safe tae go without me," Roger said with a grin.

"Could I please use your walking stick with the seat?" she asked him.

"Aye, just take it from the sittin' room when yeh leave," he said.

She put her arm around his back and squeezed. "Thanks!" she said and finished the last of her soup. When they were all finished with the meal, she asked Millie if she'd like some help with the dishes.

"Nae; go on now and get yeh up tha' hill," Millie said.

Erin stood and walked around the table; she hugged her, then kissed her soft, and now quite pink, cheek. "I love yeh, Millie!" Roger watched in amusement as she then turned to Annis and kissed her cheek, "I love you too, Ann. You are two of my favorite people! Ach, and I can't leave you out, Roger! I love you too." He blushed crimson, not expecting her to include him and feeling as though he'd been caught admiring her. "You've all been so wonderful to me, making me feel like family, *nearly* from the start." She laughed and smiled at Millie.

She went back to David and took his hand. "I'm going to go change into more suitable clothes," she said to David and then ran up the stairs.

Roger sighed as he left the house feeling warm inside until he noticed David following him.

———

A few minutes later, feeling much more energetic than she had before, Erin came back downstairs. Not seeing David, decided to go to Roger's flat to get the walking stick. As she approached the door at the top of the stairs, she heard David and Roger talking.

"*Of course I do! But no' in the way yer thinkin',*" she heard Roger say, sounding a bit defensive.

"*I only want tae be sure we understand each other,*" David said. He didn't sound angry, but she could tell it was something serious.

"*Aye, yeh ken I'd never do anathin', even if et were a romantic sort of love. Yeh ken I'm no' like tha', though I'll defend her tae the death if I need tae!*" Roger said passionately.

Erin knocked lightly on the door. "*Come in,*" she heard Roger say. She'd planned to ignore what she'd just heard, but all of a sudden, the thought of Roger defending her to the death and how he'd saved her from Bran overwhelmed her, and she had to hug him.

"I'm sorry, David, but I have to," she said. She walked over to Roger and gave him a big hug. "Thank you for what you just said, I'm sorry for eavesdropping, but it means a lot to me. Also, thank you again for saving me from Bran!"

Roger stood stiffly at first; she guessed he was looking at David to make sure he wasn't going to get possessive. After what she presumed was a nod or some other unspoken understanding between the men, he relaxed and returned the hug. "Ach, you were no' meant tae hear that!" he said and laughed when she wouldn't let go.

"Aye, but I did, and... well, thank you," she said, then she let go and kissed his cheek, very briefly. "Alright, now where did that walking stick go to?" she asked, trying to change the subject and keep herself from crying.

"I have it, darling. Are you ready tae go?" David said.

She hugged him, burying her face into his clean shirt. He smelled so good, like a manly man with a bit of poshness thrown in. "Aye, let's go," she said and stepped away from him. "Sorry, I reckon I'm in a hugging mood today."

———

When David and Erin started down the stairs, Roger listened to them talk and banter. He could still hear them through the open window as they walked down the driveway. He heard Erin saying. *"David, what did you say to him? I hope it wasn't threatening! He's been so good to me!"*

"Dinnae fash, I just wanted tae know if he was in love with yeh, because... it seemed as though he was, and I only wanted tae make sure we understood one another," he heard David say.

"Sounds threatening to me. Please don't be jealous of him; even if he were head over heels, infatuated with me, I don't think of him that way at all. To me, he's more like an awesome uncle or big brother, and I could never think of him in any other way," Erin said, and he could no longer hear what they were saying.

Roger sighed; if he were being truly honest with himself, he would admit he was just a *little* bit in love with her. Ten years ago, he might have been jealous or might've tried to win her affections, especially after what David had said to her, but not then. It was just that her smile brightened his day and her laugh made him feel better on the inside. He was going to miss her something fierce when they left in the morning.

Chapter Nine

SLEEPING BEAUTY

David and Erin decided to go to the St. Anthony's Chapel ruins instead of Arthur's seat that time. They hiked the path up Jacob's ladder to Queen's Drive, then turned left at the car park. David had worn his baseball cap and a pair of American-looking sunglasses, trying to blend in. He wore jeans that didn't cost a fortune, his T-shirt had an Iron Maiden album cover on it, and a beat-up jean shirt finished the 'American tourist' look. Erin brought a sweater in case she got cold since nothing David owned fit her.

Being a Saturday afternoon, it was rather crowded, but the disguise seemed to be working. No one bothered them until they got to a very scenic, flat, grassy spot, and two ladies asked them to take their picture. Erin instinctively did the photo-taking and then gave them back their phone.

Everything was fine until they were about to walk away, then one of them stopped and studied David's face. "Hang on! Are you... David Elliott?" she asked, more loudly than was comfortable, seeing there were so many people nearby.

Erin didn't want the whole park watching them, so she improvised. "He gets that all the time! We're here on vacation, and he's been asked that at least six times already! He's painfully shy and hard of hearing, so he doesn't say much. In a way, I'm his translator and help him with social situations."

"Aww! Y'all are so sweet!" The two women said in unison with a heavy southern drawl.

"What are yeh doin'? Let's move on already!" David whispered into Erin's ear.

She smiled sweetly at him. "He wants to know where you're from," she lied.

"Texas," The ladies said at the same time. "Where are y'all from? Sounds like you're from the Midwest?" one of them asked.

"I'm from Wisconsin. He was born in England but has lived in Wisconsin for a long time." She was having fun making up a fake story for the girls, but she could tell David was anxious. "Well, we should be going now; it was nice—"

"Wait! Do you want us to take *your* picture?" one of the women asked.

Erin hesitated but thought it would seem weird for her to say no. "That would be nice," she said and opened her camera app, then handed it to her. They stood together, and she prayed David wouldn't flash his magic smile at them. He didn't, so after the usual thank-yous, they walked away, and Erin opened the photo in her gallery.

They looked like weirdo tourists, and with the way David was smirking, he looked nothing like himself. "Good night nurse! You look like a dumb American!" she said as she showed the picture to him and laughed so hard she snorted.

He also laughed. "Verra funny, but ye're mad with yer cock and bull stories about us!" he said. "Though et was rather clever tellin' them I was hard of hearin' and shy; makes it easier tae excuse ma not sayin' anathin.'"

"Thank you; I accept your compliment. I also made you English so you could choose any accent in which to hide. I need to learn your stock accents so I can have even more fun with this!"

"Ye're mad!" he said as they trekked through the center of Holyrood Park.

Compared to the peak of Arthur's Seat, it was a cakewalk. They talked and laughed effortlessly, though the path still needed a bit of navigation and careful footing. When they reached the ancient ruins, David took her hand, meaning to assist her over a slightly precarious spot, but something made him turn his head.

"We should leave now," he said and turned his back on whatever he'd seen. "There's a man takin' pictures of us."

Erin turned and looked at the man; he looked right back at her and smiled. She had a hunch and told David she'd be right back. She walked up to the man, who didn't turn around or try to flee. He stood, watching her approach with the same smile, patiently waiting for her.

"Good afternoon!" she said cheerfully.

"Gut afternoon," he replied with a thick German accent.

"I was wondering why you were taking our picture just now?" she asked, and he smiled.

"Vell, I vas not tryink to, but you ver standink en mein shot. I said to meinself; 'vhat a pleasant-lookink couple. I will take a few photographs of zem.' I am sorry if you are upset by zis. I can remove zem from my camera if you vish it of me," he said kindly.

"Danke schoen! We would be grateful if you would," she said. "My partner is extremely shy, and he was upset about it, but you are a very kind-looking man, so I decided to come over and talk to you."

"Sprechen sie Deutsch, Fräulein?" he asked her, but Erin laughed.

"Nein, besides what I've already said. I can count to four, and not much more, but it's nice to use the little bit I know when I can," she said.

"Ja! Is very nice. I vill leaffe you alone now," he said, but Erin put her hand on his arm and shook her head.

"Nein, we will move out of your shot. Auf wiedersehen; it was nice talking with you!" she said and walked away, delighted about the conversation.

When she finally returned to David, he was shaking his head. "Auf wiedersehen? Since when do you speak German?" he said with an amazed grin on his face.

Erin took him by the arm and led him away from the spot they'd been standing. She smiled up at him. "Zere are many sings you shall learn about me, Herr Elliott!" she said and laughed. "I don't know German, only a few words, but the man meant no harm. We were standing in his shot, and he thought we looked like a nice couple. He's going to remove the photos from his camera."

David shook his head again, "What is et about you that makes yeh able tae do that? You're able tae approach a complete stranger and become fast friends in an instant. I marvel at yeh sometimes!" he said with admiration.

"Well, I'm probably still naive in thinking most people are nice and kind and don't mean to do any harm. I'll probably have it bite me in the butt eventually, but for now, it's much better to think good about people. That man was lovely! He was just a German man wanting to take some pictures of the site, and I got to speak with him. I feel blessed."

"No, love, I'm blessed tae have yeh around tae help remind me tae think that way. Ye're a breath of fresh air, yeh ken?" He bent down and kissed her. She wrapped her arms around his neck and kissed him back.

After a slight climb, they reached the mostly ruined chapel. They sat against one of the stone walls that were still standing, thankful for the bag of goodies Millie had given David before he left. "By the way, I'm sorry you had to hear about your mum and Millie that way," she said.

He gave her a look revealing just how shocked he'd been. "How'd *you* know about et? They wouldn't have just told yeh."

"Well, first of all, I have eyes, and I pay attention. Second, on the night I first ran into Bran in the kitchen, your mum and I had a lovely conversation where I spilled the beans about the baby. Millie joined us later, and I simply asked them about it."

His eyes grew wide. "Yeh... just... asked them about it? And what did you say, then? 'Are yeh lesbians?'" he said flippantly, and Erin rolled her eyes.

"You are such a man! No, I asked if they were in love with each other. I explained how I noticed that they share a bedroom and were very gentle with each other. They admitted it, and I asked them if you knew; they didn't know for sure but thought you must have some inkling. It was after that night Millie finally warmed up to me. I told them I wouldn't say anything about it to you, and, well, then I did."

They sat together, looking out at St. Margaret's Loch, enjoying each other's company. Erin put her head on his shoulder and was soon falling asleep. After the third time nodding off, she woke with a start and decided it might be a good idea to head back to the house. David agreed, and as they stood, she felt the overwhelming tiredness hit her again. She put her hand on his arm and bent over slightly. Her head felt foggy, and she wanted to lay down right there and sleep.

"What is et?" David said, bracing her up with her head on his chest.

"I'm... so... tired all of a sudden," she said, hardly able to keep her eyes open and feeling a bit frightened by the severity of it. "I... want to... lay down," she managed to say and started to slump to the ground. David caught her and helped her to sit. He resumed his position against the wall and had her put her head on his leg as a pillow. There was no use trying to get down the hill with her in that condition, so he decided to wait it out.

An hour later, David tried to wake her again. All she did was mumble something he couldn't understand, so he took his mobile out of his pocket and sent a message to Roger.

> D: *I may have a problem and need your help. Erin is sleeping, and I can't wake her. Can't carry her either.*

Roger replied:

R: *Alright, I'll leave shortly. Should bring anything?*

D: *No, unless you think we should try coffee?*

Half an hour later, his legs were falling asleep, so he took off his jean shirt and balled it up into a makeshift pillow, placing it under her head so he could stand and stretch. He watched her as he paced and waited, trying to figure out what might have caused that to happen. After fifteen minutes, he saw Roger coming closer, trying to find them.

David waved, and Roger approached them. "Ach, she's still no' awake, then?" he said, sounding shocked. He knelt and touched her shoulder, but she didn't stir.

"No, we were about tae explore the site when she seemed tae lose all strength and fell asleep like that," David said and snapped his fingers.

"A'right, then, let's sit her up," Roger said.

David knelt at her head and lifted her shoulders so she was sitting against the wall again. She woke a bit and noticed Roger. "Why are you here?" she asked, sounding tired and confused.

"I've come tae help yeh get back tae Owlgate, hen," he said. She gave him a bewildered look and then looked up at David behind her. "Come, darling, et's time tae head back home," he said, and between him and Roger, they managed to get her standing.

She was able to stay awake, though she was too weak and tired to walk by herself. A crowd had gathered to watch the spectacle of the two men trying to get the woman to stand. Some were laughing while others were shaking their heads as if something fishy was going on.

A woman who looked to be in her mid-thirties approached them and asked if they needed help. "I'm a doctor, and something is obviously wrong with this woman. Does she have a medical condition?" she asked with an American accent.

"Yes, she has the Fertilis Defect, though she is having treatments for it. Oh, and she's pregnant, as well," David replied quietly.

"How far along is she?" the woman asked, plainly surprised by what she'd been told.

David wasn't sure and quickly did the math in his head.

"Approximately... two months, I believe," he said.

The doctor looked up at him. "And are you the father?" she asked.

David wished she'd speak a bit more quietly and then heard someone in the crowd say his name. "Aye, but can we not talk about it here, please?" he whispered.

The woman looked around and saw that the crowd wasn't going anywhere, so she stood. "Alright, show's over! Clear out, or I'll make you carry her!" she said fiercely to the crowd of gawkers.

Erin looked up at David, "I like her!" she said drowsily.

"Does she have an obstetrician or midwife yet?" she asked.

Erin answered, her speech slowed with fatigue. "I didn't think I needed one until I was about three months... and—" She paused and must've forgotten what she was saying because she frowned and shook her head. "Where was I? Oh, plus, I don't live here... yet, do I, David?"

"No, darling, but you will soon," he said and looked at the doctor. "We plan tae be married, but we can't do it yet," he said under his breath.

"Yes, for a normal pregnancy, three months is normal, but in your case, the sooner, the better. Fertilis Defect and pregnant? That's rather rare as far as I know. It seems like a crazy coincidence, but I'm an obstetrician. I'm here on a four-year residency in London. One of the areas I am looking to specialize in is rare and uncommon birth disorders. The Fertilis Defect would fall under that designation, so if you'd like for me to be your doctor, I'd be glad to take you on, though I'm practicing in London," she said to Erin, who was not entirely with it.

"David, what's wrong with me? I feel drunk, or like I took a bottle of sleeping pills. I just want to go to bed now," she said with her head drooping.

"I know, darling; we'll be home soon," he said gently to her and then looked at the doctor. "We live in London and are planning to return there in a few days. If you give my mate your contact information, we will set an appointment with you," David said, eager to get Erin back to Owlgate as soon as they could manage it.

"Alright, good, and you might want to keep her from climbing this hill again!" she said. "Has she had much stress lately? I mean more than moving to another country and being pregnant?" she asked.

"Aye. It's been constant over the last two months. Also, she's only just returned from a three-day trip to America. I see now how this... adventure wasn't such a good idea after all," he said.

"It was not. I would suggest no more flying for a good month with lots of rest and as little stress as possible," the doctor said seriously.

"Aye, Doctor, no flying then. As for stress, I'll do my best, but that seems to be our lot lately," he said wearily as she handed Roger her business card.

"I look forward to seeing you again, and take it easy," she said to Erin, who gave a slight nod. Then she went back to her hike.

Roger had driven to the car park behind Holyrood Palace, so they didn't have far to go. Nevertheless, the path down was rocky, steep, and hard-going as he and David all but carried her down the hill. Eventually, they managed to get her to the SUV, then to Owlgate, and finally to David's room, which was difficult because of the stairs.

As soon as she hit the mattress, Erin said, "Thank you for helping me, boys," and fell asleep.

Exhausted, both men wanted to lay next to her and sleep as well. They sat on the edge of the bed, willing themselves to stand. Finally, they looked at each other and smiled. "I think I'll stay right here," David said.

"Aye, me too," Roger said and laughed. "Wouldn't that be somethin' for her tae wake up to? One of us on either side of her," he joked, and then his cheeks turned bright red. He stood and shook David's hand, "Yeh jammy bastard!"

David laughed, "Thanks for yer help. Oh, and have yeh got the doctor's information?" he asked, and Roger fished in his trouser pocket for the business card. He handed it to David and then left the room.

Chapter Ten

FARE THEE WELL

Two hours later, Millie knocked on David's bedroom door to tell them supper would be ready in thirty minutes. David grunted a response and then wrapped his arm around Erin. She was asleep, making little snoring and sputtering sounds, and he smiled at her. "Erin, darling, wake up. Et's nearly time tae eat."

She hardly moved, and after the fourth time trying, he got up, dressed, and went downstairs. When he entered the dining room everyone watched the doorway, waiting for her. "She's still asleep, and I can't wake her," he said.

"Ach, I'll leave her a plate in the refrigerator. If she's hungry in the night, she'll only need tae heat et," Millie said.

"Thanks, Millie. I know she'll appreciate it," David replied.

"Tha' doctor said no flyin', aye? Will yeh take the train tae London, then?" Roger asked casually but quietly to David.

"Aye, I reckon so unless she stays here whilst I go to London. I know she wants to come along, so I'll talk tae her about et when she wakes," he said.

Just as supper was wrapping up, Erin came into the dining room, looking tired and confused. "Did I miss supper?" she asked, sounding like a child who had just woken up and was truly sad.

David stood and pulled out her seat for her. "We've saved you a plate, hen. I tried tae wake yeh, but you were havin' none of et. Sit here, and we'll feed yeh," he said tenderly.

Millie hadn't made her the plate yet, and nothing had been cleared from the table, so she was able to choose what she wanted. Annis and Millie excused themselves, but Roger and David stayed at the table to keep her company.

They talked about the hike to Arthur's seat. Erin was having a hard time remembering what had actually happened and what she'd dreamed. "Was there a... woman—A doctor, maybe?" she asked. "She got the crowds to go away, right?"

"Aye, and she gave us her contact information so you can have her as your doctor. She's American and specializes in birth defects, such as the Fertilis Defect, as well," David told her. "She said yeh need tae rest, and yeh shouldn't fly for another month.

Erin put down the bite she was just about to take. "What? But what about London?" she said, and it seemed to David that she might cry.

"Dinnae fash, darling, we have a few choices. You can stay here and be taken care of by Millie, Mother, and Roger, or we can take the train. The train takes quite a long time, but ye'll be more comfortable and able to walk around tae stretch yer legs," he said.

"The scenery is bonnie as well," Roger said, trying to be helpful.

"The truth is I want yeh with me more than anathin'," David said, "However, I want you and the bairn tae be safe and healthy as well."

Erin put her elbow on the table and rested her head on her hand, closing her eyes, "I really want to go with you, David," she said. "Are you sure it won't be a bother for you to take the train?"

David smiled at her and put his hand on the back of her neck. "Et's no bother, love, though I'll have tae inform Tina right away," he said and then took out his phone and sent a message, asking her to change the plans.

The next morning, they got dressed and packed the last few remaining things for their trip since they'd packed everything else the night before. Erin had gone right back to bed after her meal and was just starting to feel a bit more energetic. Their train was meant to leave at nine, and at six-fifty, Millie came to warn them breakfast would be ready in ten minutes.

At seven, they walked into the dining room and took their seats. Annis was already seated at the head of the table, and Millie joined her after she set down the last serving dish. The mood was subdued, and no one said anything until Roger came in; he was very chipper and smiled naturally at everyone.

"Good mornin'!" he said cheerfully. His mood was infectious, and before long, everyone was talking and laughing while they ate.

Erin took a piece of toast from the rack and spread it with what she was delighted to learn were rhubarb preserves.

"Oh, Millie!" Erin said after taking a bite, "This jam is so good! It tastes like springtime! Did you make it?"

Millie smiled warmly at her. "Aye, et's ma favorite as well. I save it for special occasions. I'll send yeh home with a jar." When Erin laughed, Millie looked at her questioningly.

"You just called David's house my home," she said.

"I reckon I did—though et is yer home now, isnae?" she said.

Erin giggled; she couldn't believe she would be living with David Elliott in his London home. "I suppose so; it's all just so new," she said. "It's still hard to believe sometimes—I mean, I'm a nobody. I've never done anything remarkable in my life, and to be here as a guest of David Elliott is just crazy! If someone had told me I'd be here six months ago, I'd never have believed them."

Annis placed her soft, warm hand on hers. "Ach, we're all nobodies, dear. It's not the things we do that make us remarkable; et's how we behave and how we treat others. Et's our character, and you have one of the most remarkable characters I've known," she said tenderly. "I'm glad for the time ye've been here with us. I pray et's not too long before yeh come back to us again."

Erin had to swallow hard to fight the urge to cry. She gently squeezed David's mother's hand. "Thank you," she whispered. She couldn't say anything more without getting choked up and looked at David, who was talking with Roger. Their heads were together as if they were scheming or colluding with each other. David suddenly smiled and looked at Roger in surprise, whispering his reply.

Roger smiled and said, "I'll tell you more in the car."

David suddenly looked up and caught her eavesdropping, so she looked away and blushed. He smiled, put his hand on her thigh under the table, then leaned in and whispered, "I love you. Are yeh ready tae go?"

She nodded and wiped her mouth with her napkin. What's up with Roger?" she asked. "He's happy about something this morning."

"Aye, we'll explain et in the car. He's made a verra brave and interesting decision," David replied. Erin raised her eyebrows in curiosity.

David, Roger, and Erin stood, asking to be excused from the table as they needed to get going. There was no telling what traffic would be like, so they wanted to leave early. While Erin and David said their goodbyes, Roger went upstairs to bring down Erin's large suitcase, since it was the only bag not burned up in the fire.

"Oh, Ann, I'm going to miss you so much!" Erin said and hugged her.

"Aye, and I'll miss you as well, ma dear," Annis said.

Millie stood next to her and handed Erin a jar of preserves, a big smile bringing out the wrinkles on her face. "Ye're already family tae me, dearie, please stay in touch. I know we'll most likely see yeh in a week's time, but et'll seem much longer," she said. She hugged Erin and kissed her cheek. "Fare thee and yer wee bairn well."

Erin was about to start crying in earnest, so she simply said, "Goodbye, Millie, thank you for this." She held up the jar of jam, her eyes filling with tears, and then turned to David, who had just finished hugging his mum. Roger was waiting by the SUV, so they walked out the side door and got into the back seat.

Roger got in and started down the drive. He'd already opened the gate, and once he pulled out, exited the vehicle and then shut it with a clang. "You need a remote-control opener for that," Erin said with a laugh when he returned and put on his seatbelt.

"Ach, no! Et's part of ma job! I cannae allow tha' tae happen," he said, returning the laugh.

"Now, tell Erin what yeh said at the table," David said, "Then tell me more about why ye've decided tae do et."

Roger looked in the rearview mirror at the two of them and smiled with rosy cheeks. "I've decided tae sign up at the Fertilis Defect Registry," he said softly, and his blush deepened.

Erin's eyes grew wide; she looked at Roger and then at David. "Really? Oh, Roger! That's wonderful! The more men who sign up the better! What made you decide to do it?"

"David encouraged me—Ach, yeh just seem so happy together, yeh ken? He said tha' perhaps… if I signed up, I'd meet the woman I was born tae be with. And I wanna help someone… if I can," he said. "Et's strange tae think a treatment such as that could be a help. Et seems like a selfish thing tae do, but—"

"I ken just what yeh mean!" David said, interrupting him.

"It's not selfish—I mean, I'm sure it is for some men, but I don't believe it would be for you," Erin said, then she smiled and put her hand on Roger's shoulder.

"I ken tha' I may no' find true love, but perhaps I'll find a friend; a woman tae talk to… tae share ma dreams and hopes with, and… mebbe she could do the same with me. Or, if she's not a talker, then I reckon just havin' the touch of another person would be nice," he said quietly.

"Aye, et is," David said and took hold of Erin's hand, smiling at her.

"Aye," she said. "When is your appointment?"

"Tomorrow mornin', and frankly, I'm a more than wee bit intimidated. Do yeh have any advice, David?" Roger asked since he knew he'd been through it before.

David thought back to his visit to the Registration clinic and gave a short cough, not wanting to remember it. "Aye. Just when yeh think et can't get any more embarrassing, et will, but it'll be over before yeh know et. Just remember, it'll be worth et!"

Roger raised his eyebrows. "Aye, I reckon ye're right."

Traffic was light, so it wasn't long before Roger parked near Waverley Station. "Thank you for everything," Erin said after Roger took her suitcase out of the boot. She hugged him and kissed his cheek, "I hope you do find the love of your life."

"Thank you," he said, and shook David's hand, then he waved as they walked away. "Safe travels."

Chapter Eleven

EARLY

Erin and David were over an hour early for their train from Edinburgh to London. Since they had some time to kill, Erin thought a quick walk through the Waverley Mall would be nice. She didn't consider the fact that because he was a famous British actor it might not be such a good plan, after all.

They descended the entrance stairs on the corner of Princes Street and Waverly Bridge. The first store they came to was called the Tartan House, a tourist gift shop. Hoping for a box or two of shortbread, Erin went in and made a beeline for the 'Biscuits/Cookies' sign on the back wall. David kept his head down and browsed through a coffee table book of Highland Cows.

She took a quick peek through the kilts and souvenirs, looking for an Elliott tartan. All they had were neckties and scarves, though she did find a little booklet about the history of the Elliott clan, so she bought it, along with her shortbread.

"Okay, I'm ready," she said, and as soon as they stepped out of the store, she felt it, like a sixth sense. There were eyes following them, and she heard his name whispered everywhere. *That looks like David Elliott!* and, *"That's David Elliott... who's the woman with him?"* She noticed that David was able to ignore it, but she was beginning to feel claustrophobic and panicked, like she had just over five weeks earlier on Bourbon Street, in New Orleans.

"Are yeh a'right?" he asked, apparently noticing her distress. "Is it the recognition and attention?"

"Yeah, I'm sorry—" she began.

"Dinnae worry, this mall has security, so we'll be a'right; just relax. He smiled at her, and his calmness helped her to relax. They meandered around the mall, window-shopping and wasting time. She wished she didn't have so much luggage with her, but there wasn't anything she could do about it.

At the Williams & Johnson café, a man with a young child called out, "*Look to the future,*" a quote from *Future Explorations.* David waved at them while they stood in line, waiting for their two small coffees. Outside the café a few minutes later, a woman and a teenage boy stopped him to ask for an autograph, which of course he gave them.

———

A young, slender, blonde woman, wearing skimpy workout clothes, jogged around the corner and saw them. "Oh—My—God!" she said in a strong Californian accent. She approached David and squealed, "I can't believe it's you! I'm just so... in love with you! I want to have your babies!"

David was used to all sorts of comments, but this one was new and over the top. Honestly, he couldn't tell if she was joking or serious. He heard Erin hide a laugh as a cough and then stepped away. "Uh, hello—" he began.

"I'm fantastic in bed and also great with kids, so I'd make an amazing wife," she continued, sounding earnest, and he was almost too stunned to say anything.

"I'm sure you would make someone a fine wife, but I'm afraid it cannot be me as I'm not actually looking for a wife at the moment," he said, somehow managing to keep his composure. He started to walk away, scanning the crowd for Erin, but the woman followed him.

"But... didn't your wife just die? Don't you need someone like me to take her place, to help you with your kids?" she said and put her hand on his arm as if to comfort him for his loss.

"Are you—serious?" he said, not able to hide his shock. She looked blankly into his eyes, and it became clear, "Oh! Dear Lord, you are. Yes, she did pass away, just, and I'd appreciate it if you'd allow me some time to mourn her before making your proposal. Good day." He didn't wait for a response and walked away, hoping Erin was still nearby. He found her looking in a store window and somehow managed to control his temper enough not to explode and vent his frustration, but it wasn't easy.

"To be fair, darling," she said with a smile, "I want to have your babies, too. I also think I will make a good wife, and what was the third thing? Ah, yes, and from your reaction the last time we made love, I'd wager I'm not too bad in bed, either."

He put on a fake smile and then frowned. "I can't believe the audacity and presumption of some women."

"Put on your happy face, darling," she said quietly and nudged him with her elbow, "here comes another one."

He took a deep breath and turned around, sporting his perfect smile while Erin retreated to a nearby bench to wait. The woman seemed startled that he'd turned before she'd said anything but recovered quickly. "Uh, hello—I'm sorry to be a bother, but I wanted to let you know just how much I appreciate you and the work you've done. Would you mind posing for a selfie with me?" she asked politely.

"Well, thank you; I don't mind at all," he said briefly, the fewer words the better. She held up her phone, put her arm around his waist, and just as she took the photo, she lowered her hand, trying to grab his ass. Thankfully, he knew what she was trying to do and reached around in time to stop her. She didn't seem phased at all by it and quickly opened the gallery file on her phone to show it to him.

"If you want a copy, I can transfer it to your phone?"

David couldn't remember having ever been asked that question from a fan before. "I... appreciate the gesture, but... no thank you." He was angry about what she'd tried to do and wanted to get away from her.

"Alright, but... how will you remember me?" she said, sounding genuinely disappointed and disheartened by his refusal.

"I have a good memory. Now, if you'll please excuse me, I've—"

"Do remember me!" she said a bit too loudly and forcefully. "I believe—Well, see how lovely we look together? Maybe—"

David plastered on a smile. "I'm very sorry, but I'm not looking for a relation—"

"Oh! I know! I... never intended to be disrespectful of your wife's passing. I just thought—" she interrupted.

"I'm afraid you've thought incorrectly, now please excuse me." He knew if he said another word to that woman, it would be rude, so he decided to end the conversation by walking away. He saw Erin sitting on a nearby bench. *This is absurd,* he thought and sat next to her.

"Nice save there!" she said. "I can't believe she tried to do that! Don't people have any shame or—or ability to control themselves anymore?"

"We need tae announce our engagement *now*! Et's only gonna get worse," he said. "I'm too old for this."

———

He looked miserable, and Erin gave him a compassionate smile. Being a friendly, polite person, she knew it was difficult for him to hurt anyone's feelings or come across as rude, but it wasn't an option with those inappropriate women. "We can discuss it, but aren't you supposed to talk to your PR manager or someone before you do something like that?" She wanted to kiss him so badly, and he very much looked like he needed to be kissed, but she controlled herself.

"Always the voice of reason, you are. Don't yeh want people tae know about us so we can stop hidin' our love and so these mental women will leave me be?"

"No, I don't… well, yes, of course I do, but… right now, people look past me. To them, I'm just your overweight friend; they wouldn't dream of me as your lover, and most certainly not your wife! I think, for now anyway, I prefer it that way."

He brushed a piece of her shoulder-length, salt and pepper hair behind her ear with his fingertips and kept his hand there longer than he needed to. Then, he looked into her eyes. "Aye, tha's understandable, but these women are mad! I just hope none of them try anathin'—anathin' that will make yeh upset, as the woman by the pool did."

"Ugg, don't remind me. I don't wanna remember that day, but I get your point."

"Before I married Susannah, I would get graphic fan mail. The women who sent them described, in ghastly detail, the things they wanted tae do with me if we ever met. Some were so foul that I chose tae have them filtered before I received them. I reckon a healthy packet of them will be arriving again soon, now I'm a widower, and I dinnae look forward tae it."

"Graphic? Really?" she said, and he raised his eyebrows.

"Aye, many contained naked photos of... private female body parts. Erin, yeh must promise that if yeh see *anaone* actin' oddly around me, ye'll come to me... tae help me get out of et! I can't always get away, yeh ken? These radge women are clever and know how tae trap a man. I willnae hit or harm a woman, I just can't, so yeh need tae have ma back."

Erin would've laughed, except he looked so serious, almost to the point of panic, that she nodded. "Okay, David, I promise. I just don't want to get paranoid and walk up to every beautiful woman you end up next to... alright, I'm lying; I will, but I know I shouldn't. I don't want you to think I don't trust you if I do it too often."

His smile accentuated his crow's feet. "I'd rather it was you next tae me, no matter the situation, and will never wish yeh hadn't come."

She looked into his beautiful brown eyes, hardly able to believe she was with him. The desire to kiss him grew stronger, though she knew she couldn't. Her thoughts were interrupted when a very skinny girl with stick-straight hair dyed very bright red said, "Excuse me." Less than half his age, she was wearing a skirt so short the only way to describe it was 'micro.'

As she approached the bench, she held out her arm to him. He was about to shake her hand when Erin noticed that she was showing him her tattoo. She could hardly believe what she was seeing; the woman had David's face tattooed on her forearm. "David, look at that!" she said in awe. It was an image of him from *Future Explorations* and was done very well.

The young woman frowned at Erin, made a little *humph* sound, and then looked adoringly at David. "Would you please sign my arm? I've been hoping to meet you *my whole life*! You are my favorite actor, and it would mean so much to me if—"

"What's your name?" David cut her off.

She smiled, showing dazzlingly bright white teeth. "Jessica," she said.

"Tell me, Jessica, what do you think it means to *me* when you show contempt toward the person I'm sitting with?"

"David, it's all right, really—" Erin began, not wanting him to be upset.

He looked from the young woman to Erin. "No, it is *not* alright. She was downright rude to you just now and then expects me to do her a favor? I'm not having it any longer." He looked back at the girl and sighed. "You may apologize to my good friend here, and then I will sign your arm. Otherwise, I will not. Manners are all I ask for, not flattery."

The girl looked at Erin and then back to David as if she hadn't even realized another person was there at all. Erin blushed deep red, not wanting an apology from her. "I—I'm not sure how I was rude to her, but I'm sorry," she said to David, not even looking in Erin's direction when she said it.

David took the felt-tipped pen she offered and signed a line and a dot, which wasn't even close to his actual signature. She let out a *squee* and then jumped up and down. "May I have a small hug, as well?"

He shook his head sadly and stood, taking Erin's hand to help her up. "Let's go; I'm through here," he said and led her away while the woman gaped at the two of them.

"That's not going to teach her anything, you know?" Erin said when they were out of earshot. "She clearly doesn't understand manners; plus, I thought you didn't want a reputation for being a jerk."

He stopped and looked into her eyes. "Erin, I would rather come across as a jerk than tae allow that little... coo tae treat you that way, whether et's because of your size or because ye're a woman in the same vicinity as me. I'll not play along, and that's final." He closed his eyes and took a cleansing breath. "Oh, and by the way, I love yeh!"

Erin shook her head and smiled at him. "You're crazy! Thank you, and I love you too."

"What bothers me most is that no one *ever* said anathin' negative about Susannah, and she was downright horrible at times. You, on the other hand, are completely wonderful, yet people won't give you the time of day, or they don't even see yeh, and et's not right!"

"David, as long as you love me and as long as you take care to treat me with respect, that's all I really need," she said, seeing in him how much it was bothering him.

"Aye, but I'll be speakin' tae Becky as soon as I can about makin' an announcement—I mean, if you're a'right with et? I ken I said I'd wait a few months, but I dinnae want to."

"I'm not sure I'm ready for that kind of intense scrutiny. I reckon it will be okay, but please listen to what Becky says and make sure it's the right time to do it," she said as they made their way out of the mall and out onto the street.

"A'right, but et's my life, not the public's life lived through me. I'll do what I damn well please—"

A man, who looked to be about twenty, waved from across the street where the enormous, double-decker tour busses were waiting for passengers. "*Allons-y!*" he said, and Erin started to laugh.

"What did he say?" David asked.

The man cupped his hand around his mouth, trying to amplify the sound. "*Allons-y!*" he said again.

Erin waved at him, and David looked at her, perplexed. "He said '*allons-y*,' darling; he thinks you're David Tennant." She started laughing really hard, while the man stood there, waiting for a reply. David rolled his eyes and waved at the man, who cupped his ear, trying to hear his response. "Awww, don't leave the man hanging!" Erin teased.

"But I'm not David Tennant."

"Maybe not, but he doesn't need to know that; be a good sport."

David rolled his eyes again. "*Allons-y*," he said back to the man, who looked overjoyed.

Erin was still laughing as they continued walking toward the train station. "Now that wasn't so hard, was it? You just made his day."

David shook his head again and knit his brows. "Aye, but et was a lie. He's gonnae tell his friends he saw David Tennant today, though he didn't. I dinnae like tae do that."

Erin looked at his face, seeing the genuine concern. "I'm sorry, you're right, but if you hadn't done anything, he would now think David Tennant was a rude bastard. You kept *that* from happening, anyway," she said, trying to make him see the bright side of the story.

"Ye're mad, yeh ken."

"As a hatter, now let's find something to eat; I'm peckish."

Chapter Twelve

PECKISH

David and Erin came to a Wetherspoons and decided to get a snack there. Their waitress, who couldn't have been more than eighteen, approached the table. "What can ah get for yous?" she said, without looking at who was sitting there.

"I'd like the chips, please," Erin said. "I thought we could share unless you're hungrier than that," she said to David.

"I'm not hungry, et's fine with me," he said, and it seemed to her that he was still distracted and agitated by the day's encounters.

The young waitress looked up and finally noticed David. She opened her mouth but nothing came out at first, then she croaked, "Right! What an honor tae be servin' you! This is gonnae sound daft, but my mum loves everythin' ye've ever done. She's forever goin' on about 'David Elliott this and David Elliott that'." She laughed at how ridiculous she sounded. "Sorry, ah know ah sound mental."

Erin laughed with her and looked at David, who was smiling good-naturedly. "Aye? Well, your mum has good taste; what can I say?"

"Ah hate tae ask this while ye're trying tae enjoy a quiet meal, but would you mind signin'—Ach, shit—Ah've nothin' for you tae sign." Just then, her mobile phone started ringing. "Ah'm so sorry, but ma mum's jest out of hospital, and et's her, so… ah need tae answer et." She stepped away from the table, and they heard her say, "Mum, I'm workin'!"

Erin knew he was about to do something really sweet when he looked at her, smiled, then stood and tapped the waitress's shoulder. "One moment," he said and got her attention before she hung up. He reached for her mobile, "Do yeh mind?"

Her eyes grew large, and she put her finger up to ask him to wait. "Mum, there's someone here who'd like tae speak wi' yeh." She handed David her phone and stood there biting her nails.

He put his hand over the end of the phone and asked, "What's her name?"

"Rose," she said.

Both he and Erin smiled, so Erin explained. "His daughter's name is Rosie."

"Hello, Rose?" There was silence at first, then he said, "Yes, I am," and then they heard a noise that sounded like a cross between a laugh, a cry, and some kind of exclamation. They all laughed as David held it away from his ear. "Yes, it is… Yes, your lovely daughter is our waitress today. Thank you… Well, thank you… No, of course not; she's been lovely. Yes… You think so? Well… But… I see. No, I'm sorry, but that's simply… Alright. Yes, I will… Yes… You're welcome," he said and then laughed heartily. "I'll see what I can do… Alright… Okay. Here's your daughter; it was nice speaking with you, Rose."

He handed the mobile phone back to their waitress, who mouthed, '*thank you*' to him, and then turned away to finish the conversation with her mother.

"What did she say—" Erin began but at that moment the girl raised her voice.

"Yeh did what? Aww, Mum! Yeh didnae! Ach... But... No... Mum! Listen, ah've got tae go. Ah'll call you on break. A'right, bye... bye... bye." David raised his eyebrows as she walked quickly back to the table. "Ach, Mr. Elliott, ah'm sae sorry! Ah cannae believe she's done tha'. Ah'm beside maself over et."

"Oh dear, that doesn't sound good," Erin said with a laugh.

"Don't worry, et's alright. That'll be my—" He held up his hand and began counting on his fingers, "Third... offer of marriage today?" He looked at Erin to confirm.

"At least; possibly the fourth," she said with a laugh.

The waitress smiled sheepishly. "Aye, well, ah'm still sorry about et. Ah'll go put yer order in now," she said and hurried away.

"I assume she wanted you to marry her daughter?" Erin asked.

"Aye, a forceful Scottish woman she was, too! I'm verra glad ma mother isn't like that."

"Aye, but she could be like *my* mother and want yeh all for herself—Oh! That sounded worse out loud than it did in my head, sorry."

David scrunched up his face in disgust. "Ach! I could've lived without that thought in ma mind!" The waitress returned with their food and put it on the table along with the bill. She was about to leave, but David stopped her. "Did yeh find somethin' for me tae sign, then?"

She blushed and shook her head. "Ah thought ye'd no' bee overly keen... after my mum's—"

"Nonsense. I could sign one of your order tickets," he said and pointed at the booklet of slips in her hand.

"Okay." She shrugged, tore one off for him to sign, and handed it to him, then she stood, biting her nails as he wrote.

He showed it to Erin, who nodded her approval. She watched the girl's face as she took the slip from David's hand and read it out loud. *"Tell your mum I'm sorry I can't marry you. —David Elliott x"* Her face turned bright pink, all the way down her neck, but she laughed good-naturedly.

"Verra funny, thank you," she said and walked back to the kitchen as quickly as she could.

"We need tae get goin', love; et's nearly time tae board," David said as they finished their food. The bill was only about six pounds, so he put a twenty-pound note on the table, and they left the restaurant.

Erin was amazed at the beauty of the train station as they walked down the long, paved ramp into the belly of Waverly Station. It was like stepping back in time for her. She could picture women dressed in corsets with bustles and large hats and men with their three-piece suits, stove-pipe hats, and bushy mustaches waiting to board. The trains themselves were streamlined and modern, but the station was lovely.

The lower facade of the station was nice, with its ornate carved pillars and decor, but it was the inside of the waiting area that wowed Erin the most. While David had their tickets printed, she looked around the room in wonder. The floors were marble, and the ceiling had glass windows with wood trim, some painted with beautiful floral designs. In the center of the room, there was an enormous glass dome with wooden panels around the bottom of it, painted with garlands. The walls were covered in marble, with high windows, and she loved every inch of it. She could've sat there all day on one of the long, wooden benches, daydreaming; however, their tickets didn't take long to be printed. Soon they were headed back out to the platform, where they didn't have to wait as their train was sitting at its dock, ready for boarding.

Chapter Thirteen

A TRAIN BOUND FOR LONDON TOWNE

The first-class K car was a quiet car, which meant no cellphone usage, minimal talking, etc. They boarded it, and David placed Erin's suitcase in the designated luggage area at the end of the car, then they found their assigned seat. She had romantic ideas about the journey and smiled at David as she put her purse on the little table between them.

"I'm so excited! How old am I now—Nearly forty, and I've never been on a train," she said.

David looked surprised. "Really? Well, et's not that romantic, not like et is in films," he said, slightly quelling her enthusiasm.

It wasn't long before the train started moving, and they glided through the station, past the coffee shop and car hire kiosk. They burst into the daylight, passing the backsides of office buildings, then they whizzed through a short tunnel that plunged them into darkness, except for the interior lights of the train car, which went on. Houses and apartment buildings that sat on the edges of the train tracks were a blur as they sailed past them.

A man who called himself the Train Guard made his announcements over the speakers, telling them that their first stop would be Berwick upon Tweed, then announced that breakfast would be served shortly. Erin watched the landscape fly past. As they left town, she was disappointed that so many berms, dense rows of trees, and hedges blocked the view along the tracks.

A woman came around to the first-class passengers, asking what they wanted for breakfast from the limited menu. David chose the full Scottish breakfast and Erin chose the yogurt, though it was spelled 'yoghurt.'

They flew past several small train depots and occasionally the view would open up, then she could see the beautiful land with fields and houses scattered about. It was as though a farmer had thrown 'farm' seeds into the air, letting the wind take them. The few standing were the ones that took root and grew.

They passed the Prestonpans station, and Erin remembered the battle she'd learned about in the *Outlander* books and television series. Lost in a daydream of Highland men in kilts, brandishing blades while running through the fields, she was startled when David interrupted her thoughts. She realized she'd nodded off and was embarrassed to learn that she'd been drooling.

"Erin? Are yeh awake?"

"Hmm—I am now. I was just dreaming of… well, never mind." She smiled coyly at him, waiting to find out why he'd woken her.

"Did yeh want tea? They'll be serving et soon." He smiled and bumped her foot under the table.

She nodded at him and turned her cup right side up. *Good night nurse, he's amazing! Look at him! Could there be anyone more beautiful in all the world?* she thought. It was impossible to absorb just how insanely gorgeous he was, and sometimes when she looked at him it shocked her, as if seeing him for the first time.

She met his eyes and smiled, tapping his foot with hers. When she moved her hand to her side, she felt the small bag of shortbread cookies. She reached into the bag, took out the small Elliott Clan booklet, and started reading about the origins of the surname. It said that no one knew for sure where it originally came from, though it gave a few theories. It was pretty boring, but she really wanted to learn more so she decided to trudge through it.

"What've yeh got there?" David asked.

"Oh, I bought this at the mall. It's about the Elliott clan; would you like me to read it to you?"

He smiled at her. "Aye, love. Tell me all about ma clan, then."

She wasn't about to start over at the boring stuff, so she read snippets from where she was at. *'The Elliots were one of the great riding clans of the western Scottish borders.'* She read that there were different clan branches over time, but the leadership began initially with the Redheugh Ellots. "It says that the clan built strong towers in Liddesdale and held Hermitage castle south of Hawick sometimes, too.

"This says that The Ellots of Redheugh were involved in Border fighting during the 16th century and after the pacification of the Borders in the early 1600s, many Elliots were hanged, outlawed, and banished. It says that many Elliots drifted to Edinburgh and Glasgow. Elliot, with one 'T' and Elliott, with two 'Ts' became the main spellings, and the older forms died out. It's not the most gripping book I've ever read, but it wasted some time anyway," she said.

"Aye, et's no like I'm of the famous 'Wallace' clan, where there were larger than life characters who did brave and mighty deeds!" he said, rolling his eyes at her.

"Aye, we are a brave and mighty lot at that!" she said, smiling and wanting to hold his hand; instead, she sighed, put the book back in the bag, and looked out the window.

They heard the beverage trolly jingling down the aisle, and when it got to their seats, they both ordered tea. Erin sipped on hers and watched trees, fields, and ancient buildings go whizzing past her. She thought that perhaps some of the buildings had served weary travelers who arrived first on foot then on horseback, wagons, carriages, and then maybe on steam locomotives. She drifted off, back to sleep, imagining them standing outside of the buildings, watching and waving at them as they flew by.

She woke with a start when she heard the trolley come by, handing out toast, then a few minutes later, their breakfast was served. When they were through eating, their plates were cleared and they were offered more tea.

The train guard announced that they would be calling on Berwick upon Tweed shortly and gave the times of arrival, saying they were running on schedule. Erin needed to use the bathroom, so she stood and walked out of their car to the toilets. When she returned, someone was sitting in her seat, and David didn't look happy about it. She approached them, assuming the person would stand and leave. Instead, David stood and offered her his seat, giving the impeccably well-dressed, exceptionally beautiful woman a hint they were together, though it didn't work and she remained seated.

"I'm afraid you are in my seat," he said coldly. "I'm going to have to ask you to move now." She stood then and looked at Erin distastefully.

"Very well, but if you change your mind, you know where to find me," she said and kissed his cheek. He didn't bother to reply and sat in Erin's seat, wiping his cheek with the back of his hand.

"God! What a whore!" he said, not caring whether she'd left the train car or not.

Erin looked at him feeling dazed and confused. Her heart rate had increased when she saw the woman kiss him and wanted to know the story behind how he knew her.

"Who was she? She seemed to know you," she asked, trying to sound casual; she wanted to be objective and not jump to any conclusions.

"Aye, we met many years ago when I had a small role... before I got the part on *Future Explorations*. She told me she was havin' a small do at her flat and that I should join her. I didn't care much for her back then, but I thought it would be a chance tae get to know more of the cast. Well, a small do et was—just me and her. I wanted no part of et, but she kept blockin' the damned door. She handed me a glass of red wine and played romantic mood music that nauseated me. I didn't drink the wine, sure et was drugged, and as soon as she excused herself tae use the loo, I fled. I had hoped never tae run into her again.

"I see... well," Erin said, taking a deep breath, "I'm glad I could rescue you then." She tried to smile, but she knew it wasn't convincing. It wasn't that she thought there was anything up or that she didn't trust him; she just wished that all the beautiful women would fall off the face of the earth for the rest of her life. The way the woman had looked at her made her feel fat and ugly again. She propped her jaw on her hand and continued to look out the window.

"Don't you believe me?" he asked.

Erin nodded but didn't say anything for fear of the tears threatening to fill her eyes. *How can I marry him? How can I be with a man who will be, understandably, surrounded by the most beautiful women in the world when I'm nothing like them?* She swallowed hard, twice, but felt the prickle of unwanted tears forming; she wanted to go somewhere so he wouldn't see them, but there wasn't anywhere to hide.

"Erin?"

She jammed her eyes shut, willing herself to stop with the theatrics and calm down, but it was no use; the tears rolled down her cheeks and fell onto her palm.

"I dinnae understand; why are you upset? I didn't have any control over her settin' herself there," he said, agitation evident in his voice.

Erin shook her head. "I'm not angry," she whispered but didn't look at him. "I... just feel—" She could feel the sob rise in her chest, so she didn't finish her sentence.

David leaned forward and took hold of her hand, kissing it tenderly. "Ach. I'm sure she made yeh feel about an inch tall, my love, but she doesn't matter. She's a disgustin' slag, and *you* are my true love, and I think ye're beautiful."

Erin nodded, still unable to speak. *Where's a fucking tissue when you need one!* she thought. "I love you," was the only thing she could say, and it came out as a hoarse whisper.

Their assigned seats were singles; across the aisle, though there were unoccupied doubles, so David stood and took her hand. "Come here," he said and sat next to the window. Erin sat beside him and put her head on his arm. The tears wouldn't stop, but now they were a mixture of feeling fat and ugly and joy at having met a man who could make her feel better about it. It meant everything to her that he didn't think she was fat or ugly.

About halfway through their ride, someone came around to ask what everyone wanted for their lunch. Erin chose a warm cheese and onion pie, and David chose the roast beef sub.

She was just getting comfortable again and not hating herself as much when the woman returned. This time, she had her phone out and didn't try to hide that she took a picture of them sitting together. "What are yeh after now?" David barked, plainly irritated.

She smiled sweetly, though malevolence seeped out of her features. "I don't want anything from you... right now, David, darling," she said. "I'm just procuring a little... insurance—"

David's face went red. Erin could see the vein pop out on his forehead, as it had when she'd told him what Bran had done. He tried to stand but was pinned by the table, so Erin quickly stood, allowing him to get out of the seat.

"You have some nerve threatenin' me, yeh bitch." He quickly snatched her phone away from her and turned, walking determinedly toward the toilets. He opened the door to the men's room and stepped inside. She cried out for him to open the door, but he ignored her.

After a lot of banging on the door, he opened it and stepped out, revealing a dripping wet phone with a crushed screen. He pushed past her, and she screamed when he opened the window on the door. "Don't you dare!"

The hedges and rocks were a blur as he chucked it out of the train. "You won't be blackmailin' me," he said and went to Erin, who was standing nearby, watching with a small crowd of curious passengers.

"How dare you!" she said furiously.

David turned around and got up in her face; his Scottish temper got the best of him, and his spit flew when he spoke to her.

"If I ever hear from yeh again; if yeh bother me, ever again, or if an exposé comes out in a tabloid and I find out et was you, I will take you tae court, and I will not back down. Are we clear? You don't intimidate me; you disgust me, now go crawl back under the rock you slithered out from yeh cu—"

He didn't finish the word, although Erin wouldn't have minded if he had. Apparently, no one had ever spoken to her like that before because she turned bright red, huffing and puffing, not knowing how to reply. She turned on her heel and stormed out of the car, slamming the sliding door as best as she could for effect, except it didn't work.

Erin took his hand, and before she let him lead them back to their seat, she hugged him tightly. She wrapped her arms around his chest, holding on for dear life, then she kissed him passionately. She no longer cared if someone saw them or sold a picture of them to a tabloid or internet site; she was in love with him and wanted the world to know. He held her and kissed her right back as the people nearby clapped and then returned to their seats.

"I love you, David Elliott. That was so brave and crazy, and I love you for it! You have my permission to tell whomever you want about us; though, I'd still recommend you listen to Becky." She was pretty sure it would be bad for them to announce an engagement when she was still technically married, but they could at least be open about their love in public and tell people they meant to get engaged if the subject came up.

Erin felt like she was floating. "I can't believe you threw her phone out the window! That's priceless!" she said.

He smiled and seemed a bit embarrassed at his bravado.

"She deserved it; maybe she'll think twice about speaking that way to another man."

Erin allowed him to sit and then put her head back on his arm, holding his hand and feeling so in love. The women with the beverage trolly came round, and Erin ordered a Coke while David had coffee.

They talked and laughed through lunch; a weight had been lifted, and things seemed brighter than they had before. After their meal, Erin was tired, so she rested her head on his arm and fell asleep. She slept through the next two stops and only woke because she needed to use the bathroom again.

She got up and made her way to the toilets, hoping David would be alone when she returned. Thankfully her wish came true; he was sound asleep with his mouth open, and his head tilted back against the window. She stood and watched him for a while; if it had been in any way possible, and if there had been someone who could perform the ceremony on the train, she would've said 'I do' that very second.

She sat next to him and nudged him a bit to get him to close his mouth. He lifted his head, rubbed his hand over his stiff neck, and looked at her smiling at him.

"What? Was I snoring... or drooling?" he asked, and she shook her head.

"Neither; I just like you."

He laughed and bent down to kiss her. A businessman walked in, and they didn't care; a woman and a small child walked through, but they didn't stop snogging for them. David took out his phone and typed a message to Becky, telling her he wanted to make a formal announcement to the press or whoever cared to know, saying that he was in love and would be married as soon as possible.

"What about the reporter in the car?" Erin asked. "You promised him your next big story, didn't you?"

David kissed her hair and added that he wanted that reporter to be given the story first, then sent her a photo of the business card the man had given him.

It didn't take long for Becky to reply.

B: *Are you absolutely sure about this, David? Is this the woman you met through the FD Registry? You haven't known each other very long, have you? Also, and I hate to bring this up, did you mention that she was pregnant? If so, the press will have a field day with it. If you're heart-set on it, you should do it now, while she can still fit into a dress, or after the baby is born. Wedding photos with a belly out to here won't look very nice in the papers. Now, don't be angry, you pay me to be your voice of reason.*

"Well, she's not wrong," Erin said, feeling a bit disheartened. "I figured she might say as much."

David put his finger under her chin and turned her head to look at him. "I don't care what anaone thinks about whether or not ye're pregnant or that we haven't known each other for verra long. *I* know this is right; more right than the last eighteen years of ma life have been. I'm not marryin' you because ye're pregnant but because I love yeh. Plus, we can get married privately and then have the celebration whenever we wish. Et's nobody's business what we do with our lives, Erin," he said, and then his phone rang with a notification.

B: *One more thing, isn't she still married? I've just researched how long it would take for a divorce to be final in her state. It says she must wait a minimum of 4-6 months for the divorce to be final, sometimes longer, so you'll have to wait to get married. Now, if you're sure you want the media coverage, we can let it be known that you have a serious love interest, but do you*

honestly want it to be sent to this
guy first?

"Wow, I didn't know it took so long! Well, it sucks, but we'll just have a long engagement then," Erin said. Ultimately, she was glad things would be out in the open, although she wasn't naive enough to think things wouldn't be a pain in the butt for a while with the media hounding them. "I think you should give her your consent. Do you want to send her a photo to give the reporter? There's that nice one from our last night in New Orleans?"

"Aye, tha's good, et will make et more official and will make people see us as together." He found the photo in his gallery and attached it to his reply.

D: *Yes, send this to him, along with*
the news.

"There, it's done; she probably won't actually get it out to him for a day or two, and then he will have to write his story, so it may be a few days until it's in the papers, so just be patient."

"As a monk on Sunday!" she said, and he looked at her as if she'd gone mad.

"What?" he said.

"I'll be as patient as a monk on Sunday," she repeated.

He laughed hard and kissed her again. "Ye're mad, is what you are!"

Finally, the train guard announced they would be arriving at King's Cross station, so Erin stood to stretch her legs and use the toilet. When she returned, she could see the beginnings of the station appearing outside. David used his app to have a car waiting for them once they got there, and Erin grabbed her luggage from the rack.

They slowly rolled into the glass-domed station and came to a gentle stop, then the doors opened, and everyone piled out onto the platform. David helped her with her suitcase then they walked toward the interior of the building. The station ceiling was round, and a diamond waffle pattern wrapped around it, bringing your eyes to the center of the building, where the arrivals and departures screens were hung. On the opposite wall were shops and food.

Erin saw signs for Platform 9¾ and would've loved to see it, but being a Sunday, the lines were outrageous. She also knew David could never stand in lines like that anyway; as it was, they were being stared at and pointed to, their every move watched and recorded in photos and videos.

She saw David check his phone then he picked up his pace. "The hire car is waiting for us. Once we find it, we can relax," he said. They found their ride, and the driver opened the door for them. As soon as the door shut, Erin leaned over and kissed David. "Well, what was that for?" he asked breathlessly.

"I'm just excited to be heading to my new home with you, that's all," she said and put on her seatbelt.

Chapter Fourteen

NEW HOME, NEW RULES

The hired car pulled up to a row of wide townhouses; the driver got out and opened the door for Erin and David, then lifted Erin's suitcases out of the trunk. As the car drove away, David led Erin up five steps. She had butterflies in her stomach as she stood next to him on the stoop. He put the key into the lock and opened the large wooden door. "Et's nice to be home," he said with a sigh as they walked in.

Erin stayed close to him, looking around the room and up at the high ceilings. The last time she was there, she hadn't had a chance to look around. Now, she took the time to notice details, like the intricate crown moldings and floorboards, as well as the exquisite inlaid designs in the wood flooring.

She knew David had informed Kitty and Francie that he'd be staying for the week and that he wanted to have a staff meeting with them when he arrived, though she didn't see anyone around. They heard her before they saw her; a lilting tune and footsteps preceded the appearance of Kitty, who was wearing earbuds and clearly hadn't heard them come in.

"Cor blimey!" she said when she saw them standing there, then quickly pulled the earbuds out and stuffed them into her pocket. "Sorry, Mister Elliott, I din't 'ear ya come in. Aw, 'ellow Ms. Erin, it's nice ta see ya again."

"Hello, Kitty," she said and laughed, thinking of the Japanese cartoon character. "Sorry, I'm going to have to get used to saying that."

"Aw, no worries; I get 'at all the time." Kitty smiled, then looked at them standing in the foyer and blushed, though Erin didn't understand what was wrong. "Aw, sorry, sir; 'ere I am talkin' away—let me take your fings upstairs for ya. What room will Ms. Erin be stayin' in, sir?" she said subserviently.

"Never mind the luggage just now, Kitty," David said. "Is Francie nearby?"

Kitty looked at him gravely and then nodded. "I fink so, sir. I can go get 'er if ya want me to?" She looked at the floor and started biting her fingernail, then she realized what she was doing and put her hands at her sides.

"Yes, please find her and meet us in the sitting room."

He wasn't using his Scottish accent anymore, but Erin wasn't surprised. Kitty turned resolutely and walked away, looking a bit sad, Erin thought.

"David, I think Kitty believes you're going to fire her and Francie; she seemed to be sad and nervous just now," Erin said quietly, and he gave her a puzzled look.

"Do you think so? I never said anything about sacking them," he said, sounding shocked.

"No, but in their minds, why would you keep them around if your wife just died and you are never here; it makes sense for them to think that way," she said.

"A'right, I'm glad you said something; I'll keep it in mind." They left the suitcase at the door and walked to the sitting room, which was entirely too formal for Erin's taste. There was nothing comfortable in the room, nothing said 'sit here,' and it was supposed to be a room to sit in. Erin chose a modern, straight-backed upholstered chair to sit on, but David shook his head.

"Would yeh mind sittin' on the sofa next tae me?"

Erin smiled and stood; she'd chosen that seat so it didn't appear they were 'together,' not knowing what he was planning to say to the two women. When she crossed the room, he took her hand and kissed her cheek; that's when she noticed the sweat on his forehead. "Are you okay?"

"I'm not sure where to begin or remember what I wanted to say. Susannah was always the one to have staff meetings, so I'm out of ma comfort zone. I've a bit of a panic creeping up on me." He let out a staggered breath and smiled sheepishly at her.

She wiped the sweat off his upper lip and gave him a peck on the cheek. "You'll be brilliant, my love. I'm here with you, and there's power in numbers, right?" she said.

"Yes, you're right, as usual."

She felt nervous, too, as she sat on the sofa next to where he was standing, wondering if he'd expect her to say anything. Just as she was about to ask him, Kitty appeared at the door, and then Francie joined her. Erin could tell by their hesitancy to enter that they weren't used to being invited into that room. She smiled at Kitty and nearly waved her into the room but stopped herself; this wasn't her house, or at least David was the boss, so it fell to him to direct what was happening. He did just what Erin would have done, waving his hand to say, 'come in.'

"Please join us, ladies." He waited for them to come closer. "Please take a seat; I must speak with you about something important today."

The women looked at him, and Francie said, "If et's all the same tae you, sir, ah'd rather stand."

Ahh, so she's Scottish! Erin thought.

"That's fine," he said, and the two women stayed where they were. "My friend, Erin, seems to think you are under the impression that I've called this meeting to sack you." The two women were silent, but they bowed their heads. "Well, I'm not, so please relax."

Francie let out a long breath. "Ach, ah kent ye'd never sack us, sir. Ah told Kitty here tha' verra thing."

Kitty gave her a rankled look that plainly revealed it was Francie who'd been insinuating the sacking, not her. Erin smiled warmly at them both.

"I wish to speak with you about Mrs. Elliott and introduce you to Erin. She... well, we'll get into who she is in a moment." He took a deep breath. "As you most likely already know, Susannah and I had not been... well, seeing eye to eye of late, and I am going to let you know why."

The women looked at him wide-eyed as if it were none of their business and he shouldn't even bring it up. "Sir, we don't need—" Kitty began, but David interrupted her.

"You do need to know, as it involves Erin."

Erin thought he could have worded it better since now she would be seen as the 'other woman,' which wasn't a good start.

He told them, with minimal details, about being tricked into joining the Registry and that Martin Green was not, under any circumstances, welcome at his home any longer. He told them how he hadn't wanted to sign up but that Susannah had convinced him it was the best way to proceed. Then, he asked them if they knew what the treatments involved. When they both shook their heads, he told them that as well. Their eyes grew wide again, and they both looked at Erin as though she were diseased.

"It's not contagious, don't worry," Erin said when she saw the looks on their faces. "I was born with it. Sorry, David, they looked scared, and I—I wanted to put them at ease."

"It's quite alright," he said and gave her a quick smile. "The thing neither of us was expecting with this whole endeavor was to... well, to fall in love." There was more widening of the eyes, Erin's as well.

"Well, that was blunt," she said quietly. David looked completely out of his element, and she wondered if he wanted her to help him, but she wasn't about to say anything unless asked.

"What I'm trying to say is—I was going to petition for a divorce from Susannah, and—Well... and then she... passed on—" He was in over his head now, Erin could sense it, but she didn't know what to say either. He looked at her as though he were drowning, and she shrugged.

"What I mean to say is— If you feel you aren't able to accept this new situation, then I will accept your resignation. I understand you may feel a certain loyalty to Susannah, but if you can accept it, I'd... we'd prefer you stay on and continue as before with Erin and myself as your employers from now on."

He let out a long breath, sat next to Erin, and stood right back up. "This is the most uncomfortable furniture I've ever tried tae sit on!" he said, and Erin laughed. She stood next to him, and he took her hand. "Now, do you have any questions or comments?"

Francie looked Erin up and down as if examining her. "Ach, she looks a'right tae me; sae long as she stays oot of ma kitchen."

Erin looked at David and shook her head slightly. That condition wouldn't work; she liked to cook sometimes and would not be kept out. "Now, Francie, that won't be the way of it. Erin will have complete access to every room in this house, and that's just how it's going to be." Francie looked at her again and sniffed but didn't say anything.

Kitty stood and smiled at Erin. "I fink, if ya don't mind me bein' frank, 'at you seem nice togevah, and I fink I'll like Ms. Erin for me gov'nah, sir," she said quickly and blushed as if worried she'd said the wrong thing.

"Governor! I can't believe you just called me your governor; that's brilliant!" Erin said, forgetting herself, and looked at David, hoping she hadn't overstepped her bounds either.

He laughed good-naturedly. "Alright, now go ahead and speak with Erin if you'd like."

Francie looked at her like a stray cat someone had let in and was now saying would rule the roost. Erin walked up to her and held out her hand for a handshake, but she could see Francie was having none of it. "It's nice to meet you, Francie. I've heard you're a very good cook. I look forward to... umm... eating... here? If you know what I mean?" she said and then laughed nervously.

Francie put on a fake smile. "Aye, et's nice tae meet you as well, ma'am," she said, though it sounded like 'mum,' and walked over to David. "Mr. Elliott, ah have a joint in the oven tha' needs tendin'. If yeh dinnae mind, I'll go now."

"Before you get back to your joint, I will speak to you each individually in my office. Erin, would you care to join me? There are *comfortable* chairs in there," he said, and she smiled at him.

"Well, that depends on whether Francie and Kitty would like me to join you for their Q&A session. Francie, would you like me to be in the room or not? I won't hold it against you if you don't."

"Ah'd rather speak tae yeh alone, sir, if et's all the same?"

Erin did feel a slight sting, but she understood completely; she wouldn't be able to be as candid as she'd like with the 'invader' in the room. "That's fine, but may I just say something else to you before you leave?" Erin said. Francie turned to her with her arms crossed, looking put out. Erin was more than willing to work with the woman, but she wouldn't put up with blatant insolence. "Listen, I'm not going to just waltz into your kitchen and demand things be done my way... or tell you at the last minute that I've decided to cook supper. I want to work with you. Also, I don't know how you feel about the look and design of the kitchen the way it is now, but... it's not my taste. I plan to make it much more… homey, beautiful, old-fashioned even… I think. I want your input, for instance, the things you need, want, and would rather do without. Can we work together on it?" she asked, praying it would soften Francie's heart toward her.

Francie looked at Kitty, who nodded emphatically. She uncrossed her arms and walked up to Erin. "Ah truly do hate tha' kitchen, mum. Et's dull and gloomy, and ah start tae feelin' depressed when ah've been in et for too long. Ach, ah'm willin' tae work with yeh, mu—"

"I really wish you'd just call me Erin," she cut in and looked at Francie, smiling.

Francie gave her a wary look. "Ach, tha' may be, though ah'll be callin' yeh Ms. Erin or mum."

"Alright, Ms. Erin is fine. Go ahead and speak to David; Then, when you're done tending to your joint, you can come back here and talk with Kitty and me if you'd like to."

Francie shook her head and left the room, following David. Erin and Kitty sat together on the edge of the couch, which was the only way it was at all comfortable, though she had to convince Kitty it was all right for her to do it. "Thank ya, ma'am—" Kitty said, though again, it sounded like 'mum.'

Erin interrupted her. "Oh, don't call me mum, just call me Erin, please."

Kitty shook her head. "I can't. It ain't proper, and if the agency were ta find out, we'd be sacked! I'll call ya Ms. Erin, though, if you'd prefer."

"Alright, then, that's fine," she said resignedly. It was going to take her a while to get used to the situation.

Kitty smiled and said, "I'm real 'appy for you and Mr. Elliott. You're real nice togevah. I hope 'at's not too forward ta say."

"Thank you; I'm happy for us too. You have no idea what we've been through to get here. You know what, Kitty? To quote Anne Shirley, I knew you were a 'kindred spirit' when I first met you."

"Who's Anne Shirley, mum? I've never 'eard of 'er; is she American?"

Erin played at being shocked and appalled at her question, ignoring her use of 'mum' that time. "What? Are you telling me you've never even heard of her? *Le potage*! Surely you've heard of *Anne of Green Gables*, haven't you?" Kitty looked scared that she'd actually offended her new employer, so she nodded tentatively, but Erin saw right through it.

"Oh, Kitty, my dear girl! It's a book series from the turn of the twentieth century, set on Prince Edward Island, Canada. It's about a young, red-haired orphan girl sent to live with an older couple, who are brother and sister, to help on their farm, only they wanted a boy—It's too much to explain now, but you just have to read it! I have all the books; they are being shipped here as we speak. I will loan them to you when they arrive. If you are anything like I imagine you are, you will fall in love with them. Come to think of it, I think Rosie should read them as well! Okay, I'm getting ahead of myself." She took a deep breath and laughed lightly.

Kitty looked at her as though she were slightly mad but smiled warmly. "I love ta read, so it'd be lovely ta read somefin' you love so much," she said.

Erin placed her hand over Kitty's and squeezed it. "I'm going to be here all week, Kitty, and I'd love to get to know you better. Maybe you can show me the ins and outs of this place as well?" Kitty had an odd expression cross her face. "What is it? Did I say something wrong?"

Kitty smiled ruefully, "No, mum—I mean—Ms. Erin. Ya di'nt say anyfing wrong; it's just 'at now I can't talk ta you as a friend. I 'ave my place, you see?"

"Fiddle faddle! I'm your 'gov'nah,' right?" Kitty smiled at the way she'd said the word and nodded. "Well, then, I'd like us to be more on friendly terms. Now, David, he's your boss; give him all the deference you need to, but with me, please don't. I don't know anything about having household help; I would appreciate it if you could please teach me?

"I'm sure I'll have to go places… snobby rich people's houses, for instance, who have maids and staff, and I'll need to know what's what, but with you, I need to be myself. Unless *we* have the snooty people over here, then I'll allow you to call me mum and bow and curtsey if you want to. Is it a deal?" Erin said, feeling like she was begging for Kitty's friendship, but she knew she'd be completely lost if she didn't have someone to teach her.

She smiled hopefully at the young woman sitting next to her. In her eyes, Kitty wasn't lower than her or of lesser value. To her, they were the same, and she planned to make that evident. There was an employer/employee relationship involved, yes, but an employer didn't have to be a taskmaster.

"A'wright, Ms. Erin, but I'd feel bet'er about it wiv' Mr. Elliott's permission."

"That's a great idea! We'll speak to him when—" David walked in just then, and she turned to him. "Well, speak of the devil," she said. David looked behind him. "Yes, I meant you, dear. Would you mind coming over here?"

"Aye," he said, raising an eyebrow and approaching them cautiously.

"Aye, you mind, or aye, you will?" Erin said.

Kitty smiled and stifled a laugh.

"Well, I'm here, aren't I?" he said.

"So, do you want to talk to him about it, or should I?" Erin asked, looking at Kitty, but she raised both eyebrows and shook her head, letting her know she did not want to do the talking. "Alright—" she began, but David interrupted her.

"Wait, Erin, would you mind if we did this 'talking' in my office? This room suffocates me."

Erin smiled at him; she wanted to kiss him and tell him it suffocated her too, but she decided to be at least slightly dignified, for the moment, anyway. "Fine with me. Kitty?" she said and looked at her, asking her if she minded going to David's office. Kitty stood, seeming flummoxed, so Erin looked at David, confused at her hesitancy.

"It's alright, Kitty, she doesn't understand. Come with us, please," he said.

The timid woman smiled and nodded. "Yes, sir," she replied and seemed relieved.

David put his arm around Erin's shoulders. "I'll explain what happened later."

They walked into his perfectly crafted office; it smelled like everything David and all Erin wanted to do during her time in London was sit in there and breathe. She began to feel slightly intoxicated, and more than a little turned on. "Oh, David, I love this room!" she said as they walked in. David sat in his desk chair, and although he offered her a seat, Kitty stood before him. Erin sat on the brown leather couch; the soft leather embraced and welcomed her, unlike the horrible sofa in the sitting room.

"Thank you, love; now what was it you wanted to talk to me about?"

He was being very formal, very employer-like, and that was turning her on even more than she had been before. She wanted to pretend he was her boss and she'd been called into his office because she needed to be reprimanded. Trying to refocus, she shook her head, but it was very difficult to concentrate. "Hmm—what was it,

Kitty? Oh, right… where to begin? Her mind was spaghetti in that room; it was the most powerful aphrodisiac. *Why didn't I feel like this when I was in here before?*

"So, I'd like to be on more friendly terms with Kitty. I don't want her to call me mum or miss; I'd like her to call me Erin, though I know she won't. I want for her and me to be friends, essentially. Now, of course, I realize you are—*we* are her employers, and when we have company, it will be proper for her to do those things, and if I need something done, something that is her job to do, of course, I'll ask her to do it, but I don't want—"

David stood unexpectedly and walked up to her, then he took her hand to help her stand, and she stood, confused as he hugged her. Between the smell of his skin and the room, she melted even more. She nearly reached up and kissed him as if it were just the two of them, but she caught herself just in time. "You are not in any way like Susannah, and I love yeh so much for et." He realized he'd just said that in front of Kitty and cleared his throat.

"I am alright with it, as long as you are able to do as you say when we have company or when the circumstances call for it. I think Kitty has had a rather rough time of it, working here with Susannah, although she'd never say anything." He glanced up at his housekeeper, and she blushed, looking at the floor. "Listen, Kitty, things are going to be much different around here now, and I believe it will be for the better, don't you agree?" he asked.

She smiled and looked at Erin. "Yes, sir, I reckon so."

David stepped away from Erin, and she slid back onto the couch, feeling even more drunk. She suddenly wanted Kitty to leave so she could attack the amazing man who had just returned to the leather chair behind his desk.

"Now, Kitty, do you have any questions, comments, or concerns you'd like to talk to us about?" David said.

All Erin could do was sit and look at him, nearly drooling. She needed to snap out of this love coma she was entering into, and quick, so she stood and began pacing, but that didn't work. David and Kitty were now looking at her as though she had most definitely gone mad. "Please excuse me… I need to… to use the… loo." She opened the office door and stopped; she had no clue where the bathroom was.

"First door on your left," she heard in stereo.

As soon as she was out of the room and away from David, she felt sane again, though she knew that as soon as she went back, she'd feel all melty once more. She turned on the light, walked into the bathroom, and about peed herself. The room was gorgeous, like walking back in time about a hundred and twenty years. Everything looked to be original, although she thought they probably had outhouses and chamber pots when the place had been built.

When she was finished, she pulled the chain to flush and then washed her hands. In the mirror, she saw the slight bruising on her face, which was faded though still visible. She also looked drunk, which was not good, so she took the hand towel and ran it under the lukewarm water; it never really got cold. Trying to revive herself a little bit, she wiped it over her forehead and the back of her neck, then walked back into the office to find David sitting in his desk chair, alone.

Kitty was gone, and he looked at her with worry on his face. "Are yeh all right, love?"

Erin did feel all melty again. "Does the door to this room lock?" she asked, feeling drunk. She wanted him to take her right there, over the desk.

"Aye," he said slowly, as though completely bewildered at her behavior.

Erin peeked at the door and saw a skeleton key with a tassel hanging from it sticking out of the lock. She walked over and flipped the key, which made a satisfying little *thwip* noise. "This room... and you in it... is driving me crazy!" she breathed and stood in front of him, running her fingers through his short chestnut hair.

"Et is, is et? And what do you propose we do about et, then?" He put both hands on her neck and pulled her head down to his, kissing her passionately, then he took his hands off her neck, lifted her top, and started unfastening her bra. He struggled with the last hook, and when it finally came undone, he lifted it under her shirt and gently cupped her breasts, all the while kissing her. Then, he stood and began unfastening her jeans; he put his hands under her waistband and pulled her pants down just enough to grab her ass.

Erin couldn't resist and massaged his rock-hard cock over his trousers. She gasped and felt his cock grow even harder as she touched it. He put both hands on her ass and squeezed, pulling her up against him while also pinning her against the edge of his desk. His kisses became even more passionate as he tugged her jeans down, then he turned her around and bent her over the desk.

He unfastened his slacks and pulled them down hastily.

Erin felt him put his hard-on between her legs, making her cry out softly in anticipation. He spread her lips and entered her, making her gasp, "Oh yes! Oh—" His thrusts were like lightning striking her, filling her with energy and draining her at the same time. Things started falling off the top of the desk, a pen, and then a paperweight. Erin grabbed the front edge, moaning and panting until he released inside of her; it felt like an explosion which, in turn, made her explode in response.

She lay, bent over the desk for a long time; she felt so good, he made her feel so damn good. "Good night nurse, David! I don't know how we manage to do that every time, but it's fantastic! Fabulous, even. Thank you!" she said, still breathing heavily.

He chuckled softly. "Aye, fabulous is a good word for et, and ye're quite welcome."

They put their clothes back on and sat together on the sofa. "What time is supper?" Erin asked. She wasn't particularly hungry, she just wanted to know how much time they had before they'd be expected anywhere.

"Generally around half five. Et's only half four now; come here and let me hold yeh."

Erin sat on his lap with her head on his chest. That was where she felt most comfortable, the most at peace, in his arms. "I want to soak this up, this time with you. I know you'll be filming soon, and we may be apart more often, and I'll miss this. I wish I could put this feeling into a bottle and keep it; then, when I'm feeling lonely, I can open the bottle and take out a pinch every now and then. Hey, wait; whatever happened to Kitty? Where did she go while I was in the bathroom?

"Ach, she told me she dinnae have any questions, and she looked forward tae working for us, so I told her she could go."

Erin smiled. "I'm sorry I bailed on you; I just couldn't focus in this room. It was intoxicating me, and then when you hugged me,

I lost it and needed some fresh air. All I could think of was you bending me over that desk and taking me, just like you did."

"Aye, this room is intoxicating; tha's why I spend most of ma time in here," he said. "I almost forgot; I need tae explain what happened with Kitty in the sittin' room."

"Yeah, I'm guessing I did something wrong." She shook her head, knowing it wouldn't be the last time.

"Aye, well, not wrong, just not right; she isn't accustomed tae her employer givin' her a say in matters, such as whether she'd prefer this room or that. I say, 'follow me here,' and she says, 'yes sir;' yeh just threw her off. I know you were bein' polite; ye're a verra polite and considerate person, but that's not how things are in her line of work. Do yeh understand?"

"Aye, I guess so, but it's going to take me a while to get that one right. I'm afraid to ask what Francie said."

David smiled and laughed. "She's a stubborn one but a fine cook. You were right tae say what yeh did before we left the room; I think et made a difference. She said yeh seemed like a well-meanin' person, and she'd give you a chance—"

Erin sat up. "She'd give *ME* a chance! The nerve! Seriously, David, if she gives me too hard a time, I'll sack her myself!"

David laughed and pulled her back to him, "Aye, and you may if yeh really feel yeh need to, though I think all she wants is tae feel valued. Then again, once you taste her food, yeh may put up with her insolence and give her a bit more leeway. Susannah never liked her; if yeh didn't notice, she wasn't overly fond of the Scottish accent, but even *she* couldn't deny Francie was a valuable commodity."

Erin did a perfect imitation of Millie's *humph* sound. "All right, but I'd bet dollars to doughnuts she didn't have a joint to tend!"

David laughed and squeezed her, kissing her forehead as he did so. "Dollars tae doughnuts, eh?" He stroked her hair and inhaled. "Would yeh like tae change yer clothes and see our room before supper? I… asked Kitty tae take Susannah's things out of the master bedroom and put them into the spare room, the one you were in when we were here. I also asked her tae move ma things back into our room. She's also changed the bedding and pillows and things like that, so yeh don't feel as though ye're usin' her things, yeh ken?"

Erin looked at him and smiled. "That was very thoughtful of you, thank you—"

"What is it?" he asked, noticing her hesitation.

"Oh, I almost called you 'honey.' It's my 'go-to' term of endearment, sorry."

"I dinnae mind et as long as ye're no' thinkin' of Todd when yeh say et tae me. Et's verra American; I like et, and if tha's what yeh wannae call me, et's fine," he said and kissed her again.

"Alright, I probably won't use it often, but it's good to know it's a 'safe' word. Now, let's go to our room. Good night nurse, that sounds so good! I now share a bedroom with David Elliott; be still my heart!" she said and placed her hands over her chest.

They stood and walked toward the door. "No, love," he corrected her, "yeh share a house, a cottage… or the remains of et anaway, along with the old farmhouse; two household staff, four, no, five children, and, well, everathin' else I own, along with me, my darling."

Erin stopped and turned around to look at him. "You said you have, like, ten million pounds or some outrageous amount stashed somewhere; does that mean I'm also a millionaire?" she said, laughing but wide-eyed.

David laughed as he unlocked and opened the door. "Aye, you are," he said.

She stood in the doorway, absorbing the information until he took her hand and pulled her into the hall, closing the door behind them.

Kitty smiled when she saw Mr. Elliott and Ms. Erin pass the dining room where she was setting out the dishes. They were laughing, and she felt so much joy. She liked the way they interacted with each other; Mrs. Elliott had always been snooty and condescending to Mr. Elliott, and she'd hated it. There had been many times she'd wanted to slap her, tell her to shut up, and be thankful for the wonderful man she had and not to treat him like garbage.

She'd been living in the same house as Mrs. Elliott for the last three years, and just like Mr. Elliott had pointed out, she was glad Ms. Erin was nothing like her. She'd never have said it out loud, but she'd thought Mrs. Elliott was the most snobbish, stuck-up, mean, and selfish bitch she'd ever met. Mrs. Elliott didn't show her true self to many people, especially not to her husband, but Kitty saw it and heard it every day and had started to hate her.

Kitty knew Mrs. Elliott's opinion was that she was always wrong, no matter what she did, until she just did everything wrong without trying. Mrs. Elliott sucked the joy out of a person, and she had secretly thought about giving her notice to Mr. Elliott more than once, but she needed her job and would never have done it.

A blush spread across her cheeks when she thought of what Mr. Elliott had said about her having a hard time of things because of Mrs. Elliott; it was as though he had read her thoughts. She knew it was all going to be worth it now that he'd found a partner such as Ms. Erin, though. She would be someone worth working hard for.

The young housekeeper gave a little snort when she remembered Ms. Erin asking her if she wanted to go to the study. She had never been included in that sort of decision before and didn't know if she should answer her or wait for Mr. Elliott to correct her? The gesture meant so much to her though. Ms. Erin's reaction when entering the study gave her a thrill as well, knowing how much Mrs. Elliott hated the room and was forever trying to get Mr. Elliott to let her remodel. It was the one thing he had put his foot down about, and she was glad he had. The room was beautiful and well suited to him, and Ms. Erin as well, she reckoned.

She finished setting the table and hummed a tune as she headed back to the kitchen, thankful for the happy change in the household.

Chapter Fifteen

SHARED SPACES

When they got to the staircase, Erin noticed her suitcase was gone and presumed Kitty had taken it up for her. It wasn't light, and she felt bad, hoping Kitty didn't have any trouble with it. She and David walked hand in hand up the stairs and entered the first bedroom door they came to. The room was large, with high ceilings, a four-post bed, and a fireplace. The mantle was white alabaster, carved with a design of roses and greenery intertwined with wide ribbons.

"Oh, David," she said and ran her first two fingers over the carvings, marveling at how anyone could do such a thing with hard stone. "This is so beautiful! It's perfectly my style." She walked into a closet that was the size of the kitchen in her old house. Her clothing had been hung or put away for her; her three pairs of shoes looked lonely sitting on the empty racks which had once held hundreds of pairs of designer shoes. The room looked desolate, with her tiny wardrobe taking up less than a tenth of the space available.

"Where are your things?" she asked, not seeing any of David's clothing in the room. He smiled and led her through a door to another walk-in closet, only slightly smaller than the first one. She gasped, "What on earth!"

"I'm rather as fond of this room as I am of ma office," he said.

Erin looked around her; there were at least two dozen suits and a dozen or so separate jackets; she saw four kilts of different colors. She recognized the ancient and modern Elliott tartan and guessed the third one was for hunting or something else that was very Scottish. The last one, she thought, might've been the kilt he wore in *Future Explorations*, but she wasn't sure. She saw a rack with more ties than she could count hanging on it and rows of shelves that held over two dozen pairs of shoes, from trainers to heavy leather boots. As well as hangers and racks, there was an island of drawers in odd shapes and sizes; she put her hand on one of the pulls and looked at him for permission.

"Aye, go on; explore whatever yeh want." She opened a wide, thin drawer and saw a dozen handkerchiefs laid out neatly; the next one held cufflinks and tie tacks. He unlocked a door on the other side of the island and showed her a whole case that had several drawers full of expensive-looking watches.

Erin was overwhelmed. "This is extraordinary, David. I've never seen anything like it; I'm in awe and a little bit daunted by all of it."

David smiled at her. "If you weren't, I'd know yeh were an imposter. Et's taken a long time tae amass all these things; some of it was earned, some were gifts, others were handed down tae me from ma father, and some I'm keepin' safe for—well, for Bran, although, where he is, he'll no be needin' any of et."

"What was your dad like?" Erin asked him impulsively as she looked into his eyes. "I wish I could have met him."

David smiled and pushed a stray piece of hair behind her ear. "Ach, I'll tell yeh all about him, but no now; et's nearly time to eat, and yeh still haven't changed.

She looked at him and frowned. "Do I really need to change? Will anyone care but us?"

"No, et doesn't matter tae me; do yeh wannae go down now, then?"

At the thought of food, Erin's stomach growled. "The boss seems to think it's time," she said.

"I reckon the boss knows best." David laughed and turned out the light in his closet, then hers. They descended the stairs, and as they got closer to the dining room, the most incredible smell of roast beef filled the air.

Erin looked at David. "I repent! I was wrong, and if it tastes even half as good as it smells, I'll never doubt again!"

"Trust me, it will, ma love."

They entered the dining room, which looked like something out of a fairytale, and sat side by side, David at the head of the table and Erin at his right hand. She knew she should probably be sitting at the far end of the table; it was rather small compared to how big she was sure it could get with all the leaves added to it, but she wanted to be near him and didn't care what anyone thought of it.

Kitty brought out the wine and poured a bit for David to try; he nodded, so she poured them both a generous glass full. Erin lifted her glass and toasted, "To new beginnings." David joined her, and they clinked glasses. She took a drink and nearly spit it out.

"Don't like et?" David asked, seeing the pained look on her face as she tried to swallow.

"It's... so... dry!" she wheezed. "I'm sorry, but I can't drink this, and I bet it cost a fortune, too."

He laughed heartily. "Only half a fortune, love. I'll ask Kitty to bring out something a bit sweeter, all right?"

She stuck out her tongue and took one more tiny sip, just to be sure it really was as bad as she'd remembered. As soon as it touched her tongue, she made a face, like she'd just taken a bite of a whole lemon, rind and all. "Do you actually like this?" she asked and shook her head, trying to bring a bit of moisture back to her cotton tongue.

"Not especially, but Susannah insisted the meal start with a dry wine. I dinnae ken why, but et's not how et needs tae be any longer." Kitty brought out a tray covered with little bites of food on tiny rounds of bread and puff pastry. "Kitty, would you please bring out some sweet wine instead of—" He began, but then Erin's eyes grew wide, and she shook her head, covering her mouth with her hand. "What is et? Are yeh ill?" he asked her, but all she would do was shake her head, looking first at him and then Kitty. "Please take the wine back to the kitchen, Kitty," David said to her.

"Yes, sir." She took the bottle and, seemingly without judgment, left the room. "What's the matter, hen?" he said once Kitty was gone.

"Oh, David, I'm not supposed to drink alcohol!" she said. He nodded and put his hand over hers. "Ach, I wasn't thinking of that, though I'm sure one sip won't do any harm. I'll ask her to bring something else."

Erin sighed and felt a little bit better, but she was going to have to be more careful. "David, what is this?" She pointed to the tray arrayed with miniature works of art.

"Canapés, and by the look of et, Francie is going out of her way tae impress yeh."

"Consider me impressed! I don't want to eat them, they are too pretty, and I'm also afraid I won't like them and she'll be offended."

David put his hand on hers. "Dinnae worry, I'll help yeh choose. This one is duck pate, and that one is obviously caviar; the rest are as they look, except that one, I'm not sure what et is, looks like aubergine and courgette, but et could be anathin'. Why don't I try et and tell yeh what I think it is?" They made a game of guessing what they thought it would taste like and laughed when it proved to be something completely different.

Kitty brought out several other courses, including soup and a small plate of fish that looked disgusting but tasted amazing. The showstopper was the roast beef joint with root vegetables and homemade Yorkshire pudding with insanely delicious gravy.

"Good. Night. Nurse. She could make this every night for the rest of my life and I'd die a happy woman!"

"Agreed!" David said, and when Kitty came out to see if they needed anything, he instructed her to tell Francie word-for-word what Erin repeated for her, even though she was slightly embarrassed about it.

"Wait, Kitty. Please make sure she understands it's the joint, veg, and Yorkshire pudding I'm referring to; the rest has been lovely, but that joint is unlike anything I've ever had, and I'm from the Midwest! I've had my share of roast joints, but hers is the very best, and I love it!"

"Yes, Ms. Erin," Kitty said and left the room, smiling.

"I just don't want her to think I want all the fancy stuff every day. You were right; she's an amazing cook!"

At the end of the meal, Erin was so full she didn't think she'd have room for dessert, but when Kitty brought out two little ramekins of perfect-looking crème brûlée, she simply had to make room. "I hope this is the last course! I won't have room for anything else," Erin said, taking her first bite of the custard masterpiece in front of her. "Holy Moses, this is amazing! I can't stand it! It's all just too good! It's almost better than sex with you!"

"Ach, as long as it's only almost," he teased and held her hand.

Kitty came in to check on them, and Erin beckoned her with her finger to come close and then whispered something into her ear. "Will you do that for me? Tell her it's for the pudding, and then come back and tell me her reaction, please."

Kitty stifled a laugh and nodded. "Yes, Ms. Erin, I will." She left the room, covering her face to hide her laughter.

"And what was that about? You're up tae somethin' aren't yeh?" David said.

Erin looked at him and smiled. "Just wait until Kitty comes back, and then I'll tell you." They finished their puddings and groaned. "That was one of the best meals I've ever had; just don't tell Millie! I guess we'll be giving quite a bit of leeway in the future."

Kitty came back, her face and eyes red. Erin was startled and exclaimed, "What on earth happened? Were you... crying?"

Even David looked concerned, but Kitty shook her head. "No, Ms. Erin, well, I were, but only 'cause I were laughin' so 'ard. I done jus' as ya said, and I don't fink she'd ever 'ad anyone do 'at b'fore. She went all red in the face and put 'er apron up over 'er mouf. I fink she might still be cryin'."

At that, David got upset and stood. "Crying? What in Heaven's name did you ask her to do, Erin?" Erin wasn't listening to him; she was trying not to laugh because the look on Kitty's face told her that if she started, Kitty wouldn't be able to control herself. "Erin! What—"

Erin took his hand and pulled on it gently. "Sit down, David; it's okay. It's nothing bad; I simply asked Kitty to kiss Francie on both cheeks and give her a big hug, saying it was for the pudding. Do you really think she's crying?" she asked Kitty, who nodded with a little smile. "Well, I didn't mean to cause that, although I'm glad she appreciates my... well, appreciation. I'll go to her after David tells me we're done and make sure she's alright."

Kitty shook her head at that and looked serious for a moment. "No, Ms. Erin, I don't fink you should do 'at. I fink she'd be embarrassed."

"Okay, then… well, thank you for being such a good sport about it, Kitty."

"Please thank Francie for me as well, without the hug and kisses, if you don't mind. Also, thank you for your help tonight; it was quite a lot of work, I'm sure. Oh, and one more thing, we won't be taking any dessert wine tonight," David said.

They stood and left the dining room; Erin was so full it was uncomfortable. As they walked up the stairs, David said, "I have a mind tae take a shower; do yeh think you can entertain yerself for that long without me?"

"Gee whiz, I'm not sure! A whole big house to explore, and there *is* the 'west wing,' which I've been forbidden to enter! That's the first place I'll go!" Erin said with a hearty laugh.

———

Kitty heard them from the bottom of the stairs and smiled. *Kindred spirit, huh? I don't know what 'at is, but she's gonna be a lotta fun!*

"*A'right then, go explore if yeh want tae,*" she heard Mr. Elliott say and then continue up the stairs. She caught a glimpse of Ms. Erin as she turned to head back down, so she hurried away, afraid of being caught eavesdropping.

Chapter Sixteen

BAD PEOPLE

"Kitty?" Erin said, trying to catch her before she got too far away.

"Yes, mu… er, I mean Ms. Erin? What can I do for you?"

"What are you supposed to be doing right now?" she asked, and Kitty looked at her with surprise. Erin saw the look and rephrased what she said. "I'm sorry, what I mean is, I'd like to talk… if you have the time. I can keep you company if there's something you're supposed to be doing. I don't want you to fall behind or make things harder for you."

Kitty smiled at her warmly. "Naw, I'm meant to be emptyin' the bins and then buildin' a fire in your room, if you want one—Mrs. Elliott always did, even in summer."

"I'm sure she did," she said and shook her head, knowing that the only reason she'd want that would be to make more work for the young woman. "No, I mean, if David *really* wants one, I'll let you know, but I don't think we'll be needing a fire tonight. Thank you, though."

Kitty looked relieved. "Then I'm to turn down the bed, set out your pajamas, and fluff your pillows." Kitty listed her duties and looked startled when Erin laughed.

"You seriously fluff David's pillow? What in heaven's name has he done without you these last few weeks!" she teased, laughing hard, then she made herself stop. "I'm sorry, Kitty, I didn't mean to belittle your job, it seems so—I don't know... excessively pampered to me."

Kitty laughed and smiled. "Well, it only takes a moment, an' well, Mrs.—"

Erin nodded and then shook her head. "I see... Mrs. Elliott expected it. You know, I only met Susannah twice; both times were under terrible circumstances, and I understand that I was the 'other woman,' but everything about her was just horrible. I'm sorry to speak ill of the dead, but I can't imagine having to be in the same room as her, let alone work for a woman like her."

Kitty raised her eyebrows and nodded slowly as if holding her tongue. "It's not my place to say anything." There were a few moments of awkward silence and then she smiled up at Erin. "Mr. Elliott 'as never fanked me after a meal b'fore; I don't fink Mrs. Elliott would 'ave approved of it. I fink... aw, never mind," she began, then seemed to change her mind.

Erin gave her a sharp look. "Just tell me... what do you think, Kitty. I won't get angry or upset at you for voicing your opinion."

"Well, I jus' fink you're goin' ta be the best fing to 'appen to 'is place, is all."

Erin blushed, not knowing when she nudged her into speaking that Kitty was going to compliment her. "Oh, Kitty! You're so sweet. Thank you."

"It's true," she said with a shrug. "I reckon you've met the children, then? May I ask you 'ow ya got on wiv 'em?"

"We got on very well; I got along especially well with Rosie and Charlie; they're lovely!"

Kitty looked a bit shocked. "Ya said ya wan'ed me ta tell you the truff?"

"Yes, please," Erin said, hoping it was something nice.

"Well, I can see Charlie bein' friendly wiv ya, but not Rosie. She likes ta act like 'er mum, all 'igh an mi'ey, like." Her eyes grew large, and she covered her mouth. "I'm sorry, Ms. Erin; It's not my place ta speak like 'at."

"Don't worry about it, Kitty. I think Rosie acted that way just to please her mum, to get her approval, but take the… uh… unhealthy, shall we say, influence away, and she's really sweet. I intend to try to teach her the value of kindness, especially to the people her mother didn't think worth her time," she said and saw that Kitty looked like she wanted to say something else but was hesitating. "Spit it out, Kitty. Just say it; I won't get upset at you."

"Aw, ole' Francie says 'at you're… wiv child, but I can't see 'ow she'd know 'at; ya don't look pregnant ta me," she said.

Well, we can't pull anything over on old Francie, now can we? she thought to herself and sighed. "I don't know how she could either," Erin said and looked over at Kitty. She couldn't lie to her, and David hadn't said anything about not telling them, so she admitted it. "She's right, I am. I'm somewhere around two months along. I can't imagine how she could know—Oh, and please don't tell anyone, and don't confirm it with Francie either until I speak to David about it, okay?"

"Awright, I won't. Five children, though… at's somefin' ain't it?" Kitty said.

"It is definitely something!" She had an instant family now; she had dreamed of having a baby someday, but four already mostly grown children, and one on the way, *was* something! "Were you here when they had the nanny? David told me she was strict."

"I was… for 'er last few years; b'fore Rosie was sent to school. She were strict, too strict if ya ask me".

"Why? What did she do?" Erin asked.

Kitty's eyes widened, and she shook her head. "I don't know all the fings she done, but the housekeeper what was here b'fore me said that she convinced Mrs. Elliott 'at Mr. Elliott shouldn't 'ave any free time wiv 'is own children! It weren't right! Even I knew all he wan'ed to do was be wiv 'em, but she kep' 'im away."

Erin's eyes were brimming with tears at hearing it. "Oh, Kitty! Roger told me that Susannah would make excuses to take Peter away when he was a baby, but I just thought… I don't know… that she was being clingy or something; I didn't know it was with all of them. How could she do that? Poor David!" A tear escaped and ran down her cheek. Kitty reached into her pocket, produced a small package of tissues, and gave one to her. "It rips my heart out to know that even with all the money in the world, you can still find yourself in such an awful situation. I swear to God that won't happen this time! I'll kill, or at least maim, the person who comes between David and this baby!" she said passionately.

Kitty was now tearing up and took out a tissue for herself. "I believe ya will, Ms. Erin, as ya shou'd; I could see his 'art breakin' each time he were turned away from the nurs'ry, but 'ere was no'fin' ta do abou' it," she said.

Erin felt heartbroken. "How could someone do something like that? He'll have as much time with his bairn as he could ever want or need this time! That's for damn sure!" she said and impulsively hugged Kitty.

That night, as they got into bed, Erin watched David pound his pillow flat and couldn't understand why. "David?" she said, and he looked at her. "Why do you do that?"

"Do what, exactly?" he asked.

"Pound all the fluff out of your pillow."

"I... dinnae like ma pillow fluffed," he said and continued his mission.

"You don't? Did Susannah know that?"

"Aye, I reckon she did; why?"

"Humph! She specifically instructed Kitty to fluff your pillows every day. She's been taking care to fluff them the best she knows how, and that bitch knew you didn't like it! Was there no end to her treachery? I think you should maybe let Kitty know your preference, don't you?"

David sighed and nodded. "Aye. I'll tell her in the mornin'."

They got into bed, and Erin lay next to him, enjoying his scent and the feel of his chest hair between her fingers. She couldn't sleep with all the things she'd learned rolling around in her mind and stared at the ceiling for quite a while. "Are you awake?" she finally whispered.

"Mm-hmm," he said, not sounding at all awake.

"I just wanted to let you know something about our baby."

He took a deep breath to wake himself. "Aye? And what's tha?" he said and put his hand over hers.

"I don't know if I've already said it or not, but you can spend as much time with it as you want; I won't limit you in any way. It is your bairn as much as it is mine, and I won't allow *anyone* to tell me or you how much time or attention we can give it."

He rolled onto his side and looked at her. "And what's made yeh think of that?" he asked. He lifted her hand to his lips and kissed it.

"I... well... I asked Kitty about the nanny, and she told me that she convinced Susannah that you shouldn't be allowed to spend time with your own babies." Erin's eyes filled with tears of mourning once again for David's stolen time with them. "She was wrong, and I'm not gonna let that happen to you again! I'm sorry for crying; It just... what she and Susannah did to you, and your children, too, it... makes me so sad and really pissed off! "Kids need their dad to be in their lives! I was gonna say especially boys, but girls need their dad just as much, or maybe more! How will they know what kind of man to marry if they don't have the love and example of their daddy?" She was embarrassed to be crying over it, but she couldn't help it; it was important to her.

He rolled onto his back again and stared at the ceiling. "I... didn't know the nanny and Susannah were workin' together against me. I—I thought they knew best what was healthy for the wee things and foolishly didn't ask questions or fight et." He put his fist over his heart and took a long shaky breath. "Ach, ma heart aches, and I wanna throttle both the nanny and Susannah! I also... want tae hold ma children in ma arms right now, yeh ken?"

She couldn't help but sob at his pain and whispered, "I ken."

"Thank yeh, Erin, for knowin' what I find important and for bein' so thoughtful and considerate," he said and kissed her forehead. "I love yeh. You're goin' tae be a brilliant mum and an amazin' wife. Yeh care about the things that matter most, and I'm so verra glad ma children will have you for an example from now on."

Chapter Seventeen

ROGER'S REGISTRY

Roger woke in the morning nervous about his appointment at the Registration clinic. He got up, took a shower, and got dressed in some of his nicer clothing instead of his work attire. Though he wasn't very hungry, he went into the house if only to get his mind off the unknown things to come. The house felt empty now that Erin and David were gone. He sat at his usual spot, said good morning to Annis, and tried to hide his fear.

"Yer lookin' quite nice this mornin', Roger; what's the occasion?" Annis asked.

"Doctor," he replied, having already thought of what he would say if anyone asked. The meal was quiet, and Roger started to feel a bit gloomy. He began having second thoughts and nearly excused himself to call and cancel the appointment, but the memory of David and Erin's happiness, even after all their struggles, made him decide to follow through on his plan.

The clinic was in Leith, so he didn't have far to go; therefore, he got there much too early and had to sit in the waiting room for a long time. Two other men walked in while he was there, both looking nervous and unsure, which helped him feel less alone in his doubts, at least.

Finally, they called his name, and he walked through to a simple room with a chair, an examination table, and a computer. He'd filled out the paperwork while waiting and had given them to the man at the front desk.

He was asked to wait and remove his shirt, then, after a while, he heard a man speaking to someone near his door. There was a short knock, and the door opened, revealing a young man in a dress shirt and tie. Roger thought he was much too young to be a doctor, but he kept his mouth shut.

"Hello, I'm Dr. Mitchell, and I'll be performing your examination. So, Mr. Blackwood, tell me why you've come here today?" Roger explained how he knew a couple who had been brought together because of the treatments, and while he understood it wasn't a dating service or a way to meet women, he hoped he might meet someone whom he could help. And that even if there wasn't a love connection, at least he could meet someone to talk to and become friends with.

The doctor looked at him for a few moments before responding. "Your honesty is refreshing; we most often hear 'I want to do my part,' or 'I like to help people,' and whilst that may be true, it's not most men's motivation, I can assure you."

Roger shrugged. "Wha's the point of lyin'? This is who I am, and I've nothin' tae hide."

Doctor Mitchell did his examination, told him he could put his shirt back on, and read through Roger's paperwork. "You've not filled out how you'd like to be compensated for your time?"

"I dinnae want tae be paid; I have all I need and know people who can help me if necessary."

The doctor sat a moment, observing him. "I... believe it's compulsory, but I would imagine you can give the money back to your match or donate it to charity."

Roger squinted and thought for a moment. "What are ma options again?"

"You can be paid in pounds, deposited directly into your bank through a Bacs Payment Scheme, or you may receive a voucher toward accommodations; the details of which are in a brochure you will have received when you arrived."

"I see. I'll take the pounds, I reckon."

"Alright, I'll note it in your file. Also, you've only listed one person in your sexual history."

Roger shrugged again. "Aye. Ma wife; she died a verra long time ago, and I've never gone lookin' for anaone tae replace her."

"I see," said the doctor, "I'm compelled to ask you, then, if you are absolutely sure this is something you'll be able to do? You'll be expected to have sex with a stranger with no guarantee you'll find love or anything close to it. Is that something you are truly willing to do?"

"Aye. I am willin' tae do what yeh said; are you tryin' tae talk me out of et, then?" Roger said and then smiled, making the doctor laugh.

"No, I'm not, but you honestly don't seem like the type of person who will be able to follow through with something such as this, though I truly hope you can." He wrote some notes at the bottom of the page and then stood. "Please follow me," he said and led him to a room with a sofa. He saw racks of magazines and

DVDs, as well as a television mounted on the wall. "Use this specimen cup," he said and pointed to one that was sitting on a small cupboard next to the door. "Take as long as you need, and when you are ready, please place the sample into the cupboard and flip this light switch. Someone will come along shortly to take you to have your blood drawn. Do you have any questions before I leave?"

Roger shook his head. "No," he said, his face hot, and the doctor left, closing the door behind him. "Right," he said to himself as the door clicked shut. He pressed the lock button and then stood in place, wondering what to do next. He went to the rack of magazines and since he didn't have another plan, chose one at random, though he wasn't into pornography. He looked at the naked men and women performing sexual acts and scowled, returning the publication to the rack; it was not for him.

He removed his trousers and took the cup from off the cupboard and sat on the small sofa. He lay back and thought about his wife; she was plump and fair, with shoulder-length red hair and a million tiny freckles all over her body. He'd tried to count them all once but quit when he'd reached the insides of her thighs. The thought of that started to work.

He thought about their wedding night; they'd both been virgins, and neither one of them knew what they were doing. There'd been a lot of blushing and giggling that night, but all the laughter had stopped when they finally started to get things right. It was heaven then, and he'd prayed it would never end. After that night, he recalled not being able to stay away from her and taking her to him at any and every opportunity he could.

He wanted to picture her face, but the harder he tried the farther away it seemed; it was all blurry, without the detail he could once conjure on demand. After a long time, she started to come into focus; he was extremely turned on then and realized much too late that the face he was seeing was not that of his wife but of Erin, smiling and laughing at something he'd just said.

He felt ashamed as he twisted the cap on the small cup and placed it into the cupboard. He put his trousers back on and then hit the light switch, feeling as though he'd betrayed David somehow.

A man with scrubs and exam gloves came in to retrieve the cup and escorted him to the waiting area, where he would have his blood sample taken. "The phlebotomist will be with you shortly; please take a seat."

Roger sat in a chair that was not at all comfortable and crossed his arms; he started thinking about the woman he might be matched with, what she might look like, as well as her personality. His thoughts were interrupted by a woman's voice.

"Roger Blackwood?" He stood and followed her to a small room and sat in a small chair. She asked him to put his arm on the edge of the countertop next to the chair, and in no time, she was finished. She put a ball of cotton wool over the puncture wound and placed a plaster over the top. As she put the label on the small vial of dark red liquid, she told him if they found a match, they would contact him via telephone and that it usually took anywhere from two to four days to attain the results.

Roger left the clinic feeling only slightly the worse for wear and got back to Owlgate ready for another normal day, though he didn't feel normal at all. There was no turning back any longer, and the idea of meeting a female stranger and following through was far more frightening after the fact. He was all butterflies with a bit of nausea thrown in for good measure as he changed his clothes into something he could work in and then headed downstairs to the garage.

Chapter Eighteen

MONDAY AT HER NEW HOME

Erin woke to David rolling over and laying his arm across her chest; she heard him inhale and sigh contentedly. "Yeh smell so good. Wakin' up next tae you is a treat," he said.

Her laughter filled the room. "Are you kidding? Waking up next to you is like being in an impossible romance novel!"

He moved his hand to her belly, gently rubbed it, and then smiled as he dove under the light covers to kiss his hidden baby. His voice was muffled as he spoke to it and then kissed her belly some more. He then surprised her by moving southward, parting her legs with his chin and burying his face into her folds.

It was feeling really good when the morning sickness hit and she had to push him away. She almost panicked when she stood and didn't know where to go at first; there were too many doors. She found it, and not a moment too soon, having to run so she wasn't sick all over the floor. "Will this ever end?" she said miserably and flushed the toilet.

"Aye. Et will, hen." He stepped into the bathroom and helped her up. "I wish I could help yeh, love," he said and put his forehead against hers.

"I'll tell you what; this bathroom doesn't help very much! It's dizzying! Let me guess who remodeled it?" she said, knowing full well who it was. The room was covered from floor to ceiling with white marble streaked with jagged black slices that looked like claw marks; it looked like a skunk or zebra had exploded and stained the walls.

"Aye. Et was one of the things we strongly disagreed on, but she won out, as usual."

"It wouldn't be so bad in small quantities, but it makes my brain hurt." She hugged him and lay her head on his chest with her eyes closed and then groaned as they stood in the middle of the bathroom together. "I need to brush my teeth, but I don't want to let go of you," she said and felt his chest move as he laughed.

"Why don't yeh brush them and then head back tae bed wi me?" he asked, but she groaned again.

"I'd love to, but my stomach isn't settling down. I need toast or something to calm it. How about a little afternoon delight later?"

"A'right, but ye'd better keep your hair away from me till then, or there's no tellin' what I'll do tae yeh."

She let go of him and cocked her head to the side. "You know it's not my shampoo that you're attracted to, right? I mean, I've used at least three different kinds since I've been in the UK."

"Et's... not? But—"

"No, darling, it's pheromones. It's my smell and your animal instinct," she said and laughed at his intrigued look.

He pulled her closer and pressed himself eagerly against her. "I'll show you animal instinct—"

"Later," she said and kissed his cheek. She turned toward the sink and was amazed to find that her toiletries had been set out for her. She picked up her toothbrush, squeezed her toothpaste onto it, and started brushing while David stood at his mirror and examined his face.

"Yoo lowk so diffrnt en tha meerer," she said with the toothbrush still in her mouth and then laughed. She spit the toothpaste out and started over. "You look so different in the mirror." She rinsed her toothbrush off, placed it in the holder next to David's, and stood next to him, studying their reflections staring back at her. Hers was the same old face she saw every day, but his looked quite different. *More like Bran's face,* she thought but didn't say it out loud.

"You look different as well; I hate tae say et, but I prefer the 'real' you compared with yer reflection," he said.

"Same here." She turned away from the mirror and looked at his face "Ah, much better; it's you again."

He smiled his million-dollar smile and kissed her. "Mmmm, you taste all minty!" he said.

"I won't tell you what you taste like."

He glared at her but then picked up his toothbrush and started brushing his teeth.

They got dressed, both of them disappearing into their own respective closets and coming out ready for the day. They walked down to breakfast and greeted Kitty first, then Francie with a cheerful 'Good morning.' The dining room table was set, and they enjoyed quiche and fresh fruit, which included raspberries the size of Erin's thumbs. "Look at these Nephilim berries!" she said.

David was looking at the newspaper, which had been set out next to his place setting. He looked up and smiled. "Aye. That's the usual size of them. Haven't you seen a raspberry before?" he asked, and Erin rolled her eyes.

"Of course I have, but they're so much smaller in the states, or at least in Wisconsin. I have—I mean had," she said a little bit more quietly, "some raspberry bushes at my house, and they were only the size of my thumbnail on a good year; sometimes they were even smaller."

She picked one up from her plate and examined its perfection "What a thing of beauty," she said as Kitty walked in. "Speaking of things of beauty—" she said, making Kitty blush. "Kitty, look at this berry; have you ever seen anything so perfectly beautiful?"

Kitty smiled, obviously amused. "No mu—I mean Ms. Erin, I 'aven't," she said, looking at the specimen before her. "Can I get ya anyfing?"

"No, thanks."

"Anyfing for you, sir?" she said to David.

He looked up at her and smiled. "No, Kitty, I believe we have everything we need. Now, if Erin would stop examining her food and eat it—"

Erin looked at him and scowled playfully. "How can I eat such a lovely thing as this?" she asked, holding it up to him.

He snatched it out of her fingers and popped it into his mouth. "Like this," he said, which made Kitty laugh out loud, then she caught herself and stopped, her eyes wide.

"Did you see that, Kitty? The nerve! Well, I'll just have to find something else to examine. Kitty, would you please excuse us?"

Kitty's eyes grew even wider as she looked at Erin in surprise, but then she smiled and looked away. "Yes, mum, I mean, Ms. Erin," she said, and Erin put her hands up in surrender.

"Okay... I give up. You may call me 'mum' if it comes more naturally to you, but I'd still rather, with all my heart, that you'd just call me Erin. Now, I've got some examining to do. One of us will call for you if we need anything."

"Yes... mum," Kitty said and left the room.

Erin stood motioning for David to push out his chair. "You really shouldn't talk like that in front of—" He stopped when she knelt in front of his chair to unfasten and unzip his trousers.

She managed to pull them and his underwear down far enough for her to take him into her mouth, examining him with her tongue. "What shouldn't I do?" she asked, knowing he'd forgotten all about it.

"Nothing, never mind; that feels so good! Dinnae stop!" Erin continued for a few moments more and then took her top off. "Erin! Yeh shouldn't do that in here. What if someone comes in?" he exclaimed, but Erin only smiled.

"I highly doubt Kitty will come in here after what I said, and I'm sure she's warned Francie not to enter unless called for as well. Now, move to a chair that doesn't have arms on it, and let me sit on you; I need you now!" she said and started taking her pants off.

He watched her, wide-eyed, and then moved to another chair. "Ye're breakin' every rule of 'high-class' society and it's drivin' me crazy!" She straddled him, face to face, and kissed him as he entered her, continuing to kiss him, to keep him quiet, as she rocked back and forth. It didn't take long before he was gently biting her lip as his cock pulsed with his release and her body joined with his. "God, Woman! What will the staff say about us?"

She looked him straight in the eyes and became serious. "They will say we love each other and that we're meant to be together," she said.

He gazed into her eyes and sighed. Then he pulled her head down and touched his forehead to hers. "I reckon tha's no such a bad thing tae say, is et?" he said. "I do love yeh, and I also think we were meant tae be together."

"So do I, David."

They got dressed again, and Erin noticed she was less tired than normal. Whether it was because she wasn't climbing mountains or the increased sexual activity since their fight, she didn't know, but she was happy about it. They had only gone without sex for five days, which shouldn't have been a big deal. The only reason she could think of was that maybe, with the pregnancy, she needed to have treatments more often.

Thinking about the pregnancy made her remember the doctor they'd met in Edinburgh. "David, we should make an appointment with that doctor from Arthur's Seat."

"Aye! I'd nearly forgotten about tha'. Her business card is in the pocket of ma other trousers; I'll get et." He stood before her and placed his hand on her cheek. "Yeh make ma knees weak, you know that?" he said.

A big grin spread across her face. "Aye; it's my super-power!" she said and then laughed.

David had his mobile out, typing something when he returned with the card. "I'll send Tina—"

"Wait," she interrupted, "I'd—Well, I'd like us to make the appointment... together... without Tina. Is that okay?"

David smiled at her and sat in his chair again. "Aye, et's okay, except I've no idea what my schedule looks like from month to month."

"Wouldn't it be possible to ask Tina to send you that information?" she asked.

"A'right, I'll do that, but I'll have to make her aware of the appointments once they're made."

"That's fine with me."

David amended his message to Tina, asking for his next few months' appointment schedule. She replied with a calendar of his appointments, and they called the number on the card. Twenty minutes later, they had five dates set.

When David mentioned they had met atop Arthur's Seat, the receptionist fit them in the same week, on Wednesday, during her lunch. Erin had a suspicion she was skipping it just for her.

David sent the dates and times to Tina, who replied,

> T: *Are you unhappy with my work?*
> *Have I done something wrong?*
> *Please instruct me on how I can*
> *improve.*

He showed her the message. "Ach. Now she feels as though she's no good enough."

"Tell her... wait, may I?" she said and held out her hand for his phone. He handed it to her, and she typed;

D: *You are doing a fine job, but these are private Dr appts I want to make for myself.*

"Aye, that's good," he said and hit send. A few moments later, he showed her Tina's reply.

T: *Okay. I'll add them as personal time, then.*

"Now what shall we do?" Erin said. "I haven't actually gotten to explore the house; would you like to—" David looked at her, took her hand, and became very serious; his gaze was so earnest she stopped talking. "What? You look so intense; what's wrong?"

"There's somethin' I want tae show yeh; follow me." He led her to the back corner of his office and asked her to wait while he opened his safe.

"Safe?" She was puzzled, as she hadn't seen a safe in there. He moved the foliage of a large spider plant and opened the secret door that looked just like the paneling on the walls. She laughed and said, "Cool! Secret compartments!"

He pushed several numbers on a keypad and the door opened with a smart *click* Once the door was fully open, he turned a small brass key to open a small drawer and pulled the entire thing out.

Next, he took out a flat wooden box with a tiny clasp keeping it shut. He took his passport out of his pocket, placed it into the safe, and then brought the drawer and box over to the couch where she was sitting.

He sat next to her and set the box and drawer on his lap. He took out a string of pearls and handed it to her; the pearls felt cool in her hand as she gently held them and noticed the diamond-bejeweled clasp. "This was ma great grandmother's on my mother's side; et's verra old. It may have been her mother's before her, but I can't say for sure."

She gave it back to him, and he put it back into the drawer. Then he pulled out several heavy men's rings with various colored gems set into them, representing different clubs or organizations his forefathers had been members of. He paused and put the small drawer on the cushion next to him.

He flipped the delicate clasp open on the flat wooden box, revealing that the inside was lined in blue velvet. She saw nearly a dozen military service medals and pins laid out in neat rows. There were crosses and medallions with delicate silk ribbons in different colors and stripes. Many had bars or pins shaped like sprigs of leaves attached to them. She had read somewhere a long time ago that the bar of leaves represented more than one act of the thing that earned the medal.

"Oh, David! They're beautiful!"

"They were ma great grandfather, David's, medals from his time in both World Wars."

She saw a bronze cross; the ribbon at one time was probably red, but time had turned it into a pretty plum color. There were a few silver crosses and medallions with King George V, looking stern, and some with King George VI, looking quite likable. "You must be so proud!" she said after looking them over thoroughly.

"Aye. They are one of my prized possessions." A smile lit up his face, and his cheeks became rosy. "I'm so glad you appreciate them, though my true reason for bringin' you in here is for this." He reached back into the little drawer and took out a small, brown, leather-covered box that looked to be very old. He set the box of medals on the arm of the couch and took a deep breath.

Erin was suddenly very nervous; she knew what was coming but hadn't expected it since he'd already asked her if she'd marry him, and she'd said she would. He slid off the couch and knelt on one knee. "Erin, ma darling. This was ma great grandmother's weddin' ring. Et means a great deal tae me, just as you do." He opened the tiny box, revealing a stunning, delicate, platinum diamond ring.

She gasped; the center was slightly oval with an enormous diamond ringed by many smaller ones. There were two leaves, one on either side of the center, which also had small diamonds in what looked sort of like a Celtic knot but gave the impression it was a rose with two leaves. The band was intricate open filigree, tiny, and delicate, it was the most beautiful ring she'd ever seen. "David—" she began, but her voice cracked and she couldn't continue.

"Do you like it?" he asked, his voice also cracking a bit.

She shook her head, which made him frown, then she tried to speak, but it came out in a whisper. "I love it," she said.

He smiled and took the ring out of its box, holding it gently between his thumb and first finger. "Erin, will yeh accept this ring as a token of ma love and as a promise tae be my wife?" Several tears rolled down his face, which made him smile and roll his eyes.

Erin had never heard a more perfect proposal; she got on the floor with him and kissed him. "Aye, David; I will. I love you!" she said and held out her hand; there was still an indent from where she'd worn her first wedding band for fifteen years. He slid the ring onto her finger, and like magic, it fit. She didn't have tiny fingers, so his great grandmother must have been her size. That made her love his great grandfather even more. "It's the most beautiful thing—I'm afraid I'll ruin it!"

"Dinnae worry. It lasted sixty years on her hand and over thirty on my mother's. I am sure you'll take good care of et, or I wouldn't have given et tae yeh."

"It was your mother's as well? Why isn't she wearing it now?"

"She wore it for a few years after ma father died and… well, I reckon she was with Millie, so she didn't want to wear it any longer."

It suddenly occurred to Erin to ask, "Is… this the ring… well, that you married Susannah with?" There it was out in the open. She didn't want to be jealous, but she wasn't sure she wanted the ring if it had been.

"No, et's not. I showed it to her once, before we were married, and she turned her nose up at it. There was something else, as well; I just knew it wasn't meant for her. I should've known then she wasn't the one for me, whereas I knew ye'd like and appreciate it. I just know it's meant for you. Tha's one reason I took the time tae show you the medals; if you could appreciate them, you would appreciate the ring."

Erin was speechless; she just kept looking at it, moving her hand in different ways to show off the sparkling diamonds and the filigree work. "This must've cost a fortune back at the turn of the century!" she said, not meaning to bring up money, only it was such fine quality. "Oh! I'm sorry, that came out wrong. I meant to say it's so fine and… well, any man who could pick out something as stunning as this for his love—I don't know, it's just so pretty! It's perfectly my taste."

"Aye, I'm sure et did cost a fortune, but my great grandad wasn't hurtin' for money. He was quite industrious and managed tae make a fortune or two in his lifetime," he said with a laugh.

"Thank you for this and for asking me so sweetly; I'll be able to tell our bairn about the day you officially proposed to me," she said tenderly. He started grinning, so she could tell he was up to something.

"Why wait?" He helped her to stand so she could sit on the sofa. Then, still kneeling, he lifted her shirt, exposing her belly, and lay his ear on it. "Hello, ma love; it's your daddy. I wanted you tae know that I just asked yer mummy tae marry me, and do yeh know what she said? Hmm? I can't hear yeh—she said yes! That means we're gonna make et official; one big Elliott family. I love yeh! Grow up healthy, darling."

"I love when you do that, David. It makes me happy that you're so excited about our bairn. Come here and kiss me." She leaned forward and put her hands on his cheeks; he kissed her, and she kissed him. "You know what we need? We need a selfie to commemorate the occasion!" she said.

"A'right, your phone or mine—Or, I know, how about one on each?" he suggested.

"Yeah! Cover both bases!" They both took out their phones and opened their camera apps. Erin held hers up first, holding her new ring up, which made the phone take the shot, thinking it was a wave. That one wasn't so great, so they tried another one, which turned out very well. Next, David held his phone up, and they took a few more until they also got a really nice one on his.

"I'm going to send this to Lily if you don't mind?"

"I don't mind, but only her for now, at least until the story runs in the paper," he said, and Erin agreed.

> E: *You'll never guess what just happened! Squee!*

She typed, added the photo, and hit send.

David sent a copy to his mother, Millie, and Roger, with a message saying:

> D: *I believe a celebration is in order!*

David started getting replies immediately; from Millie, he read,

> M: *Ach, Davey! I'm so happy for you.*
> *Tell Erin we miss her!*

From his mum, he read,

> A: *Oh, David, that's wonderful news!*
> *It's lovely on her! you look so happy!*
> *We miss you both!*

From Roger, he read,

R: *Congratulations! I'm so happy for you, mate! A good celebration is long overdue around here! Tell Erin we miss her. It's just not the same without you here.*

Chapter Nineteen

DIRTY SECRETS

The next day, David had to leave in the morning to do a job for a popular mobile phone company. He didn't know when he'd be home but said he'd text her when he was on his way back.

Erin showered, dressed, fixed her hair, and went downstairs for breakfast. It was Francie's day off and a 'serve yourself' day, which meant a bowl of Nut and Honey Crunch or Weetabix. She couldn't decide, so she mixed the two, which wasn't half bad. After rinsing her bowl, she heard the mail drop inside the large wooden door in the entryway and walked over to pick it up.

Most of it was junk, but she saw one from the Fertilis Defect Registry. She decided to open it, since it didn't look private or personal, and was shocked to see the first line, in capital letters.

"THIS IS YOUR FINAL NOTIFICATION.
COMPLIANCE IS COMPULSORY IN ORDER
TO REMAIN IN THE SYSTEM."

Erin read the letter and learned they'd been trying to contact him for the last two months. He was supposed to give them information regarding the results of the treatments, give feedback, then update his status. It said that if he didn't do it within one week, he would be taken off the list and other things she didn't understand.

But why hasn't he been getting his mail? she thought. She knew he'd been away in America, and then Edinburgh, but he'd been home in between then, when he'd left her every night at the Ritz, for example. Even if he didn't get it then, for some reason, there should've been a stack of mail for him when he got back. She decided to ask Kitty and found her folding laundry, listening to music with her earbuds in. She knocked on the doorframe and walked in.

Kitty jumped and put her hand to her chest. "Core blimey! I di'n't see ya there," she said too loudly. She took the earbuds out and continued "'Ow can I 'elp ya, mum?"

"I need to know why David hasn't been getting his mail?"

The young woman frowned and looked perplexed. "I can't say, mum—"

Erin held out the envelope from the Registration Office and showed it to her. "This is very important mail, Kitty; what's been happening to the others like it?"

Kitty took the envelope and looked it over. "I've only ever seen one other like it, mum, and 'at were two months ago, I'd say. But Mrs. Elliott was the one what took the mail every day, so maybe she—ya don't fink she—" She covered her mouth in shock.

"I do think she would, but I don't understand why? What would it solve? It's not like it would split us up. Did she have a place she kept her papers, like a desk or filing cabinet?"

"I fink she used the desk in 'er and Mr. Elliott's room," she said, and Erin narrowed her eyes at her.

"It's my room now, Kitty. I know you're busy, but would you come with me to check it out?"

Kitty looked a bit frightened and glanced over her shoulder. "She told me I was never ta touch 'er desk, mum."

"Kitty, she is dead; she can't scold you anymore. I don't know what I'll find, and maybe I'm overreacting, but I don't want to be alone. I'd like you there so that if I find something—I don't know... really bad... you're a witness that I didn't put it there."

"But wha' about Mr. Elliott? Won't 'ee be upset?"

Erin shook her head. "No, I know David won't be angry; he said I can look anywhere I want, and this is my house as well as his now, so you won't get in trouble with him," she said and looked pleadingly at her.

"Awright, mum."

Erin was suddenly nervous; she didn't know if she wanted to know what Susannah was hiding in her desk or anywhere else. They headed up the stairs and into the bedroom; the desk was in the corner of the room, untouched, as far as she knew, since Susannah had died. The desk had a wide, narrow drawer with a small chair under it and a vertical row of two small and one larger file-folder-sized drawers. She opened the top drawer and all she found was stationary, stamps, pens, an electronic tablet, and a fancy letter opener. The middle drawer was empty. Next, she pulled out the chair and tried to open the narrow drawer, then the bottom one, but both were locked.

"Kitty, do you know where she kept the key?"

Kitty shrugged; she kept looking over her shoulder as though the police would come and arrest her for aiding this invasion. "No, mum."

Erin sat on the wooden chair and pondered where a woman such as Susannah Elliott would hide the key to her secret stuff. *Where would no one think to look?* "What did you do with her clothing and shoes?"

"They're in the spare room, mum."

"Okay, come with me, and stop calling me mum. I'm not your mum, and it's getting on my nerves. If you can't call me Erin, just say yes, no, or maybe, full stop," she said, her fear and anxiety getting the better of her.

They walked down the hall and opened the door to the spare room. Susannah's things were either hung up in the closet or laid neatly on the bed. Most of the shoes were in boxes; she had a hunch, so Erin conscripted Kitty into helping her go through all the shoeboxes.

There were some beautiful shoes; it was too bad they were all a European size thirty-six, which was like a US size five and a half. They turned out every pair and found nothing, though there were still shoes in the closet, not in boxes.

"Which were her favorite pair, Kitty?" The young housekeeper walked over to a pair of red heels that would kill Erin if she tried to wear them. She picked up the shoes and handed them to Erin. When she turned them over to check their size, out fell a small brass key. "I knew it!"

They returned to the master bedroom and Erin put the key into the lock in the narrow drawer. It turned freely, and inside, they found a small blue bank book, which she picked up and opened. The name on the account was Susannah Jane Sutcliffe, and the last entry was on June twelfth, two days before her death; it showed a balance of over a million pounds.

Next to the bankbook was a stack of letters. Erin opened the top one, and it was signed 'Love, Clive.' She didn't bother reading it; David could do that. Under those letters were two from the Registry; one was a welcome and thank you for signing up letter, the other one was a reminder to sign in on their website and fill out a questionnaire every month. She couldn't understand why Susannah would keep them from him.

Erin unlocked the large drawer and opened it; inside was a mess of prescription bottles that weren't empty and several large manila envelopes. She pulled one of the envelopes out, opened it, and nearly started bawling right then and there. Inside were dozens of envelopes postmarked from Scotland, with the writing of young children.

She opened one and it read, '*Happy father's day, Dad. I Miss You and I hope You will visit Soon. Love CHarLiE ELLiOtt Age 8, (ALmOst 9!).*' She handed it to Kitty, who read it and gasped, placing her hand over her mouth. "Almost none of these have been opened, Kitty! What kind of person does that! My poor David!" She set the mustard-colored envelope aside and was afraid to look at the next one, but she had to.

That one was filled with credit card statements; hundreds of thousands of pounds of purchases she doubted David was aware of. The next one had several more brown envelopes inside of it, each unopened, except one, which was full of mail addressed to "Mr. David Elliott % Tina Cullin." She opened one of the letters postmarked five years earlier. It was from a fan who had Cancer and wanted him to know how much she loved Future Explorations. Erin read some of it out loud.

"Everyone on my floor watches one episode every Thursday evening in the lounge. I know you're a very busy man, but you must do charity work, and I know we would all be chuffed to bits if you made some time to visit us. I understand if you aren't able to do that, but please think about it and please send us a signed photograph to put up on the wall. Your biggest fan, Vivian Watters."

Enclosed was a photo of her wearing a lovely floral scarf over her bald head; she handed it to Kitty, who was now in tears and sitting on the end of the bed.

Erin opened another letter from a fan, though *it* was quite different. It also had a photo, but it was a burlesque pose; not nude, but not something David would want to see, and nothing she would want him to see either! The sender wrote that she wanted to put on a show for him; to tease him and make him beg her for more— *Blah blah blah; I could just puke.*

The contents of another manila envelope made Erin scream and drop it. Several photographs of Susannah posing nude, in sexy positions, and some naked ones of David alone or with her on top of him spilled out onto the floor. David looked like he was sleeping in them and didn't look natural. Kitty picked one up and then dropped it. "Core blimey!" she said.

"This is sick! He's not even awake! Was she drugging him? But why? Oh, Fuck! When were these taken?" Erin examined one of the pictures, realizing they weren't taken in the master bedroom but in the spare room, and thought she might actually vomit, then. She looked at them all, even though they were disgusting, and in one of the pictures, saw something that did make her run to the toilet and throw up.

David's alligator tooth keychain was sitting on the bedside table and looking back at the others she saw it in all of them. He'd bought one for each of them when they were in New Orleans on their first treatment weekend. At the time, he said it was something small they could put in their pocket to remember their time together.

That meant the photos were taken some time after he'd gotten home from Louisiana and before Susannah died.

"Wait!" Erin said as she stumbled back into the room.

Kitty jumped; she was already nervous about being caught. "Core—"

"Who in the fucking hell is taking these pictures? They aren't selfies!"

Kitty's eyes grew huge. They looked at each other in horror, realizing there had been someone else in the room. "But who?" she asked.

"I don't know, but we need to find out!" Erin said. *Was it a man or woman? Were they also involved in... molesting David while he was drugged and unconscious?* she thought while she dug through the rest of the drawer. Something dawned on her, something she'd seen in so many movies and crime dramas that it seemed too stupid.

She pulled out the large bottom drawer and saw two more manilla envelopes hidden in the space under it; one was fat and one was thin. She pulled them both out and set them on her lap. The fat one was easy to open and contained thousands of pounds in cash, but the last one made her hesitate; she sat on the floor and cried for a while before she could bring herself to open it.

"Erin. Are ya sure ya wanna see 'at? Do ya wanna know, or would it be bet'er to leave it be?" Kitty said and got on the floor to kneel in front of her. "It won't 'elp ya, only hurt," she said, and Erin looked up at her.

"What if it was a man, Kitty? What if he was drugged and then raped by a man?"

Kitty put her hand on Erin's trembling ones. "And if it were a woman? Do ya want to see 'at? Do ya?"

Erin was truly torn; she did and she didn't. She wanted to know, but if she saw it, she knew she wouldn't be able to deal with either one. "What should I do, Kitty?" she said, then stood and started pacing. "I know you're right, of course. I won't be able to handle it either way, but if it was a man, he should be tested for... diseases... or—oh, God, Kitty." She stopped pacing and placed her hands on top of the desk, having trouble catching her breath.

Kitty calmly stood and took out a brown paper bag from her apron, opened it, and handed it to Erin. "Breave into it," she said calmly.

Erin started breathing into the paper bag while Kitty led her to the bed, but as soon as she sat on it, she jumped back up. "No! NO!" She grabbed hold of the envelope and tore it open. Suddenly Erin knew what Susannah was doing; she was setting David up! She was getting ready to blackmail him and leave, taking probably two million pounds with her and ruining him in the process. She pulled out a random photo; it was of David and a familiar-looking woman with long, dark hair; the next was of him and another woman; the next was with a man, but he wasn't raping him, just lying next to him on the bed, making it look like they were sleeping.

Erin was so angry that if Susannah hadn't already been dead, she'd have found her and killed her with her bare hands. *Do other people have copies of these? Where did they get them printed? Who are those people?* Erin was shaking and couldn't breathe again.

Kitty took the paper bag out again, that time holding it up to her mouth for her. Then she held her as she cried. "Let's clean up, and you can tell Mr. Elliott when 'ee gets home."

Chapter Twenty

MR. ELLIOTT RETURNS HOME

David finished the job earlier than he'd hoped, so he sent a message to Erin, telling her he was on his way home, though he didn't get a reply. He got out of the hired car and walked up to his house, looking forward to a quiet evening at home with his woman. When he opened the door, Erin was there, looking utterly unwell, as if she'd been crying and sick in the toilet all day. There were bags under her eyes, and her breath was a bit shaky.

"What's happened, ma love?" He had flashbacks of saying those words so many times and was terrified of what it might be that time. "Darling, tell me," he said.

Her eyes were sad, and she shook her head, "I found something, and I need you to try to be calm," she said.

All thoughts of calmness left him that very moment, and he went white in the face. "Ma Losh, what is et now?"

"It started with a letter from the Registry…" She told him what had happened that day, starting with the letter, then she took him upstairs to their bedroom. "Open the top middle drawer," she said.

He turned the brass key, opened the drawer, and found the bank book. "What does this mean? Sutcliffe was her maiden name, but why keep putting money—a million pounds!" He saw the pile of letters underneath where the bankbook had been laying. "Did you read these?" he asked her in shock.

"No, I only opened the last one and read the name at the bottom. He opened them and started reading.

"*Dearest Susie,* 'Susie? She wouldn't let anaone call her that. '*I want you to know how sorry I am that we couldn't meet—*" He read the whole thing out and then the next one and the next. "Clive Dawson? I dinnae remember us knowin' anaone by that name." He read more... "*I love you, my darling! When can we go? When will you run away with me? I will wait forever, but it is so very difficult, my love.*" He sat there after reading the last one, shaking his head. "And this is what yeh found? By the look of yeh, I'm guessing there's more?" Erin nodded. She stood next to him and took out the letters from the Fertilis Defect Registry. He read them and was angry. "What—why? I dinnae understand."

"Me neither; it wouldn't keep us apart, would it?"

"Maybe, in her sick head, she thought if I wasn't enrolled anamore, I'd just stop seein' yeh?"

"There's... more. Open the large drawer," she said.

He opened it and saw the half-empty bottles of pills; he read, "Valium, OxyContin, Percocet, Librium. Some of these are heavy tranquilizers; what could she possibly need with these?"

Erin didn't say anything; she reached into the drawer and pulled out a large manilla envelope. "Darling, please prepare yourself."

He didn't know in what way to prepare, but she looked like she was going to start sobbing, so he gingerly opened the envelope and pulled out an unopened letter from when Peter was nine. The envelope had their address, written in a neat, even script, and postmarked from Scotland. He looked at Erin, knowing letters from the school showed up with that postmark. He opened the sealed envelope and gasped; inside was a pressed daisy and a little boy's handwriting. He read it out loud.

"HI DaddY,
I piked thiss flowr for you. I miss you. When can I see you? Plese rite bake soon.
Love PeTer"

David was crying; he lifted the tiny little flower and sobbed. He felt like someone had ripped out his heart and locked it away in that damned desk, robbing him of the joy he might have had at reading it when Peter was small. He didn't know if he could make himself read another one right away; he wanted that one to soak in first. "I want to put them in order and then read them slowly," he whispered once he'd collected himself.

Erin wiped her face with the back of her hand and nodded. "That's a good idea." She took out the next large, yellow envelope. He hesitated to take hold of it, but she assured him it wasn't as bad as the last one, though it was still bad.

He opened it and saw dozens of credit card bills. He knew she liked nice things and spent a lot of money, but he hadn't seen those and didn't know she'd racked up that much debt. None of them were marked paid, so he reckoned they were all outstanding. "I'll show these to my accountant; there's nothing else for it. What's next?" He figured things would get easier from that point.

Erin looked sadly at him and handed him another one. She pulled out a letter and handed it to him. "I read this one and know it's safe," she said.

He looked at her and raised his eyebrows. "Safe? Ma Losh." He opened it and read a letter from a girl with Cancer. Then he read the date and looked at Erin. "But—that was—five years ago! Is she still alive? How dare Susannah hide these from me! What was she thinkin'? I dinnae understand!" He reached in and pulled out another one, but Erin touched his hand.

"You might not want to do that; I read only one other one, and it wasn't something either of us would want you to see." He nodded and dropped the letter back into the envelope as though it contained Anthrax. "I'll sort through them for you and only give you the nice ones."

He looked into the envelope it had come from and recognized the brown packets he used to get from Tina. Many of them had just been thrown in without any thought of opening them at all. He looked at her, his eyes begging for it to be over, but she shook her head and handed him the last one. The look on her face shocked him; she looked like she was in pain and was holding her breath.

———

Erin wished Kitty were still there to offer her the paper bag, but she wasn't, so she'd just have to try to remain calm.

He opened the envelope, pulled out one of the photographs, and couldn't believe his eyes. "Fer fuck's sake! But—I don't remember—FUCK. Ma eyes are closed!" He put the envelope on top of the desk and turned around.

She was startled to see that his face was red and the blue vein bulged from his forehead. He was breathing heavily, pacing, and talking under his breath. She thought maybe he'd need the paper bag until he stopped and looked at her. Tears filled his eyes, and he picked up the last photo he'd seen before setting them down.

He held it up and pointed to the alligator tooth on the nightstand.

She looked at the floor; his face was too much to bear looking at. "David—you were drugged; you didn't—" He knelt in front of her and held her; he was shaking as sobs racked his body. How could she show him the rest? It would break him; he'd lose something of himself and who he thought he was if she revealed what was in the other, hidden envelope.

"I am so—so—sorry, Erin. I swear I didn't know this was happenin'. I dinnae remember anathin' of et!'

Erin gently pushed him away and walked back to the desk. "I know, darling; I believe you. This is the worst thing I will ever have to do, and I'm so sorry. I just can't keep it from you. Brace yourself," she said.

His face became as pale as death, and she thought for a moment he might pass out, but he steadied himself and sat on the desk chair as she gently lifted the bottom drawer and pulled it out. There lay two more envelopes; she lifted the larger one and handed it to him. "There must be a hundred thousand pounds in here! What— What was she goin' tae do?"

Tears were now running down Erin's face as she slowly picked up the flat envelope. She thought about running to the kitchen and burning them in the oven or a garbage can, but instead, she looked him in the eye and handed it to him. "I still love you, no matter what it shows in there. You are still the same man I want to marry and whose baby I'm proud to be carrying." She was breathing heavily now, and he looked terrified.

"What on earth could Susannah have done to make you say something like that? Those are serious things to say to a man." He opened it while looking at her and pulled a random picture out. It was of him, lying on a bed with a woman straddling him. He stood and threw the photo on the ground. "Oh, God! I know that woman! She's been to our house for parties and—" He had goosebumps all over his arms, his face looked like death, pale and grey, and his lips looked almost purple.

Erin was startled. "David, maybe you shouldn't look at any more of them. Just give them to me and I'll get rid of them for you," she offered.

He shook his head and reached in again, this time it was of him and a man; the man was sitting on top of him, and it looked like the man was being fucked by him, but his eyes were closed, so you couldn't tell what was really happening. "God. God! Erin! What is this? I—know him as well. He's the husband of one of Susannah's friends. Is this some kind of horrible joke?" He pulled out another one; it was of a man lying next to him. There were more with different women, some with two women and him, and one with two men and one woman. After that, he put the envelope down and lay his head on the desk, over his arms. Erin wanted to go to him, to touch him, but something in her told her not to. Somehow, she knew that he needed to work things out in his mind before she said or did anything.

"Did yeh look at all of these before you showed them tae me?" he said after a while.

"I only saw three of them; two with women and then the last one that you saw with the man. I didn't want to show you, but—how could I keep it from you? That would've been no better than what she'd done. I—I'm so sorry, David," she said.

He lifted his head, turned slowly around in the chair, and looked at her. He looked very old and very tired, as though he'd been beaten; defeated at life, and was ready to give up. "I can't take much more of this," he said.

Erin saw a shiver run through his shoulders, and he suddenly stood and ran for the bathroom. She could hear him being sick as she sat on the bed, not knowing what to do. After a few minutes, she heard the shower start and then the sounds of water being splashed as he washed himself.

She stood, took her clothes off, and walked into the bathroom. He was scrubbing his skin with a hand towel, and she could see the disgusted look on his face. It was the same thing she'd done after Bran had raped her, and she suddenly realized he'd just found out that he'd been raped and sexually assaulted for who knows how long while being drugged out of his mind.

She opened the curtain and he shook his head. His face screwed up, and he looked like he wanted to run away and hide. She stepped in and took the towel away from him. "Erin, please; you dinnae want tae do this. Yeh don't understand—"

Erin glared at him, fire flashed in her eyes, and she got angry. "*I* don't understand? *I* don't understand what it's like to be raped while I'm conscious and can see and feel everything? *I* don't know what it's like to be groped, afraid Todd was going to rape me as well?"

David looked at her and understood then how his reaction to what Bran had done would have broken her heart. He saw it replay in his mind, and he was utterly ashamed of himself. "Oh, Erin," he said and took hold of her, holding her to him and cried while she did the same.

"I love you so much, David. I need you to know, no matter what those photos show or what anyone says, I'll love you the same as I did this morning and as I did a month ago and as I will for the rest of our lives." She reached up and put her hand on his cheek, looking him in the eyes, then she smiled and kissed him.

His hands were still soapy, and he ran them down her back, then back up her front, and stopped on her neck.

"Thank you, ma love; I need yeh." He turned them both around so that Erin was now under the water, and he watched as it ran over her body, how it parted when it hit her nipples and then ran down to her feet. He touched her and kissed her; he ran his fingers through her wet hair and buried his face in her neck, kissing her and biting her earlobe.

He wanted to examine her, to bathe her, and to make love to her, though how she could let him after what she'd seen and now knew about him was something he couldn't understand, but he was going to do it. He pushed her against the cold hard marble of the shower walls and then pressed himself against her.

She shivered from the cold and cried out, "Please, David, please make love to me, right now!"

He pulled her away from the wall, and she bent over, holding on to the handrail. With his fingers, he parted her lips and pressed himself against her, feeling her body accept him as he slid into her. She moaned deep and low, and it reminded him of the sound she'd made in New Orleans that drove him over the edge. "Do yeh like that?" he asked her and then thrust deeper into her, making her cry out.

"Yes, I like it!" she said, just in time for him to do it again.

"How about that?" he cried out again.

"Yes, more! Please," she said.

He grabbed her hips and thrust again and again, making her cry out and moan until he felt her shudder and then release, sending waves of energy up his cock, down through his balls, and even a little into his legs when he paid attention to it. He thrust again, and then it was his turn. "Fuck, Erin, fuck," he said as he let the waves of his orgasm wash over him.

He pulled out of her and turned her around, kissing her fiercely, then he put his hand between her legs and felt the hot liquid of their ejaculation running down her leg, then being washed away by the water. He continued to touch her, putting his fingers inside of her. Feeling its heat and how slippery it was turned him on so much.

He kissed her and touched her until he was hard again, then he laid her on the flat marble of the shower floor, and she raised her legs over his shoulders. His knees hurt like crazy, but he was going to make love to her again no matter what, and if he could manage a third time, he would do it again.

"You are mine, Erin, and I am yours. I'm not goin' tae let yeh go, ever; you can count on that. Ye're stuck with me until we die, and yeh dinnae have a choice about et anamore. Do you hear me? Yer mine, and I'm yers. Do yeh ken?" He was crying again, and she was too.

"Aye, David. I ken it, and I'm glad of it! Oh, yes—that feels so good! I'm yours until we die, and that's final; yeh can't get rid of me! Oh! Keep doing that—just like that—" He felt her body tighten up like a rope wound too tight, and just like that it was released, as though she blew up, building the pressure inside of her, and he felt it, pulsing and kneading him, bringing him closer.

He kept going, but it wasn't working any longer; images from the photos started popping up in his mind, assaulting him and torturing him until he became limp and stopped.

"Are you alright?" she asked tenderly.

He rolled so he was sitting with his back on the shower wall and put his hand up to cover his face. She sat next to him while the water rained on them, and he shook his head miserably. "How do I get the images tae stop, Erin? She's ruined me! Do you—Do you still see Bran when yer with me?"

Erin lay her head on his arm. "Sometimes, but not as often as it was in the first few days after it happened. It might not have been so bad if he didn't look so much like you. But then I feel your touch; I can sense our connection, so I know it's you, and I can relax. I don't know how to stop them; I wish I did. Sometimes I'll be doing nothing related to sex or anything, and a memory will attack me, and I don't know what triggers it," she said.

"I don't even have any memories of it, and et's killin' me from the inside out; I can't imagine what ye've gone through! And then I had tae be a fucking idiot and act the way I did—" he said and broke down again with sobs of grief and regret.

Erin shushed him and put her hand on his face. "Don't worry over it anymore; it's all over now. I'm strong, and it will all be okay in time, and as for what you said, I've forgiven you, and I don't think about it anymore. I'm only sorry you're now able to understand my side firsthand. Just be grateful that you don't have any memories of it! That would be worse! Darling, I don't know how to help you except to keep reminding you that I love you no matter what. I don't see it the same way you do, and I'm sure you're going through hell right now, but one thing that you can count on is my love, no matter how you feel about yourself, *I* love you," she said.

David nodded and lay his head on her lap, not caring that it felt as though the water was slowly etching away at his skin.

Before supper, Kitty was relieved when Ms. Erin came down and pulled her aside. She was informed that Mr. Elliott was not aware that she'd been in the room when Ms. Erin had gone through the desk, and he also didn't know that she'd seen any of the photos. Kitty was glad of it; she didn't want Mr. Elliott to question her or to be upset, knowing she'd seen him without his kit on.

Supper was quiet; Kitty brought the serving plates to the dining room, but Mr. Elliott and Ms. Erin mostly just picked at their food, not talking much. The dishes went back to the kitchen with only a spoonful missing, which upset Francie. The cook started complaining to her. "What dae I dae all day? Cook their meals, and fer what? They dinnae even touch them!"

Kitty explained, "They've 'ad a rough day, Francie. I reckon they'll eat it for lunch t'morrow. Ya know, I fink if you're smart about it, Ms. Erin might just give ya the day off t'morrow. Perhaps she's feelin' badly for putting ya out as they've done." She planned to ask Ms. Erin, herself, to give Francie the day off and was willing to fetch fish and chips for supper the next day if need be.

Mr. Elliott and Ms. Erin retired early, but Kitty caught up with Ms. Erin and told her what she'd been thinking. "If it's not too forward of me, mum, I fink the two of us, and Mr. Elliott should go frew the 'ouse, from garret to cellar ta see if she were hidin' anyfing else before the children get 'ere. You wou'nt want 'em findin' anyfing. I've suggested to Francie 'at maybe you'd give 'er the day off to fank 'er for cookin', even though you didn't eat it. If she's gone, we can all look wivout 'er gettin' all nosey like."

"Kitty, that's brilliant!" she said. "You may tell her that Ms. Erin is giving her the day off, and you may take credit for bringing it to pass if you want to. I'll talk to David about doing that tomorrow."

When Erin got to the bedroom, David was already in bed with his eyes closed; he obviously didn't want to talk. "David, I've given Francie the day off tomorrow so we can turn the place upside down... to... make sure there isn't anything else hidden that the children might find or that she's planted for them to discover," she said.

He opened his eyes and turned to look at her. "She wouldn't— never mind." He closed his eyes again but reopened them. "Francie, but not Kitty?"

"Kitty can help us; she... helped me earlier, and she will not look at what she shouldn't or tell anybody anything. I trust her," she said.

He gave her an uncomfortable look. "Kitty was with yeh when yeh found all of that—Did she—see any of et?"

Erin was torn; she couldn't remember what Kitty had seen, and she didn't want to admit she'd seen *any* of it but being honest was more important. "I—I don't know what she saw. I think she saw one that fell out of the envelope when I dropped it; one of Susannah and... possibly you, but she—"

He sat up and looked at her, his eyes wild. He stood and grabbed her by the shoulders. "How could yeh let her see that? Erin! I'm her employer; she can't see things like that." His face was pale, and in a moment, he was dashing to the toilet to be sick.

"I'm sorry, David. I didn't know I'd find anything like that in there. It's not like I was having her going through the drawers; I was doing that," she said.

He rinsed his mouth at the sink and got back into the bed. "Never mind. What's done is done."

He sounded numb, and she wanted to hold him, but something again told her to stay back for a moment, to give him time to decompress. His world was falling apart all around him, and now a member of his staff, inadvertently as it was, had possibly seen a photograph of him naked. Erin undressed and got into bed; she purposely stayed away from him, laying in the opposite direction, to give him space.

After a few minutes, he rolled over and held her tightly. "I'm sorry, hen," he said.

"I understand, and I'm not upset," she said simply.

Chapter Twenty-One

THE THINGS YOU FIND HIDDEN

Erin woke in the middle of the night and heard David weeping softly next to her. She got up to use the toilet and when she returned, lay next to him, placing her arm over his chest. "I love you," she said quietly.

"Do yeh think—" he said and then rolled onto his side, away from her. "Never mind."

Erin could guess what he wanted to ask. "If you mean whether they actually performed sexual acts on you or with you, I don't know if they did." He nodded again, and his body started to shake from the sobs he was trying to keep down. "I really don't think so, though; you are always in the same position, and I think it would be difficult to do much on an unconscious person. I think they were posed and set up to look as bad as possible," she said gently. "I think this was Susannah's last resort; I heard her say, 'You'll be sorry,' when she left on the day she died. I think she did this as a way to bully and blackmail you into coming back to her. I don't think it was real, but I don't know that for certain." He said something Erin didn't understand. "What? I didn't catch that," she said, and he rolled onto his back again.

"Yeh didn't see all the pictures, did yeh?" She shook her head. "There are some that are not just posed, Erin, you can see— Oh, God!"

"You can see what exactly? What does it show?" He lay his arm over his eyes and shook his head. "David—"

He sat up and swung his legs over the side of the bed. "Et shows both men and women... with... ma cock in their mouths, and et wasn't flaccid, either." He stood and walked into the bathroom. After a moment, she heard him vomit in the toilet again. She knew he was driving himself mad with the thought of it all. The toilet flushed, and she heard him running water to brush his teeth.

She could tell he wanted to hit or break something, so she got up and put her robe on. She went into the bathroom, holding David's robe in her hand. "Put this on, please," she said. He looked at the robe and then at her; his face was so sad and frustrated.

"I dinnae want tae go anawhere, Erin," he said miserably.

She held the robe out again, and he took it. "Please trust me," she said. He put the robe on, and she led him down the stairs and into the ugly concrete kitchen. She had brought a few pillows with her, and as they walked in, she asked, "What do you hate most about this room?"

He looked at her as though she'd gone mad. "Erin, et's one in the mornin', why—" he began, but she turned him around.

"Look at this mockery of everything beautiful and pick something you hate about it. The cabinet doors? Hit them. Take this pillow, hold it up, and hit it. Pound it all out. Take things and smash them; mind they aren't rare or one of a kind, please, but smash some old bottles or something she loved."

He remembered the day he'd told Susannah about what Martin had done. She'd been in the kitchen on a chair trying to reach a vase he'd given her for their anniversary, but it broke, and she'd seemed upset about it. "She wasnae upset about the vase breakin'; she'd broken the vase on purpose to try to hurt me or to get her anger out," he said out loud.

He reached up and opened the door to the cupboard she'd taken it from and started removing things and setting them on the counter. There were years and years' worth of vases in which he'd given her bouquets for their anniversaries, Mother's Day, St. Valentine's Day, etc., and she'd kept them all. "Why'd she keep these?" he said. "She didn't care about them; she didn't have a sentimental bone in her body, and her body was all bones."

He continued taking vase after vase out until it was empty. It was then he noticed a small hole on the shelf; it looked like something you'd run an electrical cord through, but there wasn't anything to plug in up there. He put his finger inside it and lifted the false bottom out of the cupboard.

Erin gasped and took the wooden panel from him when he handed it to her. He carefully leaned over the vases on the counter and saw a small lockbox and another manila envelope. "Oh, fuck, there's another one," he said and handed them to her, then he backed away from the counter and took them. They went to the small table Susannah had used for breakfast every day, and he set it down. The box was locked, so he opened the envelope. Inside were thousands of Pounds worth of Euros and American Dollars. He dumped the contents out on the table and out dropped a small silver key. "You've got to be kidding!"

David picked up the key and inserted it into the lock, which turned easily, opening with a *pop*. He looked at Erin, took a deep breath, and lifted the lid, then he raised his hands and backed away from the table. Inside the metal box were over a dozen, maybe two dozen little plastic bags filled with white powder.

"Holy Moses! Is that... what I think it is?" Erin asked.

He shook his head slowly. "I've no idea—I've never seen et before, except in films, so I couldn't tell yeh."

"We should call the police, David! What if you're caught with it? We need to tell someone who can help you," she said.

It was then he remembered the name he hadn't recognized, Clive Dawson. "I can't call the police," he said, breathing heavily, "Clive Dawson is a cop or investigator of some kind. I couldn't place his name before now; if we call the police, I think it'll be a setup."

"Bloody Hell! This is ridiculous!" Erin said. "The lengths Susannah went through to hurt the people who loved her... it just... pisses me off! And, now what? How do we get rid of all this?"

He looked around the kitchen, hoping to find something to bury it in, then figured that plan wouldn't work. "I think we should flush et, or... tip et down the drain. It must be completely gone before the children arrive," he said.

"But, David, I'm torn! Getting rid of it like that will make you look guilty, plus it'll put a butt load of cocaine into the water system, and no amount of treatment will take it all out. But I also know you're right; calling the police would be bad if the guy writing love letters to Susannah was a corrupt cop. I guess we have no choice, but I don't want to touch it!" Erin said.

David looked around again; he took Francie's washing-up gloves and put them on. Erin smiled at him because they were pink with purple polka dots. He took the whole box to the sink and lifted one of the little baggies of powder out as though it contained plutonium. He opened the bag and carefully poured it into the drain, then he turned the water on, and it was gone.

"I need a torch; check in the cupboard above the washer," he said.

Erin went to the cupboard and a moment later was handing the flashlight to him. They looked each other in the eyes and knew they were in over their heads as he took it out of her hand. He shined the light down the drain and shook his head. "Et's leavin' a residue; stickin' to the grease and clumpin' up. We should find a larger drain... like the shower. They went upstairs with the box; he set it just outside the shower and dumped another packet down the drain; he turned the water on, and it went down pretty well. He tried one more, and it did the same. He then walked over to the toilet and dumped one in there. It flushed easily, so he did two more.

He put one down each of the two sinks in the bathroom and then flushed several more in the spare room toilet, making sure it was impossible to see a residue. When they were all disposed of, he had a pile of small baggies he didn't know what to do with. He put them into the bathroom bin and took the bin liner out but didn't tie it shut.

First, he took the garbage and the lockbox to the kitchen and washed the box well, along with the gloves. He knew if he threw Francie's gloves away, she'd think something was up, so, wanting to avoid that, he put them right back where he'd gotten them. Next, he dried the lockbox with paper towels, which went into the bin bag, then he went throughout the house, with Erin's help, using spray cleaner to wash all the sinks, mirrors, toilet rims, and anything that might have come in contact with the drugs. They were exhausted by the time they were done, and it was already nearly time to get up.

They ran to the kitchen; David wiped the lockbox and key thoroughly to get rid of any fingerprints, then put it back into the secret compartment, which they also sprayed with cleaner, just to be sure. Finally, he quickly put all the vases back into the cupboard and had a last-minute idea. Knowing Francie would be up soon to start the coffee, he ran to the water closet and took the loo roll off the spindle.

He and Erin wrapped small bits of the paper into wads and then wet them slightly; the roll was nearly empty, so they took the rest of the loo paper off the roll and put it all in the bin liner bag. He ran it out to the large dumpster bin out back, knowing it was unlikely someone would go rooting around in there unless it was absolutely necessary.

There was still a pile of money on the table, so he used a towel to put it back into the envelope, to cut down on fingerprints, and hurried to put it into his safe until they could decide what to do with it. Then, after checking once more to make sure nothing was out of place, they picked up the pillows and headed back upstairs.

Chapter Twenty-Two

TILLY

Matilda Maxwell, known as 'Tilly,' sat at her desk. Her eyes hurt, which meant she was about to have an episode. She really hoped it would hold off until she got home, or at least someplace safe. Her symptoms had started in earnest when she had gotten her first period, the same as every other Fertilis Defect sufferer. That day, she'd complained of sore eyes and having trouble hearing. As she got older, though, it progressed into temporary blindness and usually deafness, too. Sometimes it was one or the other, but increasingly, they both happened at the same time

She was born in Galena, Illinois thirty-six years earlier, and at a young age decided that when she graduated high school she would travel and live in another country. She didn't have many prospects for a career, except that she was good at learning languages and was quick as lightning with sign language, which came in handy when it was just the deafness that hit her.

After graduation, she traveled some, making her way to Edinburgh, and fell in love with it. She found a primary school that was willing to sponsor and help her through college, so she became a teacher for the deaf and hearing impaired. She loved her job, every part of it, and was good at it too. The kids liked her, and the teachers were impressed with her ability to engage with the kids and make her lessons fun and interesting.

Everyone at the school knew about her condition. She'd told them if they heard her yell for help that she was having an episode and someone should come to find her as quickly as possible. One of her greatest fears was hurting a student if she suddenly went blind while working with them.

The Registry option had been offered to her a few months earlier, giving her some much-needed hope that they'd find her a match soon. She waited and waited, anticipating the call that could potentially change her life, but her phone never rang. Her newfound hope was quickly waning, but her doctor told her not to lose heart, as more and more men were signing up every day and that eventually, someone would turn up.

It was 4:50, and she had just finished preparing for the next day's lesson when her cell phone started going crazy. She had set the ringtone for the Registration Office to *Celebration,* by Kool and the Gang, as it seemed fitting to what the call would warrant. She was horribly nervous, and her hands were so sweaty she nearly dropped the phone. "Hello?" she said, hardly able to breathe.

"Hello, is this Matilda Maxwell?" a woman with a soft Scottish accent asked.

"Yes," she managed to squeak out.

"This is the Fertilis Defect Registry Office, and we'd like tae inform you that we've found someone who matches yer profile. Are yeh able tae give me your availability at this time?"

Tilly put her hand over her mouth and screamed silently, then she took a deep breath and answered as calmly as she could. "Yes, of course; I am available weeknights after six and weekends anytime. Can—can you give me any information about him, such as his name or age?"

"Aye, his name is Roger, he's a widower, and he lives in Edinburgh. That's all I'm allowed tae say at the moment. I'll contact him tae see if we can set up yer first treatment. We usually suggest setting aside a whole weekend or a few days in a row tae meet, whether yeh stay together or meet evera day is up tae you. That way, you can get tae know each other before having the treatment. What is yer soonest availability with that in mind?"

"Oh, okay; that makes sense. The sooner, the better. I can feel an episode approaching. I am available starting Friday then."

"A'right, someone will contact you soon; good luck," the woman said and hung up.

Tilly was beside herself with nerves and happiness. She knew the treatments meant sex with a stranger, but at that point in her life, she didn't care; she was single and could do whatever she wanted. She just hoped the guy would be nice, and even though it didn't really matter, someone she was attracted to. Feeling like she was floating, she left her classroom and made her way to the teacher's lounge to get her things out of her locker. Everyone was gone so she couldn't share her news, but she would be happy to tell anyone who cared to know in the morning.

The call couldn't have come any sooner! She knew that within a week, she'd be blind, groping for something to hold on to and most likely losing all sense of orientation when her hearing inevitably clouded over. Becoming suddenly blind **or** deaf was never fun, but when both happened at the same time, it was terrifying.

She was glad the bus stop was at the intersection in front of the school. Every day, she counted the steps to the bus stop, just in case she had an episode while on her way. That way, hopefully, she'd know where she was and wouldn't wander out into the street. So far, that hadn't happened, but she'd made sure the drivers on that route knew about her condition. She was a regular rider, and they were very accommodating, even though they had a tight schedule. They were aware to watch for her at 5:15 every night and which stops she took every day.

She wondered what it would be like to live a normal life, where she didn't have to ask people to look out for and keep an eye on her. Where she could step out of her house and do whatever she wanted to do without fear that everything would fade to black, not knowing how long it would last.

At 5:45 she was home and turned on the electric kettle for tea, then she put her Morrisons shepherd's pie into the microwave. At 6:00, she was sitting on her sofa with a TV tray, ready to watch a rerun of *Future Explorations*. Her favorite episodes were the first and second of season one, the third and last of season two, and all of the third season. *Leave it to the Brits to get something right and then cancel it after only three seasons, leaving everyone wanting more!* she thought again for the hundredth time.

The theme music started 'Dah-ah-dah—dah-ahah—', and she blew on the 'piping hot' bite on her fork until it was 'edible hot.' She watched as Joe Whitehall traveled further and further into the past, getting himself into and out of scrapes, narrowly escaping the villains every time. Joe was her favorite character, though he was only in a few of the episodes, the first and second one, and a few later on in flashbacks.

Most people adored John Thomas Fife; he was tall, slender, handsome, and wore a kilt, but he was too perfect. Joe was plain and ordinary, like her. She was pale and homely; her hair was straight, dishwater blond, and had no life at all. Wearing a bra was completely optional, as there wasn't anything to lift or separate; there were no curves to her at all. Men never cat-called or even looked twice at her, but she didn't mind; she was independent and free to do what she wanted when she wanted and didn't have to share anything, especially the remote control!

She watched till the end of episode one, where Joe walked, or more accurately, limped and stumbled, over the berm in front of an old farmhouse in the Scottish Highlands, finding a man in a kilt standing there. The kilted man looked into the sunset with one hand shielding his eyes as Joe fell and rolled down the side of the berm. He handed the tall Highlander the small device that would allow him to travel in time, just as it had for him. The Scotsman tried to ask questions, but it was too late; Joe was gone. Tilly always cried when Joe died, no matter how many times she watched it.

She started the second episode, which began where the other had ended, in front of the Highlander, John Thomas of Fife's simple farmhouse. He picks up the device and ends up moving forward in time, landing in the same spot several years into the future. His farm is overgrown, his wife and child are gone, and he doesn't know how to process what's happened. A flashback of Joe being told how to use the device reveals that if the previous user could only go back in time, the next user would only be able to go forward. In several scenes, Joe and John Thomas nearly meet, but something always prevents it.

She loved the simplicity of the show's concept; it was genius and could have lasted a lot longer, with new people taking the place of John Thomas, but to the horror of the growing fandom, it was canceled after season three. Thus, just like *Firefly* in America, the few precious seasons became a cult classic, watched over and over, memorized by its loyal and very often obsessed fans all over the world.

Future Explorations was what had made her want to live in Scotland. It had started just before she graduated, and she was instantly in love. She hadn't yet been to the Highlands or even much more north than Stirling to see the Wallace monument, but she figured she'd get there someday if it was meant to be.

Though she might have liked Joe better than John Thomas, John Thomas had one thing over Joe, and that was his Scottish accent. It was one of the biggest draws to live there, and she never grew tired of it. Granted, Edinburgh didn't have as strong an accent as many other places in the country, but it was enough.

She got up, threw the empty Morrisons container away, and then washed her fork and glass, setting them on a tea towel next to the sink. After that, she went to the bathroom to put drops in her eyes, though she knew it wouldn't do anything. Then she went back out to finish the second episode.

She could listen to John Thomas Fife talk forever; she would close her eyes and imagine Joe was speaking the lines John Thomas was saying. *I hope Roger is Scottish, with a really nice, thick accent!* she thought and pulled the blanket off the back of the couch as the end credit music lulled her to sleep.

Chapter Twenty-Three

SET UP

Breakfast in the morning was simple since Francie had left just after making the coffee. David and Erin were just barely awake; they hadn't gone back to bed, being too nervous and wound up. Instead, they put the children's letters in order by date sent and then by name. They read another one and cried. David hadn't known how much his kids missed him and didn't write to them often because he didn't want to burden them with having to write back.

"I think we should take these with us when we pick the kids up. We can explain to them how we found them hidden in their mother's things and that you didn't even know they existed before now. We can read them together, and they can see how sad you are about it. I'm sure they will like seeing their childish handwriting as well. I also think it will do a lot to heal any wounds they might have because you didn't respond."

"Aye, that's a verra good idea. I did write, but not as often as I should've. I didn't know they wanted me tae so badly," he said.

Erin noticed he had bags under his eyes. There were also streaks of grey in his hair showing through the dye job he'd had for an advertisement he'd recently shot. They seemed much thicker and more noticeable than only a few days before. His eyes were bloodshot from lack of sleep and crying, and more than just tired, he looked beat. "Do you want to lay down and try to sleep?" she asked, but he shook his head.

"No. Everatime I try, I think of the photos and feel sick," he said.

She took his hand in hers and kissed it. "I understand," she said.

After breakfast, David received a message from Becky, saying that the news of his new relationship had just been published. Therefore, when Erin and Kitty started discussing the order of what should be done first, he wasn't really paying attention. He had just gotten to the first page of the **Latest Headlines—Showbiz** section of the morning newspaper when he heard Erin say, "David should look there; there might be spiders."

"Did yeh say somethin'?" he asked.

She was holding the list of places they'd compiled to search and smiled at him. "Never mind, darling," she said, so he shrugged and went back to his paper.

"Ach! Here et is then!" He folded the paper over so that the page he wanted her to see was on the top and set it in front of her.

Kitty left the room, and Erin looked at where David was pointing. There were two photos, the one they'd sent to Becky, and a close-up of Erin, looking not very photogenic. "Uhh! Take it!" she said and turned her head.

David read the article out loud.

It has been announced in an exclusive message to reporter Doug MacDaniels that Future Explorations hunk, David Elliott, recent widower of Susannah Sutcliffe Elliott, is currently involved in a 'serious relationship' with an American woman named Erin March. They've been seen together in Edinburgh and London, and I wonder, as all of you must, just what he is doing with someone like her? Can someone say REBOUND? Or perhaps she's in a family way? Whatever the reason, these must be desperate times indeed.

"I'm sorry, ma love," he said and sighed. "That wasn't nice. Dinnae worry about et though; at least now people will know and, hopefully, leave me alone."

"I'm fine, and I hope you're right." She hadn't expected the press to be kind, and, so far, she felt able to brush off the affront and not let it ruin her day.

Kitty returned and they were soon ready to start scouring the house; they had just begun when David's mobile rang, making them all jump. He looked at the screen and sighed. "Et's the school; I wonder what Daniel has done this time?" he said with slight trepidation.

Erin guessed Susannah had been the one to deal with those calls, but now that it fell on him, she could sense his dread.

He swiped the answer icon and said, "This is David." There was a pause while he listened to the person on the other end of the line. "Excluded? Peter? What on earth could have made him that upset? He's not like that; it's usually Daniel warranting a call. May

I speak with him, please?" He gave her a look and then put it on speakerphone.

"Dad?" Peter said, miserably.

"What happened, son?" David said, sounding truly worried.

"I was in a fight, but Ted Fisher said you were—I won't say what he said, but it wasn't nice. He... showed me pictures of you and... well, a woman, and, well, he called her a slag and a whore, Dad!"

"But, Peter, I told you about the photo so you wouldn't get into this mess." He looked at Erin and rolled his eyes.

"But, Dad, it wasn't *that* picture; I saw that one as well, and it was nothing, these were worse! And they were—" He lowered his voice, presumably so no one in the office would hear him "with Erin, Dad, and she didn't have any—clothes on. I didn't want to see it, but he showed it to me before I knew what it was. He was showing them all over the school and making fun of you and the— fat slag. I didn't say that, Dad; he did!"

David looked at her, and she knew her face was red. "There were photos like that in a newspaper... of us?" he asked.

"Yeah, and they're really bad. I didn't want him talking about her that way, Dad. She's not a whore *or* a slag!"

Erin took out her phone and searched for 'David Elliott images.' The first few were headshots she'd seen many times, but when she scrolled a bit, she saw two she didn't recognize. She tapped the images, expanded them, and nearly dropped her phone. Knowing Peter was on speakerphone, she managed not to say anything, but when she showed them to David, his face grew red, and he was much gentler in the way he spoke to his young son.

"Fer fuck's sake!" he mouthed to Erin, who looked horrified. "Peter, I—just saw the photos. I'm sorry you had to see that; it wasn't fair to you. Let me think for a moment." David took a deep breath; he didn't know what to do, it was only a few days until their summer holiday. Should he pick him up or leave him there? The secretary, Margaret, had said if he stayed, he'd be made to work on the grounds, which he probably wouldn't hate, but that Fisher kid and all the rest of them would taunt him the whole time, which might get him expelled, not just excluded. He looked at Erin and mouthed, "What should I do?" She shrugged and shook her head. "A'right, son, for how many days have you been excluded?"

"Until Saturday."

"Brilliant, four days until your summer holidays begin; why would they do that at the very end of the year? I reckon Roger will have to fetch you. I'm working in London now and can't get away or I'd do it myself. I will speak with Headmaster Campbell about releasing all of you at the same time, though I don't have much hope of that. We can speak of this in more detail when I see you next. Now please hand the phone back to the secretary."

"Alright. I'm sorry, Dad," he said. He could hear him hand the phone back to Margaret.

"When shall we expect you, Mr. Elliott?"

"May I please speak to Headmaster Campbell?" he asked, and she paused.

"He is a very busy—"

"I must speak with him," he said more forcefully, so she put him on hold. A pleasant-sounding man started spewing rhetoric about how fantastic the school was, having earned this award and that honor; he was not impressed.

"Duncan Campbell, how may I help you, David?"

Just the sound of the man's voice gave David cold sweats. He had spent many hours in his office trying to defend himself for minor incidents blown out of proportion when he was his children's ages. "Yes, sir, I've been informed of Peter's behavior, and seeing it is the end of term, are you willing to release his three siblings, as we—"

"I'm afraid that won't be possible, David," the headmaster cut him off. "As you know, there are many preparatory instructions given for the next term on those days, and I cannot—"

It was David's turn to interrupt. "I understand, sir. However, I'm not planning to send my children back next term. I am planning a family holiday to the states, which we will begin before the end of term, so if you would be so kind as to have them ready." He could hear the old man sputtering, trying to find a response.

"But, David; would you break the tradition of you and your children—"

"Gladly. Without hesitation. It was my former wife who insisted on sending them there, and I intend to free them from the place. My driver will pick them up later this evening. Please allow them time to pack their belongings. Also, please include any assignments that may come due so they may finish them; we will return them in the post," David said.

"I still believe that—" the headmaster tried to argue, but David was impatient with him.

"What is it you believe, sir? What punishment did Ted Fisher receive for his actions in this fight?"

The headmaster floundered, sputtering, "I—that's not—"

"Ach, I see, I imagine his father is an honored member of the education authority or has contributed too many pounds tae embarrass *him* with an exclusion for *his* precious son, yet you believe everathin' yeh read in the tabloids about me, so a little more embarrassment won't matter tae David. Is that what you believe, Headmaster Campbell?" he said, trembling with rage, as thirty years of fear and frustration came out all at once.

Erin was wide-eyed and shaking her head vigorously, trying to get him to stop. She finally put her hand on his shoulder. "That's only going to harm the children, David, please stop," she whispered as quietly as she could.

The headmaster still hadn't answered his accusations, so he ended the conversation with, "Kindly have my children waiting at half seven, good day," and rang off. He was still shaking when he set his mobile on the table next to him.

"Are you okay? You really went off on him!" she asked.

That was a side of him he didn't often reveal and he looked at her sadly. "Aye, I probably shouldn't have done that. I reckon I should've spoken with the children tae find out if tha's what they would want me to do, but I was just so fed-up by the hypocrisy in that place. I hope the children won't be very angry with me for not allowing them tae say goodbye to their schoolmates." He placed his head on her shoulder and sighed.

"I'm sure they'll forgive you, dear. I don't think you should worry too much, they didn't want to talk about school with me, so I'm guessing they feel the same way as you. Now, why don't you call Roger and tell him he'll be taking a road trip tonight?" She kissed his hair and reached around to touch his cheek.

He lifted his head and looked at her. "Do yeh think he'll take et out on ma kids? Oh, God, I hope not," he said.

"I don't know anything about their headmaster, so I don't have an answer. I hope he doesn't, but if he does, I'll go up there and toilet paper the entire place!" she said and then laughed.

"You'll do what?" he said.

"Haven't you ever TP'd anyone before?"

He looked at her blankly. "I reckon I've heard of it, but no, I've never— I think our equivalent would be throwing eggs, especially rotten ones, which I've also never done."

"Well, I can't say I've ever actually toilet-papered anyone myself, but it's done a lot in America. It's illegal now, so it's not quite as popular as it was when I was a teenager, but it's still done. Apparently, it's hard to remove if it gets wet because instead of disintegrating, it sticks to itself and becomes like paper mache, but I'd do it for you and the kids!" she said with a smile, trying to cheer him up.

"Thank you, darling," he said and smiled at her. He picked up his phone, called Roger, and waited for him to answer until he realized that he usually texted him. He was just about to ring off when Roger answered, sounding a bit worried.

"Hullo? David? What's the matter?"

David laughed. "Ach, I rang yeh by mistake. Erin said, "Call Roger," so I did."

"Aye, I see. So, what do yeh need?"

"Ach, Peter hit another boy, gettin' himself excluded for the last few days of term, so... bein' in a foul temper, I decided tae pull them all out as of tonight."

"Well, tha' must ha' been a verra foul temper indeed!" Roger said. "I take tha' tae mean I'll be drivin' up there after supper then? And what would yeh like done wi' the lot once they're here?"

"I'll speak to ma mother about keepin' them until we can get there tomorrow night."

"That's fine wi' me, mate, though et would be much more enjoyable if I could take—what did yeh name the car?" he asked, and David laughed.

"Neela; Erin says et means blue, like the sea, or sky, or somethin' blue," he said, and it was Roger's turn to laugh.

"Neela, then, but they willnae fit. At what time did yeh tell them I'd be arrivin'?"

"Half seven." The adrenaline had worn off, and he started doubting the wisdom of his actions.

"A'right, I'll be there, oh, and give my regards tae Erin, if yeh will."

"Aye, I will. Eh, Roger, I don't reckon ye've seen the latest photographic journalism tae hit the newsstand, have yeh?" David asked.

There was a pause and Roger cleared his throat. "Aye, well, unfortunately, I have; both of them tae be exact. Is tha' what Peter's fight was about?"

"Aye."

"Ach, well, I can imagine what a group of boys his age kept locked up together day and night in tha' place would say tae him about et. I hope he walloped the boy right well!"

"Aye, don't tell—" He was about to say, 'Don't tell Susannah'; it was something he'd said to him quite often. Then he realized it was no longer possible to tell her anything. He was glad he wouldn't need to start substituting 'Erin' for the person not to tell since they agreed on most things already. "Right—Ach, I hope so as well, Roger; thank you."

"Aye," he said and rang off.

David sent a quick text to his mother and informed her the children would be staying with her and that he and Erin would be returning Thursday night. She replied that it was fine and she looked forward to seeing both of them. He put down his phone and began pacing and biting his nails.

"Penny for your thoughts?" Erin said softly.

He looked at her and tried to smile. "I've buggered some things up today. I was thinkin' about education options, and I've no idea what would be best. I can't place them into a state school; those kids would eat them alive. I reckon I'll have to find a good day school or a tutor to teach them."

"Well, you don't need to decide today, and we have much... well, more pressing and important things to discuss right now." She opened the page on her phone and showed him the photos she'd found. The first one was of him and her at the Audubon Cottages in New Orleans. He was sitting on a patio chair with her on his lap, her robe open; nothing was blurred. In the other one, she was bent over the patio table with her robe lifted over her back, and he was standing behind her, obviously having sex.

"Bloody hell!" he said.

"I'm afraid to ask, but do you know where the photos are? The ones Susannah had?" she asked.

"Aye. They're in the drawer of the—" He stood suddenly. "Ach, I hope they are still there! If Kitty saw them!" *I reckon et doesn't matter, now she's seen the other one,* he thought miserably. He left the master bedroom, which they were about to start turning inside out, and hurried to the bedside table in the spare room. He opened the drawer, saw the envelope, and sighed. "Thank God!" he said and walked back to their bedroom." He handed them to Erin but held them tight as she tried to take them from him.

"Now, brace yerself, Erin. These are not pretty; they're not as bad as the hidden ones yeh found of me, and the published ones are the worst of the lot, but just be prepared," he said and let go.

———

Erin took the packet and went into her dressing room. For some reason she was embarrassed to look while he was standing there. Pulling them out randomly, the first one she saw was of her, yelling at the bride-to-be; her face was red, and she looked really fat and just ugly.

"Good night—" She set it upside down on a shelf and took out another, which was of David kissing Champagne's hand; she was just visible in the background. The next photo was of David leaning over to talk to her in the jazz club. Those two weren't too bad; she was sitting, and you could only see her face. The next one showed David looking down at her while she looked up at him. It was beautiful, and she wanted to frame it.

Next was a photo of David kneeling on Bourbon Street after she'd gotten the brain freeze. After that was a shot of their first kiss, and she stared at it for a long time. She could remember every detail; the clean air, at least compared to Bourbon Street, the feel of the bricks on her back, the heat of the night, and the feel of his lips on hers for the first time. She closed her eyes, reliving the moment; it was still intoxicating.

"Oh, David," she said dreamily, "this one is so nice!" She turned around, and he was no longer standing where she could see him. She set that photo on top of the stack and then looked at the next one, which had been taken at the French Market. She was leaning against a support pole, and he was kissing her. In her memory, she could still feel the warm night air and smell the breeze off the water, mixed with the yeasty smell of beignets frying at the Cafe Du Monde. She took a deep breath and smiled.

He was right; most of these aren't so bad, she thought too soon because the next was one that had been published. She examined it and shook her head. *I can't believe this! Someone would've had to have been waiting and timed it perfectly! And where were they standing to get that angle?* She was laid out on David's lap; breasts, belly, hips, legs, everything exposed to the world. *Holy Moses!* she thought and turned to the next.

The next few were her and David having sex, without question. The first two weren't that bad; all you could see was her rear end and David's torso; the first of them had been printed, but the last one made her jump. "Oh, Fuck! Fuck! No way!" Her rant was interrupted by David coming into the room holding his phone in his hand.

"I decided to look up the story on their website so I'd know what they said. Would you like me to read it out loud?" he asked.

"David!" She raised the last photo of them having sex. He lay his mobile on the bed and went to her. It was the same pose and position as the last two she'd seen, except that one had been taken on an outward thrust so you could see some of his cock. The look on David's face revealed that he'd just reached his climax. "Thank

God they didn't print this one!" she said, shaking and feeling light-headed.

"I know, I know." He held her and stroked her hair. "Dinnae worry, love," he said and kissed her, then he walked back to the bed and picked up his mobile. He read the caption, then the story.

NOT SO FUTURE EXPLORATIONS

David Elliott Caught with His Pants Down in New Orleans! *Future Explorations heartthrob, David Elliott, 45, and an unknown woman were captured in a revealing pose last month, whilst David was in America shooting a small part for a crime drama programme in New Orleans, Louisiana.*

The couple have been spotted on several other occasions; in London and Edinburgh, but no one would've guessed the intimate nature of their relationship. Sources tell us it's serious and ongoing.

David Elliott is a recent widower of his late wife, Susannah Sutcliffe Elliott, who died suddenly of a heart attack earlier this month. We wonder who this new woman in David's life is, and did his poor wife die of a broken heart?

"Damn! I guess today was the best day for our announcement to run, huh?" she said, wanting to cry—to throw a fit actually, but what was the point? Nothing could be done about it anyway. "I just can't believe Peter has seen it, and maybe the others have by now, too. I hope no one at home in Wisconsin will—Well, I don't think they read the tabloids, not that this would be in the American ones, but there's the internet, and I'm pretty sure some of my girlfriends look up your name, well, often. Good thing it doesn't show my face, right? Why is Martin doing this to us? What is the point?" She didn't mention Todd; there was no way to know if he was being voyeuristic about her and David or avoiding it at all costs. Either way, he'd probably see it someday, and she didn't like the thought of that.

"This time, I reckon et's revenge. He was verra bitter and blamed me for Susannah's death at the funeral. I imagine he thought he'd win her affection once I was out of the picture," David said and then groaned. "I... may have said something which would've made him quite angry as well, but I thought that was what the woman who kissed me was about; I reckon I was wrong."

"What... did you say?"

"Ach, he was making a scene and said that I never loved her, not as much as he did. I'd had it with his outbursts by then and said... *Maybe not, but she hated you.*' I ken et was unnecessary, and I should've kept ma mouth shut, but et's done now, and—"

"Holy Moses, David! What if Kitty has seen the article and... photos— Or Francie? I can't go anywhere today! People will have seen it... me! Oh, no! We have our first doctor's appointment today! We need to call and reschedule!" She stepped away from him, breathing heavily and shaking as she began to panic.

David took her back into his arms. "Shhh, dinnae panic, love," he said as she sat on the edge of the bed. "Et's a'right, yeh dinnae have tae go anawhere, darling."

There was a knock on the door. "Excuse me, sir, I found 'is and—" Kitty said and poked her head into the room. "Oh, dear me! Are ya a'right, mum?" She walked in and produced a small paper bag from her pocket. "'Ere now, just breave as ya done b'fore. 'At's good, just relax, Erin, you're gonna be a'right. Shhh." Their housekeeper sat her on the side of the bed and spoke softly to her. After a few minutes, Erin started to relax and breathe normally again.

"Where'd yeh learn that Kitty? You were brilliant!" David asked her admiringly.

She made sure Erin was really improving before she answered. "Me mum gets 'erself all worked up about fings, sir. She starts breavin' 'eavy, just like Ms. Erin were doin', so I always 'ave a paper bag 'andy," she said. Erin started to get up, and Kitty put her hand on her arm

"Wha'ever's boverin' ya, mum? Don't suppose I can 'elp, but I'm willin' ta try.

Erin looked into Kitty's caring eyes, and it didn't matter that she was the housekeeper. "I just learned there are naked pictures of... David and... me in the tabloids, and we—we have a doctor's appointment for the baby later today. I already know poor Peter has seen them, and hundreds of other people have by now, too. I just don't want to go anywhere." She couldn't believe she was telling her all of that. It wasn't really appropriate, but she was the only friend, other than David, she had in London, and after the ordeal they'd already been through the day before, she had to let it out to another woman.

"Yes, mum, I'm sorry ta say I've seen 'em, but— if I'm 'onest, I fink ya looked lovely. Me mum's the one what showed 'em ta me. She's not a small woman, ya see, and she remarked 'ow nice it were ta see someone who looked more like 'er bein' involved wiv an 'andsome man like our Mr. Elliott. Pardon me sayin' so, sir," she said.

"It's all right, Kitty," he said and took Erin's hand to help her stand.

"I fink you shou'nt be worried all that much, as more people are on your side than ya fink, and the one's what aren't don't matter anyways. As for your Peter, 'ee'll be a'right. I reckon 'ee's seen 'is share of nudi'ty, and 'ee'll forget, or at least 'ee'll see 'at not all women are skel'tal and sickly lookin'— Sorry for saying so, but I fink you should walk out of 'ere wiv your 'ead 'eld 'igh, proud of who ya are, and not be afraid, mum. Pardon—"

Erin reached out and hugged Kitty tightly. "Kitty, you are a Godsend and a really good friend too. I needed to hear that, and if it were up to me, I'd give you a raise for acting as therapist as well as housekeeper," she said and smiled at David.

"We'll talk about that another time," he said and smiled.

"Oh, and thank your mother for me as well, please," Erin said as an afterthought.

Later that day, Kitty approached David and said, "Mr. Elliott, sir, I've found som'fin' in Rosie's room ya might wanna see." Kitty had been tasked with tearing apart the children's rooms to make sure nothing was hidden for them to 'accidentally' find. "I left it where I found it."

He and Erin followed her down the hall and up the stairs to Rosie's bedroom. It was pink, purple, and everything Erin would've wanted when she was a girl. Kitty pointed to Rosie's nightstand; the drawer was open, and laying on top of everything was a photograph, turned upside down. David stepped forward and picked it up, revealing a copy of their first kiss photo. He frowned and showed it to Erin, who furrowed her brows.

"But why this one?" She took it from him and examined it. "Oh, I know. She didn't know the children knew about me, and she wanted poor Rosie to see you with another woman. That's just evil!"

"But she did know, remember? She was tryin' tae obtain information out of them—Unless she planted this one before she tried her little crying act. But if that's the case, I reckon they would've found them by now. I don't understand," he said.

"I found a'nover one, as well, sir," Kitty said. She led them into Peter's room and pointed to his nightstand. Again, David picked up the face-down photo. This time, it was the one of him kissing Champagne's hand. Kitty then pointed to Peter's desk. The top drawer was open, and they saw another small photo on top of everything in it. "The pic'ture were buried deeper, sir; I only put it on top so's you'd see it."

He picked it up and revealed one from the envelope in his desk that Erin hadn't seen the day before. David was sitting up against the headboard with his eyes closed. A large woman, only a bit larger than Erin, wearing a black, satin negligée, was positioned with her head down, apparently giving him a blow job. You couldn't see any private body parts; the pose was only a suggestion of what was happening.

"Fuck!" Erin said when she saw it and turned her head. "To show an innocent child something like that on purpose! That's child abuse! What was wrong with her?"

David shook his head, and Kitty looked sad. "Sir? I want ya ta know 'at I never looked at 'em, the pic'tures, I mean, so ya don't need ta worry about that," she said. "When I see the back or corner of one, I set it face down on top of everyfing for you ta look at.

David closed his eyes and put his head down. "Thank you, Kitty. I appreciate et."

They spent the rest of the morning searching the house until it was time for David and Erin to leave for their appointment, then Kitty was left in charge until they came back.

Chapter Twenty-Four

ROGER'S NEWS

Roger had planned to change the oil in the SUV before David rang; he had plenty of time before he had to leave, so he was preparing for the job. His mobile rang unexpectedly, and he looked at the screen; it wasn't a number he recognized but he answered it anyway. "Hello," he said.

"Is this Mr. Blackwood?" an eager young man's voice asked him.

He was not used to people calling him by his surname and nearly rang off, thinking it was someone trying to sell him something he didn't need or want. "Aye," he said tentatively.

"I'm Jason from the Fertilis Defect Registry, and I've some good news. We've found your match, and she doesn't live far from you."

Roger set down the oil pan and funnel he was holding as everything suddenly became vibrant and he noticed all the little details around him. The cat he'd been trying to catch was seen running out of the garage with a mouse between its teeth, he noticed the stairs leading to his flat needed to be swept badly, and he saw a forgotten, empty mug sitting on his workbench from when he'd stood, talking with Erin one day. "That's... wonderful! Now what do I do?" he asked, utterly surprised they'd found someone so quickly.

"The next step is to make a treatment appointment. We recommend setting aside a few days for the first one so you can get to know one another before performing the treatment. You might consider putting her up in a hotel or someplace private where you can become comfortable together.

"Well, I hadnae thought of tha'. I live in a flat with two bedrooms, and I only use one. If she's willin' tae stay here, she'll have complete privacy. Otherwise, if she doesnae feel comfortable wi' tha', I could stay in the main house whilst she stays in the flat for the weekend… or we could leave the option open either way and she can decide when she gets here?" He was rambling, so he stopped talking.

"Alright, I will contact her to find out if she is agreeable to that situation. She did say she was hoping to start treatments as soon as possible. Are you available this weekend?"

Roger was taken aback; he wasn't sure how that would work with the four children, David, and Erin there. "Well, I reckon... if she's willin' tae come here, I'm available Friday afternoon."

"Fantastic. She's available after six on weekdays, so unless she has any objections, and I will contact you if she does, you should expect her to arrive on Friday after six," Jason said.

Roger stared at the dirty coffee mug on his workbench. "Aye, tha's grand, thank you," he said, his heart nearly beating out of his chest. He rang off and figured he'd better tell Annis before the stranger knocked on the door and Millie sent her away. He went into the main house and found her in the sitting room, knitting something small and delicate. "Excuse me, Ann," he said. She looked up, and he continued. "I need tae speak wi' you about somethin' important."

She raised her eyebrows and put her knitting down.

"Aye, what is et, Roger?"

"Well, I've—I mean, I've signed up with the Fertilis Defect Registry, and they've found a match for me. I—I wanted, first, tae tell yeh about et, before a woman shows up lookin' for me, and second, tae ask yer permission tae stay in Millie's room if she's no' keen on sharin' the flat wi' me. Ach, it'll only be for the weekend, no longer." He knew his face was red and figured she'd be able to see the rings of sweat on his shirt.

"Tha's what our Erin has, correct; the Fertilis Defect? And the Registry, that's the same one David was tricked into joinin' by Martin Green?" she asked bluntly, and Roger nodded. "And ye've joined of yer own volition then?" She sounded surprised and a bit puzzled.

"Aye. David suggested et in jest, but I got tae thinkin' tha' mebbie et's somethin' I could do for someone who needs help, as our Erin did, so I considered et and... decided," he said.

"Aye, Roger, you may use Millie's room for yourself but not anaone else; not until we meet this woman and get tae know her, as we've done our Erin. I truly wish yeh well and am sae pleased... and impressed tae hear of your decision. To learn of this admirable act only increases my already high respect for you," his employer said.

Roger hadn't expected to be praised for what he was doing and didn't know what to say. Annis looked at him with such deep emotion he felt his cheeks grow warmer in her gaze, so he said, "Thank you," and left the room.

Chapter Twenty-Five

ANTENATAL VISIT

Erin and David arrived at the clinic, or as they called it, the surgery, ten minutes early to fill out paperwork. They walked in and saw that the place was buzzing with pregnant ladies, mostly twenty-somethings of all shapes and sizes. Some were tiny little things who looked like they'd swallowed a soccer ball, while others were more average in size with differing extremes of baby belly.

Erin noticed a stand with paper masks. Thinking quickly, she took one and handed it to David. "Here, put this on and pretend you've got a light cough," she said.

He smiled, put the mask on, and played at coughing delicately until he was laughing so hard, he actually did start coughing, in earnest. His laugh was something she needed to hear. "That'll teach ya!" she said with a smile as they walked up to the registration desk. "Appointment for Erin March?" she said quietly, not wanting anyone in the waiting room to hear her name since it had been in the newspaper that morning. The receptionist handed her a clipboard with a stack of papers and asked them to find a seat.

Erin started filling out the pages, leaving blank the things she didn't know and quietly asking David the things only he did. He was all smiles; she could see it, even with the mask; he was acting excited, almost giddy, and impatient. After the events of the last couple of days, she was surprised to see it. "What is up with you? It's not like you haven't been through this several times before," she said.

He looked at her and shook his head. "I've sired four children, aye, but I was never allowed in on this part."

Erin looked at him, her eyes wide. "Are you kidding me? She didn't even let you come to the doctor's visits? The more I learn the more I don't like or understand her," she said. He was still smiling and practically bouncing up and down in his chair. Erin laughed at him and shook her head. "You're like a little boy, waiting to sit on Santa's lap to tell him what you really, really want for Christmas!"

He just shrugged and watched the door that led to the exam rooms like a hawk.

A short woman wearing scrubs with cats chasing balls of yarn came out and called Erin by her first name, then she led them down a hallway. "My name's Molly; I'm Doctor Westin's nurse," she said, then asked Erin to step on an electronic scale and took down her weight as 77 Kilograms.

"Wait, what's that in pounds?" she said.

The Nurse did the math in her head. "One hundred sixty… well, I'll just say one seventy."

"What! I've lost over thirty pounds! That's amazing," she exclaimed. David smiled at her and didn't say anything. Erin knew he'd be happy for her, but he wasn't attracted to thin women, so she figured he'd also hope that she didn't get too thin.

Molly measured her height against the wall at 165.1 cm.

"Five foot five inches, I believe?" David said, having already done the math before being asked.

The nurse nodded and asked Erin to give her a urine sample. When she'd done that, they were led into the exam room, where she was asked to sit on a chair. Her blood pressure and heart rate were taken, then she was asked half the questions she'd just answered in the paperwork.

"Everything seems fine. Doctor Westin will be in shortly," Molly said.

She left the room, and David stood next to Erin's chair, holding her hand. He took the mask off, and she saw he was still smiling from ear to ear. "I love you," she whispered.

"I love you, as well," he said.

She'd never seen him so excited before; his eyes were nearly twinkling, and his million-dollar smile never left his face.

Doctor Jill Westin came in and crossed her arms. "I hope you've been taking it easy since I saw you last," she said to Erin, looking stern and then smiled congenially.

"I have. No more mountain climbing for me!" Erin said and laughed as she made an X over her heart with her finger.

"Good! Well then, I think I should formally introduce myself. My name is Jill Westin."

Erin shook the doctor's hand and looked at David, who also shook her hand. "David Elliott," he said, and she nodded.

"I already knew that," she said with a smile and continued to speak with Erin. "To tell you the truth, Erin, you're the first pregnant Fertilis Defect sufferer I've seen. Not many of you can get pregnant, even with treatments; you're a rare specimen."

"You could say that in more ways than one," Erin said and laughed; she'd meant it sarcastically, but David smiled.

"Aye, you are," he said tenderly, though he was still excited and beaming.

Dr. Westin sat on a small rolling stool. "So, we calculate your due date from the first day of your last period, so according to what you've told us—"

"Wait, what if you know within a day when it was conceived?" Erin asked.

"Are you that confident of the date?" Erin looked at David again.

"I'm pretty sure; I mean, if I was ovulating two weeks after the start of my period, then I would've conceived on May twentieth, right? Our first treatment was on May sixteenth, and we... well— the, uh, last treatment was May twentieth, so—"

"So, you were most fertile from the seventeenth through the twentieth; In that case, we add 266 days from the actual date of conception, which would be—" She looked on her calendar and did some calculations, "February tenth."

Erin looked at David. "February tenth," she said aloud, wanting to make it real in her mind.

"Though, if you're keeping track of your progress online, it will be about two weeks off," she said.

Erin nodded; she hadn't even thought of doing that yet. The Dr. asked Erin to sit on the high examination table covered with stiff, white paper and had a pillow covered with a very thin, gauze-like pillowcase. "Now, I need to make you aware that this pregnancy would be considered high-risk by your age alone, so when you add the Fertilis Defect aspect into the equation, it makes it even more delicate. There are routine prenatal screening tests we'll be performing, such as blood tests and ultrasounds, but, according to your progress and what we find through the imaging, I may want you to consider other tests and procedures in addition. Depending on how things progress, I might recommend a specialized or targeted ultrasound, which can detect abnormal development," she said.

Erin and David nodded; hearing their pregnancy was at an overly-high risk wasn't something they wanted to hear.

"There are other tests we could do as well, but they are very risky to the fetus and could result in miscarriage, so I rarely suggest them. They would be Amniocentesis, where we take a sample of the amniotic fluid, or Chorionic villus sampling, where we take a sample of cells from the placenta. Both of them can identify certain genetic conditions, such as the Fertilis Defect."

Erin hadn't thought about possibly passing the disease to her child; she looked at David and saw that his smile was turning into a frown. His brows were furrowed, and the twinkle was nearly gone from his eyes.

"Another test would be Cordocentesis, where a sample of your baby's blood is removed from the umbilical cord for testing, which can identify the Fertilis Defect as well as blood conditions and infections."

Both Erin and David were wide-eyed; they felt a bit overwhelmed and frightened. It must have shown on their faces because the doctor put her hand on Erin's shoulder. "Now, don't be afraid; I'm only telling you this to prepare you should something happen. Though, if you can climb Arthur's seat and fly around the world in only a few days, I'm sure you'll be fine. I would imagine if you were going to miscarry, you would have done so by now. I was told that you've been under quite a lot of stress since conception, so I do want you to be aware of your body. I want you to call this clinic as soon as you can if you notice any of these symptoms." She named off a long list of things to look for including vaginal bleeding, severe headaches, pain or cramping in the lower abdomen, changes in vision, and decreased fetal activity once it starts moving, among other things. "They are warning signs and should not be dismissed or ignored. You will be sent home with all of this information, so don't worry about remembering any of it," she said.

Erin shook her head, trying to clear it a little; it was a lot of stuff to digest in such a short amount of time. "I have a question," she said. "Would you be willing to lift the ban on flying if it's just from London to Edinburgh and if it's not frequent? We need to go back to—" She didn't know what David wanted to share with people about their private lives, but she needed a reasonable explanation for wanting to fly instead of traveling by train again.

"We'll be retrieving my children for their summer holidays this weekend," David inserted for her.

"It's just that the train is so tedious and takes so long," Erin said.

"How long will you be staying in Edinburgh before heading back to London?" Doctor Jill asked.

"Three days, I reckon," David said.

"I guess that will be okay but the more time in between flights, the better, so if it's possible to stay longer, I'd suggest doing so," she said.

Erin sighed with relief. "Taking one elementary school, one high school, and two middle school-age kids on a long train ride doesn't seem like a pleasant afternoon, no matter how amazing they are," she said and smiled at David.

"I can imagine. I have a thirteen-year-old, and just having him to deal with on a train wouldn't be much fun after an hour or so," Doctor Jill said sympathetically. "So, tell me, Erin, what were your Fertilis Defect symptoms before starting treatments?" Erin explained her symptoms, and the doctor typed everything into the computer. "And did you plan to conceive?"

Erin looked at her with her eyebrows raised. "Ah, no. I was told I was infertile; it was during my first treatment session that it happened. I didn't even think to use birth control."

"Alright; and have you had any episodes since starting the treatments?"

Erin looked at David. "I had one a few days after starting them. It was the worst one I'd ever had, but I haven't had any since."

"When did you say you started treatments, mid-May? And how far apart were your episodes at that time?"

"They varied, usually it was about a month apart, but I started having minor ones in between the big ones," Erin said.

"So, it's been over five weeks since you've had symptoms then?"

"Yes, but I did notice… well, we didn't—I didn't have a treatment for five days in a row. That's when I had the thing on Arthur's seat. We'd gone ten days without… when we went home after our first session, and I seemed fine; before I knew I was pregnant. I was tired after the first week, but it wasn't that bad. Oh, and just recently, I am experiencing fainting spells and start to hyperventilate much easier than ever before in my life. I think the fainting and hyperventilating are brought on by extreme stress, though. I wonder if the pregnancy... or the advancement of it, is affecting the treatments, though I haven't had any of my usual F.D. symptoms."

"Have you had any more extreme fatigue since Arthur's seat?"

"No, but I did hyperventilate yesterday... and... this morning," Erin said.

Dr. Westin looked at her, her eyebrows raised. "And what do you think brought them on?"

Erin didn't want to talk about it and looked at David, who shrugged. "Well, I... found some... things that his late wife had been hiding. They were really bad, and, well, I lost my composure. This morning, I learned that someone we know sold a revealing and horrible photo of me—I mean us... to a tabloid. I was afraid to leave the house and come here, knowing that people would have seen it."

"And you say you've never had that issue before now?" Doctor Westin asked.

"Yeah, but I've also never been under so much stress; everything seems to be going wrong at once. We can't seem to get out of this cycle of really crazy and most often bad things happening to us since we met, I guess, and it's just so stressful." Tears were now falling down Erin's face. She hadn't meant to cry, but the strain was taking its toll on her. David put his hand on her shoulder, and she leaned against him. "Otherwise, now that we're having treatments daily again, I don't feel the exhaustion anymore," she said.

The doctor looked at her and then at David. "Perhaps seeing a therapist or a counselor might help you to deal with all the new things you're having to deal with? Being in a new relationship with... a celebrity. I imagine it would be full of stress, and getting it all out would be healthier than keeping it inside of you," she said gently, handing Erin a tissue.

"I'm sorry for crying; I've been crying at the drop of a hat lately, and I never used to cry! I'll consider a therapist, thank you," she said as Doctor Jill continued typing.

"And the fainting? Do you know what might have been causing that?"

"I think it was just from standing too quickly and then with the stress on top of it—"

"Well, it's common for women in their first trimester to faint or become dizzy when they stand. Your baby is taking quite a bit of your blood supply now, and your body is having to adjust. I think we should add those things to the list of what to call me about. You are likely to feel more and more tired throughout your pregnancy, but if it becomes severe again, make sure you call and I'll fit you in. Also, it might be a good idea to continue daily treatments as much as you are able. I know things happen and finding the time every day can be a challenge, but the more the better is my way of thinking."

"If we must," Erin said and smiled.

Dr. Westin asked her to lay back on the exam table. She asked her to unfasten her pants and lift her shirt, revealing her belly. She started probing Erin's belly with her fingers and then rolled a small cart with a machine on it over to them. "You should recognize this," she said to David, but he shook his head. "Didn't you go to the pre—I mean antenatal appointments for your other children?"

"No, I wasn't included in any of this with them. I would've liked to—but—" he said and shrugged.

"That's too bad," she said. "So then, I'll start from scratch. This is a fetal Doppler; it's what we are now going to try to hear your baby's heartbeat with. She turned the small machine on and then picked up a white bottle sitting next to it. She turned it upside down and hit it against her palm to get whatever was in the bottle to fall to the tip. "I'm sorry, but this will be cold." She squirted a plentiful amount of clear jelly onto Erin's lower belly, which made her inhale sharply but then smile.

"Whoo! You weren't kidding!" she gasped.

Doctor Westin then picked up something that looked like a flashlight or a small toy microphone. She touched the top of it to Erin's belly, and instantly they heard *whoosh whoosh—whoosh whoosh*—in a familiar steady rhythm from the machine's speaker. "That is your heartbeat, Erin; your baby's will be much faster."

She pressed the microphone into her belly and moved it this way and that, causing the machine to make lots of strange noises and feedback, until finally, they heard a faint *whow-whow-whow-whow-whow-whow* coming from the speakers.

"That's your baby's heartbeat," Doctor Westin said.

Erin looked up at David, who was standing next to her. He was trying to hide it, but she saw the tears welling up in his eyes. He looked down at her, which caused them to fall down his face. "That's one of the bonniest sounds I've ever heard," he said and kissed Erin's hand. "I love yeh."

Erin took his hand and smiled. "I love you too. It's just amazing; so fast and strong!"

"Yes, that's how it's supposed to sound. Your baby's heart rate is at about 135 to 140 beats per minute, which is very good." The doctor took some tissues from a box on the cart, wiped the gel off

Erin's belly, and then told her she could sit up. "Are you taking a prenatal vitamin?"

"Oh, no, I'm not. I didn't even think of it."

"You need to start taking one right away, and don't bother to get the cheap ones—" She looked at David and laughed, "Well, I suppose I don't need to worry about that with the two of you. Just make sure it has folic acid, which is vital, especially in the first trimester."

"Okay, we'll get some today," Erin said.

"Alright then, unless you have any questions for me, I'll send my nurse in with the information I mentioned earlier. Do you have more appointments scheduled?"

"Yes, I've booked five more, once per month. Is that enough?" David said.

"Yes, that's good. It was nice to meet you, now that you are awake and coherent, Erin, and you also, Mr.—"

"Please, call me David," he said.

"Okay, David, it was nice to see you again. I look forward to assisting you both in delivering a perfect, healthy baby in about seven months," she said and walked out of the room.

Erin stood, refastened her pants, and sighed. They looked at each other, hardly able to believe what they'd just heard. "We've just heard our bairn's heartbeat," David said, then wrapped his arms around her and kissed her hair.

She hugged him back and relaxed in his arms. "I love you so much, and I'm glad you were here!"

The nurse came back with a folder of pamphlets and printed pages. "If you have any questions, please ring the number on the folder, and I'll see you in a month's time." She led Erin and David down the hall to a sign which read, 'lobby,' and then walked away.

David put the mask back on, and they walked out into the crowd of mostly women, unscathed and not bothered. "I may have tae bring one of these masks everawhere I go from now on! Et worked brilliantly," David said.

"Aye, and then I'll start calling you Michael Jackson," she said and laughed.

They returned home after stopping to pick up a few bottles of prenatal vitamins. They were excited about the baby yet wary of what Kitty might have found while they were gone. "This has been a crazy day! I hope it gets better!" Erin said as they walked in the door. They couldn't see or hear Kitty, so they climbed the stairs and still didn't hear her.

"Kitty?" David called out.

"Up 'ere, sir," they heard coming from the attic.

David followed Erin up the steep stairs to the uppermost floor, which had once housed the female servants of the family who'd built the house.

"Oh! I love this!" Erin said. "This is the kind of place where you find a stack of love letters like you did in *Houlihan's Flat*! I could spend hours up here."

David laughed, which was nice to hear. Even Kitty turned around when she heard it. "I believe ye'll get tae do just that, darling," he said, thinking they'd be spending at least the rest of the day scouring it. They went to Kitty, who was digging through a stack of boxes that looked like they'd been untouched for decades.

"I've been frew every inch of the children's rooms, sir, and I've found nofing else. I'm nearly finished 'ere as well. I'm sorry, Ms. Erin, but I've not found any love let'ers," she said with a grin.

Erin smiled and noticed the contents of some of the boxes. "Are those Halloween costumes?" she asked David.

"I dinnae ken," he said and picked up a wig that had fallen out. "Looks as though they are." He lifted it for her to see.

"Remind me to come up here when we get home from—" She smiled and looked at David. "Home—that's nice. What was I saying? Oh, yes, home from Scotland," she smiled even bigger. "That sounds nice too! I think I have a game idea to play with the children!"

Kitty smiled at them. "I know it's not my place, but I'm so glad ta see someone with an 'eart full of fun living 'ere."

"Me too, Kitty," David said.

Chapter Twenty-Six

ROGER'S LONG HAUL

As soon as he finished his supper, Roger excused himself from the table and returned to the garage. He wanted to change his clothes and at least wash his face before leaving for that high and mighty school. After washing his face, he combed his hair, which was getting a bit too long for his taste; he made a mental note to get a haircut the next day.

A few minutes later, he was in the SUV, putting a CD into the player; "Queen's Greatest Hits" would make the drive a lot less tedious. He pulled out of the garage and backed down the drive, stopping at the closed gate. *"You need a remote-control opener for that,"* Erin had said. He smiled at the memory as he got out, opened the heavy iron gate, then returned to the vehicle, and backed out, only to get out to close it again.

He knew he thought about Erin far too often, and if he didn't nip the innocent thoughts in the bud, they would turn into something not only inappropriate but they'd be much more difficult to stop. He decided to think about what the woman from the F. D. Registry would be like; would she be anything like his late wife? Would she be plump and pretty or slender and elegant?

He'd seen slender and elegant with Susannah, and it wasn't to his taste. She'd been sickly and haughty and not in any way pleasant; he'd honestly prefer a full-figured, curvy woman to a gaunt bag of bones. He wondered how old she was. *Why didn't I think tae ask anathin' about her whilst speaking with them?* Would she be fair and freckled or dark and swarthy? Straight hair or curly; blue or brown eyes; red hair or blonde?

He started subconsciously constructing an image of what she might look like, which made him smile and then miss his turn.

"Damn!" he said as he turned onto the next road to make his way back around. He'd also forgotten to turn up the volume on the stereo, so he turned the dial and heard the end lines of *Somebody to Love.* Instead of starting the disk over at track one, he let it go to the next song.

As he merged onto the motorway, he sang along to *Fat Bottomed Girls* with Freddie Mercury.

Before he knew it, he was more than halfway to the school, and by the end of the last song, he was only a few miles away. He would start the disk from the beginning when the children were with him, knowing how much they liked to sing along with *We Will Rock You.* It was something he knew for a fact Susannah would have hated, which made it all the more fun. He'd been driving back and forth to the boarding school for six years; since Peter had started, at age eight. Each time he picked them up, he would prepare that song for them to sing along with as they headed down the long drive away from the dismal place.

He found a stall in the car park, and as he walked toward the main building, he saw David's four children standing at the top of the concrete landing, their luggage in a pile next to them. That was something new; in the past, they'd been kept in the office until he came inside to sign them out. He went to Peter, who was looking at his shoes with his hands in his pockets. "What's all this?" he asked, not understanding.

"Our Headmaster told us Dad doesn't want us to come back next term, so he said we could wait outside," the boy said quietly.

Roger was angry; his face was burning with rage. He wanted to barge into the building, making as much fuss as possible and give that bastard headmaster a piece of his mind. More than that, he wanted to remove those poor, innocent children from the retched institution. "A'right then; good riddance to bad rubbish, I say," Roger said.

The four of them looked up at him with astonishment; they had never heard Roger give a personal opinion so boldly and didn't know how to react. He took the heaviest of the luggage, and the boys carried the rest to the SUV. Some things were strapped securely to the roof and the rest stuffed in the back or under their feet.

The mood wasn't very lively as they all piled in and put on their seatbelts. Roger wondered if they would even want to hear the song, but as soon as they started down the drive, Daniel began chanting, "Rock you! Rock you!" Roger laughed. Peter had essentially gotten them all booted out of school, and then they'd been stood on the stoop to be humiliated, but they knew he wouldn't pass judgment or punish them.

He pushed the audio power button, and the kids started clapping and stomping along with the music. They didn't know all the words, but when it got to the chorus, they raised their voices and forgot about good manners, class, or being well-behaved children; they just sang and laughed and smiled. After the first three songs, Roger turned off the music, and they sat for a while in their own thoughts, Peter looking out the window.

"Yeh know, Peter, yer dad told me what happened, and I know yeh got in trouble for et, but I'm proud of you for stickin' up for him and Erin," Roger said.

"Thank you," Peter said simply.

"I reckon ye're also worried and unsure of what'll happen for yer schoolin' next year," he said, and the teen shrugged his shoulders. "You should also know I'm proud of yer da' for stickin' up for you and takin' yeh out of tha' horrible place." Peter didn't say anything as he stared out the window at the passing hedges.

"Did yeh no' hear me? Yer dad went and—"

"I'm not in the mood for another lecture, Roger, please," he said.

"Another— What part of 'I'm proud of yeh' makes et a lecture?" Roger said.

"I don't want to talk about it; any of it," Peter said hotly and put his earbuds in.

———

The rest of the drive was silent. When they pulled up to the house, Roger got out to open the gate.

"That wasn't very nice, Peter; he was only trying—" Charlie began, but Roger got back in.

Peter sighed deeply and said, "I'm sorry, Roger, but do you know how it is to see your dad and his partner in a newspaper—like that?"

Roger paused for a moment. "No, Peter, I dinnae ken at all, but I consider yer da' and Erin to be ma mates, and et wasnae pleasant tae see them like tha' for me either. I reckon et's traumatic for you tae see things like tha, but yer da' has done somthin' about et, don't yeh see? Instead of jest apologizin' and tip-toein' around the situation wi' you and tha' boy, he's tried his best tae help yeh. I ken ye're too young tae understand, but takin' yeh out was brave, not cowardly. He kens well enough you were punished unfairly. Remember, he was sent tae tha' school as well, and he knows all about the headmaster and the things tha' go on there."

"Why then, if he knows how unpleasant it is, did he send us there, to begin with?" Peter said in a huff.

Roger took a deep breath as if deciding what to say next. Peter was about to open the door when the older man put his hand on his forearm and turned to look at them all. "I'm goin' tae tell yeh why, but yeh may not tell anaone I've told yeh. No', because I'm lyin', but because I dinnae want yer da' tae think I've overstepped ma place, yeh ken? Now, you already know tha' some of the ways of yer mother were no' verra nice?" They nodded. "Well, I reckon, and et's only my opinion, mind, that she didn't ken how tae deal wi' children in any way whatsoever, so once you became too much for her and the nanny, *she* sent yeh off. I'm no tryin' tae be unkind, but she was no' the motherin' sort, no' like our Erin. So, she sent yeh off tae be raised by a system instead of parents. I know for a fact yer da' didn't want yeh tae go there, but yer mother had a way of gettin' yer da' tae do things tha' I dinnae understand."

He stopped talking and watched to see if anyone was upset by what he'd said. They were all nodding and listening patiently, so he kept going. "Now tha' she's no longer here, God rest her soul, yer da' is finally able tae do wi' yeh what HE wants, and has **always** wanted, which is tae be wi' you. Tae have yeh near tae him and Erin, who I can tell loves yeh as though you were her own flesh and blood.

Another thing for yeh tae think on is tha' you'll want tae make sure tae be good tae our Erin, you willnae be findin' anaone like her again!"

They all smiled at the thought of Erin. "We love her a lot, and we're happy Dad has found her, or at least I am," Rosie said from the backseat. The rest of them, even Peter, nodded their agreement.

"I ken you do. I know, in many ways, yeh have et rough havin' a famous person for yer da'; et's somethin' you didn't choose, but yer da' is a good man who's tryin' tae do what's right and good for yeh. He has no control over what the paparazzi and money mongers are willin' tae do for the money shot of him, so please try tae understand. If et weren't for his line of work, you wouldnae have the nice things yeh do, and yeh might have been born wishin' yeh did." He paused to let it all sink in. "Tha's all I'll say. I wanted you tae know so yeh didn't take et out on yer da'. Please be patient whilst he tries tae get things in order, and do tell him, truthfully, what ye'd like him tae do as far as schoolin' if he asks yeh."

"I'm hungry! When can we eat?" Daniel said from the back.

Roger smiled and shook his head. "I'm sure Millie will have somethin' for yeh. Go on, and I'll bring yer things in for yeh."

Everyone but Peter got out and headed to the house; he stayed in the front seat, looked at Roger for a few seconds, and then back out the window. "Thank you for telling us... about Mum, I mean. I—we all know she wasn't a good mother, and we know Erin will be. I'll try not to be upset at Dad. Do you really think all he's ever wanted was to be with us?"

"I know et's true, Peter."

The young man frowned, having his own reasons for doubting it. "I know you're right; he can't stop things from happening, but it can be crushing for us when it does." He opened the door and got out, closing it gently behind him.

———

Roger sat for a minute and watched the young man slowly walk into the house; he could hear the dogs going mental with the arrival of the children. *He's so verra mature. Poor thing, havin' tae see tha' sort of thing at his age,* he thought sadly as he turned the ignition off. He unloaded the luggage and began delivering the children's things to their respective rooms. *I'm so glad they have Erin now.* On his way down the stairs after his last load of luggage, he met Peter going up.

"Do you know when my dad will be arriving here?" the young man asked.

"I'll be collecting them from the airport tomorrow night," Roger said, and Peter nodded.

"Alright, would you please tell him I'd like to speak with him when you see him?"

Roger smiled at how adult he was becoming. "Of course I will," he said and headed back to the garage to park the SUV and give it a spot clean, if necessary.

Chapter Twenty-Seven

DREAMS

In the morning, Erin ran to the toilet again to be sick; David was already in his closet getting dressed and preparing for the ads he would be doing that day. He heard her retching and felt his stomach lurch a bit. *Poor thing,* he thought for the umpteenth time since she'd started having morning sickness. He heard the toilet flush and poked his head around the doorway to ask if she was okay.

"I'm as good as I can be with… well, I'm fine. No use in complaining; it won't make it any better. You know what, I had a dream sometime this morning; it was about the cabin up north."

"Oh? I'd like to hear about it. Come sit in here with me," he said and took his suit coat off the burgundy, tufted, leather, Queen Anne-style armchair. She sat, crossed her legs, and shivered; the leather was cold on her bare body. David went out and brought her a blanket from the end of the bed.

She wrapped herself in it and began, "Okay, let me think. First, I was at a recording studio where Sting and some other guy were supposed to be recording something but instead they were goofing around and acting like they were doing the Tango. Then, it changed so that I was someplace where people were actually dancing. There were several men who wanted to dance with me; one of them was Viggo Mortensen and one was another actor that I don't know the name of but he was in a movie I saw last year.

"Anyway, you were there, and I knew you really wanted to dance with me, but Viggo asked me first, and well... it was Viggo Mortensen! So, we started dancing, but then I saw you. You looked so sad, and I knew I was supposed to be dancing with you—it was what I was meant to do, like fate or something.

"Mental note, never introduce you to Viggo Mortensen!" David said.

"You know him?"

"No, but if we ever become acquainted, I'll need to remember this," he said and laughed.

"Next, we were at the cabin up north; we were in Neela and parked right up close to the front door. We were about to walk inside, and... there was a young boy with us; he was about four, and I recognized him as one of the kids I had on my bus years ago. He was a bit of a stinker but not a bad kid. He walked in with us, and I noticed a small bag of fruit snacks—you'd probably call them jelly babies or wine gums, but that doesn't matter. At one point, I saw him eating them, even though I hadn't told him he could. I was pretending to scold him about it, then I took him up in my arms and sat, holding him like a baby and laughing. The real kid probably wouldn't have let me do that; he was always on the go, but this one did. I knew we were fostering him or keeping him for someone, and all he needed was love.

"The next thing I knew, we were having a get-together at the cottage with a small group of friends. You were standing at a barbeque grill with an apron on, cooking food and serving drinks to our friends, but an evil-looking man showed up. He had an evil-sounding name, but I can't remember what it was, so I'll call him Lucifer. Lucifer had brought a bunch of people with him and just walked into our cottage. I knew you had to let him do whatever he wanted to do for some reason—as though he owned the property or something.

"I was sitting at a picnic table, watching you and talking with our friends, when he came over and started playing death metal music. He and his friends sat at a table behind me, and suddenly my friends became his. The lady sitting next to me started licking my forearm, it was gross and weird, but I wasn't scared until she started acting like she was going to bite me, then I called out your name; you dropped everything and came to me.

"We decided to let Lucifer take over the party, and you asked him, very politely, for permission, 'if he didn't mind' for us to return to the house and have some privacy. He nodded, and we walked back inside the cottage. That's when I woke up." She sat there for a moment, and he looked at her with his eyebrows raised.

"Wow! You remember all that from your dream! I really hope none of it comes to pass!"

Erin's eyes twinkled, "Dancing with Viggo Mortensen wouldn't be too bad," she said and laughed while he shook his head. "I think Lucifer, looked a tiny little bit like—what was his name—Oscar; the one who—took Bran away."

"...took Bran away," David finished with her.

Erin felt a shiver run up her neck. "I know it's illogical, Jim, especially after the last part of the dream, but I think you—I mean we, should rebuild the cottage," she said, and David looked at her as if she were mad.

"Jim? Who's Jim?" He looked slightly worried, but Erin laughed.

"Jim... Captain James T. Kirk—Spock... it's illogical? Star Trek?"

David rolled his eyes. "You are a verra peculiar person, my love, and I've been thinkin' about that. Et would be nice tae have a place tae bring the children again. I dinnae ken if the foundation is still good; if it is, we can rebuild on top of it. We'll have tae look into et, but for now, I've gotta get goin'."

Erin stood and let the blanket fall to the floor.

David gave her a look that screamed, 'LUST!' "Ach, tha's not fair!" He stood in front of her and touched her face. "I'm gonna need tae postpone this for later today, hen, but I'll look forward tae seein' yeh then."

"I'll look forward to it too." She took his hand and placed it on her breast. He wrapped his hand around it and gently squeezed. Closing her eyes, she inhaled and then gave him a peck on the cheek. He tried to kiss her lips, but she turned her head.

"You don't want to do that! Morning breath *and* morning sickness? It's just not a good idea to kiss me right now." He grabbed hold of her ass and pressed himself against her leg. She could feel him through his trousers, hard and ready for her, and longed to release him from his trouser prison. Instead, she allowed him to kiss her with their mouths closed.

"I want yeh so badly, darling! If we have any time whatsoever when I get home, I'll be bringin' yeh up here straight away." He reluctantly let her go, then left the room.

She flopped onto the bed and closed her eyes. He turned her on so much she was tempted to please herself a little bit, like she used to need to do with Todd, but decided to wait for David to get home. Being with him would be so much better than anything she could do to herself. Instead, she got up, brushed her teeth, and took a shower.

David returned home tired of smiling and posing. He wanted to sit and veg in front of the telly, but he had to get ready to go back to Edinburgh; the plane wouldn't wait for them. He opened the front door and saw Erin talking with Kitty about something. She turned and smiled at him, and Kitty left the room. "I'm so glad you're home! I missed you today!" she said and went to him.

She wrapped her arms around his waist and laid her head on his chest. He could smell her scent; he still thought of it as her shampoo, even though he'd been told it was pheromones and was instantly revitalized. He looked at his watch; it was half-past one, which meant they had three and a half hours until they had to be on the plane.

"Ye're what I've been lookin' forward to all day; come upstairs with me?" He kissed her passionately and then took her hand.

She laughed and followed after him. "Okay," she said.

As soon as the bedroom door was closed, they started peeling layers of clothing off themselves and each other. "Come with me," he said and pulled her by the hand into his closet. He set her on the leather wingback chair and knelt in front of her.

"Oooh! That's cold!" she said, and then as he started kissing the insides of her thighs, it changed to, "Oooh! That's nice!" She lay back and allowed him to touch her and kiss her. He entered her with his fingers, making her gasp. "Darling—this feels amazing, but we don't have much time—" He took his fingers out and touched her clitoris. "Never mind, I don't care anymore; we can walk to Scotland for all I care."

He started moving in large circles, watching her as he hit a spot that felt especially good. She was getting closer, breathing heavier, and little moans and gasps started escaping from her mouth. Just like that, he felt her start to clench and knew it was his turn, so he stood her up and bent her over the chair. He could still feel her pulsing around his cock as he entered her. He thrust, making her moan again and again until he felt it once more, that strong pulsing and twitching her body did when she had an orgasm. He loved the feeling of her releasing, which usually caused him to climax too.

They were both out of breath and wishing they had time to lay with their naked bodies together for a nap, but they had to get going or they'd miss the plane for certain. "I set out some of the basics I've noticed you always pack; I hope it helps," she said.

He saw his things laid neatly on the end of the bed and hugged her. "Thank yeh, love; ye're so thoughtful." He took a small travel case from a shelf in his closet and put them into it.

"I'm already packed; I used one of Susannah's small travel cases. I only needed to get dressed to be ready to go.

David watched as she checked her hair and makeup while he brushed his teeth and combed his hair. He smiled at her. "I love standin' next tae yeh at these sinks; ye're lovely tae look at," he said and then leaned over to kiss her.

"You're not all that bad yourself," she said and then looked away, frowning. "People are going to recognize me, aren't they, especially when they see me with you?"

David smoothed an errant hair and smiled. "Aye. They will, but just think of all the jealous women out there who envy you! Ach, that sounded egotistical, but yeh ken there are women out there who would love tae be you. And for those who think anything unkind, who cares what they think? I love you Erin March, and nothin' is gonna change that. Also, we dinnae need tae be secretive or hide anymore; I can hold yer hand and even kiss yeh whenever I please!" he said with a twinkle in his eye. "Beware!"

"I'd like that—having you kiss me in public—or I think I would. I reserve the right to change my mind. And of course you're right; who cares what people think, but it's hard to think that way right now," she said.

There was a knock on the door. "Mr. Elliott, sir, your car is waiting for you and Ms. Erin. Do ya need 'elp wiv your luggage?" Kitty said through the closed door.

David opened it and smiled at her. "No, Kitty. Thank you. Have a nice weekend off. We'll see you on Monday, most likely; otherwise, I'll text yeh," he said. He reached out for Erin's hand, and they walked down the stairs together. At the bottom of the steps, he grabbed her ass, making her laugh. "How about that? Can I do that in public?" he asked and opened the front door for her.

Erin shook her head. "Absolutely not!" she said emphatically and then got into the hired car.

Arriving at the airport, they rushed through the terminal, making it to the departure gate with only ten minutes to spare, which was cutting it too close for anyone's comfort. Winded and laughing, they found their seats and got settled in.

Chapter Twenty-Eight

RETURN TO EDINBURGH

David and Erin's flight was only an hour and a half long and touched down at 5:55, just as their tickets said it would. They made it through to the arrivals gate and saw Roger with a cardboard sign with **'March'** in block letters written on it. Erin laughed out loud and hugged him. "Alright, David, I'll see you later; Roger and I need to be going now." She lifted his arm around her shoulders, and they turned, walking away.

"But he always gets the girl! Et's not fair," David said, and they all laughed as he caught up and they walked together through the terminal toward the car park. As they rounded a corner, a middle-aged man stopped them asking for a photo. David smiled and said, "Sure."

The man shook his head and pointed to Erin. "With her, please," he said.

Erin didn't know what to say. Why would anyone want a photo with her? She shrugged and took a selfie with the man, who was beaming. He thanked her and went on his way. By then there was a group of people standing around waiting for a picture with whomever the celebrity was. A woman asked for a photo, and again,

David said, "Sure." The woman was elated but asked if Erin could be in it as well, so she obliged.

Three more sets of people wanted their picture taken with David and Erin, but the fourth wanted nothing to do with Erin at all. She stared dreamy-eyed at David, not taking her eyes off him, even when she snapped the selfie with her selfie stick. Then, she began to look at his lips as if she were about to try to kiss him, so Erin stepped in. "I'm sorry, but Mr. Elliott needs to—"

The woman shot daggers out of her eyes at her. She continued hanging on David and licking her lips as if getting ready for her chance. Erin could see David was agitated after he tried to move away from her, but she held onto his arm with a death grip. "I'm sorry, but I really do need to—" he began.

She stopped suddenly and managed to catch him off guard, swinging him around as he lost his balance and tried not to fall on top of her. She pressed her lips to his and tried using her tongue, but both Roger and Erin got her off him. When a security officer walked by to see what the commotion was about, David accused her of sexual assault and asked him to take her away. The man grabbed the woman by the arm and ushered her away though she pulled and tugged, trying to get back to David.

David, Erin, and Roger booked it and managed to get to the SUV before anyone else could molest them. David kept wiping his mouth and frowning. "God, that was disgusting! What made her think she could do that tae me? I'm sorry, Erin. I didn't know—"

Erin smiled at him. "We'll wash your face when we get to your mum's. She was a sicko; there's no way you could've known she'd do that, though I did see her eyeing up your lips—that's when I tried to intervene."

"I'm glad I dinnae have tha' problem! What a foul twat!" Roger said.

"Well said!" David agreed. "Argg, I just wannae spread hand sanitizer all over ma face!"

"Oh, before I forget," Roger said, "young, Master Peter has informed me tha' he would like tae have a word with his father when he arrives... that is if he doesnae mind."

David's eyebrows went up and Roger laughed. "A'right, perhaps he didn't say it quite like tha', but he was so grown up and formal about et."

"Thanks for the message," David said. "I'll make sure he has a chance tae do that."

They arrived at Owlgate, happy to be somewhere safe from molestation. David went straight to the WC to wash his face. The stress from the last few days was catching up to them, and between turning the house inside-out, rushing to catch the plane, and posing with so many people, they were knackered.

The reunion with the children was a happy one; they crowded around Erin, each wanting her attention and not bothering much with David when he returned from washing his face. "Erin, I drew this for you!" Rosie said and handed her a picture of a house with a stone fence and a big yellow sun in the sky.

"Oh, that's lovely, Rosie! Thank you!" she said.

"That's where I'd like us to live someday... together, as a family, when you and Daddy get married." Erin smiled and hugged her, looking at David.

"I wrote you a letter, Erin, but I sent it to London, so you won't get it until we get home," Charlie said proudly.

"Oh, Charlie! That's so sweet of you! I can't wait to get it. It'll be the first piece of mail sent to me at that address! You are just so sweet." She hugged him and kissed the top of his head. She looked at David standing nearby; he was smiling, obviously enjoying how much his kids liked her.

Daniel approached her. "Hi, Erin. I'm glad you're here," he said quietly, then under his breath, he said, "Now can I play with Gertie?"

Erin knew Gertie was his favorite dog and that he loved to run around the house and garden with her. She laughed and tousled his hair. "It's nice to see you, Dan. Go on and play." He smiled up at her, revealing his set of dimples, and then ran off, Gertie following at his heels.

Peter stepped up to her and smiled. "Hi, Erin! I agree with Dan; I'm glad you're here, and I've... missed you, actually. I'm chuffed that you're coming back to London with us as well," he said, sounding so sincere.

"Thank you, Peter! I've missed you too," she said, accepting a hug from him.

"I thought... perhaps... we can have a cricket match together... at the park?"

He sounded so hopeful; how could she refuse. "That sounds like fun, but you'll have to teach me the rules," she said.

"I can do that," he said and flashed his father's brilliant smile at her.

"I've missed you all so much!" she said to the three remaining Elliott children. "Thank you for the warm welcome; I can't tell you how much it means to me, but I think your dad might be feeling a bit left out." She pointed to him standing in the doorway, holding a large shoebox, watching his children and fiancée bonding.

Peter turned and looked at him, smiling brightly, plainly happy to see him. "Hi, Dad," he said and then turned back to Erin, which made David put his hands up as if to say, 'what?' Erin laughed, and Peter gave her another hug. The young man then turned to face his dad again, laughing. "Only joking," he said and went to him, giving him a quick hug. "Dad, can we talk?" he asked.

"Yes, we can, son—" he began, but Peter was already heading to his room.

———

David set the shoebox on the sideboard at the bottom of the stairs and followed his eldest son, having no idea what he might want to talk to him about. When he entered the bedroom he saw Peter staring at the floor, looking suddenly shy and humble. "Dad, I—I'm sorry for getting myself excluded, and I wanted to thank you for not being angry." He wrapped his arms around his dad's waist, and David held him.

"Ach, Peter, I'm proud of you for standin' up for us. I know those pictures were dreadful, and you shouldn't have had to see them. Ye're so much more of an adult every time I see yeh—you; it almost breaks ma—my heart." He was still embracing his eldest boy and didn't want to let go. "There's something we've brought with us from London that I'd like tae—to show you. Will yeh—you please—"

"Dad, it's a'right if you speak like Gran in front of me. I was just sore before... when I—well, it's okay now," Peter interrupted him and stepped back from the hug.

"Good, et's exhaustin', tryin' tae choose ma words," David said. "Let's go down, and I'll show yeh what I've brought from London."

They walked back downstairs and joined the rest of the family, sitting around a small fire in the inglenook fireplace. They were laughing at something Daniel had just said; that is, everyone was laughing except Daniel. Erin turned and smiled at the two of them as they entered the room and patted either side of the sofa she was sitting on. David sat on one side of her and Peter on the other.

Erin nudged Peter with her shoulder and smiled. "It really is good to see you all again," she said.

Peter smiled at her. "I've truly missed you as well, Erin," he responded.

David heard their conversation and felt as though his heart would burst. He cleared his throat and got everyone's attention. "Erin, would you mind fetchin' the box from the sideboard?" he asked. She left the sitting room and he continued. "Erin found somethin' at the house in London the other day, and I want tae share et with yeh." Returning with a long shoebox meant for tall boots, Erin handed it to him then went back to her seat.

"There were things I wasn't made aware of whilst yer mother was alive. She kept things from me, and I am just now learnin' how... unwell she was... in her head. I'm sorry tae say that, but et's true." He held up the shoebox. "Children, inside this box is every card or letter ye've sent me from Carnoch over the years. They were hidden in a locked drawer, and most of them weren't even opened."

The children's eyes were wide, and so were Annis's, Millie's, and Roger's. "So, what ye're sayin' is she hid them from you all these years? And ye've no' seen any of them?" Annis said. She was flushing red, starting at her neck and working its way up like a thermometer.

David nodded, and his eyes filled with tears. "Aye," he whispered. "I didn't know about them. I never read how yeh missed me, or that yeh wanted me tae write yeh back. You must've thought I didn't care or was too busy for yeh, but that's no' true. I have missed you... every single day since yer mother sent you away from me—tae that wretched school."

Every person in the room was in tears, so Millie passed around a box of tissues. Even Daniel was crying with his knees pulled up to his chest and a dog lying close beside him. "I want... no, need tae open them and read them out, so they aren't forgotten anamore, and so we can share them together. There are too many to get through tonight, but for as long as et takes, I want tae set here with yeh every night and have this time with yeh."

Peter looked at his dad, and a tear escaped his soft blue eyes; it ran down his cheek and dropped onto his clean blue t-shirt, leaving a dark round spot where it landed.

David took out the earliest one from Peter.

Dear DaD,
I am at scool nowe, and I miss you anD mummy anD nanny.
Plese writ too me allot.
I LoVE you
Peter Elliott AgE 8

He handed the letter to Peter, who laughed at his handwriting and spelling, then he looked up at his dad. "I'm glad you've brought these. Open another, please?"

He opened another one from Peter, the one that had the pressed flower in it, and then one from Charlie.

Hi Dad.

I Miss You. I Love You. I wish I coulde Give you a Hug!! Dan said he is to old for Hugs, but We are the Same age and Im Not to old for Hugs! Can someone be to Old for Hugs, daddy? I will never be to Old for Hugs. Hugs make me feel better. I wish I had more Hugs from you daddy. Please Write to me.

Love CHarLiE ELLiOtt Age 8

Everyone laughed at how many times he'd said the word 'hug.' When he was done reading, David held out his arms to him. "No, Charlie, you can never be too old for hugs," he said, and the boy went to him. David held on as long as his son wanted, and Charlie needed a very long hug. He also whispered, "I love you, Charlie. I'm so sorry I never wrote back."

"Mine next!" Dan said, so David reached into the box and pulled out a letter from him. It was stained with dirt and something that, at one time, was probably sticky. "Sorry about the jam; I forgot to wash my hands," he said.

Dad

I want you To writE to mE. PLEasE. I nEvEr got any maiL bEfore, and I want somEthig to opEn LiKE thE OthER boys HavE.

DaniEl EllIOtt AgE 8

David read one from Rosie next; this had been her first year in boarding school, so there weren't many from her. He opened it, and inside was a drawing of a cat with a crown.

Deer Daddy,

This is A CAT. I Love CATs and I want A cat. Cats are flufy and soft. Can we pleese get A CAT?

Love, Rosie Mae Elliott Age 8

P.S. This CAT has A crown. It is A princess.

P.P.S. I mis You and I Love you and rite back to ME and tell me if you like my CAT.

David got on the floor where Rosie was sitting and looked closely at the cat. He pointed out details about the drawing and then smiled brightly. "Rosebud, this cat has five legs!" he said.

She shook her head. "No it doesn't, Daddy."

David pointed to each one, and Rosie's eyes grew wide. Then she laughed, and the whole room joined in with her, laughing and crying at how heartbreaking the whole thing was.

"Rosie, I love this drawing. I think et's beautiful. Thank yeh for sendin' et tae me," he said and then opened another one from Charlie.

Dear Daddy,

I miSS you very much. How are You? I loSt a tooth today! Dan Said the Tooth Farey iSn't real, but he LieS a lot.

I can't wait to See you at ChriStmaSS. May I come down for the party thiS year?

Love, your Son,

Charlie Elliott Age 8 1/2

"Will we have a Christmas party this year, Dad?" he asked.

"I'm not sure. Yer mother was the one who organized them, so I think we may have to take a year off," David said, not wanting to overwhelm Erin with the task.

The next letter was from Daniel.

Dad.

I did NOT get a letter from You today. I Asked you too Send one. That makes me Mad at you.

Please Write to me.

Dan Elliott

P.S. I still love you.

David was choked-up at that one. He looked at Dan, who still had his face buried in his knees. "Dan, yeh have no idea how gutted I am that I made yeh so upset. I wish with all ma heart that I could go back and write tae yeh every week."

Daniel kept his head down and nodded.

He read several more, and then it was time for bed. The children went to him and had a nice, long group hug. After a minute or so, Rosie pulled Erin down to join them so that they were a pile of Elliotts and one March on the floor. Erin, somehow, 'accidentally' tickled Rosie, then Charlie, and then Dan, which had them all laughing. She wasn't sure Peter would want her to do that, but he was smiling, so she pinched his knee, which got him giggling. That made them a laughing pile of Elliotts and one March.

David and Erin walked upstairs with the children after they'd said goodnight to their grandma, Millie, and Roger. David overheard Charlie tell Rosie that he 'couldn't wait for the next night so they could open more letters,' and that 'it was like Christmas!' Erin joined David as the three younger ones were tucked in and kissed on their cheek or forehead; Daniel even allowed her to hug him.

"I said that to Charlie to make him angry. I don't actually think I'm too old for hugs, I just don't like too many of them," he said in her ear.

David went into Peter's room alone. The boy watched the door after him and frowned. "Why didn't Erin come with you?"

David raised his eyebrows and went to the door so that he'd be heard down the hall. "Erin? Would you join us, please," he called to her.

Erin came in and sat on the edge of the bed behind David. "I would love to," she said and smiled at Peter.

"Dad, I need to tell you that the last few letters I sent to you were... not very nice. I was upset because you never wrote back," he said, and David put his hand on his arm.

"Et's all right, son; I understand. I would be angry at me as well!"

Peter looked at Erin and then at his dad. "Sometimes I hate Mum," he said quietly. "She was a terrible person; she never once told me that she missed me... or any of us! She didn't love us, and I—hate her!" He pulled his knees up and hugged them, burying his face in the blanket that was covering them.

David pulled his boy close as he sobbed. "I must tell yeh the truth, son. I didn't know how... well, who yer mum really was until now, and there are times when I hate her as well, but I love you and your sister and brothers so verra, verra much."

"I know you do, Dad," Peter said, still sniffling. "Roger spoke to us in the car when we arrived yesterday. He helped us see why we shouldn't be angry at you. He's very smart, Roger. He said we should make sure to be good to Erin, as well, because she's awesome. Well, he didn't say it that way, but that's what I think. I'm sorry, Erin, for being angry and moody with you at first. I know now that you're a good person, and I am glad you're part of our family now."

———

Erin was shocked; she'd never heard a young man, especially a teenager, speak to an adult like that before, and still sniffling from when Peter started crying earlier, it broke her up even more. "All is forgiven and forgotten. I'm glad I'm part of this family more than I can say." She sniffed again and wiped her eyes with the back of her hand. "Thank you for accepting me." She felt like she was in a Hallmark movie; everything was all warm fuzzies and tearjerkers. "I'm going to get ready for bed now; you two finish saying goodnight." She bent and kissed Peter's forehead. "Goodnight, Peter."

As she headed back to David's room, her mind played, *'Goodnight, John Boy. Goodnight, Grandma. Goodnight, Mary Ellen. Goodnight, Ma. Goodnight, Elizabeth. Goodnight, Pa. Goodnight, Grandpa,'* and she smiled. She put on her pajamas thinking, *'Goodnight, David. Goodnight, Ann. Goodnight, Peter. Goodnight, Millie. Goodnight, Rosie. Goodnight, Charlie. Goodnight, Erin. Goodnight, Daniel. Goodnight, Roger.'* It was a nice thought.

———

Roger said goodnight to Annis and Millie then walked back to his flat. It occurred to him that he'd forgotten to tell David and Erin about his first treatment the next day. *I reckon it can wait till tomorrow*, he thought, and then got ready for bed. He looked in the bathroom mirror and examined his face; he was all wrinkles, and his skin looked leathery from years of not wearing sunscreen.

His hair was too long; he'd planned to get it cut but had forgotten all about it. *It probably doesnae matter much, anaway.* He stood back and looked at himself naked; he wasn't very muscular anymore, and much of his skin sagged, but he didn't think he looked too bad. He only hoped the woman he was meant to make love to would feel the same way. He got undressed and into his bed thinking about her, though as he fell asleep, she morphed into Erin again.

Chapter Twenty-Nine

A BUSY, BUSY DAY AT OWLGATE

Everyone at Owlgate woke up late, except for Millie and Annis. Millie was knocking on doors all morning trying to rouse people until eventually it worked. One by one, the household and their guests arrived at the table, droopy-eyed and seeking coffee.

———

Roger walked in looking like he was the one with morning sickness. "Woah, Roger! You look like you're hungover," Erin said.

He gave her a wry smile. "And yeh look lovely, as well, hen."

Erin laughed. "Sorry. I deserved that. I didn't mean—"

"Dinnae worry, I didn't sleep well last night," he said with a soft laugh.

"Worried about something, are you?" she said, teasingly.

"Actually, I was—"

He was interrupted by Millie who had come in with the last serving dish, filled with roasted tomatoes. "Ach, Roger, would yeh mind helpin' me in the kitchen for a moment?"

"Aye," he said and followed her out of the room. When he returned, Erin was in a conversation with Annis and David, so his news was forgotten again. At lunch, he meant to tell David, but everyone needed his attention, so he wasn't able to tell anyone.

The day wore on; at times it went so slow it felt like slow motion and at other times it flew. Before he knew it, it was five o'clock and he had to run up to the flat to take a shower and change his clothes. He'd been sitting on the back patio with David and Erin, drinking a cold Irn Bru and laughing at David as he recounted the offers of marriage he'd received before they'd boarded the train to London. He was just about to tell them about his match, who would be there at six, when he looked at his watch. He stood and ran, pell-mell, toward the garage, knocking his drink over, leaving Erin and David to stare after him.

———

"Well, that was sudden! Wonder what that's all about?" Erin said.

David was also curious; it wasn't like Roger to behave that way. "I'll find out," he said and started toward the garage.

Tilly managed to get everything ready early and was out of school in time to take the bus on the other side of the building. It arrived forty minutes earlier and was a much faster route home, but it usually took her too long to get herself out the door, so she settled for the longer way.

She was home by 4:10 and in the shower by 4:20.

The night before, she'd spent an hour pondering what to wear, eventually deciding that something comfortable would be better than anything revealing. It wasn't a date after all, and she didn't want to give anyone the impression that she was slutty or loose. The only consideration she made with regard to wearing anything even close to sexy was her underwear, but they were pretty, not sexy. She was packed already, so she grabbed her bag and was out the door in no time.

Instead of the bus, she'd decided to take a cab to Roger's house and saw it waiting for her from her bedroom window. She was in the taxi by 4:45 and on her way, knowing she'd arrive early, but what would she do if she waited for another hour? She only hoped he would be okay with it, and if he wasn't home from work yet, she'd just sit on the front step and wait. The taxi driver somehow got her there in record time, twelve minutes, so she was an hour early and really nervous about his reaction as the taxi stopped in front of the address she'd been given.

She gave the driver a tip, got out, and stepped up to the large ironwork gate with sweet little owls fashioned into the design. *Ah, Owlgate; now I get it.* She found the latch on the service door and let herself into the grounds, closing the door as quietly as she could. As she walked up the horseshoe-shaped driveway, she saw a grand, stately home with a large garage and yard.

She heard a man's voice and followed it toward the back garden. She heard, '*I'll find out.*' and suddenly, she was standing less than ten feet away from David Elliott. He hadn't yet seen her and was headed straight for her. She wasn't sure what to do, but if she didn't do anything, she'd probably get run over by him, which, she thought, wouldn't be all that bad, actually.

She put her hands out to brace herself. "Excuse me—" she said bravely.

David looked up just in time to avoid her and stopped, obviously startled to find an unfamiliar woman in the garden. "Oh! Ah, hello. Where'd you come from?" he asked kindly.

She blushed and stammered, completely taken off guard. "I'm—but you're—John Thomas—I mean—David Elliott. I think I might be—at the wrong address, but the sheet said Owlgate; this is Owlgate, isn't it?" She was rambling and felt ridiculous.

"Aye, that's who I am, and that's where yeh are, but who are you, and who are yeh lookin' for?"

He doesn't sound upset—yet, she thought until she saw a woman come out from behind the house, then she wanted to bolt. She didn't want anyone to think she was a stalker or fangirl who'd found out where David Elliott lived.

The woman approached them and smiled. "Hello, can we help you?" she asked.

Tilly was surprised to hear another Midwestern American accent and smiled at something familiar. "I'm really sorry to disturb you, but I'm looking for someone named Roger Blackwood. My paperwork says he lives here, but obviously he doesn't. As I said, I'm really—" she said quickly, but the woman interrupted her.

"Sure, Roger's in the garage. He was about to say something, looked at his watch, and deserted us," she said.

"I'll inform him he has company. Is he expectin' you?" David asked, smiling at her.

She looked up at the tall, uncommonly handsome man she'd been watching on her television for the last fifteen or so years and nodded. "Yes, but I'm horribly early, so don't rush him. I'll just wait—umm." She looked around, trying to find somewhere to sit, and the woman laughed good-naturedly.

"Go on, David; I'm sure he'll want to know right away," she said.

"Aye, I believe you're right," David said and walked toward the garage, disappearing into the darkness.

"Oh, my God! That was crazy! I can't believe that was David—" Tilly began to say out loud to herself and then remembered someone was still standing there. "Crap! I'm so sorry! I shouldn't have said that, but—I never in my wildest dreams expected to see him today—or, well, ever for that matter." Tilly laughed nervously and watched to see the other woman's reaction.

She smiled at her. "Trust me, I understand completely! I'm Erin, by the way. I'm his—well, his partner; I think that's what people around here would call it. I'd say girlfriend, but that's just a bit too middle school for someone my age."

Tilly was shocked. "You're... dating him? Woah! But you seem so—I don't know, normal," she blurted out and then turned bright red.

"I say that to myself in the mirror all the time. As for normal, I don't know about that. Come and sit with me on the patio," Erin said and led her around the house to a lovely brick patio. Erin sat on a bench swing, so Tilly sat on a patio chair across from her. "Now, I can tell you're from the Midwest; I'm guessing Illinois?"

It was Tilly's turn to laugh. "Not bad! I'm from Galena, and I'd say you're from... Wisconsin?" she guessed, and Erin smiled.

"Yep, spot-on; Green Bay, to be exact. I've been to Galena; it's beautiful with all those hills and old houses. So, how'd you end up here?"

"Well, it's a long story, but I guess I have some time, don't I?" she said, and Erin nodded.

"I reckon you do, though it doesn't take men as long to get themselves ready for a date as it does us," Erin said.

"I'm… not here for a… date, exactly," she said defensively, not knowing why it made any difference whether it was or not.

"Oh, I'm sorry; I assumed… way to put my foot in my mouth," Erin said.

"It's all right; I can understand why you'd think that. No, I have—a disease, and he's going to help me with—"

"You're his match?" Erin interrupted, wide-eyed.

Tilly looked at her again, this time with concern. "He—told you about it?" she said, frowning and feeling uncomfortable.

"Oh, there I go again, saying the wrong thing; I'm sorry. I also have the Fertilis Defect, and David is my match."

Tilly's eyes grew wide, and her mouth hung open in disbelief, but then she shook her head a bit. "You do? He is? I can't believe it. That's just crazy!"

Erin raised her eyebrow at her. "Tell me about it! David offhandedly suggested to Roger that he should register, and, well, we didn't think he would. So, since we've been through the process, he told us about his decision and asked for any advice we might have. Roger is a diamond in the rough—Ah, wait, what's your name?"

"Oh, sorry, I'm Tilly—I mean Matilda Maxwell, but everyone calls me Tilly. You said your name is Erin, right?" Erin nodded. "Can you tell me, Erin," she asked, tentatively, "have the treatments worked for you, and can I ask what your symptoms are?"

"First of all, I love your name; it's perfect! The housekeeper here is named Millie! That won't be at all confusing! Anyway, yes, the treatments are working for me. I've had one episode since we…

uh, started them, but they hadn't had time to take effect yet," Erin said and explained what her symptoms had been. Just as Tilly was about to tell Erin hers, Roger and David came walking around the corner.

The two women stood, and Tilly's eyes involuntarily went to David. It was unnerving to see him there, and she was losing her cool rapidly. She consciously looked away from him and saw Roger; he wasn't as tall or as handsome as David, but he had very kind eyes, and she liked the way he looked.

Erin spoke up. "I reckon an introduction is in order; Roger, this is Tilly, and now we'll leave you—" she began.

"No!" they both said at the same time, and then blushed. "Ah, okay; we can stay then," Erin said.

There was some sorting out of seats to be made; David and Erin sat on the bench swing while Roger and Tilly sat next to each other in Adirondack chairs. Tilly noticed that Roger's hair was still wet, and his shirt was buttoned wrong, but she wasn't going to bring it up. "I'm sorry to say this, but I just have to get it out of the way so I can move past it," she said to David, breaking the silence which had fallen over them. "I—can't tell you what *Future Explorations* has meant to me. It's what made me want to travel and why I came to Scotland in the first place. Someday, I'll get to the Highlands and see those mountains for myself," she said, her face burning. "I know you're probably tired of hearing that, but it's true." She started biting her bottom lip and looked down at the moss-covered bricks under her feet.

"I'm not tired of hearin' et from people who mean et, and especially those who've had their lives changed so greatly by et. I'm the one who should be thankin' you for watchin'. I can't believe people are still so passionate about the old episodes. I hope you do get tae see the Highlands, they're stunnin'," he said and smiled as he put his arm around Erin's shoulders, pulling her closer to him.

———

Roger sat, not knowing what to say. He didn't know what he'd expected, but it was nothing like the woman sitting next to him. He wanted to stare at her, to study her, but he couldn't do that.

"So, how'd yeh meet, then?" David asked, not having heard the women's conversation, and Erin nudged him.

"We havnae met before now," Roger said. It was the first thing he'd said, other than 'no' since he'd walked up with David.

Erin whispered into David's ear, and he nodded emphatically. "Oh, I see," he said, and then everything got quiet and awkward again; no one knew what to say.

"Can I... make a suggestion?" Erin asked after several minutes of silence and everyone looked at her.

"Please do," Roger said, relieved that someone said something.

"Well, when David and I first met, knowing what we were there for— and, well, with him being who he is—" she said and looked up at him, smiling. He bent down to kiss her temple. "Anyway, we weren't all that comfortable, so we went for a nice long walk. It was perfect because we didn't have to sit staring at each other, like we're doing now, trying to think of something to say. A walk really helped to break the ice—well, that and falling flat on my ass in front of the man of my dreams... that worked as well. There's nothing like humiliation to make you feel like things couldn't get any worse, at least."

"Et's true," David said, smiling, "and she did such a fine job of et!"

Erin reached up and gently patted David's cheek as though she were slapping it. "Let's go in and ask Millie if she needs help with supper—" Erin began, but Roger stood suddenly.

"Damn! I forgot all about supper, and I didn't tell anaone I'd have a guest."

Erin and David were already standing, and Erin put her hand on Roger's shoulder. "Dinnae worry, Roger. I'll speak with Millie and see if she'd be willing to send some food to the flat. That way you don't have to meet even more people and you can have some privacy."

Roger sighed. "That'd be grand, Erin. Thank yeh!" he said.

———

They heard them before they saw them; the children had gone to Dr. Neil's to burn off some energy and came home just as wound up as they'd been when they left. Charlie and Rosie walked around the house together, holding some wildflowers, followed by Peter. Daniel could be heard but not seen until one of the dogs was let loose, then he was briefly glimpsed chasing it and howling like a hound dog.

"*Le potage*!" Erin said, making Tilly laugh at the reference.

Charlie and Rosie went to Erin and handed her two large bunches of white daisies and red poppies. "We've picked these for you, Erin. They came from the roadside, not Dr. Neil's, so don't worry," Charlie said proudly.

"Peter wouldn't allow us to pick any at the garden anyway," Rosie said and glared at her eldest brother.

Peter shrugged and put his hands up. "The sign says—" he started, obviously having said it many times before, and all three children said at the same time, "Do not pick the flowers." Rosie rolled her eyes when she said it.

Erin laughed and hugged Charlie and Rosie first. "They're beautiful! It was sweet of you to think of me." She walked over to Peter and put her arm around his shoulder. "You're such a good leader; what would we do without you? Just think what Dr. Neil's would look like if you weren't there to make sure your siblings didn't destroy it!" She pulled one of the poppies out of the bunch and handed it to him. He reached for it with a slight smile, but Erin snatched it away. She held it out again, and he rolled his eyes.

"Common Poppy; Papaver rhoeas," he said.

Erin kissed his forehead and handed him the flower.

———

None of the children had noticed Tilly, and she didn't mind; she was happy just to see the dynamic of Erin and those children, who, by the look of them, were David's.

"Okay, people," Erin said, meaning the children. "let's go inside and wash up for supper. I'm sure you're all as filthy as an earthworm after a rainstorm." Rosie noticed Tilly then and started to ask, but Erin diverted her attention. "She's just a friend of Roger's, now no dilly-dallying. Mind your evil stepmother... or... I won't let you go to the ball to meet Prince Charming. Muah ah ah ah!"

"You're not evil—at least not much of the time," Charlie said and then laughed as he ducked, avoiding Erin's pretend slap.

"But, Erin, you've already met Prince Charming, remember?" Rosie said and looked at her dad.

Erin looked over at David, who was holding the door and smiled. "Aye, Rosie, I have," she said.

They disappeared into the house, leaving Roger and Tilly standing there alone, except for a dog and a boy, both barking maniacally in the side yard. Roger was smiling, watching the family. He turned to Tilly and held out his hand. "Now that the hullabaloo is over, I reckon it would be proper to introduce myself properly. Roger Blackwood, pleased to meet you," he said with a smile.

She smiled back and shook his hand, feeling a sensation she couldn't describe. "Matilda Maxwell, or just Tilly; it's a pleasure to make your acquaintance." They both laughed gently and looked into each other's eyes for the first time. They were still holding hands, and suddenly things weren't quite as awkward as they had been a few minutes before. "I... like your accent," she said softly.

"Thank you... uh, would yeh like tae take a walk, or I could show yeh ma flat? Et's above the garage." He pointed to the large brick structure where David had disappeared earlier.

Tilly's eyes were hurting and her ears ringing. She was torn between taking a walk and getting to know the attractive older man or just getting the treatment over with so she could hopefully relax. That woman, Erin, had said that even after a treatment she'd had an episode, yet she hoped beyond hope it would keep her from having the one she could feel coming. "I'd like to see the flat first if you don't mind; then I can put my things down." *And maybe we can just get this over with too,* she thought.

Roger led her into the garage and up the stairs, he'd thankfully remembered to sweep that morning. "Et's nothin' much, but et works for ma needs." He opened the door and they walked inside. "Ma room is tae the left, and the spare is tae the right. You can help yerself tae anathin' in the kitchen, as well, oh, and the toilet is the door at the end of the hall."

Tilly set her bag on the floor next to the spare room door, and then everything went black.

Chapter Thirty

AN EPISODE TO REMEMBER

Erin's cell phone rang; it was Roger's number, but she knew he was in the flat with Tilly. *Why would he be calling me?* She answered it but didn't hear anything. "Roger? What's wrong?" She heard heavy breathing and very nearly hung up, thinking he'd somehow butt-dialed her.

"Erin—I need yer help. I think—I think she's havin' a—I dinnae ken what yeh call them—a fit?" he said, sounding panicked.

She knew there wouldn't be anything she or anyone else could do other than wait it out, no matter how scary her symptoms were. She also knew how embarrassing it was and it only made things worse to have too many people paying attention to you. Tilly needed to relax and feel safe. Roger was freaking out, so the only way to help at that point was for her to remain calm and talk him through it. "Okay, what's happening? Can you tell what her symptoms are?" She could hear a slight whimpering and Roger's heavy, frightened breathing.

"She cannae see, and I dinnae think she can hear either. I dinnae ken what tae do."

"Okay, where are you? Are you near the sofa?"

"Aye. We're in the kitchenette."

"Put your arm around her shoulders and take her hand. Lead her to the couch and help her to sit next to you—"

David walked into the sitting room and mouthed, "Who is it?"

Erin shook her head and held up her finger, asking him to wait a minute. "Then take her hand, palm up, and use your finger to write out, slowly 'How can I help,' in capital letters, okay? Now set the phone down, do that, and then tell me what happens."

"A'right," he said. Erin heard him put the phone down and waited.

———

Tilly stood still like a deer in the woods, tears of frustration rolling down her face. She didn't know what to say, and she didn't want to yell at him by accident either, so she stayed quiet. She felt him lead her to the sofa, and they sat together. After a few moments, she felt him spelling something out on her hand, each touch filled with energy.

"How can I help?" he wrote.

No man had ever been as thoughtful as that for her before. She shook her head and whispered, "Nothing. It just has to wear off. It usually lasts about thirty minutes or so; I'm so sorry!"

"Then we wait," he spelled out on her palm.

More tears fell down her face. *Is he for real? He signed up to have sex with me, not to care about me or do anything extra, like 'put up with' one of my episodes. He doesn't even know me; why should he care enough to sit here with me like this?*

———

Erin heard her response and said, "ROGER!" as loud as she dared, not wanting to startle anyone. It ended up alarming her with memories of the day Bran had raped her. Then, she'd yelled for Roger to help her; this time it was to help him."

"Sorry," he said into the phone.

"It's okay. Are you alright now? Do you need me to come help you?" His breathing was regular, and he sounded calmer.

"No, I think we'll be a'right. Thanks for yer help, Erin; I owe yeh."

"You owe me nothing. If anything changes for the worse, or if you need anything, just call me back. I'm glad to help if I can." She hung up and sighed, then went in search of David. He was found on the patio, petting one of the dogs, who had jumped onto his lap.

"What was that about? I heard yeh yell for Roger; is everathin' a'right?" he asked.

"Aye, it is now. Poor Tilly is having an episode, and he was scared. I think things are under control now, though."

David raised his eyebrows. "Are yeh sure? Do yeh think we should go and—make sure? What are her symptoms?" he asked, sounding genuinely concerned.

Erin looked sadly at him. "He said she couldn't see, and it seemed like she couldn't hear, either. Oh, David, that would be so scary! I'd be petrified I'd fall off something or get lost or hurt," she said.

David lifted the dog off his lap and patted the cushion next to him for her to sit there. "Aye. I'm so glad ye're bein' treated now, and yeh needn't tae worry about et anamore." Erin looked at him and shrugged. "What? Am I not right?"

"I just think we should try to make love every day, to be safe. I don't like the way I felt when we went a week without."

"Well, if yeh think it'll help, I'm willin', but et won't be easy!"

———

Roger sat with Tilly for a good twenty minutes. Eventually, she looked at him and shook her head. "Why did you do that?" she asked, and he looked shocked.

"What do yeh mean? Did I do somethin' wrong?" he asked.

She shook her head again and smiled. "No, it's just that I've never been with a guy who was as patient and thoughtful as you were just then; you did everything right. How did you know to do that with my hand?"

His pride wanted him to take the credit, but his nature had to admit he'd had help. "I have tae tell the truth; I panicked and called Erin. She helped calm me down and told me what tae try. I'm just glad et worked."

"Well, remind me to thank Erin the next time I see her. You were really great, and I appreciate it," she said and leaned over to kiss him on the mouth. It started as a simple kiss, and then she began to kiss him with a bit more passion. He responded to her, and before long they were vigorously making out.

"Tilly," he said after things started getting more intense. "I need for you tae tell me if yeh want me tae stop, a'right?"

"I don't want you to stop at all; I think now's the time to keep going," she said and laughed gently.

He looked into her eyes and then stood. He took her hand and helped her up, then walked to the front door and locked it. After leading her into his bedroom, he locked that door as well; he wasn't going to let anything interrupt them. "Et's been a verra long time for me, so please be patient with this old man," he said, but she didn't seem to notice.

She took her top off and revealed she wasn't wearing a bra. He didn't know if he should touch her or wait, but she decided for him, taking his hand and placing it over her breast. Her nipple was hard, and she gasped as his hand closed around it, so he kissed her and allowed her to unfasten his trousers. He was worried that he might do something wrong, but she seemed to sense it and took a lot of the initiative, which he was grateful for. She pulled his trousers and pants down then gently touched him. Her hands were so small and soft, and he was ready for her.

"Oh, God!" she said, inhaling sharply, but he didn't know why. He took his shirt off and then unfastened her jeans. As they fell to the floor, she pressed herself against him, and he couldn't take it any longer. He led her to the bed, and she lay on her back, then he pulled down her delicate panties and looked at her. She wasn't plump at all, and her body was not remarkable in any way; she was plain and small with no curves or even an ounce of fat on her, but he was entranced. He wanted her right then and lay on top of her, hesitating as he was about to enter her.

She looked into his eyes, smiling at him, and nodded. "Go on," she said quietly.

He pressed himself into her and could feel her body yield to him. He remembered the feeling he'd had with his wife, but this was different; there was something else, something more profound and even more fulfilling. She gasped loudly, as if in pain, and he would've stopped, but it was already too late. "Ma Losh, I'm sorry," he said, unable to stop himself from finishing sooner than he'd planned, but then he felt her body behaving differently. She was obviously experiencing something similar to what he was. He felt her contracting on the inside, sending shock waves through his now overly sensitive cock.

"I—I can't believe that just happened!" Tilly said when it was over. "I usually need a lot more time before I can climax like that. You're so—large, I mean—wow! That was amazing! When can we do it again?" she said, which made them both laugh.

"Dinnae worry, I'll let yeh know just as soon as et's possible," he said. He couldn't believe it either; he'd never had sex like that with his wife. With her, it was always good, and he'd loved her more than anything, but it was never… electric, like what had just happened in his bed. The look on her face, the look of satisfaction and contentment; he remembered seeing it on David and Erin's faces a few times and could now appreciate what they had between them. "Large, eh?" he said.

He rolled onto his back, and she snuggled into him, laying her small arm over his burly chest. "Yes, very large," she said and sighed. I think I'll sleep in here tonight if it's okay with you?" she said, and he smiled.

"Aye; et's all right wi' me. I think I will as well," he said, and they were both asleep within minutes.

Chapter Thirty-One

SUPPER WITH A STRANGER

Roger heard his mobile from the table in the kitchenette start vibrating and playing the *Imperial March* from *Star Wars;* the song played for Darth Vader's entrance. He woke up and knew if he didn't answer her message quickly, Millie would be up there in a flash, making sure he would be on time for supper. He tried to roll out of bed in a way that wouldn't wake Tilly, but when he walked back in with his phone, he saw that her eyes were open and watching him.

"Et's Millie, the—housekeeper. She's makin' sure I'll be down tae supper on time; she's rather particular about tha'. Erin must've forgotten tae ask her about sendin' somethin' up. I'll tell her I willnae be dinin' wi' them tonight. I dinnae want yeh tae have tae—"

"I don't mind, and to tell you the truth, I'm really hungry, so if she doesn't mind an extra mouth to feed, I'd love to—be your guest?" she interrupted him.

Roger looked up from his mobile and smiled. She was lovely, dainty almost, but not frail. Her eyes were too large, and her nose was too small; she didn't have lips either, just thin lines showing where her mouth was, but he thought she was beautiful.

"Aye, I'll ask her tae put out another setting," he said and started typing slowly; he wasn't very fast at it. He sat on the edge of the bed, suddenly feeling strange being naked with a woman in the room with him.

> R: *I'm sorry, I forgot to mention it, but I have a guest. Erin was meant to tell you. Do you have enough for her as well?*

A few moments later he got a reply.

> M: *Aye, Erin told me, but you'll eat with us. I'll not be sending plates up there to get broken or forgotten. Your woman can just come eat in here with the rest of us.*

'Yer woman,' that has a nice ring to it, he thought, but he wasn't about to start thinking of her that way—not yet. He knew Millie was only being that way because she wanted to meet Tilly, though she would never have admitted it.

Tilly rolled over and sat next to him on the edge of the bed. "Doesn't she want me there?" she asked, sounding slightly worried.

"No, she's fine wi' et. I need tae warn yeh though, tha' Millie comes across as a wee bit—crabbit and no' easy tae please, but underneath she's as sweet as her homemade rhubarb preserves. She just needs tae get tae know yeh," he said.

"I'll keep that in mind," she said and seemed pleased. "It was a shock to see David Elliott earlier. Does he live here all the time?"

Roger had hoped David wouldn't be there when he first met with his match; after all, how could any man compare to him? "No, this is his mother's home; I'm the caretaker and driver for the family. He and Erin are here tae retrieve his children for their summer holidays."

"They're out already? Ours runs for a few more days," she said.

"No, their boardin' school's term ends Monday, but one of them got intae a fight and was excluded. Et was David's late wife who insisted they go there, so he's pulled them out early. Are you a teacher, then?"

"Yes, I teach at a school for the deaf. I thought it would be a good occupation for me, seeing that I go blind and deaf once every other month, give or take."

He took her small hand into his and kissed it. "I hope tha' will be all over for yeh now," he said, then looked at the alarm clock and nearly jumped up. Damn! We'll be late if we dinnae hurry. Millie abhors tardiness; please get yerself dressed."

They threw their clothes on, made a mad dash to the main house, and entered the dining room out of breath and laughing. All conversation at the table died as the crowd sitting around the large dining table stared at them; David, Erin, and the children smiled warmly.

Roger noticed the flowers the children had given Erin were in a beautiful, etched glass vase in the center of the table. The red poppies and white daisies were striking against the white linen tablecloth and robin's egg blue china. "Everyone, I'd like yeh tae meet ma friend, Tilly," he said nervously.

"Tilly rhymes with Millie!" Rosie said, forgetting her manners. Tilly and Erin smiled, but the young girl covered her mouth with her hand and put her head down. "Sorry," she said, and Roger smiled at her.

"She will be here for a few days—I think—" he said and looked at her. Now that their treatment was over, he wasn't sure if she'd still want to stay. She smiled and nodded, so he continued, "Ye've met David and Erin, but ye've no' met the rest of the household. At the head of the table is Annis Elliott, David's mother and head of the household. Then there's Millie; she runs the house—verra well I might add," he said with a wink, "And this lot are David's children—"

"Sorry, mate," David interjected, "but if yeh dinnae mind, could yeh say David and Erin's children, please?" Erin looked at him with shock, and so did the kids, but then they all smiled and started talking at the same time. Millie had to stand and clear her throat before they would calm down.

"Of course I will," Roger replied. "Tilly, these are David and Erin's children. Ach, and I cannae forget about the one on the way." Everyone at the table froze and you could hear a pin drop. Roger knew immediately he'd stepped in it and was in deep. "Damn—was I no' supposed tae say anathin' about tha'? Ach! I'm sorry; truly, I am." The children were looking between David and Erin, clearly shocked.

"Aye, we'll talk about it after supper," David said, looking at the children.

"A'right, now, take yer seats, or you'll be to blame for a cold meal," Millie scolded.

Roger pulled out the chair between him and Erin and pushed it in when Tilly sat, then he took his seat, feeling stupid.

"Uhm, it's nice to meet you all, and thank you so much for allowing me to join you on such short notice," Tilly said.

Everyone looked at Millie, and she looked at Annis, who closed her eyes. "For what we're about tae eat, may we be truly grateful, Amen." Everyone at the table said, 'Amen,' then Annis responded to Tilly. "Et's nice tae meet you as well, dear."

Roger listened as Erin and Tilly talked about the Fertilis Defect; he heard Tilly thank her for giving him such thoughtful, perfect advice, and he smiled, thankful for it as well. Occasionally, his hand would touch Tilly's, for instance, when they reached for the same serving dish or when they both reached for a napkin that had fallen on the floor. Each time they touched, lightning would pass from her to him, making him want to stop everything and make love right then and there.

———

"Well, that must have set a record!" Erin whispered into David's ear at one point during the meal. He looked at her, confused. "Well, isn't it obvious? They've already had their first treatment."

He raised his eyebrows and looked over at them, smiling and laughing, every so often looking at each other and blushing. "I can't believe et! Ye're right," he said and watched them a while longer. He took Erin's hand in his and leaned in closer, "Were we that obvious in New Orleans, do yeh think?"

"Umm, I think we're that obvious now! At least sometimes," she said and kissed his cheek.

David wanted to kiss and touch her more. The electricity between Tilly and Roger was contagious; even Millie and Annis were gazing fondly at each other. The mood was light as everyone ate and talked and laughed, and soon, all mention of babies was forgotten, at least for the time being.

291

Chapter Thirty-Two

LETTERS FOR REBUILDING

After supper, Erin warned the children not to go too far because they would be reading more letters once everything was cleaned up. Tilly asked her what she meant, and she briefly told her about finding some letters from the children and said she was welcome to join them, so Tilly said she wouldn't miss it.

Erin helped Millie clear the table and then dried the dishes for her. They talked about London and how Millie was so happy to have them back, even if it was just for the weekend. "My new doctor says I can't climb Arthur's seat anymore, and I should wait as long as possible between flights, so maybe we'll stay a few extra days," Erin said hopefully, then she looked around the room, making sure no one had entered without her noticing. "Millie, did you know Susannah never allowed David to come to any of her baby doctor appointments?"

Millie stopped washing the pot she was scrubbing and turned to Erin. "No!" she gasped, looking sad and angry as she brought her attention back to the pot. "I did not ken tha'," she said quietly and with emotion. "I knew she was no' a good person; she wouldnae look at me like a human being, and she never wanted tae be with the children at all. She wanted David's attention at all times, but then, when she had et, she was rude and nasty tae him. And tae find out she'd been keepin' those letters from him!"

Erin could see she was working herself up; her face was red, and the poor pan she'd just started washing got the full brunt of her anger as she scrubbed the living daylight out of it. "What sort of person would do tha' tae someone they said they loved?" Millie said and wiped a tear threatening to escape her eye with the back of her wrist. "Ma heart was breakin' for our poor Davey and the bairns last night. They are such good wee beasties, and tae have a mother such as her is jest no' fair." The older woman turned her head and smiled fondly at her. "Except now they'll have you, Erin!" she said with a full, genuine smile. "Ye'll make a lovely mother, ma dear; yeh already do, yeh ken? I've never seen those bairns act as carefree and happy as they do when ye're with them."

"They're so sweet; I already love them dearly!" Erin said.

"Whom do yeh love dearly?" David said as he entered the kitchen.

Erin smiled and flicked a few drops of water at him from her wet hands. "All y'all. I love you all, but I was referring to your children," she said.

"Speakin' of **our** children," he said with a smile, "they're askin' for more letters; would yeh mind gatherin' the brood whilst I get the box?"

Erin stepped up to him and kissed him, placing her wet hand on the back of his neck. "Sure."

He scrunched up his face and moaned. "Ahhh! Tha's just—evil! I'll get yeh back; ye'd better beware!" Quick as a flash, he had the wet tea towel she'd been drying the dishes with and was trying to snap her with it. He missed her all but once; the third time, he got her good on the leg, making involuntary tears smart her eyes.

"Oww!" She wasn't upset, but her eyes betrayed the pain she'd just felt, and he dropped the towel.

"Oh, ma love, I didn't mean for et tae hurt yeh! Are yeh a'right?" he asked and hugged her.

"You should know better than tae hit a girl! I taught yeh better than tha'?" Millie scolded him.

"It's okay, I'm not really hurt; it just stung a bit. I didn't mean to scare you," she said and wiped a tear away, just as Rosie walked in and saw her.

The young girl ran to her and hugged her around the middle, looking up at her with big, concerned eyes. "Are you alright, Erin? Your eyes are red; were you crying? Did you stub your toe? I once stubbed my toe in here, and it hurt so badly I cried as well," she said so sweetly that Erin nearly started crying out of sheer love for her.

"No, sweetheart, I didn't stub my toe, but it was sort of the same thing. It didn't hurt bad; it just made tears come to my eyes. I'm fine, darling; thank you for the hug, it helped so much!" Rosie smiled and stood on her tippy toes. Erin bent down a bit, thinking she was going to whisper something in her ear. Instead, she kissed her cheek, which did bring more tears to her eyes. She looked up at David, and he had watery eyes as well. "Oh, Rosie, you are just the most precious girl I know! Thank you for that!" Rosie started to walk away, but Erin remembered her task, "Wait, Rosie, we're going to open more letters in a few minutes; would you mind helping me gather your brothers?"

———

Rosie smiled, happy to be given a task to do for the person she hoped with all her heart would be her new mother someday. She wanted to try it out... to call Erin 'Mummy,' but she didn't know if it was a good idea yet. She might not like it, or her dad might not like it, so she said, "Sure," instead.

———

The family was gathered in the sitting room, talking and laughing. Erin saw Tilly standing in the doorway, waiting for Roger, so she waved her into the room, and Tilly took a seat on the sofa. When Roger came looking for her, Erin pointed her out, and he sat next to her.

Erin looked around the room then cleared her throat. "Okay, everyone— Wait, where's Dan?" she asked, not seeing him.

"He's under the coffee table," Rosie said, sounding exasperated.

"Dan, I need you to listen up; this is important. Can you please come out now?"

Daniel crawled out only enough that his head, shoulders, and arms were sticking out. He folded his arms, laid his chin on them, and then looked at her hopefully. She could just tell that he wasn't being naughty; something in his features made her understand that he didn't want anyone to see him cry again. "Thank you," she said with a smile and then sat on the sofa, waiting for David.

When he entered the room, all talking stopped, and they watched him sit next to Erin. "I'll read more of yer letters in a few moments, but first, I need to address what Roger brought up at supper," he said and shot him a look.

Roger shrugged and mouthed, *'Sorry.'*

David smiled at him and continued. "Et's true, Erin and I are indeed expectin' a child." All four children gasped and looked between one another, as well as David and Erin, with their mouths open. They each looked at Erin's stomach, then her face, in unison; it was quite comical, and she laughed.

"I'm not showing yet; it's still very early, so it will be a long time before you can tell there's a baby in there."

Charlie scooched himself up to her and smiled excitedly. "I'm very happy for you, and Dad—" he began, but stopped, squinted, and tilted his head to the side like a dog who's trying to understand a human when they speak. "… and all of us," he finished, and surprised her by kissing her cheek. He then crawled back to the spot he'd been at on the floor, leaving Erin speechless. The other three did similar things, each taking Charlie's lead and kissing her on the cheek.

"Well! That was… beautiful! Thank you," she said and then paused; she was thrilled but also a bit suspicious. "I need to know something, though; do all of you really feel that way, or are you only saying it because you don't want anyone to be upset with you? I mean, if you are, that's great, but if you have questions or want to talk about it, it's okay; you can tell us, and we won't be angry."

Daniel looked up at his dad. "But aren't you too old to have more babies, and aren't four enough?" he asked.

———

David smiled at his young son's honest question. "I'm not too old, Dan, and neither is Erin. As for four bein' enough, well, et's not really about that. We're not havin' a bairn because we feel as if we dinnae have enough, et's because we love each other, and—"

"Was it an accident?" Peter asked bluntly.

David felt the color rise in his cheeks and glanced at Erin, then he sighed and looked back at Peter. "Did we plan tae get pregnant? No, but now that we are, we're verra happy about et," he said, and Peter nodded, apparently satisfied with the answer he was given. David looked around the room, waiting for more questions, but everyone was silent. "Are there anamore questions, or shall I continue readin' your letters?" he asked, more than a little relieved that everything was now out in the open. Everyone looked at each other and shook their heads, so David pulled a letter out from Peter.

Dear Dad,

Which sport did you choose whilst you were here? I want to join whichever one you chose so we can practice together whilst on holiday. Please write soon, as registration ends in two weeks.

Love, Peter

David looked at Peter; his head was down, and he was tracing the pattern on the carpet with his index finger. "I—" David began and realized there were no 'I'm sorrys' to cover it. He knew Peter had chosen football; all his children played it, but it wasn't because he'd told him to, and they hadn't the chance to bond over it. "Yeh chose football then?" he said sadly.

"Football was chosen for me, as I missed the cut-off," Peter said, not looking up.

"Wait," Tilly said, and everyone looked at her. "Oh, sorry, I meant to ask Roger—"

"Well, go on and ask us then," Annis said patiently.

Tilly looked at Roger, and he nodded, so she continued. "Umm, well, I must not have understood what Erin told me earlier.

You found these letters in your house, but you didn't know about them? I mean, how did that happen?"

David sighed softly. He was embarrassed that he hadn't been more proactive in his household and felt the blame did land somewhat on him for not paying attention and allowing Susannah to run everything. "Ma late wife hid them from me in a locked drawer, and I never thought tae ask. I was too absorbed in ma own little world tae think about why ma children didn't write tae me," he said, full of regret, but Erin looked at him.

"David! I don't believe that about you," she said sharply.

"Yeah, Dad, it was Mum's fault for hiding them from you, not yours. None of us blame you, do we?" Peter asked his siblings, looking for backup. They all shook their heads and said 'no.'

"Aye, maybe not, but I feel as though I should've written tae yeh evera now and then to say hello, at least," he said, ashamed of himself.

"David, what's done is done, and dwellin' on et won't fix et. Read them out, and then things can heal," Annis said.

"But—I'm sorry—I still don't understand; why did she do that? Was she angry about something?" Tilly said.

"We don't know, Tilly. She must have had mental problems or some—" Erin began, but David cut her off.

"She did et because she didn't want anaone else tae have ma time or attention. I can see et now," David said, realizing it for the first time. "When I was home, at least in the beginnin' of our marriage, she wanted a hundred percent of ma time, and if I was answerin' letters, I'd not be givin' that time tae her. Recently, she didn't seem tae want tae look at me, let alone have ma time, but she still took the letters and hid them away, perhaps out of habit, or—sheer selfishness. I dinnae ken."

"What a horrible thing to do!" Tilly said and started crying. "I'm sorry, but that's just unforgivable."

Roger put his arm around her shoulders, handed her a tissue, and soothed her gently. "We all feel the same way, hen. Continue, David," Roger said, and David took one out from Charlie next.

Dear Daddy,

My friend Billy says your programme isn't as good as the space films he likes, but I think it is. I think it's better than the dumb space films he likes. Can I be in a space film with you someday? I think that would be cool.

Well, I miss you, Dad!
Love Charlie Age 9 ½
P.S. Please write back.

Charlie was blushing. "He likes *Star Trek*, and I don't. He said your show was dumb."

David was touched by his son's loyalty. "Quite a few people think my show is dumb, Charlie, and many people think *Star Trek* is cool. That's a'right, you can like mine, and he can like his... or you can like them both. I won't feel slighted if yeh do," he said, and Charlie shrugged.

Next, he read one from Dan and then one from Rosie. The next one was from Peter, again.

Dear Dad,

We started learning about plants in biology today. I think that plants are very interesting! I think I want to be a botanist when I'm an adult, or do you think that's a bad idea? I could try to become an actor, like you if you'd like me to.

Please tell me what you think.

I love you,

Peter

P.S. Maybe we could take a walk in Dr Neil's the next time we're at Gran's, and I can tell you some of the things I've learned. Would you like to do that?

David was heartbroken anew at how much his son wanted to please him and cared about his opinion. "I think ye'll make a fantastic Botanist, Peter. I very much enjoyed our walk through Dr. Neil's when we were here last; how yeh knew so verra much about every plant you laid yer eyes on. I was so proud of you, and I'd love tae do et again. Maybe we'll have time tomorrow, though if somethin' comes up, we will stay in Scotland until we make the time," he said.

Peter smiled at his dad and nodded. "You can come along as well, Erin. I wasn't much in the mood the last few times we were there, but I'd like for you to come... that is if you'd like to," Peter said to her, beaming at his dad's affirmation.

"I wouldn't miss it, Peter!" Erin said proudly.

David reached into the shoebox and took a letter out from Charlie.

Hi Dad,

Daniel is a butthead. I know I'm not supposed to say that, but it's true. Peter said I shouldn't bother to write you anymore because you never write back. He is angry at you. I shouldn't tell you that either, but it's also true.

I miss you! Can we watch Star Trek together when I'm home on holiday?

Love, your favourite son,
Charlie Elliott

David laughed. "My favorite son, eh?"

"I'm just calling it as I see it," Charlie said and then laughed happily.

"Why did you say Daniel was a butthead?" he asked, and Charlie shrugged.

"Do I need a reason? I don't remember why he was back then; it was a long time—ago," he said and lowered his head. "Sorry—"

David reached over and touched his knee. "Et's a'right; et was far too long ago. I love yeh, son, and we'll have tae make time tae watch *Star Wars*," he said, making Charlie laugh harder.

"Not *Star Wars*, Dad, *Star Trek*, though I'd like to watch *Star Wars* with you, as well."

"Right, sorry," he said and took out another letter. That one was from Daniel.

Dear Dad,

Charlie is a jerk. He won't share his comb with me. He said I have lice, and I don't! My head itches sometimes, that's all.

Everyone in the room looked at him, and he put his head on his arms.

Anyway, the nurses checked everyone for lice the other day, and I didn't have it at all.

Will you tell him he has to share with me?
You're more favouritest son,
Dan

"Dan, et's probably better if yeh use yer own comb," David said with a smile.

"But, Dad! I wrote and told you it broke. No, wait, I wrote to Mum and told *her* it broke because you never write back. She sent me a new one," he said, not even considering whether or not it sounded rude.

David's heart hurt hearing him say it so matter-of-factly. Peter shot Daniel a look, telling him he shouldn't have said it. Daniel was about to say something when David spoke up. "I'm glad of et," he said, not knowing what else to say and feeling so sad it physically hurt. "Now... who's next?" It took a lot of effort to sound casual when he felt so utterly miserable. "Ach, Rosie." He pulled one out with her little girl's handwriting on the sealed envelope. He ripped it open carefully and read:

Dear Daddy,
There is a boy here named Simon who calls me names and pulls my hair. Peter says he likes me, but that doesn't make sense! If you like someone, why be mean to them? He is a year older than me, and I don't like him. I wish I never had to see him again.
Love,
Your Rosebud

David took a deep breath and smiled at Peter, who shrugged, then they both looked at Rosie. "Aye, Rosebud, he liked yeh, but you'll never have tae see him again now," he said.

Rosie's eyes grew large, and her eyebrows shot up. "But—he liked me! What if no one ever likes me again, Daddy!" she said, and it looked like she was about to cry.

"If a boy is mean to you, he's not worth your time, sweetheart," Erin said. "The boy to watch for is the one who is thoughtful and kind and who does nice things for you; he's the one to like back. Mean boys are immature and need to grow up before a girl should like them; otherwise, they might grow up thinking that being mean works on women."

There was a noise near Roger, and everyone looked in that direction. Tilly had started crying, and everyone watched her run to the kitchen, leaving Roger sitting alone, looking confused. He actually looked a bit frightened, so Erin stood and followed her.

———

Tilly was standing at the sink staring out the window when she heard Erin come in. "I'm sorry I caused a fuss out there; I feel like an idiot," she said and saw her new friend approach holding out a tissue in the reflection on the glass.

"It's okay; I've done more than my share of similar things since I met David. Do you want to talk about it?" she asked.

Tilly considered her; *She wouldn't understand, would she?* "I've... never had a nice guy for a boyfriend. I seem to attract the bad ones—the ones who, like you said, have grown up thinking that being mean is okay. I've been called names like cunt and whore most of my life, and I've been beaten and slapped more times than I can count. Also, not a single man has ever helped me during an episode, not even my dad. They seemed to think I was acting or something and that it wasn't as bad as I was making it out to be. They'd back away and then yell at me for trying to get attention."

"Oh, Tilly! That's terrible! Those men are a waste of space! Roger isn't one of them, though, if that's something you're worried about," Erin said.

"Oh, no, I realized that right away! Instead of backing away, he did just what I needed him to do. I now know it was with your help, but he cared enough to *get* help and not leave me there to cower in a ball on the floor until I could see again. He's a man I could fall in love with, Erin. Do you think it's premature to say that after only knowing him for, what, three hours?" she said and then laughed softly.

"Honestly, I don't know how these treatments work, but if I've learned anything, it's that premature affection is a way of life with us. I fell head over heels in love with David after only a day and a half, and that was after talking myself out of it about three times. And yeah, I loved him as an actor, but then I fell for the real person."

Tilly looked at her, unsure if she should say what was on her mind but decided it wouldn't hurt. "Can I ask you a very personal question?"

"Is it about the 'electricity'?"

Tilly cocked her head to the side. "Really? You too? I've never had sex like it before! It's driving me crazy thinking about it even now. I find myself wanting to run back to his flat and—" Roger walked in then, and both women started laughing like schoolgirls. He stopped dead in his tracks and turned around.

"Wait, Roger," Erin called after him, and he turned, clearly waiting for the punchline. "We're sorry, we'd just complimented you, and then you walked in, and it was perfect timing, that's all, I swear! We weren't making fun of you in any way," she assured him.

He relaxed a bit and then looked at Tilly. "Are yeh a'right? Ye've been gone for so long; I thought I'd come to see if yeh needed anathin'?"

Tilly smiled at his sweetness and then went to him. "No. I'm okay now; Erin is really good at making a person feel better," she said, and Roger smiled at Erin.

"Aye, she is, at that."

Tilly saw the tender look he was giving Erin. She dismissed it as part of the strange disease, or maybe she'd helped him through something big that she didn't know about yet, but had it been any other man, or under any other circumstances, she might have been concerned about it.

———

"Oh! David!" Erin said and rushed back into the sitting room. Roger and Tilly followed her and returned to their seats.

David looked up at Erin and smiled. "Everathin' a'right?" he asked.

She nodded and sat next to him. "Fine, did I miss anything?"

"I've just finished the last letter from Rosie. We can read the ones you missed later," he offered.

"Okay, so who's next?" she said and smiled at the faces sitting in front of her.

"Peter is next," David said and pulled out the last letter from Peter. It had arrived in the post just before they'd left London, and he had decided to wait to read it. It was slightly thicker than the others had been, and when he opened it, he saw there were two sheets of paper.

Peter stood suddenly and said, "Please don't read it out loud."

David looked at him and gave a slight nod. "A'right." He held it out in front of him and read silently while Erin read it over his shoulder.

Dear Dad,

I don't know why I bother writing to you since you never reply. I think this will be the last letter I write to you.

Charlie was crying last night because he missed you and wanted a hug. I hugged him for you, Dad. I think he would feel better if you sent him a letter.

Peter

David was trying to hold back the tears as he flipped the page.

Dad,

I know I said I wouldn't write you anymore, but you should know Rosie had a nightmare last night and was crying out for you. I know if you sent her a letter, she would feel better. Even a short note would be nice, but I know you won't, you never do, and it makes me angry. I'm not the dad, but I'm forced to act like one when a head boy comes to wake me in the middle of the night in order to quiet my little sister or one of my brothers. It's not fair, Dad, and sometimes I hate it.

Peter

P.S. If you're too busy to send a letter to her, I think she would love one from Erin, any of us would.

Tears were now rolling down David's and Erin's faces, and because of their reaction, the rest of the room was in tears as well. The tissue box made its way to David, and he pulled one out. He couldn't look his son in the eyes; he covered his face with the tissue in his hand and wept.

Peter went to him and knelt at his feet. "Dad, I didn't know you weren't getting the letters. I'm sorry for making you feel guilty and saying those things. I know you would've written back if Mum had given them to you. Please, don't cry," he said and started crying himself.

David leaned forward and held his son, and the rest of the kids, even Daniel, gathered and hugged each other for a long time. David saw Erin watching them, finally healing after years of anger and resentment, and let go for just a moment to look for her. He held out his arm and invited her into the hug, so she moved closer and allowed them to embrace her.

After a few moments, Peter sat up. "This is nice, but my legs are falling asleep," he said, and maybe it was the stress, or perhaps it was just because she was a kid, but Rosie got the giggles really bad, which set Charlie off. Soon, the whole room was laughing, and the dogs were barking.

After everyone calmed down, except for a few giggles still coming from Rosie, David spoke quietly to his brood. "I love yeh, ma wee bairns, and I promise tae never let you forget et!" He looked at Erin with red eyes and an exhausted smile. "I love you as well, my darling." He leaned over and kissed her.

The twins said, "Eww," in unison, which set Rosie off again.

"Alright, you lot, it's time to get ready for bed—" Erin said, but Daniel interrupted her.

"But it's too early! We still have an hour!" he said, and Erin smiled.

"Aye, but you all need a shower or bath. You smell like something the cat dragged in!" she said and stood, leading them, like the pied piper, toward the stairs.

Daniel was bouncing around, saying, "Erin! But Erin!" over, and over until she whirled around and stopped in front of him with her hand out. Her palm landed dead-center on his forehead, and she looked him in the eyes.

"What is it, Dan?" she said, managing to keep her cool. He was caught off guard, and Charlie stood with his mouth hanging open. Peter looked admiringly at her, and Rosie was already halfway up the stairs.

"But we don't have a cat!" he said, and everyone who'd been holding their breath, not knowing what Erin was going to do, started laughing.

"Oh, Daniel, it's a figure of speech. Get yer wee hinder up those stairs. If I'm not mistaken, Millie will help you with your bathing requirements," she said and shot a pleading look at Millie, silently asking for assistance. The kind woman stood, all business, and herded them upstairs. As soon as they were out of sight, the room broke out in applause.

"What? What's that for?" Erin said, slightly taken aback.

"Where'd you learn that? You were like a Jedi, using the force or something," Tilly said and held her hand out the way Erin had when she'd placed it on Dan's forehead.

"I don't know," Erin said, with a shrug. "I just turned around, and he was right there, so I put my hand on his head to stop him; I didn't know it would work like that. I guess it *was* pretty cool, huh?"

———

"Aye. Peter was looking at yeh as if you were Wonder Woman or somethin'," Roger said, and Tilly noticed that Roger had looked at her the exact same way, though she didn't know what that meant. Erin was obviously in love with David, but the way Roger looked at her sometimes made her think that maybe he was in love with her too. He might not even realize it, but it seemed obvious to her.

*What's it to you if he **is** in love with her? He's not your lover; he's treating you for your disease, and that's all. So what if it feels like heaven on earth when he's inside you; that doesn't mean it's love.* Tilly's inner voice chastised her.

Roger turned and looked at her; he was smiling, and her heart melted. At that moment, she didn't care if Roger was in love with Erin or not; he was looking at her, and she was the one going back to his flat with him. "Do yeh wannae go back—" he began, and she didn't let him finish.

"Yes, I do," she said and looked into his dark grey eyes. His smile grew bigger, which made his crow's feet stand out prominently on his weathered face.

Oh, Tilly! You'd better be careful, or you'll have a mess on your hands with this one.

But he's only just met you; maybe he'll fall in love with you and forget about her?

Or maybe he won't, and you'll end up chasing after his heart and never truly gain it.

She didn't know where it would go, but she didn't need to right then. He took her hand and told David they were going to head back to his flat, then he found Annis and thanked her for being so gracious in allowing Tilly to join the family for dinner.

"Ach, et's nothin', Roger; ye've been such a blessin' tae this family that we feel as though ye're one of us. Tilly is welcome here anatime, though I'm sure Millie would appreciate a wee bit more notice in the future," she said warmly.

Roger smiled, and Tilly noticed he was actually blushing a tiny bit. "Aye, I imagine she would," he said. "Good night."

Tilly felt as though she should curtsey; Annis was very stately, commanding respect, yet she was kind and gentle about it. She wished she were like that, but she was too plain and featureless to command anything except indifference and disdain. "Yes, thank you, and goodnight," Tilly said meekly.

Chapter Thirty-Three

TIME FOR BED

"What an amazing night," Tilly remarked as they walked between the house and garage. "They have such an interesting dynamic; how long have David and Erin been together?"

Roger had to think about it; it seemed like Erin had been part of the family for years. "I'm no' exactly sure, but et's no more than two months, at most," he said.

Tilly stopped walking and stared at him. "Two months?"

"Aye. Et feels like much longer, though."

"But she and the children have bonded… Well, I suppose with everything being new, they would get along. Give it a year or so, and the kids will start to—" she began, but Roger was frowning at her.

"Start tae what?" he said, not caring much for what she seemed to be implying.

"Well, I just mean, once the newness wears off, sometimes kids will start acting out and resenting—"

Roger was getting a bit hot under the collar; she didn't know those kids, or Erin, either. "I see what yer tryin' tae say, but did yeh no' hear what their birth mother did tae David, and in turn tae them? And tha's just the beginnin' of et. They're finally findin' love from a good woman, and I think they'll appreciate et—" he started to say.

"I didn't mean to say anything offensive," she said. "It's just that in my experience…Well, that's my experience, and these people are different than anyone I've ever met. I really hope you're right."

They quietly climbed the stairs to his flat, and he turned on the light. When they stepped inside, he closed and locked the door behind them. He'd felt the energy level drop between them after their disagreement and took her hand. "I'm sorry I took offense, Tilly, but I've seen what those poor wee things have had for a mother, and ma heart has broken so many times for them. I only want them tae be happy and loved, and I know our Erin can give them tha' love." He felt his cheeks get hot though he didn't know why.

"Does she know?" she asked and sat on his small sofa.

"Does who know what?" he said, not knowing what she meant.

"Does Erin know you're in love with her?" she said, and Roger's face burned even hotter.

"I'm not—that's just ridiculous! Sure, I care about her; she's a fine woman, but no like tha'!" he said defensively. He couldn't believe both she and David had confronted him with that— accusation. He didn't love her, she was his friend, and they got on really well, but Erin got on with everyone. He realized he was sweating; his shirt was absorbing it, and he imagined his armpits were soaked. A line of sweat was beading up on his upper lip and forehead; he could feel it, and the look on Tilly's face betrayed that she didn't believe him. *I can't be in love with her; it's... wrong and dangerous.* He sat on one of his dining chairs, the red-hot embarrassment being replaced with chills as realization washed over him.

Tilly went to him and took his hand. "It's understandable, Roger; she *is* a fine woman," she said tenderly.

He looked up at the sweet, lovely creature in front of him and felt despair washing over him in waves. *How could I have let et happen?*

"It would be hard for a lot of men not to... fall for a woman like her. You don't need to feel bad; I only want to know how strong it is, I mean... if I'm going to have any chance to gain—well—" she continued but then faltered.

He looked at her. *Is she saying what I think she is?* "Yeh want tae know if I could love you—above, whatever love you believe I have for—Erin?" he said. He looked into her hazel-green eyes and marveled that she had any doubt of it. He stood and put his hands on her waist, "Aye, I know I could, but do yeh reckon you could love me... someday?" he asked, completely flummoxed at the thought of the subject coming up so soon.

He hadn't had time to shave before she'd shown up, so he had the start of a fine beard. Tilly ran her fingers through it, then through his hair, from his forehead to the nape of his neck, which made him shiver and break out in goosebumps all over his arms. "I could," she said and then pulled his head down, kissing him passionately. He lifted her into his arms, carried her into his bedroom, and closed the door.

Once the children were bathed and in their pajamas, David and Erin went to tuck each of them in. Erin thought about how her mother used to read a chapter or two to her every night from some wonderful books, *Little House in the Big Woods*, *Anne of Green Gables*, *Little Women*, and so many more. She knew Rosie would enjoy her doing that, and she thought at least Charlie would as well.

"David," she said. "I'd like to buy some of the books I loved as a child so I can read them to Rosie and whoever else would like to hear them at bedtime. I already own the ones I'd like to read, but they're still in transit across the pond, and I'd like to start tomorrow night if that's all right?"

Rosie sat up and began bouncing up and down and clapped her hands gently. "Oh, yes, please, Daddy," she said, and when Erin stole a glance at the twins, they were both smiling, though Dan tried to hide it when he noticed her look at them.

"Aye, that would be lovely. I think you and Rosie should go out tomorrow and get whatever yeh want. I was thinkin' about taking the boys up Arthur's seat, and ye're not allowed up there anamore," he said. The twins did nearly the same thing Rosie had done, sitting up and looking as though it were Christmas morning.

"Sounds like a plan," Erin said and kissed Rosie's forehead. She got up from the edge of Rosie's bed and walked across the room to the bunk bed the twins shared. She stood on the bottom rung of the ladder to give Dan a peck on the cheek and then sat on the edge of the bottom bunk to hug Charlie and also kiss him on the cheek.

Next, David and Erin went hand in hand to Peter's room and said their goodnights. David told him about his plan to take them to Arthur's Seat, and Erin told him he was more than welcome to join them when she read to the younger kids. He seemed very happy when they left his room, after a hug and kiss from both her and David. When they got back into the hallway, David stopped her and bent down for a long kiss. "Mmm, what was that for?" she said, feeling a bit tipsy. She looked into his big, brown eyes, with their little crow's feet, and saw his perfect smile, feeling more than a little intoxicated by him.

"Ye're an amazin' mother; did yeh know? And you help tae make me a better father as well," he said.

She lay her head on his chest and wrapped her arms around him. He was everything she had ever wanted and had given her everything she'd ever wanted in his children, and their child still to come. "Take me to bed; I need you to hold me. This all feels like a dream, and I don't want it to end," she said.

"As you wish, my love," he said as they walked together to their room, and he closed the door.

Chapter Thirty-Four

THE MORNING AFTER

Breakfast that morning was charged with energy; having two Fertilis Defect sufferers on treatments in the same room made the molecular structure change in the atmosphere, or at least that's what it felt like. Everyone seemed to be affected by it; even the children were happy and smiling more than usual. It might have been partly due to the adventures they were anticipating, but Erin liked to think it was because of her and Tilly.

The only person Erin thought was acting strangely was Roger; he didn't seem upset, but he wouldn't make eye contact with her. He'd only said three words to her all morning, *'Good mornin', Erin,'* and seemed to be avoiding her at all costs. She tried to be herself around him, but after a while, it became oppressive.

She spent the morning helping David and the boys prepare for their outing, making sure they each had a light jacket or long-sleeved shirt for when they reached the top of the hill. Millie was busy all morning fussing over what to send with them, and in the end, they left with more snacks than any of them would be able to eat in a day.

At one point, Erin wanted to ask Roger a question and found him in the garage, alone. When she approached him, he seemed startled by her sudden appearance and kept looking over her shoulder instead of into her eyes. It reminded her of the many times she'd been with a guy only to have him disrespect her the morning after. *But we haven't ever done anything like that, so I don't understand! He was acting normal with me yesterday; what changed?* "Roger? What's the matter? Are you—mad at me?" she asked timidly. His friendship meant so much to her that the thought of him being mad at her made unexpected tears smart her eyes.

———

Roger finally looked at her and saw her eyes were filling with tears. His stomach fluttered slightly; he felt guilty for making her cry as well as for the feelings he was trying with all his might to suppress. "Ach, Erin, I'm no' angry at yeh. How could I be?" he said, his voice soft and calming. A tear escaped her eye, and he gently wiped it away with his thumb, hoping neither David nor Tilly would come in and see him as he touched her face.

"I didn't mean to cry; I don't know what's wrong with me. It must be hormones, I guess, but your friendship means so much to me, and to think of you being angry… well, I don't like it," she said and then smiled sheepishly up at him.

His heart palpitated again, and he had to look away. *Dammit, Roger! Ye're gonnae have tae get yerself together.* "Did yeh… need somethin'?" he asked abruptly. He figured that finding out what she wanted and doing whatever it was quickly would be the fastest way to get her away from him.

She took a small step back and faltered. "I—only wanted to ask if—if you would mind if I invited Tilly to go shopping with

Rosie and me—today? Sorry for bothering you. I'll just go now," she said haltingly and started to walk away.

"Aye, I dinnae mind if yeh ask Tilly tae go wi' yeh; I'm sure she'd like et," he said, not sure why he'd said that; he didn't know anything about what Tilly liked or didn't like.

"What would I like?" Tilly asked as she descended the stairs from the flat. Erin didn't say anything right away, so Roger came and stood next to Tilly, putting his arm around her shoulders.

"Erin was just asking if—" he began, but Erin finished for him.

"If you'd like to come with Rosie and me to find some books? There's also a really great shop in the old town I'd like to visit again."

Tilly smiled at her and then looked at Roger. "Do you mind?" she asked him.

Roger would have preferred to spend the whole day in bed with her, but he didn't want to be selfish. "I don't mind."

"Maybe you can see if David—" Erin started to say boldly to him, but when he turned away from her, she finished a bit less confidently "…would—like for you—to join them?"

He picked something up from his workbench and acted like it was the most important thing in the world at that moment. "Huh? Oh, aye, that's a fine idea," he said and then went back to studying the thing in his hand.

Tilly put her hand on Erin's shoulder in a friendly manner. "So, how are we gonna get there?" she asked, and Roger hurried over to them, forgetting the box of spark plugs he'd been examining so carefully.

"I can take yeh—I mean, et's ma job, after all," he said and smiled at Tilly.

"Okay, if it's not too much trouble," Erin said, sounding utterly deflated and very sad. "We'll be leaving in about half an hour; we'll meet you in here, Tilly."

———

Erin walked out of the garage, not really wanting to go shopping anymore. She was also kinda sorry she'd invited Tilly. It was apparent something was going on with her and Roger, making him all anxious around her. She knew all about jealousy, but she couldn't imagine why Tilly would be jealous of her with Roger. She didn't want to ruin the day with Rosie, so she tried to put it all behind her to think about later. Taking a deep breath, she went back into the house, smiling, and found Rosie sitting patiently at the breakfast bar in the kitchen.

"Can we leave now, Erin?" Rosie asked.

Her excitement was contagious, and Erin soon forgot about how Roger was acting. "Aye, sweety, I'll be ready in a few minutes. I invited Tilly to come along; I hope you don't mind?" she said.

Rosie smiled up at her. "I don't mind…" she said and then trailed off.

Erin noticed her hesitate. "What is it, Rosie? I can tell you want to say something."

Rosie looked at her and then at the floor. "I—I was thinking how nice it would be to call you 'mummy.' I know it's silly, I mean you're not married to Daddy yet, but—"

Erin had to turn around to hide the tidal wave of tears that had started falling from her eyes. Rosie pushed herself off the high bar seat and timidly went to her. Erin was shaking, and a tear fell from her chin hitting the floor with a tiny splash. "Erin? I—I'm sorry I made you cry. I won't talk about that again, I promise!" she said, sounding frightened and mortified.

Erin whirled around and sat on the floor in front of her, then pulled the girl onto her lap. She rocked her, more for her own comfort than for Rosie's until she was more under control. "Rosie, you darling, beautiful girl, I'm not crying because I'm upset at you. I'm just so very happy. I know it might be hard for you to understand, but I've wanted with all my heart and for all my life to have children who would call me mummy and who would let me rock them as I'm doing now. I was told when I was young that I wouldn't be able to have babies of my own because I was born with—

"Fertilizer Prefect? Daddy told us about that on the day Daniel sent you a selfie of us," she said, and Erin laughed so hard she snorted.

"Fertilis Defect, yes. Most women who are born with it can't have babies, and because your daddy is—well, making me better, I'm going to have a real baby." Rosie looked at Erin's stomach and then at her face. "Having you say that to me has made me so happy, and I won't stop you if you'd like to call me that. I can't wait to be your mummy for real," she said as tears rolled freely down her face.

"Can you feel the new baby inside you?" Rosie asked and tentatively put her little hand on Erin's belly.

"No, darling, not just yet. It won't be until maybe... September or October before I'll be able to feel it moving, and then I'll make sure you get to feel it as often as you'd like before it's born," she promised.

Rosie looked excited and smiled up at her. "Okay," she said and put her head on Erin's shoulder.

———

Tilly had come in about halfway through what Erin was saying to the youngest of David's children. *"...Fertilis Defect, yes. Most women who are born with it can't have babies, and because your daddy is—well, making me better, I'm going to have a real baby."* She wanted to have babies, too, at least one of them. Her dream had been shattered too when she'd learned she was infertile. Not that she'd ever found anyone she wanted to have a kid with, well, not until then, maybe. She didn't know if she'd be 'healed' enough to have children of her own, like Erin, but if she did, she could imagine Roger being a very good man to have them with.

She coughed a little as she came around the island and saw Erin jump. "Sorry, I didn't mean to startle you." She watched her hug Rosie and then kiss her cheek. Tilly laughed, seeing her on the floor like that. "How'd you end up down there? Here, let me help you," she said. She took one hand, Rosie took the other, and they smiled as Erin groaned, making a show of getting up off the floor. "Are you ready to go?" she asked once Erin was upright.

"I just need to get my purse from our room. I'll be right back down," Erin said. She turned and started for the stairs, but at that moment, Roger came into the house, and they collided in the kitchen doorway.

Rosie laughed as they ended up in a very awkward bear hug. Roger froze, apparently not knowing what to do, and Erin backed away, letting him enter the room. She walked out the door meekly and left the room with her head down.

Tilly felt terrible; she knew it was her fault Roger was behaving so awkwardly with Erin, but she'd also felt like it was important to say something about it to him the night before. She wasn't jealous of her, she only wanted Roger to see what he obviously hadn't before, but now it was a mess.

———

When Erin got to the bedroom, she was flustered from her encounter with Roger, knowing that the day before, they would have laughed about it. Now, for some unknown reason, he was acting weird and unnatural with her, and it was starting to piss her off. She grabbed her purse and some of the money she'd saved from the times David had left large piles of pound notes for her in the past. Then, when she turned around, she saw more money lying on the nightstand. She rolled her eyes, then took most of it and put it in her pocket.

She quickly checked the mirror and realized it was no use; the crying had made her face all splotchy and red and she'd successfully wiped off the little bit of makeup she'd put on that morning. "Damn!" she said and then headed back down the stairs and into the kitchen, trying to avoid Roger, but he was no longer in the house, and neither were Tilly and Rosie.

Part of her thought it would be more pleasant to walk all the way to the Old Town rather than ride in the car with Roger, but that would take all day, and she didn't want to bother with the busses either. Hardening herself against his coolness, she walked outside, expecting the SUV to be waiting near the door for her. She was surprised to see it at the end of the driveway.

Roger was standing by the gate, having just opened it, and walked over to open the door for her. He had never once done that before. He'd always waited until all the passengers had gotten in before moving the vehicle to the gate. Now she knew there was something wrong, but she closed her eyes and tried not to take it personally. Tilly was sat next to Roger in the front seat, and he smiled at her when he got back in the second time, after closing the gate behind them.

"Where to?" he asked brightly, but Erin wasn't feeling very bright at the moment.

"Old Town, please," she said as if he were just a taxi driver. She felt sick and disappointed at the character change she attributed to Tilly's influence. She needed to regain some of her joy, so she took out the card Tim had given her and told Roger the address of the curiosity shop. She couldn't remember what hours Tim had told her he worked on Saturday, so she hoped with all her heart he'd be there.

Chapter Thirty-Five

BOOKS AND CURIOUS THINGS

Roger pulled the SUV up outside the shop, but before he could get out to open her door, Erin opened it and got out, helping Rosie after her. As he approached Tilly's door, Erin went into the shop, not waiting for her. He opened the door for Tilly and watched as Erin walked away without even saying 'goodbye,' or 'thanks,' which was not like her at all. He was torn; he wanted Erin's friendship more than—well, more than nearly anything, but he couldn't be around her without thinking about what Tilly had said.

Tilly got out and gave him a light kiss. "I'm sorry, Roger," she said unexpectedly. "I shouldn't have said anything, and now I can see you're having a hard time. I never meant to drive a wedge between you and Erin, I honestly didn't, and now I don't know how to fix it."

He looked at her, not knowing what to say; he could see the enormous iron wedge that he, not she, was pounding into his relationship with Erin, but what other choice did he have? "I—" he started, but couldn't admit his feelings, not there, on the street. How could he tell that lovely woman that it was nearly impossible for him not to love Erin and that he wanted nothing more than to run into that shop and apologize to her, trying to make things alright again? He knew he needed to be mindful of Tilly's feelings, but he didn't know how to balance it all, so instead, he smiled and said, "Et'll be a'right." Then he shut the door and got back into the driver's seat. He drove off, upset about how he was treating Erin; it was obviously affecting her, but he also wanted to please Tilly, yet not knowing how, and it was almost too much for him.

Back at Owlgate, he pulled directly into the garage instead of parking it outside; he needed to think, to breathe. He shut off the engine and walked up to his flat. Tilly's overnight bag was sitting on his bed, her toothbrush was on his sink in the bathroom, and he could smell her perfume on the shirt she'd taken off the night before and left on the chair in the corner of the room.

"What do I do?" he said quietly to himself and sat on the end of his bed. It was quiet in the flat. All he could hear was the tiny refrigerator and a branch from one of the large trees outside scraping on the roof. *I'll have to get to that soon*, he thought. He knew he could never have Erin. That was never a serious thought in his mind, but he liked being around her, and he thought she was so very beautiful, whether the rest of the world agreed with him or not.

He lay back on his bed and thought about his dear wife. *What would Maggie say about all this?* He closed his eyes and was able, that time, to visualize her face, with her rosy, freckled cheeks and her bright blue eyes. Her red hair was being picked up by the breeze and blown over her eyes. She was laughing and smiling, her deep, soft dimples showing, and his heart ached. "Oh, darling, I wish yeh were here! I dinnae ken what tae do." And then he heard, almost as if it were a real voice in the room, his wife, still laughing and speaking tenderly to him.

"Yeh dinnae need tae do anathin', Roger," he heard. "Tilly said she understands why yeh would love Erin; yeh just need tae refocus yer love and energy. Dinnae avoid Erin, just be yer wonderful, sensible self. Love Erin as a friend; admire the things yeh find lovely about her without pursuing et and put all the love yeh can ontae Tilly. The way I see et, darling, if yeh cannae do tha', you may just lose the both of them in yer quest for neutrality. Et's changin' yer character, love, and tha's one of yer greatest strengths."

Roger woke about twenty minutes later, feeling like a weight had been lifted off him. It was so simple, "Thank yeh, ma darling," he said to the ghost of his dear wife and then went back downstairs and into the house.

Erin saw Tilly walk into the shop on Victoria Street, looking around in wonderment. She knew it was like stepping into a grown-up kid's dream and could see that she loved it immediately. She stepped up to her and Rosie, near the *Doctor Who* merchandise, and picked up a little Matt Smith figure, turning it over in her hand. "I think David would make a fantastic Doctor, don't you?" she said casually.

Erin didn't want to be mad at Tilly; it wasn't her fault, or at least she hoped it wasn't her fault Roger was acting like a jerk. "Yeah. I think so too," she said, really making an effort.

Rosie got very excited when she saw the *Future Explorations* display. "That's my daddy's signature!" she said and pointed to the name signed on the cardboard cut-out of a scene from the show with David's face as the focal point. "What does it say? It's all messy," she asked.

"Tae Tim and th' staff— Thes shop es brilliant! Good luck on all yer Future Explorations—David Elliott," said a voice coming from the back room, then a young man walked into the shop.

"Tim! I'm so glad to see you! How have you been?" Erin said and practically ran to him, hugging him tightly.

"Is that what it really says?" Rosie asked, sounding unsure whether to believe the man or not.

"Yes, darling, that's what it says," Erin confirmed, "This is Tim, the person your dad signed it for. Tim, this is Rosie; she's David's youngest child. Tim works here and has become someone I consider to be a friend. We are kindred spirits." She exchanged a smile with him. "You will learn all about what they are when I start reading *Anne of Green Gables* to you."

Tim smiled broadly when she said that. "Ach, tha's one eh mah favorite books! Ah know, ah dinnae seem the type tae be readin' tha' mushy, girly stuff, but mah mum would read et tae mah sister, and ah overheard et."

"I like you even more knowing that about you," she said.

"And, aye, Erin, ah believe we're kendred spirets as well!" he said and held out his hand for Rosie to shake. "Et's nice tae meet yeh, Rosie; ah'm glad ye're here!"

Rosie timidly held out her hand for him to shake. "If you like him, Erin, I will as well."

"You may choose whom you like, darling, but thanks for your faith in my taste of friends," Erin said

"Can ah help yeh find anathin'?" he said to Erin with a smile.

"To be honest, I just wanted your good company to make me feel a bit better." Tilly was heading toward the other side of the store, so Erin took her chance to speak openly. "I think I've had a row with one of my good friends. First, I don't know what I did, and second, I don't know how to fix it. I'm feeling really bad about it, so I thought seeing you would cheer me up; so far, it's working."

"Ach, Erin! Ah dinnae ken what yeh couldae done without knowin' et, but ah reckon tha' ef she's a true friend, she'll come tae her senses and at least tell yeh what the trouble is so yous can work et out," he said.

Erin smiled warmly at him. "Aye, words of wisdom! I'm sure *he* will," she said and laughed.

"Et's no'—David, es it?" he said, looking truly worried.

"No, et's no' him," she said and shook her head. "I mean, it's not him," she repeated in her own accent. "It's someone else."

Tim looked relieved and then laughed. "If et's a man, most likely, he's in love wi' yeh, and cannae bring himself tae say et," he said and continued laughing.

Erin looked at Tilly, who was helping Rosie find Edinburgh on the large, freestanding globe near them. *Holy Moses! Is that what this is about?* she thought, and it all became clear to her. *That's why it took Tilly in the mix to make him freak out. Good night nurse, now what do I do?* "Tim? Can I ask you a hypothetical question?" she said and smiled with a slight wink.

"Anathin' at-all," he said.

"Let's say—hypothetically, that this person *was* actually in love with me... like you said, and another woman came onto the scene; how might said hypothetical man behave? Asking for a friend, of course."

Tim frowned at her and then raised his brows, seeming to understand that she was serious. "Well, ah'd say, hypothetically, if et were me, and ah met a new bird, ah'd most likely start tae push yeh away, though et would break mah heart tae do et," he said.

Erin sighed deeply and put her hand on his bicep. "Tim, you have been so very, very helpful today, in ways you have no idea about. I am in debt to you, my friend!" she said.

"Glad ah could help," he said, looking pleased with himself.

Erin saw Rosie looking at the small cottage figurine she and David had admired when they'd been there. It was on a shelf that was over her head, and she couldn't quite see it.

"Did you want to look at something, Rosie?" Erin asked.

"Yes, Mummy, I'd like to see the cottage, please," she said politely. Erin froze for a second as Rosie turned around and smiled at her. "I did it; I said it to you. Did you like it?" she asked sweetly.

Erin was beside herself; she crouched and took Rosie by both hands. "You have made me feel like a million buck—er, I mean pounds just now!" she said. She kissed the small girl's cheek and then stood with the help of Tim, who'd followed her. She smiled and handed the small farmhouse to Rosie.

"You may open et for a closer look ef ye'd like," Tim said to her.

Rosie looked at him like he was all-powerful. "Really? You'll actually allow me to do that... before I buy it?" she asked with awe and disbelief.

"Aye, just try no' tae rip the box."

She handed the cardboard box to Erin, who opened it, and then gave the miniature house to Rosie, who smiled broadly. "It's exactly the same, isn't it, Mummy? Wait, have you been there? Has Daddy taken you to see it yet?" she asked.

Tim's eyes grew large, and he mouthed, 'really?'

Erin laughed and said, "Aye, Rosebud, he did. It *is* perfect, isn't it? Except for the flowers and things on the outside; they aren't there anymore."

"And the inside doesn't really look like that either; it's all—" Rosie began.

"Dark and sooty," Erin and Rosie said in unison and then laughed. "Your dad and I bought one of these, but I'd like to buy this one for you, to have for your very own if you'd like that," she offered.

Rosie smiled and looked at the little cottage in her hands. "I would like it very much, Mummy, thank you," she said, then carefully handed the figurine to Erin and hugged her. "I like this store! I think my brothers would like it as well! We should bring them and Daddy here to see it."

"That's a great idea, darling," Erin said as Tilly walked over and looked at the shelf. She watched her scan the Pop Vinyl figures until her eyes came to rest on one of Joe Whitehall, holding the traveling device.

She lifted it gingerly and examined it closely. "This is amazing! Look at this, Erin! I've never seen any figures of Joe, only of David. It's—beautiful," she said and grinned. "I have the perfect spot for it, next to my TV." She laughed and continued to study the miniature vinyl man.

"Oh, Tilly, you have to see something!" Erin said, her resentments fading now that she understood what was happening with Roger. "Tim? Do you have another View-Master?" she asked.

"Aye." He did an about-face and put his finger up to say he was on it and to give him a minute. He disappeared into the back room and came out a few minutes later with one still in the box. Setting it on the sales counter, he took it out and opened the small envelope with the reels in it. He popped reel number one into the top and then handed it to Rosie, who had stopped what she was doing to watch him, completely engaged.

She looked at Erin for permission, and when she nodded, Rosie took hold of the machine and put it up to her eyes.

"Et helps ef yeh hold et toward a light," Tim said and gently turned her to face the large picture window. She allowed him to help her and then gasped when she saw the first image.

"That's my daddy! He's standing by the old farmhouse near our cottage!" Tim showed her how to pull the lever to change the picture, and she smiled at him.

Rosie was truly a miniature Susannah and as she watched her, Erin wondered if David's former wife had ever smiled so joyfully in her horrid, hate-filled life.

"Oh, and there's Baz, I mean Mr. Thompson, rolling down the hill!" she exclaimed.

Tilly looked at Erin and then at Rosie. "Do you know Barry Thompson? The man who played Joe Whitehall in the show?" Tilly asked her.

Rosie reluctantly looked away from the toy in her hand and answered her politely. "Yes, I do. He comes to our house every Christmas when my daddy and mum—" she frowned, "When they have their Christmas party. My brothers and I are only allowed to stay up for a little while, and we aren't allowed to come downstairs—unless—my mother gives us permission. Will you and Daddy have a Christmas party, Mum?" she asked Erin.

"Oh, well, I don't know. Maybe, though it might not be as large since I don't know as many people as your mother did." She thought about all the people who had been in those nasty photos of David and felt a bit sick. "I'll ask your father later today. Do you think he and the boys are having fun on top of Arthur's seat?" Rosie shrugged; she clearly thought the View-Master was much more interesting than her dumb brothers. "Okay, Rosie, go ahead and look through the rest of the reels," Erin relented.

Tim showed Rosie how to change the small white disk with the tiny, see-through images on them. Erin watched them interacting, and when Tim finished explaining everything to her, she smiled at his grin. It looked like he was about to explode as he approached. "All right, out with it," she said.

"The farmhouse—et exists? And yeh ken where et is?" he nearly whispered as if saying it out loud might change the answer.

She laughed and put her hand on his shoulder. "Aye! I know where it exists. David owns it, but I'm not saying where it is; not even for a Kindred Spirit, sorry," she said, and Tim shrugged.

"Ach, ah dinnae need tae ken where et es, Erin, only tha' et's still somewhere!"

Tilly looked excited as she joined them. "Did you just say David owns the farmhouse? Really? Oh, wow! Wouldn't it be amazing to see that in person! She looked at Tim, and he smiled, raising his eyebrows.

"Well, maybe once we rebuild the main cottage, David will invite you—"

Rosie made a noise that caused Erin to turn and look at her. She'd stopped looking at the View-Master and was staring at the group of grown-ups. Her little chin was quivering and huge alligator tears were falling down her face.

"Rosie! What's the matter? Oh, my darling girl!" Erin rushed over to her and held her in her arms.

"What happened to the cottage, Erin?" Rosie asked softly.

Erin hadn't thought about Rosie overhearing them and felt terrible that she'd find out like that. "Oh, Rosie, I'm afraid it burned down," she said, and Rosie looked horrified.

"How? What happened to it?" she asked, sniffling.

"Well, your daddy and I were there. He wanted to show me the old farmhouse, and I started the oven, to bake something, and— I guess it started an electrical fire."

"Were you in the house? Did you get burned?" she asked, looking at Erin with real concern.

Erin didn't want to scare her, but she couldn't lie. "The caretaker had come by to change some light bulbs and didn't have enough, so he came back, and he saved your daddy's life by pulling him out just in time."

"Old John saved Daddy's life? But where were you?" she asked and took a deep, shaky breath.

"I had gone for a walk, darling, while your daddy took a nap, and I didn't know about the fire until I heard the fire trucks. That's when I turned around and came back as fast as I could," she said.

Rosie's eyes were each as large as a two-pound coin. "Daddy almost… died?" she said, suddenly registering what Erin had said about John pulling David out just in time. There was true terror in her voice."

Erin held her and rocked her, sitting on the floor of a curiosity shop in Edinburgh. "Aye, my darling, he could have died, but Old John came back and saved him, and now he's as good as new," she said.

Rosie cried, fear filling her small body. "I want to be with my daddy now," she said between sobs.

Erin's heart felt like it had been ripped out. *The poor baby*, she thought. "Alright, sweetheart, I'll send him a message and ask him where he is."

Rosie nodded and moved enough for Erin to take her phone out of her pocket. People came into the shop and then left, not paying much attention to the mother and daughter they saw sitting on the floor. Erin sent a message to David:

E: *Where are you now, darling?*

D: *Still on the mountain. Roger has joined us. Do you need a ride back?*

E: *No...well, maybe. I mentioned something about the cottage needing to be rebuilt, and Rosie overheard me. She knows about the fire and that you could have died, and she wants to be with you. I'm sorry...I didn't think she was listening.*

D: *Oh my. It'll be over an hour before I can get back to the house, and*

then however long it takes Roger to
get to you. I'll come with him when
he picks you up, I reckon.

E: *Ok, I'll let her know. I love You.*
xoxo

"Alright, my love," she said to Rosie, "your daddy is still on top of Arthur's seat with Roger and your brothers. He's going to start heading back to your gran's now, and he'll come with Roger when he picks us up. Why don't we look for those books before they get here? Will that be okay with you?"

Rosie nodded and stood. Her little eyes were red, and she was still sniffling a bit. "Yes, Mummy, thank you for doing that for me. My—my mother wouldn't have done that; she—she didn't understand me as you do. She'd have told me to stop crying and not to act like a baby, but I think you understand me. I think you know why I want my daddy, and—and I love you," she said, then fell into Erin's arms and hugged her.

Tim and Tilly watched with their mouths open; Tilly was crying silently. Erin heard her explain to Tim, in a whisper, that she hadn't known the children for very long, and for Rosie to be telling her she loved her was nothing short of a miracle.

"I love you too, baby girl. I know you're not a baby anymore, but my mother used to call me that when I was your age; sometimes she still does, and it just feels right," she said.

Rosie let go of her and smiled. "Just like it feels right to call you mummy?"

"Yes, just the same. Now, if someone will help me up, my rear end is fast asleep! We have at least one book to buy today; I just hope we can find it!"

"Are yeh lookin' for *Anne of Green Gables*?" Tim asked.

"Yes, and a few others," Erin said.

Tim smiled, "Well, if yeh cannae find a copy of et, send me a text, and ah'll allow you tae borrow mah copy. Ah'll bring et from home tomorrow, if yeh need et," he said casually.

"Oh, Tim! That's so sweet. I'll take you up on your offer if it comes to that. I'm not sure how easy it will be to find a one-hundred-year-old Canadian book in Scotland."

"Ach, have yeh heard of Nova Scotia? Et means New Scotland, so yeh may no' have much trouble," Tim said, seeming proud of his North American geography knowledge.

"Aye, you're right! I never thought of that; well done, you! We'd better go now, though. We'll come back in about an hour; thank you for putting up with us today!" Erin said as she and Tilly paid for the things they wanted to purchase, then she hugged him as they walked out the door.

Chapter Thirty-Six

FAMILY MEETING AT THE CURIOSITY SHOP

An hour later, Erin, Tilly, and Rosie returned to the shop, looking tired and defeated. "Ach! Et doesnae look as though ye've had much success!" Tim said.

Erin was very tired, and she was glad David and Roger would be coming to get them soon. "We found *Harry Potter and the Philosopher's Stone*, which will do, but not any of the others. It doesn't surprise me too much. They were all American books, like the *Little House* series and *Little Women*. I'll just buy them on Amazon, no big deal."

"Ah must tell yeh," he said bashfully, and his cheeks flushed, dark pink, "ah've—uhh—managed tae get mah copy here for yeh, jest in case yeh couldnae find et. Mah flatmate brought et here when he… delivered mah lunch… which… ah forgot… thes mornin'." He pointed to the sales counter.

Erin saw a much-loved copy of the first book in the *Anne of Green Gables* series and wanted to kiss him. "I know you're lying, Tim, but I can't thank you enough! I really do owe you now! Are you sure you want me to take it with me? What if it gets ruined?" she asked.

"Ah dinnae reckon ye'd let tha' happen, but ef et does, ah'll get a new one. Et's no' the only one in existence," he said with a shrug.

Erin laughed and put her arm around his waist. "Rosie, I want you to look at this man, please."

She looked at Erin and then at Tim, seeming a bit confused.

"Tonight, I'll be able to read to you from one of the loveliest book series there is, and it's because this man was unselfish and went out of his way for us. If there is anything I'd like for you to learn in life it would be that kindness is worth more than gold and thoughtfulness is more valuable than silver."

"Ach, Erin, et was nothin', really. Plus, et wasnae completely altruistic, yeh ken. Ah hate tae admit et, but the thought of havin' mah book in the hands of David Elliott is crackin," he said, pink-cheeked, and looking at his shoes.

Erin smiled, having already guessed that was part of his thinking. "And honesty is more valuable than fame or riches or any priceless gem." Tim's blush deepened as he took the book off the counter. "I know you would've done it for me even if David Elliott had nothing to do with it because we are kindred spirits. That's the kind of thing we do," Erin said and saw the SUV pull up in front of the building.

David got out of the vehicle, and Erin's heart fluttered at seeing him like that. She could still very easily imagine they didn't know one another and she was only catching a glimpse of him out on the street.

Rosie looked out the window too and squeed, clapping her hands. "Daddy!" she cried.

He saw her through the window and smiled his best smile. Erin saw he'd brought the boys along, which was really nice. Once they were all out of the SUV, Roger drove away and everyone came into the shop. David lifted Rosie into his arms and held her for a long time. "Hello, ma Rosebud," he said softly.

"Oh, Daddy!" she said and buried her face into his neck, sniffling but not crying as hard as she had done earlier.

"Shhh. Et's a'right, darling. I'm here, and I'm not goin' anawhere. I ken you were frightened about the fire, but I'm safe now, and everathin's okay," he said. Her little head nodded, but she continued to hold him tightly.

The shop was quite crowded, so Tim said, "Ah realize et's Saturday, but et's heavin' in here, so ah'm gonnae turn the sign sayin' we're closed and lock the door."

David set Rosie down and then walked up to Tim. "Good thinkin', mate," he said and shook Tim's hand.

Erin saw the younger man blush and start to go into 'deer in the headlights' mode. She caught his eye and smiled, hoping he'd remember the last time they'd been there. He returned her smile and added a slight nod, then turned back to David, who pointed to the book in Tim's hand.

He held it up and said, "I was just gonnae hand this tae Erin," then handed it to David instead.

———

David scanned the front cover. "*Anne of Green Gables*, by L. M. Montgomery," he read out loud. "And yeh say this is one of yer favorite books?"

"Aye, et is," Tim answered, then realized he hadn't been talking to him and blushed.

Erin laughed. "Aye, it's one of mine, too—oh, I'll be right back," she said and walked away.

"Ye've read this?" David asked Tim, surprised.

Tim shrugged and explained how his mum had read it to his sister and he'd fallen in love with the characters and settings. "And yeh cannae go wrong wi' a plucky red-heided girl, can yeh?" Tim added.

David laughed heartily and put his hand on Tim's shoulder. He turned, spotted Erin talking with Charlie, and smiled, leaning in. "I prefer brunettes, maself," he said.

Tim smiled, and they both watched Erin talk to the boy; she was laughing and looked so sure of herself. "Aye; cannae go wrong wi' one-a them either. There's one en the book as well, yeh ken," he said.

"This is yer copy, then?" David asked, flipping through the dog-eared pages. The leaves were yellowed and the edges were now softened by time and use. "Didn't Erin find one?"

"Naw, sae ah'm lendin' her mah own copy sae she can get et started, at least. She said she was verra eager tae start t'night... if possible," he said, and David looked at the young man standing in front of him, smiling.

"Tha's verra kind of yeh, Tim! Thank you."

Tim blushed so that the tops of his ears nearly glowed. "Ach, et's nothin', truly," he said.

——

Tilly approached Erin and asked, "Why do you think Roger drove off like that? I was hoping he would stay."

"Well, usually, he's just the driver, and he doesn't hang out with the family, but seeing you're here, I'm not sure. I'll ask David," she offered. She stepped up next to him and took his hand.

He looked down at her and smiled. "Hallo! Fancy meetin' you here like this!" he said.

She smiled back at him, knowing she was the luckiest girl in the world. "Tilly's wondering if Roger is coming back?"

"Aye, he's tryin' tae find a place tae park, but bein' Saturday, et's a bit crowded. I'm sure he'll be here verra soon."

"Okay, I'll let her know," she said and brushed a hair off her mouth with her left hand. Tim gasped loudly and she looked at him, slightly bemused at his reaction to her moving a hair off her face. "What is it, Tim?" she asked.

He shrugged and gently took her hand in his, lifting it as if he were going to kiss it. David furrowed his brow until Tim said, "Yer ring, Erin; et's stunnin'! Et looks verra old; is et?"

Erin smiled and touched the center diamond. "It is; it was David's great grandmother's ring," she said. She looked up at David and he kissed her.

"Ach, sae ye're engaged, then?" he said. "Tha's brilliant! Ah'm sae happy for yeh."

David touched her face. "Thank yeh. I'm quite pleased with et maself," he replied.

"Erin! Did you see this?" It was Peter; he was holding the View-Master and laughing.

Erin kissed David on the cheek and said, "You'll have to excuse me, boys, I'm being beckoned by a *very* handsome young man, and I've had enough of this tired banter." Then she laughed and shook her head. "I have no idea where that came from; I'm just being silly."

She walked away, and the two men watched her go. "She's an amazin' woman, Erin is," Tim said, unable to stay quiet, and David grinned.

"Aye," he said.

———

Erin put her finger up to Peter to say to hold on a minute so she could find Tilly. It was too late, though; she saw Roger at the door trying to open it, but it was locked. She looked at him through the window and went to the door. The lock turned easily and unbolted with a *thump*. She pushed the little thumb latch on the old door handle, and it opened.

Roger looked at Erin, standing in front of him, and hung his head, "May I come in Erin?" he asked contritely.

She smiled at the little boy he'd just become and swung the door open. "Aye, you may; Tilly is—" she began, but he shook his head at her and waited for her to close and lock the door behind him. "I don't understand," she said as he took hold of her hand.

He found Tilly in the crowd and approached her. "I need tae speak wi' Erin; please dinnae be cross," he said.

Tilly's eyes were wide, and she looked flummoxed. "Why would I be cross?" she said and smiled at them both. Erin looked at her with her eyebrows raised and shrugged to say she had no idea what was going on either.

Roger looked around the store. "Come wi' me," he said, then pulled her to a very short hallway that led to the back storeroom and a small toilet. The space was filled with boxes and merchandise that had yet to find a home on the shop floor. "Erin, I've been an eejit and an ass, and I need tae ask yer forgiveness," he said, still holding her hand.

Erin frowned; he **had** behaved like an idiot, and she thought she knew why, *Why is he saying all of this now; why the sudden change?* "I—don't know what to say," she said hesitantly. "I—forgive you?" He looked frustrated and anxious, so she put her hand on his arm and looked him in the eyes. "Roger, I'm not sure what's going on with you, but thank you for your apology. I won't ask you to explain it to me; I just hope we can be as we were before?" she said hopefully.

He took a deep breath, seeming relieved. "Aye. Thank yeh, Erin," he said and gave her a very short hug.

"Now, Peter wanted my attention, so I'll talk to you later," she said and headed toward where she'd seen him last, while Roger watched her.

Tilly watched her as well and then walked up to Roger.

"Is everything okay?" she asked him and took his hand.

"Aye, et is now." He bent and kissed her, then looked at where they were standing. "What sort of shop is this, exactly?" he asked.

Tilly smiled broadly. "It's the most awesome store I've ever been in; come and look around with me," she said and led him to the *Future Explorations* displays.

They spent a good forty-five minutes in the store, and then it was time to go. Millie would have lunch ready soon, and everyone was getting tired. Roger left to bring the car around, and Tilly went with him.

"Will we all fit into the SUV?" Erin asked David as he examined the enormous globe positioned near the center of the main room; he looked up to answer her question.

"Aye, et holds eight people. Show me where Green Bay is on here?" he asked and looked down again.

Erin walked over to the globe that was already turned to America. Tim and the children gathered around it as well.

"Is tha' where ye're fae, Erin? I'd like tae see et as well," Tim said.

Now that she had an audience, she decided to give them a tiny geography lesson. "Okay, here, is America—" she said, trying to sound mysterious and making the younger children laugh. "If you were to cut the continent in half... like so," She used the side of her hand to cut an imaginary line through the whole of the country. "...and head north, then east until you got to the cluster of lakes, you'd be in Wisconsin, or... Minnesota, but let's pretend you're in Wisconsin.

She pointed to the state and showed them how it looked sorta like a hand with the thumb sticking out. Everyone looked at the state and tried to imagine it was a hand, but it seemed a stretch for everyone but her.

"Well, it's easier if you can imagine it." She held out her hand, pointed to the crotch of her hand and thumb, and said proudly, "I'm from the crotch of Wisconsin." They all looked at her, startled, and then laughed. She pointed to the map at the tiny dot that said Green Bay, then moved her finger down to the one that said Milwaukee. "I was born just about halfway between Milwaukee and Green Bay." Everyone took turns getting close to the globe, expecting to see what, she didn't know, but it was fun to watch them.

"Do you see the tip of the thumb?" She pointed to it on the map. "That is one of the most beautiful places God ever created. They call it Door County, and it's got coastlines and caves and trees and hills and cliffs; it's a lot like England. I just remembered, David; one of my friends is having a wedding vow renewal next month. I promised her I'd go, so… I think it might be fun to crash the party, with her knowledge, of course. Children are welcome, and you can meet my friends. I know Carrie and Steve would be thrilled beyond words to have you— I mean us—there. We can make it part of the children's holiday. Maybe we could rent a house in Green Bay, a big one that's on the way to Door County, and we can do some exploring!"

"Aye, I'll check into that," David said, enjoying her enthusiasm. "What do yeh think, children? Would yeh like tae visit the place where Erin is from?"

They all started talking at the same time:

"Oh, yes, please!"

"Yes! That would be smashing!"

"I'd like that!"

"When can we go?"

"Dae yeh think ah'd fit intae yer suitcase, Erin?" Tim asked.

Erin and David both laughed, and Erin put her hand on his back. "Oh, Tim! I don't think so, but that would be fun! If the kids were younger, I'd try to convince David to bring you along as our au pair to mind them, but I'm afraid they're just too old. I hope you get to go there someday; you'd love it! If you ever do get a chance to go, you must promise you'll tell me so I can give you a list of the best places to visit. I'll put my contact information on the back of the cover on your book," she said and winked.

"A'right, I promise." He smiled at her and looked out the window. "And 'ere es your chauffeur, *mesdames et messieurs*," he said in a thick French/Scottish accent and with a flourish and bow.

Erin looked at him quizzically. "Where on earth did that come from?"

"An au pair should practice 'is Frahnch, no?" he said in explanation.

Erin shook her head and laughed. "You are one of a kind!"

Tim went to the door as they left the store, "Haste yeh back!" he said and turned the sign around to read OPEN.

As they piled into the vehicle, the children were all laughing and smiling while putting on horrible French accents. Daniel repeated, '*oui*,' again and again, giggling at how it sounded like 'wee,' and Erin didn't want it to end.

Chapter Thirty-Seven

TIRED AND HUNGRY

Roger, Tilly, and the Elliott family arrived at Owlgate without any time to spare. Millie was waiting at the door when they pulled up, tapping an imaginary watch on her wrist. "I know, Millie; I'm sorry, but parking was a nightmare, and I had tae—" Roger began apologetically.

"Ach, no excuses; yeh have less than ten minutes before I'll expect you at the table," she interrupted him.

Erin looked at David. "Will you help me gather the children and get them washed? We can bring our things in after supper, alright?"

He looked at her adoringly and took hold of Daniel's shirt sleeve as he tried to run. "Ach, yeh heard Millie, now go directly upstairs and wash yer face. There will be plenty of time for runnin' about after lunch."

Dan put his head down and started toward the door. "Yes, sir," he said sadly.

Erin smiled at him, following Rosie and Charlie into the house. Peter was old enough to not need prodding and went on his own.

They were all back downstairs with about thirty seconds to spare since Daniel decided to have a water fight with Charlie in the bathroom, so they both had to change their clothes. Annis smiled at them as they sat, and Erin drew a cleansing breath. "Whew! We did it," she said.

When Millie was finished bringing serving dishes out to the table, Annis said her quick prayer, and they started eating. Everything felt like it had before; Roger was happy and smiled at her more than once. Tilly looked much more comfortable and spoke with Peter about her job at the deaf school. Rosie had her head leaning on Erin's arm and was holding her hand.

"Do yeh truly wanna go tae Wisconsin on holiday?" David asked her.

"Aye, I'd like to go to Carrie's vow renewal, and maybe we can see Door County, too; it's beautiful! Too bad it's not May; the cherry blossoms are usually in full bloom by then, and it's *all* cherry trees up there. Oh, and you haven't lived until you've been to Cave Point! It's absolutely stunning," she said.

David smiled at the tourism scheme she was starting to plan already. "A'right, I'm sold. I'll have Tina work it out."

"Yay! I'll send a message to Carrie after lunch," Erin said and kissed his cheek.

Erin had already put out some feelers on her girlfriend's group messenger chat. Miraculously, none of them had heard anything about her and David Elliott's relationship, so she knew it would be a surprise to show up with him. After lunch, and when she was done helping Millie with the dishes, she sent Carrie a personal message.

E: *Hey Carrie. I noticed everyone has mentioned that they've gotten their invite to your shindig in the chat. I'd really love to celebrate with you and Steve! If I'm still invited, I'd like to RSVP for 6, please. Thanks.*

A few minutes later, Carrie sent a reply.

C: *SIX! Really? I mean, I just want to know if you're serious, or joking?*

E: *I'm serious. I'd like to bring my match and his four kids, if you're ok with that?*

C: *Four kids! Wow, instant family, huh? Sure, bring the whole troop! It'll be nice to meet Mr. Miracle Man!*

E: *Ok, good. I know you'll like him, and his kids are really great.*

C: *How old are they?*

E: *Peter is 16, Charlie and Dan are 10, but I think they'll be 11 by*

then, and Rosie is 9. Oh, and
David is 45. LOL

C: *Funny! David, huh? And you say*
the kids are amazing?

E: *LOL Yes, actually, they are. I know,*
it's hard to believe at those ages.

C: *I'll take your word for it. I can't*
wait to see you! I'm so glad you're
coming!

E: *Me too! I've missed you guys so*
much! See ya then!

"Well, it's all set," Erin said to David, finding him waiting for her in the sitting room. "Carrie said she can't wait to see me and meet my Mr. Miracle Man." She laughed at the face he made. "That's what they call you since I didn't tell them your name."

"A tough name to live up to!"

"I think it fits rather nicely. Oh, by the way, I thought we could go to the arcade in Portobello today and then head to Dr. Neil's, as we promised the boys."

David groaned. "I was hopin' tae do that tomorrow. We've had a full day already. Ma belly is full, and ma legs are aching from the hike," he said and rubbed the top of his thigh for effect.

Erin smiled at him and held his hand. "Well, how about a compromise? What if we get the arcade out of the way today, seeing it's kinda cloudy, and make a day of it at Dr. Niel's tomorrow? It's supposed to be sunny and beautiful then. You can put on your hat and dorky glasses; it'll be fun!" she said, really selling it as she held out her hand to help him stand. David hadn't shaved since Thursday morning and had the beginnings of a nice beard taking shape. "You've also got a nice disguise right there on your face," she said and ran her fingers over it, scratching his chin.

He moaned and started moving his jaw and cheeks so she'd find the itchiest spots, making her chuckle. "A'right, ye've talked me into et. Just keep doing that for a while longer," he said, and she obliged him.

"Let's round up the posse and move 'em out, cowboy," she said, not knowing why she'd decided to say it that way, but it got a laugh, so she was pleased.

They had just stepped into the hallway when his phone made a noise, so he looked at it. "Ach, good, et's a message from Kitty." he said, "Yer boxes have arrived from America. She's keen tae know if she may put yer things away for yeh."

Erin could imagine her standing in front of them, dying to get her hands in there to organize everything and make sure it was all tidy for when they returned home. "Tell her she may, but she shouldn't feel obligated to do it."

David started typing, and Erin watched him. He made a delicious face when he was concentrating and was making it then. He looked at her, and she smiled at him.

"What is et now? Do I have somethin' in ma teeth?" he asked.

"No, not in your teeth, but on your lips. Let me lick it off for you," she said and touched her tongue to his bottom lip. "Mmm, tastes good, I think there's more... over here," she said and ran her tongue all the way across his upper lip, ending up with it in his mouth, kissing him, and feeling her insides do flip flops.

Millie stepped into the hall, said, "Humph," and walked away again.

———

David *really* didn't want to go to the arcade after that; he wanted to snog Erin and perhaps do a bit more with her in his room. He took her by the hand and pulled her toward the stairs, but she stopped him. "Wait—we can do that later," she said with a grin. "Let's find the kids and let Roger know our plans." David gave her the cutest little pout and stamped his foot like a child who wasn't getting his way, making Erin laugh.

Peter came in at that moment and began laughing, too. "Goh—Dad! That... was great! Do it again!" he said, holding his side and leaning against the sideboard. His reaction made Erin laugh harder, and finding an audience, David decided to play it up a bit. He pulled the face again, making Peter and Erin laugh so hard, Erin snorted, which made David lose it.

Millie came back out to see what was happening; she saw David pull the face the third time and got the giggles. "Ach, Davey! Yeh used tae make tha' face when you were wee! Et took all I had no' tae laugh evera time yeh did et," she said, holding her side.

Erin was laughing so hard tears were rolling down her face, and when Millie saw them, she laughed even harder. Before long, Annis and the three younger children were standing around, wondering what was happening. "What's so funny, Daddy?" Rosie said and then saw Erin's tears. She frowned until David looked at her, pouting.

"But I don't wanna go to the arcade!" he said and stamped his foot, crossing his arms in front of him petulantly. The three kids looked at each other and then their grandma, as if their father had officially lost it, but then joined in the laughter.

"Did you say the arcade?" Daniel asked.

"Yes, Dan. We thought we'd go today, so everyone get ready while we talk to Roger," Erin said, wiping the tears off her face. Then, she wrapped her arm around Millie, trying to help her to stand straight again.

"Ach, Losh, tha' felt good! I havnae laughed tha' hard in decades!" Millie said and stepped up to David. She kissed him on the cheek and shook her head as she returned to the kitchen.

"Come with me," Erin said and pulled David's arm toward the side door. "I wanna find Roger—"

"Do yeh reckon we ought tae... mebbe... text him first? I wouldn't wanna—eh, disturb—anathin', yeh ken?"

Erin's eyebrows went up, and she nodded. "Good thinking. Why don't you do that? Ask him if it's safe to enter his love nest," she said and laughed. "By the way, I love you, David Elliott. That was so much fun just now! I hope for many more days of acting silly with you."

He took out his mobile, sent Roger a quick text, and then wrapped his arms around her. "Aye, I do as well. I havn't allowed maself tae act like that in a verra, verra long time, and it felt good." David received a reply from Roger, telling them it was safe, so they made their way to the garage.

Roger and Tilly were just coming down the stairs, laughing, faces flushed, and Erin was glad they hadn't just come knocking at the door. "Well, you look happy," Erin commented wryly, and Tilly smiled at her.

"I am," she whispered as David and Roger talked near his workbench.

"Erin! Dad! Are you ready yet?" Daniel said as he ran into the garage.

"Calm down," Erin said, knowing it was a foolish thing to say to a ten-year-old boy.

"Where are you going?" Tilly asked him.

"Erin promised me a day at the arcades if I went clothes shopping for my mum's funeral," Dan said so bluntly that Tilly looked at Erin with raised eyebrows.

"I did," she said simply, marveling at his lack of emotion concerning the death of his mother.

"Daniel, please tell everyone tae meet out here when they're ready," David said, then turned to Erin. "I'll be back in a few minutes; I must change into my secret identity."

Chapter Thirty-Eight

AMUSEMENTS

Thirty minutes later, the Elliott family was assembled, so they piled into the SUV and were on their way to the arcade. Tilly didn't come along, so she opened and closed the gate for them, waving as they drove away. Fifteen minutes later, they were getting out of the SUV in front of a large building near Portobello beach with an enormous red sign that read 'Nobels Amusements.'

The roar of the sea and the crying gulls filled Erin's ears. She loved the sounds of the ocean, but it was overcast, and a chilly wind whipped around the side of the building, making her shiver. She waved as Roger drove away, headed back to Owlgate and Tilly.

David came up behind her and took her hand. "I reckon he wants tae get back as soon as possible," he said with a smile as they approached the doors that Peter was holding open for them. They walked in and were met with flashing lights, crazy music coming from everywhere at once, and carpeting in a pattern that looked as though someone had been sick all over it. *Probably to hide all the times children do get sick on it.* Erin thought.

The children gathered around David, but all he had were large bills, so Erin went to the counter to get change. Each child was given £10.00 to do whatever they wanted, then scattered like a school of fish when you put your foot into the water. David and Erin watched their brood as they went from machine to machine, except Daniel; he found a game he liked and stayed put.

Every now and then, one of them would come and show off how many tickets they'd won, but essentially Erin and David walked around holding hands and enjoying the anonymity David's disguise seemed to be affording them. They meandered through the building until Erin saw something she liked. "Ooh! I love Skee-Ball," she said excitedly, so David put coins into the machine and heavy, grapefruit-sized balls rolled down the shoot. She rubbed her hands together and lifted the first ball as the game came to life and began making noises. She held the ball up to David, who at first tried to take it from her, but she shook her head. "Kiss it, for luck," she said, and he scrunched up his face.

"I'm not puttin' ma mouth anawhere near that thing!" he said, making her laugh.

"Oh, alright, then kiss *me* for luck," she said and puckered up. He smiled and kissed her, then pushed his fake glasses up his nose like Clark Kent. Erin made a show of aiming and rolled the ball down the lane. It went way up to the top, missing all the holes, and dropped into the machine, giving her only ten points. "Well, I haven't played in a very long time. I need to get a feel for this machine!" she excused herself. She tried several more times and still didn't get many points.

David picked up her last ball. "Allow me," he said and launched it down the lane. The orb hit the curved-up end of the lane and landed in the fifty-point hole. "That's how et's done," he said and put his arm around Erin's shoulders.

She looked up at him, not believing what she'd just seen. The machine spat out a long line of tickets, but David was just getting started. He put more coins into the machine and waited for the balls to roll down the shoot.

"Okay, you got that one, but I bet you can't do it again," she said.

"Kiss it for luck?" he asked, holding the ball to her face. She shook her head, but she did kiss him instead. He rolled the ball up the lane, and it went straight into the fifty-point hole again.

"Okay, you're a Skee-Ball world champion, aren't you? You've played this game so often you dream about it, don't you?" Erin teased, but he shook his head as the tickets rolled out of the machine like a long yellow tongue.

"No, I've also not played this in years. I dinnae get tae go tae the arcade verra often, yeh ken," he said and threw the next ball. It did the same, and so did the next two, as well. He threw the next one, and it went into the twenty-point hole. "I didn't want yeh tae feel bad," he said with a laugh, and Erin nudged him with her shoulder. He used up his eight balls, and at the end, there was a pile of golden tickets laying on the floor at their feet.

Peter walked past and saw their cache as they picked them up. "Wow! How'd you manage that?" he asked.

"Your father, the Skee-Ball wizard," Erin said.

Peter looked at him proudly. "Show me, Dad," he said, and David pretended to be reluctant to play again, but Erin knew he wanted nothing more than to play with his eldest son.

He put more coins into the machine and tried to explain how it was done, doing it once for him, and then allowed him to throw one. It was obviously not as easy as he made it look since Peter's ball did the same thing Erin's had.

Eventually, Rosie and Charlie came to see what was happening, and they all took a lane. Rosie got hers in the twenty-point hole once, and Charlie got one in each hole but couldn't do it again. Peter was getting better but still hadn't made it into the fifty-point hole. Finally, Dan showed up with his arms full of tickets.

"Woah, Dan!" Erin said, and the rest of the family looked at him.

"I sussed out how to get loads of tickets from one machine." Will you help me cash them in, Erin?" he asked. Erin wanted to hug him tightly but knew he didn't care for things like that, so she gave him a really quick leaning squeeze.

"Of course I will," she said and picked up a length he'd dropped. Just then, they heard a noise that sounded like a cat screeching. A group of middle-aged mothers came tearing through the arcade like a herd of buffalo, all speaking at once.

"OH! It's you!"

"David Elliott! It's like a dream come true!"

"Can I have your autograph?"

"Please, could I get a selfie with you?"

"Are these your kids? How sweet."

They swarmed David, and he had to give them his attention. The children finished their games and gathered their tickets. Erin whispered to Charlie to grab his father's tickets, and they slipped away to the counting machine, which spat out a slip of paper with the total on it. Dan had the most, even with Peter's, Charlie's, Rosie's, and David's put together. As they perused the many glass-covered shelves deciding what they wanted, Erin saw the women walk away from David. When they passed by the children, she heard them commenting on how adorable they were, then one of them looked right at her.

"Oh, my God! That's the woman in the picture! Homewrecker," she said, plain as day, and gave Erin a cold stare. The rest of the women looked at her like she'd killed someone.

Erin's face turned red, and Peter's did too. "Piss off! You've gotten what you wanted, now go," he said to them angrily.

Erin put her arm around him and shushed him, seeing hot, angry tears threatening to fall from his eyes. "You are the sweetest thing, Peter. Thank you for that," she said as David approached them.

"What was that about?" he asked, apparently hearing his son's outburst but not knowing what had caused it. Erin was about to say something vague about the ladies being rude, but Dan spoke up before she could.

"Those COWS just insulted Erin!" he said loud enough that the women heard him and gasped, leaving the arcade as fast as they could.

"Okay, I reckon it's time to go," David said.

Peter was still red in the face as he said, "They called her a homewrecker, Dad!"

"Okay, we'll talk about et at yer gran's; this isn't the place, a'right," he said. Erin sensed the situation was about to get out of control and knew David was trying to keep them from making an even bigger scene.

"But our tickets, Dad!" Dan said, and David sighed.

"Erin, would yeh mind helpin' them whilst I send a message to Roger tae come for us?"

"Of course, darling," she said, and David made his way to a corner to type out his message. They decided to pool all the tickets and got a large bubble wand that looked like a lightsaber, while Rosie got a purple pinwheel.

On his way back, David was asked for his signature and a selfie by two teenage boys who'd seen the women and heard the comments by them, and by Peter.

One of the boys said to his friend, "I saw the photo of her online; et was hot as fuck!"

Peter ran at him, but David managed to catch him by his shirt sleeve just in time. "Woah! Just ignore them, Peter. Et won't do any good tae fight over et," he said, "I understand your anger, but we dinnae want—"

"But, Dad! They're talking about Erin!" Peter's face was beet red, and the blue vein was sticking out on his forehead like his father's when he was really angry.

"I ken et, son, come with me," he said. The family followed them outside, and David led Peter around the side of the building.

Erin and the others were followed by the two teens. The first one was filming them and laughing while making rude comments. The second boy was showing the picture of Erin in New Orleans, laying with her robe open on David's lap, to anyone who would look.

Roger pulled up and got out of the SUV, just as one of the boys said, "Come lay yerself on ma lap, love. I'm on the pull, and ye're pure braw!" Roger, who was much more built than David or

Peter, approached the boys and said something Erin couldn't hear. When the boys just laughed, he grabbed the one filming them by the shirt and pushed him against the stucco exterior of the arcade. Roger said something menacing to the boy while the one who'd been showing the photo around tried to get him away from his friend.

"Ach! Roger!" David exclaimed, coming back from talking with Peter and seeing what he was doing. He took him by the arm and said, "Let's go." Roger reluctantly released the boy, who began yelling at him until he raised his fist, then the two boys rushed back into the building.

By then Erin had gotten herself and the rest of the children into the SUV and opened the door for David and Peter when they came near. "I'm sorry, David," she said, not knowing what else to say or do and feeling horrible.

"Yeh didn't do anathin' tae apologize for, darling," David said.

"If anyone should be apologizing, it should be those—those—" Peter began but didn't finish.

"What was all that about?" Roger asked as he got in and turned around to head back home. The car exploded with everyone talking at the same time.

"They called Erin something bad!"

"They were being very rude to Erin!"

"They were showing that horrible picture to everyone."

David had to raise his voice to get them to be quiet. "Rude people, Roger," was all he said.

"Dad! Those boys were disgusting! They needed a thrashing! And those women were—" Peter said.

"Daddy, what's a homewrecker?" Rosie interrupted.

"A homewrecker?" Roger said, having to pull over so he didn't get into an accident. "Did someone say tha' about our Erin?"

"Those gannet, pikey, mingin', women, who'd just begged Dad for selfies and autographs, were so daft as to insult her... *to her face!*" Peter said, not able to hold his tongue.

"Gannet? That's a new one to me," Erin said, trying to lighten the mood a bit.

"Greedy, white trash, filthy women," he said, still so angry he was red in the face.

"Peter, darling, thank you for sticking up for me, but why are you so angry?" Erin asked him, reaching past David and putting her hand on his shoulder. He crossed his arms and lay his head against the window. David put his hand on Erin's knee and shook his head, silently asking her to leave it for the moment.

"But what is that?" Rosie asked again.

"It means someone who does something to break up a husband and wife; usually a woman, who tries to get someone's husband to leave his wife for her," Erin explained.

Rosie scrunched up her forehead and cocked her head to the side. "Did you do that, Erin?" she asked innocently, and Peter shot her an angry look.

"No, Rosebud, she didn't do that," David said.

"What does 'hot as fuck' mean?" Daniel asked, not caring that he'd just used a swear word in front of his whole family.

"Daniel! Where'd yeh hear that?" David asked, obviously having not heard the teen say it in the arcade.

"The chav said he'd seen the picture of Erin, and that it was hot as—" Dan began, but Charlie put his hand over his brother's mouth so he didn't say it again. He pulled Charlie's hand away and said, in his defense, "But he asked!"

Roger looked really angry, and David did as well. Erin's face was hot, and she wanted to crawl into a hole to hide. "It's not a big deal," she said quietly.

Roger, David, and Peter all started arguing with her at the same time, and Roger had to pull over again to calm down. "But it *is* a big deal," Peter said as alligator tears rolled down his face. "You're the best thing to happen to us, and you shouldn't be spoken about like that. We all love you, and—and you're not a homewrecker or—or—someone that those bell-end plonkers should be drooling over. I don't want you to be treated like that... it makes me so… angry!"

"Well said," Roger exclaimed.

"Et's over now; let's calm down, a'right?" David said as Roger pulled back into traffic.

When they eventually made it back to Owlgate, they all got out of the vehicle, quiet and sedate. "What do you think it means to be hot as—the f-word?" the three adults overheard Dan ask Charlie.

"I think it means they thought Erin was pretty—to look at, but I'm not sure," Charlie said quietly.

"So what if she's pretty to look at? Why get mad about that? I think she's pretty to look at as well," Dan said, making them all smile in spite of themselves at his sweet innocence.

Tilly came out from the garage and met them near the door to the house. "How did it go?" she said and then noticed that they didn't look happy. "That well, huh?"

Erin shrugged and tried to smile at her. "I'm tired, I'm going to lay down," she said, just wanting to go to sleep and forget about the whole thing.

"I'll be right up, darling," David said as he grabbed the bubble wand and pinwheel from the floor bed of the SUV.

———

"Is she alright?" Tilly asked as she watched Erin go into the house.

"What happened, David?" Roger asked him, and he explained to the best of his knowledge.

He began with how they'd been having a brilliant time and then how the appearance of the women interrupted it. "I was told they insulted Erin by calling her a homewrecker to her face."

"No!" Tilly said.

"I didn't hear et, but Peter was angry and told them to piss off," David said, and then told them about the teen boys and how Peter had lashed out at them, as well.

"Don't people have filters anymore? Whatever happened to being polite and keeping your mouth shut?" Tilly said, shaking her head. "Poor Erin!"

"Aye. Fame isn't much fun sometimes," he said and then went into the house to find Erin. When he got to his room, he heard the shower running, so he got undressed, longing for the hot water and the feel of Erin's wet skin. He entered the bathroom and heard gentle sobs behind the glass shower door. "Darling, are yeh a'right? May I join you?" he asked gently and stepped up to the edge of the basin. She nodded and then held him tightly when he got in with her.

"Oh, David! That was horrible! I mean, I don't care what people think of me, though being called a homewrecker stings a bit. But they said it in front of the children; how can people be so rude and insensitive? Poor Peter! He doesn't need to hear assholes calling his almost stepmother hot and talking about her like they did. It was really bad, David. They said some really disgusting things about me. He's so protective of me, and I know it hurts him to hear that kind of stuff coming from kids his age. It's so difficult!"

"Aye, and I'm so sorry you had tae deal with et," David said, rubbing her back and stroking her hair.

"I can deal with it; it's the kids I worry about. Let's move somewhere where no one knows who you are and hide away where no one can find us. We can buy an island and live like the Swiss Family Robinson or Robinson Crusoe! You can be 'My Man Friday,' and I'll order you around, telling you what to do," she said.

"I wish we could, but as soon as we escape, that's when they'll come after us, wantin' interviews and sendin' paparazzi tae catch us doin' whatever they think we left society tae do.

"Aye, I know you're right. What have I gotten myself into with you?" she asked and then looked up, smiling at him. "To be completely honest, I was just a teeny-tiny bit flattered that those kids said I was sexy. I never imagined they'd think that in a million years."

"Well, I think that picture is hot as fuck maself if that counts," he said and took a whiff of her hair, becoming excited.

Erin stood on her tiptoes to kiss him. "It counts very much!" she said, and he felt her touch his erection. He wasn't in the mood for foreplay, so he turned her around and entered her from behind, making love to her while the hot water ran over their bodies.

When they were done in the shower, it was time for supper, so Erin threw her hair up in a messy bun to deal with later, and they got dressed. They came downstairs feeling much better than they had earlier and were laughing as they entered the dining room. All laughter died away when they saw the state of the children. Peter's eyes were red, and the way his face was set reminded Erin of the first time they'd met when he was grieving over his mother's death.

The rest of the children were taking his lead, sitting quietly with their heads down as though if they did anything that bothered Peter, he'd lash out at them. Erin looked at Annis, and she shrugged, shaking her head to say she didn't know what was going on.

Erin went to him and put her hand on his shoulder. "Please come with me, Peter," she said and then turned to Annis. "Please start without us; I need to have a word with my son." She didn't know what she would say to him or what he was so upset about, but it was obviously more than just what had happened at the arcade. Peter looked at his gran then David, and when they nodded, he stood and lay his napkin on his plate.

Erin led him to the back patio and sat on the bench swing, patting the spot next to her for him to sit. It was a beautiful evening, cloudy, but now that they were away from the seaside, it was warm enough to be comfortable. Peter sat next to her, staring at the herringbone-patterned floor, which had moss growing between the bricks, making a lovely red and green mosaic. She put her hand gently on his shoulder and waited, knowing there was a dam inside of him ready to break, though she didn't want to rush him. "Peter, please talk to me. Tell me what's got you so upset. I really care about how you're feeling and want to try and help you deal with it," she said after a few minutes of rocking silently.

At first, his muscles were tense, as though he was ready to stand and start storming, but then he took a deep breath and looked at her. He shook his head and leaned over, burying his face into her neck. He began sobbing, with his arm around her in an uncomfortable hug. Erin let him cry, rocking the bench and petting his hair as his tears ran down her neck. "My darling boy, how can I help you? What are you afraid of… is that it? Are you afraid—or do you just not know what it is? Let's try to figure it out so we can get past it and move on, alright? You know I won't make fun of you or make you feel bad, don't you?"

He sat up, wiped his eyes with his sleeves, and lifted his shirt to wipe his nose. He took another deep breath and looked back down at his feet. "I've—always wanted a mum like you. I know that's terrible, but our mum was so—unmotherly. She would never have held me and allowed me to cry. She would've pushed me away and told me to grow up or to stop being a Nancy, or something to make me feel even worse, and hate her as well. You know just what to do for us, well, for me, when I feel bad, and—and when those… horrible people say such awful things about you, it makes me want to beat on them. A rage comes over me, and I want to hit them. I don't know how to stop it," he said, pinching the bridge of his nose as she'd seen his father do.

"I wouldn't have hit the women, but I wanted to pound those knobs for saying what they did about you. I wanted to thrash them until they couldn't talk anymore. They don't know you, or… love you. They're idiots," he said. "And for those women to call you a homewrecker! What do they know? You're not a homewrecker!

You're a home—saver, and we all owe you… for… making us a family again."

"Oh, Peter!" Erin said as she began to cry softly. Thank you for that," she said, but Peter wasn't finished. He stood and began pacing in front of her, biting his nails and looking at her, then looking away. He did it several times, obviously wanting to say something difficult. "What is it?" she finally asked.

He looked at her again, and a look of fear and dread came over his face. "I'm—I'm afraid those people are going to make you so upset that—you'll not want to marry Dad, and… you'll leave us," he said suddenly as if just realizing it himself for the first time. He stopped pacing and knelt in front of her. "Please don't leave us, Erin," he said and put his head on her lap.

Erin was beside herself; she couldn't believe he'd be afraid of that, though she could understand it. "Peter, look at me," she said, and he looked up into her eyes. "You are my family now, and I'm not going to let anyone tear us apart. I think of you as my son, and I need you! I need you and your father, and your brothers and sister, too… and having some asshole call me a homewrecker or… slut or… hot as—whatever, isn't going to send me away, I promise!" She placed her hand on her belly, then took his hand and placed it over hers. "Your little brother or sister in here is also a guarantee that I'm staying put, do you understand?"

He looked at his hand and then looked at her again, smiling. "I understand," he said and sighed. "Thank you for listening to me and for your promise."

"You're welcome, darling. Now, let's go back to the table; I'm starving!"

He helped her to stand and then opened the door for her. They could hear everyone at the table talking and laughing as they approached the dining room, but when they came back in, it all stopped. Peter stood before them all, looking contrite. "I'm sorry for my behavior. I feel much better now," he said. Everyone at the table gave a silent sigh of relief and resumed their conversations.

Erin kissed David's cheek and smiled at him. "Your—*our* kids are the most amazing people I've ever met," she said to him.

Chapter Thirty-Nine

ACT YOUR AGE

When supper was over, Erin offered, as usual, to help Millie with the dishes, and as usual, Millie declined. Tilly remarked that a walk might be nice. Roger agreed and suggested inviting David and Erin to join them. "I'd like that," Tilly said sincerely. The foursome walked down the paved drive, bordered on one side with a low stone and brick wall in front of well-tended bushes and on the other side with accent stones to highlight the landscaping and lawn. "I just love the ironwork on this gate; it's so much fun," Tilly said as they headed for the service door next to one of the two iron gates.

David told them about his great grandfather, David, who built the house. "It was rumored that he kept several owls in the garret and that at night, he'd let them out to hunt mice and whatever owls eat. I've been told he was so fond of owls that he had them worked into everythin'. On the ironwork here, and if yeh look closely on the old fire grates and shields for the fireplaces, ye'll see owls in them, as well as some of the tiles that surround them," he said.

"Just the other day, I noticed that the newel post on the main staircase had owls carved in it," Erin said and held David's hand as they walked to Dr. Neil's and headed to the Loch, as was their habit. The women talked about their common interests, including *Future Explorations,* and the men stood to the side to watch them. "Which are your favorite episodes?" Erin asked Tilly.

"Well, in season one—" she began and told her all about her favorites, explaining why she liked them so much.

"So, you were head over heels over Joe and not John Thomas? That's so interesting. It's always been John Thomas for me; well, him and the tenth Doctor, but don't tell David that," Erin said quietly.

"I heard you!" David said from the stand of trees he and Roger were watching them from. "Look at them, acting like girls, talking about their favorite television characters and episodes," David said and smiled.

"They are lovely though, eh?" Roger said, and David looked at him; he was staring at Tilly as though she were a cheeseburger to a man stranded on a deserted island. The realization dawned on him that he'd never seen Roger with a woman before; he had been Roger and only Roger for well over twenty years. That was a long time to be alone, and with the way he was gazing at Tilly, David knew that he and Erin should make themselves scarce. "Erin?" he said and walked toward her. She looked at him and smiled; he loved her smile. "I'd like tae show yeh... somethin'. We'll be back... in a while—" he said to Roger and took hold of Erin's hand, leading her down a path away from him and Tilly.

When they were a good distance away, he stopped, and Erin turned to look at him. "What was that abo—" He bent and kissed her passionately, catching her off-guard, but it only took a moment for her to melt into his arms. He wanted to lay her down in the tall grass behind them and make love to her right there.

"We need tae make an excuse tae leave; have yeh seen the way Roger is lookin' at her? He's been single for over twenty years. I think they need tae be alone, even if they don't know et. Also, just bein' around them is makin' me radge! Do yeh think we can sneak into the house without the children noticin'?" he asked.

Erin smiled at him and kissed him some more before she answered. "I really hope so," she said, and they walked back to where Roger and Tilly had been standing, but they were gone.

David called out, "Roger?" and then saw his head pop out from behind a tree. "Ach, Roger, dinnae stop what ye're doin'. Erin and I are gonna head back now; we'll see yeh tomorrow." He took Erin's hand and started toward the exit, trying to hurry back. Unfortunately, before they made it to safety, he saw a couple running toward them, the woman squealing like a stuck pig.

"EEEE—It's you! I can't believe you're here! We are huge fans of *everything* you've done! *Houlihan's Flat* was just brilliant! Would you mind signing my shirt?" the woman said, speaking really fast.

David noticed she was wearing a *Future Explorations* t-shirt with one of his quotes written on the front, '*The future is never far away*,' it said. She handed him a felt-tipped pen that she'd dug out of her handbag and then turned around. On the back of her shirt was an image of him in a kilt, standing in front of the old farmhouse.

"Sure—ah, what's your name?" he asked, using his R.P. English accent once more.

"Donna and Steve White," the man said.

He opened the pen and wrote, '*Donna and Steve— Thanks for watching —David Elliott*' on her shoulder blade.

She turned around and took the pen back. "Thank you so much! Would you mind taking a selfie with us?" she asked politely.

David put on a smile and nodded. "Sure," he said. Erin took the phone from the lady and snapped a few shots of them all together. The couple thanked them again and then walked away.

"Thanks for always bein' my right-hand-man; takin' photos and helpin' me as yeh do," he said on their walk back to Owlgate.

"You're welcome. I enjoy being part of it, both for you and for the person asking."

"Aye? Well, et's easier for me tae give a genuine smile when I'm lookin' at you, love."

"You say the sweetest things," she said and put her arm around his waist.

"What did you say to Peter to cause him to change his attitude so drastically," David asked as they wound around the small Duddingston streets.

"Oh, David! He's so sweet! I didn't say much, except that I cared about how he felt and that I wouldn't make fun of anything he told me. I don't think he even knew what he was so upset about, not until he started talking about it. He told me how he's always wanted a mum like me and that his mum wouldn't have listened to him or let him cry on her shoulder like he did on mine. He told me how angry he was to hear people say bad things about me and that he wanted to beat them all up," she said and raised her eyebrows. "But then, it was like he finally realized what was really bothering him. He said he's afraid people like those at the arcade today will make me not want to marry you and that I'll leave... he—he knelt in front of me, David, and asked me not to leave. It was all I could do not to bawl my eyes out!"

"He said that?" David asked. "And what did yeh tell him?" he asked, wanting to know for himself as well.

"I told him that you and the kids are my family now, that I think of him as my son, and that I need all of you. I told him that it didn't matter what some asshole called me, I wasn't going to leave. Then I told him that the baby meant I'd never leave as well. I promised it to him," she said. He didn't say anything, so she looked up at him. "What's wrong?" she said, and he shook his head.

"Nothing," he said as he opened the service door, and they stepped into the secluded yard. He shut the gate behind them and then pushed Erin up against the brick part of the wall. "I'm glad ye're not goin' tae leave us," he said and kissed her neck, then he lifted her leg up by the knee and pressed his hard-on against her. "I—need yeh, Erin! Let's go tae the house."

They walked up to the house and saw that the place was abuzz with activity. They knew they'd never get to their room without being seen, but there was another option, the garage. "Roger and Tilly are still at Dr. Neils, so we have some choices," David said. "We can run upstairs and use the spare room in the flat or... make love in the SUV with the seats down."

"I don't think using the flat is a good idea; that would be an invasion of privacy," Erin said. "I mean, it's one thing for a nap in the middle of the day, but not at night when he has a guest. Also, what if they come back before we're done?"

"Whatever's goin' on with Roger and that girl, it's contagious! I want yeh like I did when we first met," he said urgently and looked at the SUV. "It might work." He walked over and opened the back seat door, then looked at Erin. The seats flipped down to make a nice flat surface, which would be fine, as long as no one walked by. The windows were darkly tinted, though it wasn't a guarantee of privacy.

"You're crazy," she said and laughed. They quickly folded the seats down and then climbed in, giggling like kids. They tried to take off their clothes, but it wasn't easy in the cramped quarters, though they managed to get mostly naked. When Erin lay on her back, David was on her in a flash. She needed him, and when he entered her, she felt that energy course through her body. She closed her eyes, and then opened them, finding herself in the claustrophobic space. A vivid flashback of Bran on top of her, casually laying there, letting her fight and thrash hit her hard. In an instant, she was gasping for breath.

David seemed to take it as sounds of pleasure, not noticing her distress right away. "Ach, Erin," he whispered.

"Stop—please—" she tried desperately to say, but she couldn't speak; her voice was caught in her throat. David had just started to climax when her voice returned, and she cried out again, pushing him away and crying hard. "Please stop! STOP!" she cried out loudly, needing some fresh air.

———

Roger had just walked through the side door of the garage when he saw the SUV moving erratically and heard Erin yelling— again. He didn't think; he just ran to the door, opened it, and then froze as the dome light flooded the small area. He stood, staring at Erin and David, who were mostly naked. Erin was crying and gasping for breath, and David lay next to her, obviously confused, not knowing what had happened. They both looked up at him, and then Erin curled up into a ball, crying even harder.

"For fuck's sake!" Roger said, trying to catch his own breath after the adrenaline rush. "What're yeh doin' in here, and why's Erin cryin'?" He then had his own flashback of that day. "Never mind," he said quietly and closed the door, though it didn't quite close all the way. He turned and took Tilly's hand, leading her toward the house.

———

Tilly had stood by the garage door, completely confused. She couldn't see into the back of the car, but she'd heard Erin's cry for help and now questioned her and David's relationship. "Is Erin okay?" she asked, wondering why nothing was being done to help her. She could still hear Erin sobbing and gasping for air, while David didn't seem to be saying anything; at least she couldn't hear it. *What did he do to her in there,* she thought, unsure if she should still trust him.

"Let's go back tae the house. I'll explain et tae yeh, and then if yeh have more questions, Erin can tell you herself." Roger said, visibly shaken.

"Did he—hurt—her?" she asked quietly.

Roger shook his head. "No, lass, someone else did, and she was only rememberin' et."

"Oh, okay." Tilly was still confused, but she no longer distrusted David.

———

Erin hadn't panicked on the day Bran Elliott, David's look-alike cousin, had raped her in Roger's flat. It was too surreal as it happened, but as she lay on the scratchy carpeting of the SUV, she couldn't stop crying and flashing back to odd details. Memories assaulted her of the way his hair had hung over his forehead and of how the eyes on his snake tattoo had stared at her. She wished, with her whole heart, that she could go back in time and sleep in David's room instead of Roger's spare room, and every time the thought came to her, it made her cry more.

David held her and let her cry. "I'm sorry, ma love. I didn't ken you were upset—I didn't hear yeh say tae stop," he said.

"I was stunned by the vividness of the memories, and I couldn't speak. Why did he do it, David? He could've stopped me or gotten out of the bed, but he chose to do it!" she said between sobs.

———

David didn't really want to hear any more details; it made him physically ill to think about it. "He never was able to control his impulses, and I imagine—a—soft, warm, naked woman in the bed was somethin' he couldn't resist," he said and had to swallow the bile threatening to erupt if he said anything more about it. "I'm so sorry—"

"I'm not angry at you," she said. "I'm only sorry Roger had to witness it."

"His woman—" David began to say, but Erin interrupted him.

"Her name is Tilly."

"Tilly then—I heard her ask Roger if I'd hurt yeh! That truly tears ma heart out."

"I know, darling; I'm sorry I made such a fuss," she said as she began to calm down.

David held her hand and shushed her. "Dinnae fret, darling. This was a radge idea and bound tae go pear-shaped. If yer ready, I reckon we should go back to the house. You can talk to Tilly, and we can get things straightened out."

"I'm okay now; let's go find them," she said.

Roger and Tilly walked out to the back patio and sat on the swinging bench. Roger told her what had happened that day in the spare room. That David had been in London, that Bran had been raping her, and that he'd ended up rescuing her in much the same way as he'd meant to do only a few minutes earlier. "You see, she thought et was David—"

"But how is it she didn't know it was the other guy?" she asked, and Roger stood.

"Come with me," he said and led her into the house. He took her to a wall of framed photographs of various family members, including quite a few of David.

He really was a pet, she thought.

"Now, point out the pictures of David on this wall."

She looked at him quizzically, thinking it was a trick question. She pointed to every photo that looked like David and shrugged. "There are quite a few of him that look the same, though. How many fifth-grade photos do you need to frame and hang on the wall?" she said.

"Exactly," Roger said and pointed out every other one she'd pointed to. "These aren't David; they're his cousin, Bran."

Tilly looked at him, wide-eyed and shaking her head. "No way! But how do you know? How can you tell?" she said, reexamining them. Roger pointed to David's eyes in one of the pictures. "David's eyes are brown, and can you see... in this one here," he said, pointing to another picture, "Bran's eyes are—"

"Hazel," David finished for him.

Tilly jumped and grabbed Roger's arm. She hadn't heard him come in and was startled.

"Aye, and David was kind and gentle, whereas Bran was impulsive, reckless, and downright mean," Roger said, finishing his comparison.

"I can't tell yeh how sorry I am about—well, about findin' us the way yeh did," David said, red in the face.

"It's really my fault," Erin said as she stepped up next to him. "I—thought I was over it, but apparently I wasn't." She looked at the photo of Bran that Roger had been pointing to and shuddered. "He doesn't look as much like David now as he does in these pictures, but his voice is very much the same. The room was dark, and I'd been in a deep sleep. In my half-awake—half-asleep brain, I must have assumed David had come back from London... or not remembered he was gone at all. All I know is that I woke up with him—on top of me. Apparently, I invited him, but I thought he was David, and he knew it. When I said to stop, he wouldn't, so he was essentially raping me. I managed to yell for help, and Roger rushed in and grabbed him, which I am eternally grateful for."

"Aye, when I heard yeh yell tonight, my heart nearly jumped out of ma chest, Erin! I dinnae know what I thought was happenin', but et scared the bejesus out of me. Are you a'right now?" he asked gently.

She nodded and moved quickly out of the way of Daniel, who was chasing Gertie up the stairs. A moment later, Charlie came running after him, yelling up the stairs that Millie wanted him to stop running around the house and get his pajamas on. "That's why we didn't bother to come into the house. We thought the SUV would be, I don't know, safer or something," she said and shook her head, realizing how ridiculous it all sounded in hindsight. "I'm really sorry I scared the both of you. I feel terrible about it," Erin said and leaned against David.

"I really was scared for you, Erin," Tilly said and took her hand, "but I'm glad you're alright." She looked at Roger "Let's go back to the flat now, okay?"

Roger nodded and looked at Erin. He went to her and hugged her tightly, not caring about what Tilly or David thought. "I'm glad ye're a'right as well," he said tenderly. He let her go and then took Tilly's hand, leading her back out to the garage.

"Let's help Millie get the children into bed," Erin said to David. "I've got a chapter to read to them tonight."

"Aye." David looked at her. "I can't believe everathin' you've been through in so short a time. Ye're sae strong and bounce back from every setback and trial we encounter. Are yeh sure ye're okay?"

"Aye. I'm okay now. I love you."

That night Erin read the first two chapters of *Anne of Green Gables* to the children. The first chapter wasn't her favorite because it's told from the perspective of the neighborhood busy body, but as she began chapter two, she remembered just how much she loved the story. The bachelor, Matthew Cuthbert is meant to pick up a young orphan boy but waiting for him on the platform is a wide-eyed, red-headed *girl* named Anne. Being a very shy man, he's forced to listen to Anne's imaginative discourse and falls head-over-heels for her. His only worry is what his sister, Marilla, will say about the mistake.

After the fresh air and activities of the day, the family were all droopy-eyed as Erin finished the chapter. She decided to stop there, and everyone got a hug and a kiss, then David and Erin went straight to their room. "That was nice, wasn't it?" she said as they got ready for bed.

"Aye, darling, et was lovely," David said, and they both got under the covers. "I can't wait to learn what happens tae poor, wee Anne."

Chapter Forty

BAD DREAMS AND FAMILY BONDING

That night, Erin woke to David sitting on the side of the mattress, leaning forward. "What's wrong?" she asked and touched his back. It was sweaty, and she felt goosebumps on his skin. "Are you sick?" David shook his head, and she felt a shiver run through his body. "What is it, David?" She felt another ripple flow over his skin before he launched himself toward the bathroom and then she heard him retching.

When he returned to bed, he looked pale and miserable. "Nightmare," he said and got under the covers. At first, he laid on his back, staring at the ceiling, then he rolled onto his side and wrapped his arm around her, nearly smothering her.

"Woah! That must've been a terrible nightmare! Tell me about it."

He shook his head, and then everything began to tumble out of his mouth. "I reckon it was your flashback that brought them back into ma mind, but the photographs you found were in the bathtub… It was completely full, and I was being forced to get into the tub with them. As I put my foot in, I felt a hand grab et and pull… I was bein' pushed and pulled into the photos and… I felt skin… hands, legs, arms… and lips touchin' me… everawhere. I had nothin' tae grab or tae stop me from bein' drown in them, Erin! I tried callin' out to yeh, but a strong, male hand was over my mouth, and I couldn't say anathin'! I—felt a… oh, God, Erin, a… hard cock trying tae… from behind me… and that's when I woke up. Did yeh touch me a'tall?"

Erin was stunned; it took a moment for her to respond. "No, I don't think so. I was asleep. Oh, David, that sounds so horrible! How can I help you… or can I?"

"I dinnae ken, just dinnae go anawhere, okay?"

"Let me use the toilet, and you can hold me all night if you need to," she said.

He seemed reluctant to let her go, but finally, he did, and she hurried to the bathroom. When she returned, he was sitting up in bed, hugging his knees, and when she laid in front of him, as the little spoon, he quickly put his arm over her. He shook as he held her until she felt him slowly relax and heard his breathing change, knowing he was asleep.

The next morning, David and Erin got dressed and went down to breakfast. Tilly was leaving that day, and Roger seemed a bit sad. Tilly and the children were already at their places and smiled at them when they walked in. "Good morning," Erin said, and they all responded in like kind. David's mobile sounded his notification bell, so he stepped away from the table to read it. He beckoned Erin to join him and showed her the message from Tina. "Oh, good!" she said, reading the itinerary for their family holiday to America.

After breakfast, just as the meal was wrapping up, David made an announcement. "Before you run off, children, you need to know we'll be spendin' part of the day today at Dr. Neil's to fulfill the promise I made tae Peter. You may join us or come and go as yeh please, but I wanted tae make you aware of our plans. I reckon we'll leave in an hour, so if yeh wanna come along, please be ready on time." The children were then excused from the table.

"I thought you'd tell them about the trip," Erin said.

"They've already had a full weekend. I thought I'd save that for another time; I dinnae want their wee heads tae explode," he said.

An hour later, Roger returned from taking Tilly home and loitered in the driveway with David and Erin as they waited for the children. "So, how are you doing, Roger?" Erin asked with a wink.

He smiled, and his cheeks turned a bit pink. "I feel good. Et's nice tae have someone tae think of and dream about. She'll be back at the weekend again, so I'll have a bit more time tae be wi' her without havin' tae take anaone anawhere, yeh ken?"

"Millie's gonna have a hard time getting you to leave the flat for meals!" Erin said, teasing.

"She just might," he said and chuckled. "When do yeh wannae be taken to the airport, then?"

"The plane leaves at ten tomorrow morning, so I reckon we should leave at half eight, though I'll tell the children quarter past," David said. He looked at his watch and shook his head. "Three minutes of—"

One by one, the children exited the house and came to stand at the ready. "Daniel isn't coming, at least not now. Said he may show up later," Charlie said.

"Okay then, let's go!" Erin said, looking forward to spending the day with her new family. She felt light and full of energy for a change and wanted to be present and involved. She looked at David, who was also smiling, but just as she looked away, she thought she saw a shadow pass over his handsome features. It only lasted a split second, so she began to think she'd imagined it.

The children stayed close to them, laughing and speaking easily, as though they'd been together always. Rosie held the hand that David wasn't holding, and Peter walked on the other side of his dad, nearly the same height as him. Charlie stayed in front, walking backward.

Erin began laughing, and they all looked at her, waiting to be let in on the joke. "I just had the strangest thought cross my mind," she said.

"Why doesn't that surprise me?" David said and laughed when she scowled at him.

"In America, we say 'counterclockwise,' and 'prenatal,' whereas here, you say—"

"Anticlockwise," Rosie said.

"And antenatal," Charlie said, smiling because he just knew whatever she was going to say would be really funny.

"Exactly. What is Charlie doing right now?" she asked, and they all frowned.

"He's walking—" Rosie began.

"Antiforward!" Peter said and stopped walking. All the forward walkers turned to watch him as he laughed. It started out as a small chuckle, but they could tell when the idea would cross his mind again because his laugh would grow stronger and louder until it became contagious. Before long, they were all laughing and walking once more. "You crack me up, Erin!"

"I didn't think it was *that* funny, but thanks," she replied. As they walked into the Gardens, Charlie became very quiet and contemplative. "What's going on in your head, Charlie?" Erin stepped forward and put her arm around his shoulders. He smiled at her and then looked back at his dad. His smile faded, becoming a frown. "Oh, dear, what's wrong?"

"Well, nothing's really wrong, exactly," he said with his head down.

"Go on, son, spit it out," David said.

"Mum wouldn't allow us to ask for things… for our birthdays, and I wanted to ask for… something. I don't want—oh, never mind," he said and kicked at the gravel under his feet.

"Hey," Erin said and lifted his chin. "My mother would give me a whole catalog of toys to look through and write in every year before Christmas. She told me to circle the things I wanted. I might only get one of those things, but she let me dream, you know? I can't promise that you'll get everything you ask for, Charlie, but I will never deny you the opportunity to ask. I mean, I don't think we'll have room for a pony at the house in London, but I might get you a stuffed one with crossed eyes to make you think of me every time you look at it."

He looked at his dad again. David smiled at him and then walked a few yards away. Charlie looked back to Erin, and they exchanged a mystified look, but then he smiled and hugged her tightly. "Thanks, Mu—"

"Go on and say it, Charlie; she said it was okay for me, right, Mummy?" Rosie asked, beaming.

"That's right, Rosie. You may call me mum if you feel comfortable with it, Charlie, but you—"

"Thanks, Mum," Charlie said and squeezed her even tighter.

"So—" Erin choked out. "Are you gonna squeeze the life out of me, or tell me what you want for your birthday? Wait, when is your birthday?"

He let her go and laughed. "Sorry, got a bit carried away. I just want to spend the day laughing with you… with us… together as a… family. I don't remember ever doing that, in my whole life, do you, Dad?" he asked and then remembered that he'd walked away.

"I don't either," Peter said.

"Me neither, but that's what I want for my birthday as well!" Rosie said.

"Oh, and our birthday is the eighteenth of July," Charlie said.

"And you'll be eleven?"

"Yeah."

"Well, if it's at all up to me, I would love to grant you that birthday wish, darling boy. I'll even throw in all the hugs you want; that is *if* you still like hugs. You're not too old for hugs, are you? I'm really old, and I still like hugs," Erin said, poking fun of the letter he'd sent a few years earlier.

David came back and began walking with them again, seeming to be his happy, normal self though Erin knew something was bothering him. "You lot run along, and we'll catch up," she said to the children. They walked ahead, and she turned to him. "What happened back there?"

"Et was nothin'. Nothin' tae worry about."

"I don't believe you," she said, but before she could continue, his face changed to something close to anger.

"Yeh dinnae believe me? Yeh think I'm lyin' to you, then?"

Erin froze, and her heart skipped a beat. He *was* lying to her and getting defensive about it just proved it to her. It was exactly what Todd would do when she suspected he had porn in the house. If she mentioned it, he'd throw the suspicion back at her, making her feel like he was hurt that she didn't trust him. That was when she'd find it—within a day or two of the encounter. Always. "Fine… okay, if that's the way you're going to deal with my concern, then… I guess—you know, I thought we had a level of trust—" she stammered, feeling hurt and walking faster to get to the children.

"Wait! Erin!" he said, and she stopped.

She whirled around and glared at him, then she lowered her head. "What? Are you going to tell me the truth or lay another guilt trip on me?" she asked quietly, not wanting to make a scene since the children were watching them from a distance.

"I'm sorry," he whispered and put his forehead against hers. "Ye're right. I … had a flashback of the nightmare I had last night. I'm afraid tae look at them all, Erin. I'm afraid of what I'll see. I stopped lookin' after I saw the ones where ma cock was… well, I'm afraid they only get worse. I didn't want tae ruin the day by talkin' about et here."

She placed her hands on his head and stroked his hair. "Okay, darling, I understand why you wouldn't want to talk about it here, but in the future, please just say that instead of avoiding it, or worse, getting defensive. I really can't stand that."

"Aye, I should've known that wouldn't work on you. I'm sorry, love. We can… well, I dinnae want tae talk about et later, but I will if yeh need me to."

"No, we don't need to, but please talk to me if it gets worse, okay?"

"A'right, now let's have a good day," he said and kissed her.

"Sweet Woodruff, or Galium odoratuma," Peter said. "It's a flowering perennial in the Rubiaceae family, native to much of Europe and as far away as China and Japan." They walked a few more feet, and he continued. "This is called Common Motherwort, or Leonurus cardiaca. It's an herbaceous perennial plant in the mint family, Lamiaceae."

"So, what is the name of that spiny tree near the gate?" Erin asked.

"That's one of my favorites, though you can get hurt quite badly if you touch it the wrong way. The spines are very sharp. It's called a Monkey Puzzle tree or Araucaria araucana; it's an evergreen native to central and southern Chile and western Argentina."

"Daddy! I know the name of this one!" Rosie said proudly. "Rose, Hybrid Tea, Prince… William?"

"Well done, Rosie, and you're very close, but that one is named Ruby Wedding. It looks very much like the Royal Prince William, though." Peter said.

"This isn't very much fun; he knows everything. Next, he'll tell us the name of each type of lawn," Rosie said and crossed her arms in a huff.

"I understand, Rosie, but this is Peter's day to be here with his dad. Is there something you'd like to do—"

"I'd like to have tea at the Garden Room with you!" Rosie interrupted.

"I would like that as well," Charlie chimed in. "I'm not all that interested in the names of plants; I just like to look at them."

Erin glanced at David; they had spent well over two hours walking around the garden. She could understand how the other children might be getting bored of hearing the Latin names for every plant they came to. "Let me speak to your dad." Before she could say anything, Rosie ran over to David and began pulling on his sleeve impatiently. "Rosie—" she began and went to them.

"…to the Garden Room for tea… may we?" the young girl was saying excitedly.

"Rosie, I said that *I* would speak to your dad," Erin said.

"I'm sorry, Mummy," she said and put her head down.

Erin smiled at David. He crouched before her and lifted her chin. "Ach, ma wee lass, yeh want your tea now?"

"Yes, Daddy."

"I'm not sure if they're open just now, love. How about we head that way next?"

The family made their way to the café, but they weren't open yet. Rosie was sad, but then Peter said he was getting tired, so he didn't mind heading back to Owlgate. They laughed and talked as they walked the cobblestone streets of Duddingston, and when they stepped through the door, the dogs greeted them. Daniel ran in through the back door, and they heard him yell, "I'm famished," apparently hoping Millie would hear him.

"Daniel, that's no way to talk tae Millie!" David said, and the boy stepped into the hallway, red in the face.

"Sorry, Dad, I didn't know you were here," he said.

"Aye, and ye'll not speak tae her that way when I'm not here either," he said.

"Yes, sir," Daniel said resignedly.

"I'm famished as well," Charlie said to his sister.

"I think we could all use a snack and a rest," Erin said. "Let's find Millie."

That afternoon, they rested and played board games. They got to know each other and came away feeling like a real family for the first time. After supper, the children played by themselves, then at bedtime, Peter joined them in the younger kids' room, and Erin read to them. She was in chapter three of *Anne of Green Gables*; Matthew had just returned from Bright Station with a little girl instead of the boy he and his sister, Marilla, had expected. The older woman is surprised by the mistake and is determined to send Anne back to the orphanage. Anne is, understandably, very upset and cries herself to sleep.

"I would also be heartbroken if that happened to me, Mummy, wouldn't you?" Rosie said.

"Yes, I would!" she said.

"Are you sorry I'm not a boy, Mummy?"

Erin laughed and put her arm around the small girl. "Not in the least! There are far too many boys around here; we girls need each other to even things out a bit."

"Do you want a boy or a girl, Eri— I mean, Mum," Charlie asked.

"To be honest, I'm not sure. Everyone says things like, 'I don't care, as long as it's healthy.' I never believed them until now. I know I'll love it and be thrilled no matter what it is, won't you?"

The three younger children smiled and nodded, then Peter grinned and said, "As will I." He stood and said goodnight to his siblings, then went to his bedroom.

Erin and David tucked them all in, making sure to give them plenty of hugs and kisses. "I was right," she said as they headed downstairs.

"I'm sure yeh were… what was et about this time?" David said with a laugh.

"I love your kids; they're really special."

"Ach, they are, aren't they? They've taken to you like—"

"A swan to water?"

"Aye, exactly, and I'm so pleased," David said.

Chapter Forty-One

ANOTHER NIGHTMARE

Erin woke to David sitting up, gasping for breath. She rolled over to talk to him, but she had to hurry to the bathroom to be sick. When she came back to bed, it looked like he was asleep again, but when she laid down, he spooned with her and held her tightly. "Another nightmare?" she asked. She felt him nod, though he didn't say anything. "Are you okay?" He nodded again, then he shook his head. "Tell me about it?"

"I dinnae want tae tell yeh. You'll think et turns me on or somethin', but et doesn't."

"Oh, okay." She wasn't sure she wanted to hear it after that lead-in, but she wanted to be supportive. "Go ahead."

"Again, et doesn't turn me on, Erin. I was on the guestroom bed, but I couldn't move or speak. Susannah... was—"

"Okay! I don't need to hear any more; I'm sorry, but I can't listen to a sex dream about Susannah!" She was nauseated again and hoped she wouldn't need to run to the bathroom a second time.

"A'right, but it wasn't sex with her, et was... different. She was directing a film where various people were brought in to do sexual things to me. All I could think about was you and getting back to you, but I couldn't move."

"Do you think... they're memories?" she asked.

"I dinnae ken, but et feels so real. Et's suffocatin'," he said miserably.

"I wish I could help you, darling," she said and allowed him to hold her until they fell back to sleep.

It was a stressful morning; it seemed everyone had gotten up on the wrong side of the bed. The children bickered during breakfast and again while everyone searched the large house for any belongings they might've missed. At eight-thirty, Roger took them to the airport, and they all said goodbye to him. "Safe travels!" he said after many hugs and then drove away.

They headed into the terminal, carrying their luggage. David wore a hat and ugly glasses, trying to blend in, and they made it to the check-in counter unscathed. After they were through security, they made a beeline for the VIP lounge to wait for their flight. They didn't have to wait long, only forty-five minutes, then they boarded with the first round of passengers. About midway through their one-and-a-half-hour flight, a passenger approached David and asked for a selfie, so he obliged.

They got to the airport in good time, but as they entered the terminal, the press went crazy. There were photographers, videographers, vloggers, and reporters with microphones. "What in the hell?" Erin said under her breath as they were barraged with questions and people took photos with bright flashes, nearly blinding them.

"Is it true you took your children out of school because you're moving to America, David?" one of them called out.

"Were the provocative photos of the two of you taken before your wife died?"

"David, do you feel guilty for cheating on your wife?"

"Kids, do you miss your mum?"

"Erin March, do you feel embarrassed by the revealing photos of you?"

"Erin, did you kill Susannah Elliott, have her killed, or want her dead?"

"David, are you moving to America to be with your new lover?"

"Kids, how do you feel about your dad cheating on your mum with Erin?"

"Erin, is it true you started a house fire as a distraction so you could get rid of his wife?"

"Children, do you think your mum died of a broken heart?"

Oh, my God! Erin thought, wanting to yell at them for bringing the children into it as they were. She had her arm protectively around Rosie's shoulders; the young girl was crying and holding onto her while she tried to shield her from the photographers. David was checking his phone; she presumed he was trying to find out where their hired car was parked.

To make matters worse, they had their school luggage with them. As the media pressed in, suitcases were being knocked over, and the kids were being jostled around. Erin was getting really angry as they followed David to the large, black SUV he'd hired, which was waiting for them. They couldn't relax until all the doors were closed, then Erin said, "Holy Moses! Where, in the hell, did that come from?"

Rosie was sitting next to her, just calming down herself, hiccoughs staggering her breath, and Erin stroked her hair. David didn't say anything; he shook his head and looked over the back of his seat, making sure the boys were holding up alright. Erin got the hint and didn't say anything more until they were safe within their house.

Kitty greeted them cheerfully as they walked in and then saw the looks on their faces. "Core blimey! I reckon somefing bad's 'appened at the airport then?" she said and started gathering their bags. David's face was red; he was obviously angry and holding it in, not wanting to upset the children any more than they already were.

"A'right, children, I fink you need an 'ot choc'lot," Kitty said, trying to cheer them up. They obediently followed her toward the kitchen, though none of them seemed excited about it.

As soon as they were out of the room, David said, "How dare they! I dinnae care so much if they ask one of us their cruel questions, but tae do et tae the children is inexcusable! I dinnae ken what they think will happen by doin' that; we're not gonna say anathin' tae them."

"I know, darling," she said, still reeling, especially since they accused her of murder. "The older children are smart; they'll be okay. They know it's just to get a reaction, right?" she said, and David looked at her.

"Oh, darling, you must be so upset!" he said. "Tae blame you for Susannah's death is—"

Erin shook her head. "Don't worry about me; I know their tricks. I know they'll say anything, and I'm okay, but we may need to sit with Rosie; she was really upset and crying," she said. "She does know about them, right?"

"I dinnae ken," he said. "The media have never attacked like that when they were with me before."

"Well then, we need to talk to them. No time like the present, right?"

David nodded reluctantly and followed her to the kitchen. The children were sitting at the breakfast table with their hot chocolate, quiet and gloomy, whilst Kitty flitted around, chattering like a mother hen, trying to cheer them up. Erin looked at David, who very subtly shook his head to say he had nothing, so she spoke up.

"Okay, everyone, let's get it all out now. What happened at the airport was horrible! We don't know why they would attack like that—"

"They asked so many bizarre questions, like if we're moving to America, and if you started a house fire to get rid of our mum," Peter said.

"Yeah, and if you killed her!" Charlie said.

"Why did they ask if we were upset that you met Erin whilst you were still married to Mum? And—did Mummy die of a broken heart? And why do they think you killed her, Erin?" Rosie asked softly.

Erin sighed and stood next to her. "They asked really bad questions, I know, but that's their job. They get paid to ask really awful questions to get a reaction from us. If they can get a photo of us looking upset, they can sell it, and people will pay money to read about it in the tabloids and online. It's the same for videos; they want us to say things... to answer them and get angry or upset. That way, they will have a video to put online for people to see. They make a lot of money from that kind of thing."

"But... did Mummy die of a broken heart? And why do they think you killed her?" Rosie asked again, her lip quivering.

"Oh, Rosebud," David said, "yer mummy died of a heart attack, which means her heart was worn out and stopped beating, but not because of anathin' Erin or I did. She was sick for a verra long time, and her heart just couldn't handle it any longer. The doctors told me as much in hospital on the day she died. The reporters only asked if Erin killed her tae get a rise from us. Erin had nothin' tae do with her death."

"What does 'cheating on your wife' mean?" she asked next, and he looked to Erin for help.

"I'd have thought you were old enough to understand what that meant, Rosie," Erin said, and Rosie shrugged. "I see, you want to know the real meaning of it. I don't know if I can do that without it looking like your dad was a bad guy when he wasn't. Well, I don't think he was," she said, hoping she could say it in a way that made sense to them, but David put his hand on her arm.

"When I met yer mum, I truly thought I loved her, but I didn't know what real love was. I liked her, and I wanted to be with her, but I didn't love her, and I honestly dinnae believe she loved me. We didn't know it wasn't love, but we got married anaway. When you marry someone, you promise to love them, take care of them, and—tae be intimate with only them until yeh die. I tried to love her; I took verra good care of her, and I was only intimate with her until... I signed up for the Registry to help people like Erin, who are sick."

"Erin is sick?" Rosie said, wide-eyed and looking completely shocked. "She doesn't look sick to me! And what does 'intimate' mean?"

"We talked about it in my office, remember? Erin has a disease called the Fertilis Defect, which is very serious. The only way to treat it is for her to be intimate with someone—someone whom the doctors matched her with specifically. The doctors matched her and me together."

"But what does—"

"To be intimate—is—when you hug and kiss and sleep in the same bed together. You will understand when you get older, darling," David explained.

"But if you promised to only be intimate with Mum until you died, why did you do what Uncle Martin told you to do? Didn't Mum tell you not to?" Charlie asked.

"Well, a lot of things happened so that if I hadn't done it, Martin would've done things to make me look bad in the tabloids... and, well, your mum didn't want that to happen, so she told me to do it. She was hoping there wouldn't be a match for me, but there was," he said and looked at Erin.

"But a promise is a promise, isn't it, Dad?" Peter asked anxiously.

"Yes, son, promises are verra important. I thought I could love your mum forever, but you knew her; was she easy to love?" he asked, and they all shook their heads. "Right, now tell me, is Erin easy to love?"

They all looked at her and smiled, saying, "Yes."

"When I met Erin, I knew I could love her in a way I'd never loved your mum, and I knew she could love me too. There were many reasons why I had to break ma promise to yer mum. There wasn't an easy solution, but I couldn't pretend tae love yer mum anamore, and she's stopped pretending long ago. I was willin' tae continue taking care of her, but I could no longer be intimate with her. I chose Erin, and I don't regret it. I plan tae make a solemn promise tae her as soon as we're able, and I'll *never* break that promise, *ever*. No one knew your mum was goin' tae die, but there was nothin' anyone could do about et, and et was no one's fault.

"I'm glad you broke your promise to Mum. I think that if you're going to have children, you should promise to love them, but Mum never loved us! She didn't love you either, Dad. I heard her say it often," Daniel said. "She—she didn't deserve us; she didn't deserve to be a mum, but Erin does! I choose Erin, and the reporters can go—"

"Daniel!" David said.

"I agree!" Charlie and Rosie said together.

"I can't help but agree as well, Dad," Peter said. "We'll be alright; we were only shocked by what they said. We believe you, and… to answer one of their questions, we don't miss her. I'm gonna go up and unpack now."

"Aye, we'll see you later," David said, and Erin thought he looked a bit run down.

The rest of the day was unproductive; Erin was still getting used to her new home, and David seemed a bit distant and stressed. He appeared to be daydreaming most of the time, and when someone wanted his attention, his first reaction was to snap at them and then apologize. There were so many things that had happened over the last week, Erin didn't know which part of it he was upset about, and she didn't have the opportunity to take him aside and ask.

She received the letter Charlie had sent from school and read it as soon as she could.

Dear Erin,

I am writing to you from school. I had tonnes of fun with you at Doctor Neil's Garden! I hope to do it again soon! I especially liked being 'King of the Garden,' though it was for one day only.

I shouldn't say this, maybe, but I am chuffed you are my dad's partner now! I hope he marries you so you can be our new mother someday! I think we will be a better family if he does. Rosie hasn't stopped talking about you. I know she likes you a lot. Daniel told me that you are a lot of fun. He won't shut up about going to the arcade with you. Peter hasn't said anything to me about you, but I know he likes you, even though he tried not to. You are a very likeable person. I like you very much.

I can't wait to see you again during our summer holidays. I want to show you my bedroom and watch a film with you in our media room as well. Do you like Star Trek and space films? My friend, Billy, likes space films.

Sincerely,
Your friend,
Charlie Elliott Age 10 years, 11 months

It made her smile, though when she tried to show it to David, he acted like he was interested in it, but she knew he wasn't truly giving her his full attention.

Supper was a bit more formal than Erin was prepared for. David had changed his clothes and suggested she do the same. She had balked at the idea at first, but then his attitude seemed to change a tiny bit, so she did as he said. When they entered the dining room, it was set with fine china, real silver utensils, and delicate, lead-glass stemware. There was a fresh floral arrangement and candles in the center of the table, too.

The children were also dressed up as they sat, looking bored, but resigned to how things were done. When they saw her, they smiled and became more lively, but then David raised his eyebrows at them, and they went back to their dower selves. Erin frowned and sat at the foot of the table, where David had pulled the chair out for her, waiting for her to sit so he could push it in. "I don't understand," she said, but David had reached the head of the table, and everyone held hands and put their heads down.

"God bless this food and those who partake of it. Amen," David said, and everyone echoed his amen.

"David? What am I missing? This is just so… odd. Oh, let me guess," she said and then bit her tongue.

"Mother liked for supper to be formal," Peter explained.

"I see, and what do you think of that, David?"

"Now is not the time—" he almost snapped and then took a deep breath. "We can discuss it after dinner."

She knew that was his final word on the subject, so she tried to make the best of it. "Okay, but you will all have to instruct me on proper etiquette. I've never needed to be so formal in my own home before," she said.

The children were eager to teach her and began saying things like, "Elbows off the table," and "sit up straight."

"Never speak unless spoken to," Dan said and sighed deeply.

Erin's eyes grew large, and she put her hand over her mouth. David wasn't paying much attention, but the children looked at her curiously. She began making hand gestures as if trying to communicate, but no one seemed to understand her. "What's the matter, Mummy?" Rosie said, trying not to laugh.

"Oh! Thank you! No one had spoken to me, so I couldn't speak! Wait, but no one spoke to you, so you weren't really supposed to say anything either!"

"But that's not—" Charlie began and started giggling. All the children were smiling at her by then.

"How are we supposed to communicate if the only time we can speak is if someone—"

"That's enough," David said sternly.

Erin gasped; her cheeks turned red, and she put her head down. "Sorry," she whispered.

"Can we just have a quiet meal?" he began, and then Kitty came in to fill drinks.

The atmosphere was strained, so she poured in silence. Erin didn't look up when she got to her; she didn't want to make a scene, but it was taking everything she had in her to push down the desire to go off on David. "Water, please," she whispered. Kitty went to the sideboard where there was a decanter filled with ice water. She poured it out and then left the room quickly.

The room was silent until she returned with the first dish of food. Erin glanced up at David; he looked pale and distracted as he waited to be served. *What's going on in his mind?* she thought. Kitty dished a ladle of soup into the bowl that sat on top of several plates in front of her. It smelled fishy, and she didn't much care for seafood. She lifted one of the spoons and heard a small gasp come from Rosie. "What?" she said.

None of the children had started eating yet, and Kitty was just finished serving Peter, who was last, sitting next to David. Rosie looked at her dad and then nodded her head in his direction. "We must wait for Daddy to start," she whispered.

Erin nodded and whispered, "Okay, thank you."

"I said that's enough," David barked, and Erin lost her temper.

"You're quite right, David; I've had quite enough of this as well. You told me that this is my house now, too, right? Well, I'm not going to be treated like a child in my own house. If this is how dinner is going to be every night, then I will not be joining you. I respect that you are the head of the house, I really do, but I can't… no, I don't want to live like this—" She waved her arm around the room to show him what she meant. The tears were back, making her angry and frustrated, but she took a deep breath and continued without raising her voice. "Can we please stop this ridiculous charade that Susannah started just to control you, or may I please be excused and take my meal in the kitchen?" She was shaking and tried to brace herself for whatever reaction David might have.

Everyone in the room, including Kitty, who had come back to check on them, looked at her, wide-eyed. David had his head cocked to the side and had an odd expression on his face. He scanned the faces of the people in the room and then stood, which made Erin jump, thinking he was upset. He suddenly looked very sad, and his eyes became red. He nodded and put his hands on the table, leaning forward over it, then he shook his head. "I'm… sorry. Of course you're right, ma love." Erin rushed to his side, and he turned, embracing her tightly. "I was wrong to speak to you as I did, ma darling. I've just so much on ma mind, and… well, that's no excuse. Please forgive me?" he said.

"Don't be silly, of course I forgive you! I love you! Now, let's eat like a normal family, okay?"

"Okay, Kitty, please take this soup away; I don't like fish soup. Never have, never will."

"Oh, good!" Erin said. I don't like it either. Oh, Kitty, please tell Francie that it's not that the soup is bad… it's just—"

The housekeeper smiled warmly at her and put her hand up. "Don't you worry, Ms. Erin, I 'appen ta know ole' Francie doesn't care much for makin' it, neither."

The rest of the meal was much merrier; they talked and laughed together as a family.

After supper, they decided to watch a movie in the basement media room. There was a whole wall of DVDs and Blu-Rays, plus any and every streaming service you could think of to choose from. The twins wanted to watch *Lost in Vengeance*; a horror film David had played the lead role in many years earlier. Peter had just been allowed to watch it, and they were jealous.

"You'd have nightmares if you did!" Peter said. "The final scene was enough to make me want to sleep with the lights on for a few nights, I'll admit it!"

"Ooo! I found one!" Erin said and took a plastic case off the shelf. She held up Disney's *Tangled* and bounced on the balls of her feet.

"I love that film!" Rosie said.

She handed David the case and gave him and the boys her best puppy-dog-eyes, hoping they'd concede.

The movie turned out to be a hit, but the best part was during the lantern scene when David and Erin sang the duet, *I See the Light,* to each other.

On the way up the stairs later, Erin overheard Dan say to Charlie, "Our mum was like the evil witch in the film, and I'm glad she's gone."

Charlie nodded, "Me too," he whispered and looked behind him. When he saw Erin, he blushed and quickened his step.

At bedtime, Erin read two more chapters to them that night. It seemed to her that the children were completely immersed in the story already, which made her very happy. When that was done, she and David tucked them all in and said goodnight, then they headed down one flight of stairs to their bedroom. It had been a very stressful day, so they got into their nightclothes and went to bed early.

Chapter Forty-Two

DAVID TAKES ISSUE WITH THE SPARE ROOM

Erin woke from a sound sleep with a start. Kitty was at the side of her bed, saying, "Mum! Wake up, Mum." "Hmmm—what's wrong, Kitty?" she asked, not fully awake.

"It's Mr. Elliott, mum; 'ee's in the spare room, and somethin's not right," she said, sounding truly frightened. Erin sat up on her elbow, trying to process what she was hearing. "I were checkin' the 'alls, as I do when the children are 'ere, and I 'eard a noise comin' from the spare room. Please find out what's wrong wif 'im, mum."

"Okay—thank you for waking me, Kitty," Erin said. She put her robe on and left the bedroom, knowing if David was in that room, it wouldn't be good. She stepped up to the door and knocked gently, then she tried the doorknob, but it was locked. Through the door she could hear him crying and talking to himself. When she heard something hard hit the wall, she knocked a bit louder.

"David... darling... please let me in. Are you okay?" The noises stopped, but he didn't come to the door. "Please let me in; I'm so worried about you."

"Ih'm finne," he slurred. "Go bachk teh bhed."

"Are you—drunk? David, open this door or so help me I'll ask Kitty to help me pick the lock unless she has some kind of master key—or—" Erin had never been good at ultimatums. She heard him stumble to the door and turn the key; it clicked, but he didn't open it, so she did.

"Whaht dae yeh whannt," he asked, swaying a bit as he stood in the faint glow of the nightlight coming from the bathroom.

She went to him and put her hands on his arms, smelling the distinct odor of strong alcohol on him. "What's going on, David?" she asked.

He pointed at her several times before he gave up and sat on the small chair in the corner of the room. "Thiss iss nothinn' teh do wi' you. Ettss b'tweeen mhe, and thess rhoom, sae yeh shu-huld go... now." He put his elbows on the narrow arms of the chair and hung his head.

"I'm not leaving you alone in here," she said, and he looked up in her general direction.

"Ehrin, I dinnae whant teh—hurt yeh, and... I whant tehh get dru-nk," he slurred.

"Well, you've done a fine job of it already," she said. Erin hadn't actually been in the spare bedroom much since he'd brought her there in June and they'd made love on the bed. She looked at it and remembered how they'd each played as if they were forcing the other one. At the time, it had been fun and felt dangerous, in a way, but after everything that had happened to them, it was bittersweet.

"I— mhade love teh yeh on thess bed after—after Sussannahh ha-ad me raped on et," he said and looked at the bed as though it had been a conspirator and needed to be tried.

"David, you don't know that's what—"

His eyes filled with tears again. "Yeh dinnae ken? I ken et wh-ell e-nough, now! Lhook!" He stood, staggered to the bed, and pulled a photo from under the mattress. "Lhookett what I found, Ehrin; et wass right there—uhnder the mattresss... where anaone could fa-hind ett— if we h-had a guesst..." He slapped it onto her chest and patted it. Then, he went back to the corner, slid himself down the wall, and sat on the floor next to a bottle of alcohol with his head down.

"David—I don't want to—" she started to say, not wanting to see it.

"Jesst lhook at the feckin' pic-shure, Ehrin," he hissed.

She held it up and nearly dropped it. It took all her willpower and self-control not to gasp or scream. It showed a young attractive man standing behind David, who was kneeling on the edge of the bed. There was no doubt whatsoever what the man was doing to him. Erin wanted to rip it up, set it on fire and erase it from off the face of the earth. She looked at David sitting on the floor, taking long drinks from the bottle of alcohol in his hand, and her heart melted at what he must be going through.

"Oh, David. Oh, my darling. How can I help you? What can I do?" She went to him and was about to sit next to him, but he shook his head and tried to stand.

"Yehh can lheave me ahlone en here. I am gonna finishh thess bottle, and mayhbe start anotherone," he said.

Erin knew she had to do something. She steeled herself, determined to stop him, no matter how much he fought her. He had to end the destructive behavior and see what it would eventually do to his family. She stood, holding the photo out in front of them;

she knew he'd be livid, but she tore it up into as many pieces as she could before he could stop her.

"Whhat the fuck arr yeh doin'? Stop et! Ehrin!" He stumbled as he tried to stand and ended up on his hands and knees in front of her, bawling.

She took the nearly empty bottle out of his hand, tipped it into the sink in the bathroom, and then went back to him. "I don't care what this fucking photo shows! I love you, and I—I want to help you. What do you think, David? Do you think that I won't love you anymore, or that I'll be disgusted? Do you think that you're less of a man, or—that—maybe you enjoyed it?" He looked up at her, his eyes blazing. "Are you imagining that you can remember hurting when you woke up one morning and didn't know why?" She knelt in front of him; he was still on his hands and knees and had just put his head down on the carpet. "Are you attracted to men? Tell me the truth."

He raised his head off the floor and gave her the most disgusted, hateful look. "Fuck you!" he said to her and sat on his heels.

———

David wanted to slap her, but even at that level of drunkenness, he could never hurt her.

"I take that as a no," she said calmly "Do you love me, and are you attracted to me?"

He tried to get to his feet again, but he was too dizzy and off-balance, so he flopped onto his back, staring at the blurry ceiling. "Yeh ken I dhoo," he said and put his arm over his eyes. She got on the floor next to him and lay her arm over his chest. He tried to roll over, but it took too much effort, so he gave up. "I've been wi' anoth-er man, Ehrin, h-how can yeh act as iff etss no-thin'?" Suddenly he felt ill and launched himself to the bathroom, though he didn't make it and was sick all over the floor. He wanted to lie in it; he didn't even care. He was starting to think that he wanted to die, but he knew that wasn't the answer, so the next best thing was to make himself suffer.

———

Erin took a very expensive-looking towel from the counter and laid it on the floor, then she sat next to him as he knelt in front of his sick. "David, my love. I don't think that it's nothing; you've got to be hurting so badly right now, but behaving this way isn't going to help. You're only going to make things worse—" she said tenderly.

David crawled to the door frame and managed to stand. He took hold of her arm, grabbing it too tightly and hurting her, then he started leading her to the door. "Yeh need tehh leave nhow—" he said.

She'd had enough, and knew if he had another bottle in there, he'd end up killing himself with alcohol poisoning, so she jerked her hand out of his grasp. He lost his balance and ended up half sitting, half lying on the floor. "David Elliott!" she said with all the authority she could muster. "If you think I'm going to let you behave this way, trying to kill yourself while we have our bairn to think of, you've got another thing coming! I will *not* raise this baby without its father, so either you pull yourself together and—and seek help, or—or—I'm going to—to—" She didn't want to say it; it was the very last thing on earth she wanted to do, but she was desperate. She was breathing heavily and looked at him, tears filling her eyes. "I'll—have an abortion," she said quietly, losing her steam and then fell to her knees.

He looked at her, suddenly much more sober. His eyes grew enormous, and he started shaking his head. "No! No, Erin—take that back! Dinnae even say that!" he said anxiously. He crawled over to her and laid his head on her lap with his face pointed at her stomach. "Mummy didn't mean that, darling! She loves yeh, and so do I! I won't allow her tae hurt yeh!" He was crying and had his mouth pressed against her nightgown, kissing her belly.

She wanted to back down and tell him that she wouldn't ever do it, but she needed him to promise her he'd find a way to get help first. "You'll find a way to get help, or... or, to get through this, or so help me, David, I will," she said.

He looked up at her as if completely and utterly terrified. "I—I—dinnae ken how! I—dinnae think I can, Erin! Please, please, I'm beggin' yeh! Dinnae kill our baby!" He was back on his knees, hands clasped in front of him, literally begging her.

"Promise me you'll never lock yourself away, trying to kill yourself with alcohol again, and that you'll get rid of those photos. Whether you burn them or give them to your lawyer for safekeeping, I don't care."

"Aye, anathin'; I promise," he sobbed.

Erin smoothed his hair and took a deep breath. "God, David, it's alright to cry and to be upset and angry, but it's not okay to hurt yourself. Do you know what I'm saying? I can't live without you in so many ways. If you kill yourself, what will happen to me? I'll be pregnant and won't have any more treatments. I'll start having episodes again, and it will just get worse, so that, who knows, I might lose the baby anyway. I need you; I need your love! We were meant for each other, remember? You said so yourself," she said, and he nodded, putting his head back on her lap. "Also, what about your children? What do you think will happen to them if you end up killing yourself, either on purpose or by accident? We're not married yet; I can't just take custody of them. We all need you, and we all love you, no matter what someone did to you without your knowledge or consent."

"Aye. Please promise me yeh won't harm our bairn," he said with his face against her belly as if shielding it from danger.

"Aye, David. I promise I won't hurt our bairn." She was exhausted, but the mess in the bathroom needed to be cleaned up, so she gently lifted his head and stood. She doubted there were any cleaning supplies in there, so she helped David stand and led him to their bedroom. "I'm going to see if Kitty's awake so we can clean the bathroom. Go to bed, darling. I'll be right back.

He nodded and did as he was told. She helped him get into the bed and then covered him up, kissing his forehead. She left the room and saw Kitty sitting on the bottom stair, far enough away so as not to hear them but close enough so that she could come running if she'd been called. Kitty stood and went to Erin, holding her as the adrenaline wore off and she cried. "He was sick all over the bathroom floor. I'll help you clean it," she said.

Kitty stroked her hair and shushed her. "Naw, don't you worry about that, Erin. Just go on back ta Mr. Elliott and comfort 'im. I'm glad you were able to 'elp 'im. I were so frigh'ened he'd hurt 'imself, mum."

"You did good coming to get me. Thank you for caring so much! I don't know what I'd do without you!" she said and started crying again. "Oh, Kitty, Susannah was the most hateful, wicked person. She was truly and completely evil to the core."

"Yes, mum, and I'm ever so glad I don't work for 'er anamore! Now, let's get ya to bed." She put her arm around Erin's waist and helped her up the stairs. When they got to her bedroom door, she looked her in the eye, smoothed a hair off her face, and brushed a tear off her cheek. "You're a good wife—well, partner, I mean, and a good mum, and a brilliant employer. Get some rest now, a'right?"

"Alright, thanks again," Erin said and shut the door.

Chapter Forty-Three

REPERCUSSIONS

Erin woke again to David rushing to the toilet to be sick; she'd counted at least three times that night. "Are you okay?" she asked when he crawled back into the bed.

"Mnnhnn," was his reply.

Erin rolled toward him, wrapped her arm around his chest, and then snuggled up close to his backside. Instead of welcoming her, as he usually did, he lifted her arm by the wrist, returned it to her, then leaned forward.

He'd never done anything like that before; he was never cool to her, at least not without saying something, but now, he was ice cold. "What's— wrong?" she asked gently, though she had the distinct feeling that the last thing he wanted to do was talk to her. He moaned and shook his head. "David?"

"Not—now—" he said sharply, so she backed away from him and lay on her back.

She didn't know what to do; should she let it go and then spend the whole day worried and have it be ruined, or should she push a little, expecting an explosion that would take less time to get past? She decided to let him sleep a little longer while she took a shower, hoping he'd be less angry then, though she wasn't sure what he was upset about. *I probably saved his life last night, and now he's angry at me?* She started to get up, but he rolled over and grabbed her arm. When she looked back at him, what she saw scared her. His face was red, and the dark blue vein on his forehead was sticking out. Though he wasn't hurting her, she tried to pull her arm away, and he held it tight.

"Lemme make sure I remember what happened last night, a'right? Did you actually threaten our bairn's life if I didn't get over this—trauma?" he asked. His eyes were blazing, and she could feel a slight tremor in his hand.

She shook her head, really frightened at this side of him. "No, that's not what I said. What I said was I—wouldn't—let you kill yourself—" His eyes were burning through her, and she couldn't focus. "David, you're scaring me; please stop looking at me like that, and please let me go.

"Aye, yeh wouldn't let me kill maself, but ye'd kill our bairn without a problem? I see," he yelled.

Erin shook her head. "No, David, you're twisting what I said—that's not what happened. I—I made you promise to get help—because you were hurting yourself, and if I hadn't done something drastic, you would've continued drinking and would probably be dead now!"

"I—would suggest yeh stay away from me today. I've never hit a woman before, but et's takin' all ma self-control tae not haul off and slap yeh. If you EVER threaten the life of ANY of ma children again, ye'll not be seein' me again! Do yeh understand what I'm sayin'?"

All she could do was nod. He let go of her arm with a slight jerk, and she jumped off the bed. He rolled away from her, and she backed away, not knowing what to do. She heard the children running past their door on their way to breakfast and tried to remember what she'd said to him the previous night. *He was pushing me out the door, ready to drink another bottle of booze. I had to think fast— Shit, I don't remember everything I said.* She looked at his back, wanting to touch it and tell him she was sorry, but she didn't want to ever see his face look at her like that again. "I'm sorry. I—I was wrong. Please forgive me," she said, then she walked into the zebra-striped bathroom and turned on the shower.

She gathered some towels and took off her nightgown, then she looked at the door, trying to visualize him lying there, and hoped his face would be softer toward her when she came out. As she stepped in, she remembered holding him after they'd found the photos; how he'd made love to her twice right there. Methodically, she washed her hair and body, then rinsed off. She closed her eyes as she spread cleanser on her face, then used a washcloth to rinse it off. When she opened her eyes, she saw David standing on the other side of the glass shower door, watching her. She froze, afraid he'd changed his mind and had come in to slap her.

He was still intense as he stepped into the shower, staring at her, but the vein was gone, and it didn't seem like he wanted to hit her any longer. She closed her eyes and stood still, not knowing what to expect, until she felt his hand near her face, then she flinched, but he laid it gently on her cheek. When she opened her eyes, she saw that he was crying and his face was the one she knew and loved once more.

He kissed her forehead and then gently pushed her against the wall, making her gasp, not expecting it. She wasn't sure what he was doing; he was furious with her but wanted to make love? It didn't make sense. "David—" she said, but he put his finger over her lips to shush her, then pressed himself against her. He put his hand behind her head and grabbed a handful of her hair, tugging it so that she gasped again.

He turned her around and used his foot to spread her legs apart. She grabbed the handrail and held on as he took her from behind, thrusting hard to the point that it started to hurt. "David—please—that—hurts!" she said, so he slowed down a bit and kept going, building speed, only not pounding her quite as hard. She wanted to cry out, to be loud, and express how good he was making her feel, but she couldn't risk the children hearing her. She could feel herself getting closer—closer, until her body shook with a powerful orgasm that made him groan and shudder as he reached his climax. They were still for a few moments, letting the intensity die down a bit. "I—don't understand—" she said breathlessly, "I've never seen you so angry—"

He covered her mouth with his hand, startling her. "Shh, let me have this," he said quietly into her ear and then stood behind her, breathing heavily for a long time. She relaxed and enjoyed the feel of him holding her as the water ran over her back. After a while, he took one very deep breath and let it out slowly. "I—didn't expect yer reply. Et was so honest and humble; I could also tell you were verra scared of me then, and et broke ma heart. I'm sorry I threatened you, ma love. I ken you were only tryin' tae help me last night," he said, then he let her go.

She turned and wrapped her arms around him. "I love you. You were pushing me out the door, getting ready to drink the other bottle, so I panicked and said the one thing I knew would at least make you stop. I'm so sorry! I could never hurt our baby! Just please stop hurting yourself."

"Aye, with yer help I'll get past this, and I won't do that again. Also—there wasn't another bottle."

She looked up at him, and he smiled sheepishly. "Well, I'm glad," she said and lay her head back on his chest.

"I'm afraid to ask, but how did yeh know I was in there? You were asleep when I left the room."

She sighed, not wanting to tell him, afraid he'd think Kitty had been meddling. "Please don't be upset, but Kitty came and woke me. She was checking the halls upstairs to make sure the children were in bed and safe. I guess she always does that when they're here. She said she heard you in the spare room, and it sounded like something was wrong, so she begged me to make sure you were all right. She's just amazing, David, and I really love her."

"Aye, I was wrong. She's not flighty or absent-minded; she's observant and astute, and I'll be raising her salary, startin' today," he said.

"Good, I'm glad; now I need to rinse out my conditioner and get dressed; the children will be finishing their breakfast soon and wondering where we are." She looked up at him, and he kissed her, then he let her go, allowing her to rinse her hair. She laughed when she opened her eyes and saw him standing with his back against the shower wall, watching her.

"You are lovely," he said with his million-dollar smile. "Go down tae breakfast without me, and I'll join yeh when I'm done."

Erin arrived at the breakfast table after everyone was finished eating, and only Francie was still in the kitchen. "I'm sorry I'm so late, Francie; we had a rough night last night and didn't sleep well. We can eat cereal if you have other things you need to do."

Francie made a very Scottish grunt-like noise and shrugged. "Et's none of ma business, mum; I'm jest the hired help. I'll dae whatever yeh wish for me tae dae," she said.

Erin went to her and placed her arm around the older woman's shoulders. She was obviously not used to her employer behaving in that manner and stiffened up. "Francie, you are much more to me than 'the hired help,'" she said with a mocking, overly posh accent and saw the corners of Francie's mouth twitch a little. "You make all the difference in the world to this household! There is no way I could manage it, all the cooking and the clean-up afterward, plus meal planning and shopping! I'm tired just thinking about it. I have always wanted a cook but never thought my wish would come true, and now I have the best cook that anyone could have!" Francie was smiling full out now, so Erin leaned in a bit closer, whispering, "Just don't tell Millie I said that, or I'll be in serious trouble."

"In serious trouble with whom?" David said as he walked into the room and sat at the table." His eyes were red and he looked tired.

Erin knew he must be dealing with a terrible hangover, but he didn't complain or act like anything was wrong at all. She smiled at Francie, who smiled back warmly. "I was just telling Francie how much I appreciate her; how she's the best cook I could ask for but asked her not to tell Millie, or—"

David smiled as he poured himself a cup of tea from the pot on the table. "Or ye'll be in serious trouble," he finished with her.

Francie saw him pouring the tea, and her eyes grew wide. "Och, sir! Tha' must be cold by noow! I'll make yeh a fresh pot," she exclaimed and whisked it away from him before he could protest.

He managed to save the half cup he'd already poured and held onto it tightly when she returned to give him a new one. "I'll keep this if yeh don't mind; I need a cuppa, cold or not."

After breakfast, Erin noticed Peter loitering outside David's study, so she went to him. "What's up, Peter?"

The boy seemed startled and looked at the closed door. "Oh, I thought you and dad were in there," he said and pointed to it just as David stepped out of the kitchen and approached them.

"Good mornin', Peter," he said and opened the door, ushering everyone in. "What do you need?"

"I don't need anything, really. I'd planned to ask if we might go to the park for a bit of cricket today, but—"

"But?" Erin said and sat on the leather sofa. "Sit next to me."

"Well, I didn't mean to, but I heard you having a row earlier, so I wasn't sure you'd be up for it," he said, still standing and wringing his hands a bit.

Erin patted the cushion next to her, and the boy sat beside her. "I'm sorry you heard that Peter, but everything is okay between us now."

"Aye, son, I ken what yeh must've been thinkin', but Erin isn't the kind tae hold a grudge. We've sorted et all out, so dinnae worry about that. I reckon cricket may be a bit much; I didn't sleep well last night, but I'd be up for a game of quoits, instead? What do you say, darling?" he said and smiled at Erin.

"Quoits? Sounds like a disease; 'I'm down with the quoits today,'" she said, holding her stomach.

Peter giggled and then bounced up and down like a child. "It's a fun, easy game. I know you'll like it!"

"I'm sure I don't know what I'm getting myself into, but it sounds like a good learning experience, and I wouldn't miss it," she said and put her hand over Peter's.

The young man's face beamed at her, and he leaned over to kiss her lightly on the cheek. "Fantastic! I'll tell the others and gather the equipment," he said and jumped off the couch. He rushed up to David, who was leaning on the back edge of his desk, and hugged him. Then he smiled at them and hurried out the door, shutting it behind him with a *bang*, leaving the couple stunned.

"Wow! You think he's just a little bit excited?" Erin said and patted the couch where Peter had just been seated.

"A wee bit, I reckon," he said and sat beside her.

"I could take a guess, but why was he worried about talking to us?" she asked.

"Ach, when his mother and I had a row, no matter who was at fault, she'd not let et be for hours, sometimes days. Et was oppressive, tae say the least, and if one of the children asked her anathin', she may take her bitterness out on them."

"How those children ended up being so precious, I'll never know!" she said. "I guess having them far away from her in boarding school was a positive thing in the end. Was she an only child or something that she thought that behavior was acceptable?"

"No, she had a younger sister who was the family pet and then died of cancer shortly before we were married. I'd rather not talk about or think about Susannah, though. If it were up tae me, I'd prefer tae never speak of her again."

"Agreed," she said and leaned against him. "So, tell me, what is quoits?"

"Et's a simple game of tossing a rope ring over a dowel," he explained and then heard the children talking excitedly by the door. "*Leave them be! They'll come out when they're ready,*" Peter said.

"*But how will they know that we're ready if we don't tell them?*" Charlie said in a hoarse whisper.

"I reckon we shouldn't keep them waiting," David said and stood, then he helped Erin up. They went to the door, and as he turned the doorknob, it opened, and Dan fell into the room.

"I tried to pull him away, Dad, but he had his ear up to the door, trying to—" Peter began, but David put his hand up to stop him.

He took Daniel's hand to help him stand, then smiled at his children. "What're yeh waiting for? We're wasting daylight!"

The sun was shining as they walked a few blocks away to the park, and they got in an hour and a half of play before it became overcast. The rain came down in sheets, and they had to run for it, back to the house, laughing, wet, and hungry.

The rest of the day was spent indoors, thinking up skits to do with the costumes that had been in the attic. Erin delighted in how inventive and funny the children were, and she thought she couldn't be happier than she was that day with her new family.

That night, when they were tucked in, the children were still laughing and talking about things that had happened in the park and thinking up more things to do in 'fancy dress,' as they called the costumes. Peter mentioned a panto, which had the rest of the kids coming up with ideas and talking non-stop. Even once the lights were out and Erin and David were going downstairs to their room, they heard them planning and laughing.

Now, the children were all energy but the adults were knackered. They decided it was no use trying to stay up and went to bed, holding each other close. "I had one of the best days today, well, maybe I should say best weeks," Erin said, her eyelids heavy.

David yawned and said, "Aye, me too."

They were sound asleep when they heard a knock on their bedroom door. David opened it to find Rosie standing there, crying. He crouched down to her level and asked, "What's the matter, Rosebud?"

She looked at the floor. "May I come in, please?" she asked, sounding so mature and yet like a small child.

"Of course yeh may," he said and opened the door wider to let her pass by him.

"What is it, darling?" Erin asked; she had gotten up, put her robe on, and was sitting in the armchair near the fireplace.

"I was laying in bed, trying to sleep when I had a terrible thought." She went to Erin, and she helped her onto her lap. The young girl laid her head on Erin's shoulder and continued. "What if... I wake up in the morning, and everything is opposite, Daddy?" She looked at him, seeming really frightened.

"What do yeh mean, Rosebud?" he asked and sat on the edge of the bed.

"What if it's really you who's dead, and— Mummy—is still alive? And what if, instead of Erin, Mummy is with Uncle Martin, or the other one, Uncle Clive?"

Erin got goosebumps all over her body, and the hair on the back of her neck stood up. She looked at David, who had gone completely pale. "Who is Clive, darling?" he said, sounding as calm as he'd ever been.

She looked at him with a confused look on her face and said, "Daddy! You know Uncle Clive. He comes here sometimes and talks to you and—and—Mummy in your bedroom, or he did when Mummy was still alive."

David calmly stood and went to the bathroom, shutting the door behind him. Erin could just barely hear the sound of him being sick. "What did you think of the shop we went to in Edinburgh, Rosie?" she said, trying to distract her from the sounds of crying and retching coming from the bathroom.

"Is Daddy alright?" she asked, ignoring Erin's question.

"Yes, darling, I think—maybe he ate something bad today; he'll be fine. Now, tell me, did you like it?"

Rosie continued to look at the bathroom door.

"I thought it was very... nice—"

They heard the water running for a while as David obviously brushed his teeth. He came out with red eyes and was sniffling a bit.

Rosie looked concerned. "Are you sick, Daddy? Erin said she thought you ate something bad today, did you?"

"Aye, ma Rosebud, but I'll be a'right. Dinnae worry about wakin' tae things bein' opposite; et won't happen, I promise. Now, go back tae bed, love."

Rosie looked at Erin, and she nodded. "He's right; everything will be just as it is now in the morning. I'll go with you and tuck you in again, okay?"

Rosie nodded, looking sadly at her father. She got off Erin's lap and walked over to David. "I love you, Daddy, and I'm glad you aren't dead."

David took her into his arms, tears running down his face. "Aye, I'm glad of it as well," he said, and put her down, then he turned so she wouldn't see his tears.

Erin took her to her bedroom and then returned to their room. David was in bed, lying on his back and staring at the ceiling, so she took off her robe and climbed into the bed next to him. He didn't say anything as he rolled over and turned out the light.

Chapter Forty-Four

WHAT TO DO?

Erin woke needing the toilet, knowing that once she got up, she would be hit with morning sickness. She heard a noise coming from the end of the bed, but couldn't see in the darkness, so she felt the mattress next to her, where David should've been. He wasn't there, so she made her way, blindly, to the bathroom and left the light on so she could see to get back. That's when she saw that David was sitting with his knees drawn up on the floor against the footboard, his face covered by his arm. She sat next to him, and he lay on his side, his head in her lap. He was shivering, and she was worried about him.

"Ma children saw him, Erin. What could they have thought we were doin' in there? And another thing, why were there no pictures of him?" he asked.

"I—think he was the cameraman. Someone had to take those photos, and if he's a bad cop, he wouldn't want to be in any of them," she said.

"I dinnae understand any of et. Why go through all this when all she needed tae do was tell me she wanted a divorce? I'd have given her anathin' she wanted tae be rid of her," he said, and Erin put her hand on his hair.

"I'm guessing it was revenge for... well, for me. It seems like she was compiling every scenario she could come up with to frame or humiliate you. It's like she was setting everything up to go off at the right time—probably when she got home, but she didn't make it that far."

"I reckon ye're right. I only hope there aren't more plans in the works... yet tae come. I dinnae think I can take much more than this," he said, then wrapped his arm around his stomach and groaned.

"I'm worried about you, darling... I mean, I know, in a way, how you feel, but—you don't seem to be—moving past it—or, I mean, dealing with it in a healthy way, and—"

"But, Erin, it's—and I ken et sounds sexist, but et's different for me. I can't think on et without bein' sick. If someone told you that ye'd been forced tae have sex with another woman et would be upsettin', and ye'd feel violated, but for a man—tae do that tae another man? Et's much more violent of an act, yeh ken? It's every straight man's nightmare."

"Yes, you're right, it is different. I understand what you're saying, I honestly do, but I'm not asking you to—somehow learn to like it or even appreciate it. However, you have to learn how to live with it and deal with the possibility that it might have happened. Maybe you need to talk to a therapist? Didn't you say you already had one?" she asked.

David looked at her like she had two heads. "Are yeh havin' me on? I'm not going to tell *anaone* about this! No one but you can know!" he said vehemently, then he wrapped his arm tighter around his stomach and moaned.

"But David, if you don't deal with it, you'll get really sick, sicker than you are now. What do you think will happen if you don't eat, or when you do, you can't keep it down? You're already a slender man; you don't have much to lose before you end up like… well, like Susannah, and I can't bear that!"

"I ken ye're right, but there's no chance that I'll walk into ma therapist's office and tell him anything I'm feelin', or what probably happened to me." He stood and began pacing. "How could et not have? What might possibly keep them from followin' through? Even if et was just a game or… joke, someone would have done somethin', surely. Erin, ma insides feel as if they're on fire; I can't be sick with nothin' in ma wame again, or I feel as though I'll die," he said miserably.

"We need to get your mind off it—" she began, but then she saw his eyes grow wide. "What?" she said, shocked at the look on his face, then she jumped when he knelt in front of her and took hold of her arms.

"We can't make love until I get tested—for—"

He looked like a frightened child, and Erin didn't know what to do to help him. "Okay, darling," she said and held him. "Where can you go? Do you think the Registry clinic would be able to help you?" she asked, grasping at straws.

"I dinnae ken, mebbe," he said.

He was still shaking and felt cold to the touch. "I'll call them right now, alright?" she said. "I'll get my phone." She stood and grabbed her phone off the nightstand, then returned to him on the floor at the foot of the bed. When she unlocked the screen, she saw the time, 12:07 am and groaned. "They won't be open now, darling; it's midnight," she said. "Let's get back into bed, and I'll hold you until it's time to get up.

They slept fitfully until they heard the children running through the hallway on their way to breakfast. Erin took her phone off the table and swiped the screen to unlock it. She touched the microphone icon on the Google search bar. "Fertilis," she said and saw the autofill had 'registry near me' as one of its options, so she tapped it and then touched call.

The phone rang three times, and a lilting Irish voice answered with, "National Fertilis Defect Registration; this is Sean. How may I be of service?"

Erin wasn't sure what to say. "Uh, yes, hello, Sean—I have a strange question for you, and I'm hoping that you can help me."

There was a pause. "I'm sorry, but I can't help you find out if your partner is registered or not; that information is private—"

"No, that's not what I need to know—I already know he is—" she interrupted. "My... partner has just found out that he may—what I mean is—would you be able to do a private and confidential screening for STD's including—" She swallowed hard, "AIDS? I wouldn't ask, except that he's, well, he's well known, and he'd rather not be seen walking into a clinic and asking for that, you know?" She had started rambling and felt like an idiot.

"Yes, I believe I understand what you're sayin', but we aren't meant for that sort of visit. I'm sorry, but I'll have to say we can't." Erin felt deflated. "Can he not just call his normal physician and ask for a check-up, or even purchase a test at the chemist, then?" Sean asked, showing that he at least cared enough to try to help them.

"Yes, I suppose he can. Thank you for your help," she said, feeling very tired, and ended the call. "Wait, did he just say you could get HIV tests at the drugstore—er—chemists, I mean? We could do that... I mean, I could go to Boots or wherever and get every kind of STD test on the shelf, and you could take them all, just to be safe."

David looked at her, relief washing over his handsome yet careworn features. "Ach, I'm so thankful ye're here to help me in this moment, darling. I—wish I didn't need for yeh to do et, but I reckon et would be—wise. I'll at least have some peace of mind," he said.

"It's okay; I'm glad I'm here for you too. Let's go downstairs and have some breakfast, alright?"

"Ach, I dinnae think I can eat anathin' just now, would yeh please tell Francie I'm not feelin' well at present, but I'll be down for lunch."

"Okay, darling, I'll do that and then head out to the nearest chemist. You rest now, my love, and I'll wake you when I get back," she said and kissed him. She wasn't hungry either, but her stomach was still queasy, and she didn't want to have to hurry to the toilet to be sick again.

David was sound asleep when she came out of the bathroom after getting dressed and ready to go. She took a moment to watch him, so peaceful, after everything he was going through. He was terrified, and she knew it, though she didn't know how to help him cope.

She quietly left the room and headed downstairs, meeting Rosie and Charlie at the bottom of the staircase.

"And what are you up to today?" she asked. They looked conspiratorially at one another and shrugged. Erin narrowed her eyes at them, having no clue what they might be planning. "Out with it," she said, not letting them pass by her.

"We want to ask Dad if—" Charlie began, but Erin shook her head at them.

"I'm sorry, but your father isn't feeling well right now. He's asleep and needs to stay in that condition for a while yet," she said and watched as their faces fell.

"Is Daddy still sick from last night?" Rosie asked, looking worried.

"Sort of; I'm going to run to the chemist to get him something to make him feel better. You'll need to find something to do that won't wake him until I get back. Then we can find something to do together, okay?"

The children nodded sadly. "Will the medicine cure him?" Charlie asked, and Rosie looked up at her, obviously wanting to know the answer as well.

"I don't know, but I hope it'll help. Now, I've got to get a bite to eat, and then I'll be off. Please remember to be as quiet as you can be whilst I'm gone, and please tell Dan to do the same."

"Yes, Mum," they both said, and hugged her, then they ran off.

Erin went into the kitchen and took a piece of toast out of the rack. She spread it with soft butter and then raspberry jam. Francie brought out the teapot, and Erin poured herself a cuppa. "David isn't feeling well this morning, so he won't be down for breakfast. He thinks he'll be well enough for lunch, though, so please plan on him eating with us," she said to their cook. "Have you made anything special this morning?

"Ah made porridge, with fruit for the children, and will make more for you, mum," she said.

"Thank you, but this will be enough. I'm off to the chemist; do you need anything?" she asked, trying to be helpful.

"Nae, but thank you for askin'," she said, which was the first time Erin could remember her thanking her for anything.

"Okay, see you later, then," she said and went to the door. Peter came around the corner and asked her where she was going. She knew he'd like to come along, but she couldn't bring him for that trip, and it made her a bit sad since she enjoyed his company. "I'm off to the chemist; do you need anything?" she asked.

"No, but may I come with you?" he asked, predictably.

"I would love for you to come along, but I'm shopping for—unmentionable things, and I would rather do it alone this time. We'll have to take a walk or do some fun shopping soon," she said, hoping that would appease him.

"Yeah, alone is probably better," he said with his father's smile and easy way about him. "Well, uhh, have fun?" he said and then laughed.

"Oh, by the way, Peter, your dad isn't feeling well, so please make sure everyone stays relatively quiet and doesn't go barging into our room, okay?"

"What's wrong? Is he sick?" He looked genuinely worried about him.

"No, not really. He didn't sleep well last night, and he's worried about some things. He needs rest, that's all. He'll be right as rain in a little bit. Don't you worry, sweet boy," she said, seeing the same look of concern, even after her explanation.

She wondered why he would look so unsettled about his dad feeling a bit ill, and then it dawned on her that they'd probably never seen him sick. David was a very healthy man, and even if he wasn't, he'd pretend he was because that's the kind of man he was. On top of that, their mother had appeared to be perfectly fine and then died, seemingly out of nowhere.

She put her hand on his arm and brushed a lock of hair off his forehead. "Please, believe me, darling. He's not actually sick; he's tired and worried, that's all. He's not going to die... or be sick for a long time—or anything, so please, don't worry," she said, trying to keep eye contact with him.

He smiled at her and nodded. "Okay, Mum. I believe you. Thanks for taking the time to talk to me and not pushing me away—it really helps," he said, and the worried look was replaced by a smile.

Erin smiled at the dear young man standing before her. It was the first time he'd called her 'Mum', and it seemed so natural for him. "You're welcome, Peter."

He hugged her and said, "I liked calling you that."

"Me too," she whispered.

Erin stepped out her front door, opened her phone, and typed in, 'chemists near me.' The nearest one was a Superdrug, only a few blocks away, so she went down the five steps, through the small gate, and onto the sidewalk in front of their home. She took a deep breath of the warm summer air.

She enjoyed her short walk to the drugstore and went inside, heading straight to the pharmacist. She had to wait for a few minutes and then asked to speak to the man privately. She told him about her partner having just found out that he may have been exposed to any number of STDs whilst he was drugged and assaulted against his will. He nodded when she told him that she wanted every kind of test they had so he could gain some peace of mind. He helped her find what she was looking for and told her the HIV test would need to be mailed or brought back for them to analyze; the results would then be returned in three days. The total was several hundred pounds when he rang her up, but it didn't matter; it meant he would be able to sleep again, she hoped.

An hour after she'd left, she returned and went straight to their room. David was still in his pajamas, pacing at the end of the bed when she let herself in. "Did you find…" he began but didn't want to say it, "…everything?" he finished anxiously.

He was biting his fingernails, and Erin could see traces of redness in his eyes. "Yes, darling, the chemist helped me find everything," she said, laying the bag on the bed. She went to him for a hug, but he was distracted, so it was brief. He picked up the bag and pulled out two Kit-Kat bars, a Mars bar, and three Curly Wurlys. He frowned at her, and she shrugged, "What? They aren't for me! They're for the children and… us," she said and took them from him.

"Where's the—important one?" he asked, flustered and agitated.

Erin stepped over to the bed and opened the bag. She found it and pulled it out for him. He immediately grabbed it out of her hand and started to open the package, but she had to stop him. "Wait! Hold on, David," she said and took the box away from him. "We need to read the package carefully. This test will only show results six weeks or longer after exposure, but do we know when it happened? Was it over six weeks ago?" she asked.

David frowned and knit his eyebrows together. "I—dinnae ken!" he said, and Erin could see him starting to panic.

"Okay, darling, calm down. You're working yourself up, and that's not going to help you at all. Let's think. Today is July... third; our first treatment was May sixteenth, so I would assume it happened sometime between then and now. You said she knew about us when you called, after my episode, right?" she asked, and he nodded. "Well, if she did it right when you got back from New Orleans, then—I need a calendar!" she said.

David unlocked his phone and opened the calendar app for her. "You got home on May twenty-first? No, it would've been May twenty-second by then for you. So, if she managed to drug you the next day—but that's a Wednesday, and Kitty and Francie's day off is Tuesday." She was mainly speaking to herself, but David was listening intently. "I doubt she'd do it while they were here, would she? Well, if she did, that would be six weeks... tomorrow, unless she did more than one of them, then who knows. Either way, you'll need to wait until at least tomorrow before you take it, though it might be better to wait until Tuesday... this next week. Then it's gotta go back to the chemist for analysis—" She was still talking when David grabbed the box again.

"We have tae send et back?" He read the back of the box. "Three days!" he said. "This is torture! I can't stand et! I need tae be with you, I need tae love you, but I dinnae want yeh tae get sick. I need yeh, Erin."

She held him, and he kissed her urgently. He was hard and pulled her up to him by the butt cheek, making her want him. "But... David—how many times have we made love since this happened? Twenty times, probably much more. I imagine if I were going to get it, it would already be too late, wouldn't it?" she said, breathing heavily and gasping as he touched her breasts.

He started to unfasten her slacks and then stopped after running his hand over her belly. "No! I can't do et! I can't risk our bairn's wee life for ma selfish lust."

Erin was so ready for him that it was hard to think about stopping, but she knew he was right. "Could we—help each other out? I need your touch, at least! I could—" she said and placed her hand over his pajamas, feeling him react to her touch. He gasped and untied the drawstring, pulling them down, revealing his erect penis. Erin wanted to take it into her mouth but wasn't sure how dangerous that was, so she took hold of it firmly in her hand and started stroking it slowly.

He unfastened her slacks and pulled them off her, which was difficult with her hand attached to his cock, but he managed it and then took hold of her hand, and she let go. He got up on the bed and asked her to join him in the sixty-nine position. She gasped and tried hard not to make any noise as he used his tongue to explore her and his fingers to enter her.

She took hold of him once more, and carefully licked his shaft, making sure not to come in contact with any potential fluids. She stroked him and felt herself getting closer and closer with each flick of his tongue and each probe of his fingers. It was all she could do to not cry out as her body reached its climax, and she felt the release wash over her in waves, making her body contract and pulse.

She redoubled her efforts, but he sat up. "Roll over," he said, and he got off her. She rolled onto her back, and he lay on top of her, rubbing his hard-on between her breasts. He watched as she pressed her breasts against him on either side, then he closed his eyes and moaned, and she felt his semen, hot and wet, on her sternum. He immediately got out of bed and handed her the box of tissues before walking into the bathroom.

She didn't know what to think as she cleaned herself up. He hadn't done that before; usually, he held her or at least spoke to her after sex. After waiting several minutes, she knocked lightly on the bathroom door. "David? Are you—okay?" She didn't hear anything. "Can—I come in?" she asked, with no reply. A hundred scenarios flooded her mind, each one more horrible than the next, trying to explain why he wasn't saying anything. "David?" She was beginning to panic, imagining that he'd tried killing himself or something. "I'm going to open the door!" She turned the knob and slowly swung the door open. Not seeing him at first, she said, "David?" very quietly.

"I can't take this, Erin!" she heard from the bathtub where he was sitting, his head in his hands. "It's too much, and—I'm not strong enough."

She stepped up to the tub and saw a nearly broken man. He looked old and tired and not healthy. "Susannah did this to ruin you, darling. She wanted you to suffer, but you can't let her win!

You finally have your children back from both the school and from their pain and resentment. You—are finally able to be a family—"

"Because of you," he said quietly.

"All the more reason to fight, right? The children are worried about you, David. Please don't let her ruin your life. We love you, no matter what," she said and took his hand.

"Erin?" he croaked in a whisper.

"What is it, my love?"

"What if—" His words were strained and filled with emotion. "I have a disease, and I'm no longer able tae give you yer treatments? I—can't live with that!"

She sat with her back against the side of the tub and sighed. "I don't know—I just don't know, but you can't allow that to paralyze you until we find out, right? I know it's hard, but you've gotta try to keep a stiff upper lip and act tough for the children. If you can't function, they will think you're gonna die, just like their mom did. Please try to be strong for them—for us."

"I dinnae—"

"You need to get your mind off it. What do you think of going back to the park with the children today? Maybe... play some cricket, or soccer, or something? It's lovely outside right now."

David groaned; "I dinnae wanna go anawhere, but ye're right, dwelling on the 'what ifs' won't help. A'right, let's talk tae them," he said.

"Let me help you up," she said and then tried to get herself off the floor, groaning and grunting in the process. She took his hand to pull him to his feet, but instead, he pulled her down so that she was lying in the tub with him. "David! How am I gonna get out of here now?" He smiled and began kissing her. He made out with her for a long time, touching her with his hands down her slacks until she had another orgasm.

"Don't," he said.

"Don't what?"

"Don't get up from here. Lay with me until we both shrivel up and die together, then our bodies can decompose; the ooze going neatly down the drain," he said.

"I—don't know how to take that, David," she said, worried he meant it but was trying to hide it in a joke.

He chuckled lightly and kissed her again. "I didn't mean et, love. Now let's find a way out of here, a'right?"

They spent the afternoon at the park, where Peter taught Erin to play cricket, though there was quite a learning curve. There weren't enough players for a match, but they still had a lot of fun goofing around. She was glad to see David laughing and playing with his family; she only hoped it would last.

Chapter Forty-Five

REALLY?

In the middle of the night, Erin woke from an incredibly upsetting dream in which she was being held down by someone and crying. Her senses told her that it was Bran, but she couldn't see his face. She could only see his arms, neck, and one earlobe, each of them scarred from the many fights he'd been in. His earlobe had a small wedge torn from it.

She rolled over, wanting David to hold her and tell her that it was okay, but he wasn't there. She looked at the clock; it read 1:13 am. The bathroom door was open, and there wasn't a light on, so she got up and put on her robe, hoping with all her heart he wasn't in the spare bedroom, though something in her told her he was.

She opened their bedroom door and saw the tiniest bit of light shining through the crack under the closed spare room door. After taking a deep breath, she padded barefoot down the hall, feeling the cool, waxed hardwood under her feet. *Oh, David,* she thought as she gently knocked on the door, and the light went out.

"David? Can I come in?" she asked, though what she really wanted to do was barge into the room and see what he was doing in there, alone, in the middle of the night. "David?" She heard him moving, and then she heard the key being turned and the bolt *thunked* quietly back into its home inside the door, so she hesitantly turned the knob and let herself in.

David was standing, facing the window, with his arms crossed, and she was unsure whether she should speak or wait for him to say something. After a few moments, she chose to speak. "Are you okay, darling?" He bowed his head and put one of his hands up to his eyes.

She went to him and put her hand on his shoulder. "Can I help you?" He turned suddenly and wrapped his arms around her, and she didn't smell any alcohol, which was a relief. She could feel him shaking as he let out huge sobs, so she held him, letting him get it out and praying that he could somehow find peace, though she knew it would take a miracle for that to happen.

"I—I had a bad dream, and when I rolled over to hold you, you were gone," she explained, and he nodded his head. She could smell his scent, mingled with his soap on his neck and the detergent on his t-shirt. He smelled so good, and she wanted to stay in his embrace all night, but they needed to talk.

"Tell me yer dream, darling," he said and sat in the small wing-back chair in the corner of the room, pulling her onto his lap.

She told him what she'd dreamed, and then something occurred to her. "Do you still have any of those photos we found?" she asked, figuring he hadn't destroyed all of them like she'd asked him to do. He didn't answer right away, and she sighed, so he nodded. "Can I please see them?" she asked. She had a hunch and wanted to know if she was right.

"I dinnae have the photos themselves... I—took pictures of them on ma mobile and then destroyed them. I'm sorry I lied to yeh," he said, sounding ashamed of himself.

"Is that what you were doing in here? Looking at them and brooding?" He nodded again. "Please let me see them," she said, slightly annoyed. She could understand, in a way, the need to dwell on it all, but he'd promised to talk to her.

"Ach, please dinnae make me show them to yeh, Erin. They're disgustin'," he said, making a face which said as much.

"Is that why you sit in here when you think I'm asleep, to look at disgusting pictures? Or is it for another reason? Is there something about them that turns you on, maybe?" She asked, truly not understanding why he needed to stare at them in the locked room without her knowing.

He gasped and then gently but firmly pushed her off his lap. "How dare yeh say somethin' like that tae me?" he said.

She walked to the switch and turned on the light, making them both squint as their eyes adjusted to the bright light. "How dare you sit in here looking at them with the door locked, even though you promised me you'd talk to me instead of doing it again? Show me the pictures—please," she said, calm but firm.

He took his mobile out of his pocket, unlocked it, found the photos, and then handed it to her. "There! Are yeh happy?" he said, sounding vexed.

She found one that showed his earlobe and zoomed in on it. It was hard to tell, but she thought she could see a small chunk missing from it and gasped. "Oh, my—God!" she said.

"Humph. Aye, they're just as bad as before; now may I please have my—"

"David! I—I don't think this is you!" she said, staring at him, wide-eyed, but he shook his head sadly. She sat on his lap again and showed him the zoomed-in portion of his earlobe. Does it look like a chunk is missing?" she asked.

He took the phone and gave her an unconvinced look. "Erin, et's me, a'right," he began, but looked closer at the photo and then back at Erin. "What else did yeh dream about?" he asked, as goosebumps made the hair on his arms and neck raise up, standing at attention.

"Scars on his neck and arms. David—this isn't you! It's—Bran!" she said, completely shocked.

He flipped to another photo and saw very faint scars on his arm. The next one showed more scars, though they were so faded, you wouldn't notice them unless you were looking. "But you said he had a snake tattoo on his chest. There's no tattoo on this person," he said, sounding hopeless again.

Erin took his phone and searched through all the ones which showed his chest. He was right... there was no tattoo. She tried to think about the night she'd seen Bran in Annis's kitchen. The lights were off and though the last rays of sunlight were still shining through the windows, it was dim in the room. She couldn't remember why she'd noticed his tattoo so vividly, then it occurred to her. "Chest hair!" she exclaimed, startling David.

"What?" he said, frowning.

"Chest hair! When I saw him in your mother's kitchen, he had no chest hair, and the same when he... well, the next time I saw him. Those fucking snake eyes stared at me the whole time. Here, he either has chest hair hiding the tattoo, or he hasn't gotten it yet—or, maybe he'd gotten it started, but didn't get it finished until he got to Edinburgh, and that's why his chest was shaved—because there was fresh ink." She zoomed in and saw something, barely visible, under the hair—very muted colors. "Look! Can you see that?"

"I can," he said after looking closely. "So that means—I wasn't raped? Oh, God, Erin!" he cried and wrapped his arms around her, holding her tightly. "Wait, but what about Rosie saying that Uncle Clive spoke with Susannah and me in our bedroom? Do yeh think she could've been fooled by Bran?" he asked.

"If we were, then she could've been as well."

"Erin! Et's not me! I'm clean—" He put his head in his free hand, and she thought he was crying until he lifted his head and looked at her, then she saw that he was laughing and smiling. "Get up!" he said suddenly and pushed her away. They both stood, and she took the hand he held out to her. He smiled and led her in a double spin, then brought her into a closed position. The quick snap of his movement and the rigidity of the pose had her thinking he would lead her in a tango, so she readied herself to follow him. He pulled her closer, his hand just below her shoulder blade, arms up, elbows high. She could feel him becoming aroused and began breathing deeply. "I'm going to make love tae you… in here… right now." His hold on her loosened, and he led her into a spot turn away from him, facing the closed door. "Please turn the lock."

Epilogue

CLIVE MAKES HIS MOVE

On the first Friday in July, David had an interview with *Impressive Male* magazine. He'd been forced to cancel it after the fire at his cottage in the Highlands, but Tina had rescheduled it for him, and he would be gone for the day. Kitty was upstairs, helping the children sort through their closets and dressers for clothes they'd outgrown. Erin was sitting in the kitchen with Francie, deciding on the menus for the week when the doorbell rang.

"I'll get it," Erin said and jumped up to answer the door. She looked through the peephole and saw quite a few police officers standing on their front stoop. She opened the door and froze; the man closest to her was large, tall, and thick. His hands were big and plump, and as they held up his warrant card, which had his name and photo, similar to a badge, she could see on just his thumb and first two fingers, how beat up they were. He was obviously a violent man.

"I am Detective Chief Superintendent Clive Dawson," he said. "We've had a report that there may be illegal activity being conducted inside this residence. We are prepared to do a search and seizure. Please allow us entry."

ACKNOWLEDGEMENTS

First, I must thank my husband, Scott, for his patience and forbearance over the last few years. He has been my rock and encourager when I began hating everything I'd written, though only because I'd read and reread it too many times to count.

To my daughter, Elizabeth, for her support and long-suffering.

Thank you to all my family, friends, and beta readers for being cheerleaders and for your much-needed support!

A special thanks to Marni MacRae for editing and Rehman for creating another amazing cover. I'm so thankful that I found you both. I hope we'll share many more years of David and Erin's story together!

www.ingramcontent.com/pod-product-compliance
Lightning Source LLC
Chambersburg PA
CBHW050848210726
48290CB00004B/1129